# A SKY OF STORMS

# A SKY OF STORMS

## THE TERRULIAN TRIALS

### BOOK ONE

CHLOE HODGE

REBECCA CAMM

A Sky of Storms
Copyright © 2023 by Stormcrest Ink
First edition: May 2023

Find us at: www.chloehodge.com | www.rebeccacamm.com
Instagram: @chloeschapters | @readingwritingdaydreaming
TikTok: @chloehodgeauthor | @readingwritingdaydream
Facebook: Chloe Hodge Author | Rebecca Camm

Reading Groups:
Chloe Hodge's Reading Coven -- www.facebook.com/groups/
chloesreadingcoven

Rebecca Camm's Reader Group --www.facebook.com/groups/
rebeccacammsreadergroup

Printed in Australia.

Paperback ISBN: 978-0-6456250-1-1

Special thanks and acknowledgements to:
Editor; Emily Morrison
Cover Design; Cover Dungeon
Character Art; Simarts_
Formatter; Rebecca Camm

# THE TERRULIAN TRIALS

A SKY OF STORMS

A FOREST OF FIRE

A SEA OF SECRETS

A CITY OF SMOKE

A DESERT OF DESPAIR

A KINGDOM OF CONQUERORS

**Content Notes**

A Sky of Storms is a why choose urban fantasy romance novel.
It contains cursing, sexual references, violence, assault, bullying,
sexual assualt, and other adult themes.
A full list can be found on rebeccacamm.com or by scanning the
QR code below.

Verdant Plateau

Stormcrest City

Damascon Hollow

# THE HOUSES

## HOUSE JUPITER

### STORMCREST CITY

### AUGER FAMILY

Victrus and Eliana

Victoria, Fallon, Ethan, and Hadley

## HOUSE NEPTUNE

### TRITOSA CITY

### LOCH FAMILY

Zale

Zane, Zuri, Zara, Zeke, Zach, Zion, and Zariah

## HOUSE CERES

### THE VERDANT PLATEAU

### HAWTHORN FAMILY

Gabriella and Rosa

Wren and Noah

# OF TERRULIA

## HOUSE PLUTO

### DAMASCON HOLLOW

### THE DRAKES

Cormac

Ace

## HOUSE MARS

### THE CRIMSON STEPPES

### HALE FAMILY

Barrett and Myra

Kayden

## NOTABLE CHARACTERS

Kendra Reynolds - The Crimson Steppes
Flynn Stewart - The Crimson Steppes
Dick Jobs - Tritosa City
Mark Leroy - The Verdant Plateau
Celeste, The Overseer - The House of Ascension
Master Nolan - The House of Ascension
Master Luna - The House of Ascension
Master Jeremiah - The House of Ascension
Julian, Advisor - The Palace

# FALLON

I circled my prey, letting him stew in his fear for a moment before I pounced, plunging my blade into his thigh like a knife into butter. This guy was toast, and his actions today had gotten him burnt.

The dude squealed like a pig, his eyes wide as he stared past me, pupils dilated like round discs and his skin gleaming with sweat. High as a mother-freaking-kite. I could almost laugh, were it not for me playing the role of his torturer.

"Look, man, neither of us want to be here, so just tell me who you were going to sell the crystals to, and we can both get on with our day."

He jerked in the wooden chair he was tied to, hiccupping and laughing like a creepy clown as he watched something imaginary fly through the air. I clicked my hands in front of his face, which made him go a bit cross-eyed as he focused.

"Two angels. Pretty, pretty angels," he said, then exploded into hysterical laughter.

I clapped him on the back, rolling my eyes. "Okay Chuckles. That's enough crystoxx for you. Now tell me what you were planning or the pretty angels are going to chop your little dick off inch by inch."

He blinked, his eyes bugging out of his head. Yeah, I thought that might get a reaction, not that I had any plans of following through with that. I might've been ruthless when I needed but a dude could die with *some* dignity.

I had to give him credit though. This runt had big fucking balls. But what was he thinking trying to steal crystals from the mine? They were the most precious resources in Terrulia, responsible for powering the grid, weaponry—all manner of things. Not only that, but they were also only sourced from Stormcrest City and our surrounding orbit.

Which of course, was all managed by Auger Enterprises, the biggest corporation in Terrulia and also the most corrupt. My parents weren't just the beautiful faces of this business, they were the ringleaders of the biggest crime syndicate in our country and the head of House Jupiter.

So, yeah, stealing from a member of the mafia was sheer fucking stupidity. Stealing from an Auger and the most elite family in Stormcrest City? That was signing your own death warrant.

Unfortunately for me, I was the executioner today.

I pulled my blade from his flesh and he barely even flinched, so high on the drugs he'd managed to sniff—definitely crystoxx, a substance made from the very crystals he had tried to steal—before my father's cronies had found him attempting to flee near the edge of the mine.

The fucker never stood a chance. He was an employee of Auger Enterprises, and no one escaped the mine once they'd signed a contract with my parents. No one.

I crinkled my nose at the smell of iron and the pungent waft of urine that trickled down his chair and formed a puddle on the ground. Sucked to be the cleaning crew.

My sister stood beside me, her copper eyes gleaming with approval, her perfect blond hair coiled into a tight bun, nails immaculate even as she studied them. We were similar in appearance—the same eyes stained copper from proximity to the crystals, the same straight nose. Only, my hair was long and black, and my lips were fuller, maybe from my lack of sneering that she constantly did.

I stepped back, waving a lazy hand at my victim whose eyes had gone vacant again. "Victoria, he's not going to tell us anything. The guy's checked out to cloud nine for the day."

And I wouldn't mind packing my bags, flipping my sister the bird, and going on that little trip with him. Anything would be better than having to play this part and being around her.

Victoria's lips curled into a smile. Damn viper knew how much I hated this. Knew and exploited that fact. "Again." She had the nerve to look bored as she glanced at me. "And Fallon, make it hurt, or I might find someone else to torture. Someone like Ethan."

I smiled sweetly, coating my words with venom. "Lay a hand on him, Victoria, and I'll cut your pretty fingers off."

"Aw, but I just got them done." Her nails did indeed look fresh, glimmering in a blood-red hue. How predictable. "If you don't have the stomach to do what's needed Fallon, I'll be sure to tell Father you're not cut out for it."

Oh I bet she'd just *love* that, knowing I would be severely punished once she did.

"Don't bother," I snapped. "Wouldn't want you to get your claws dirty."

This was the game we always played. I would rebel, she would threaten to hurt my brother, and inevitably, I would give in. The alternative was too horrible to think of. I would never let my younger siblings, Ethan and Hadley, be harmed while I was around.

Problem was, my parents and Victoria knew it. Pricks.

I couldn't count on my hands how many times Victrus, Eliana and Victoria had beaten the ever-living shit out of me for daring to say 'no'. When I'd reached my breaking point, they'd changed their tactics, threatening to punish my brother Ethan instead.

I never wanted my younger siblings to go through that. They were both still innocent, still pure. When my parents had threatened me with their safety, that was it for me. The moment I had decided that once I got Ethan and my sister Hadley out of this hellhole, I'd come back for my parents. And when I did?

I'd kill them.

Without a single sorry bone in my body. Not after everything they've done to me, and certainly not after all the people they've killed, abused, extorted, or forced out of house and home.

Victoria grinned wider, as if knowing what I was thinking, and gods damn did I want to punch that fucking smirk off her face.

Instead, I pictured it in place of the man's and clocked his jaw, then again on his nose, causing it to *crack*. My sister cackled behind me, clapping her hands.

Interrogations were Victoria's favourite thing, mostly because our father, Victrus, gave her full authority to run them. Assholes. Power hungry, corrupt, and cruel, Victoria and Victrus were the biggest cunts in high society.

I've told her that more than once too. I received lashings and beatings for it, but it was totally worth it. And maybe I was naïve, but I still had hope for Victoria. Our parents had fucked her up good and proper, but maybe I could get her to see the light. To change her allegiances and remind her that we'd loved each other once. Back when she taught me to fly, when we'd play hide-and-seek in the house or when she shielded me from our parent's wrath.

But then she'd been forced to enter an initiation week with Auger Enterprises. She's never been the same since.

I looked back at the dude before me. "You gotta give me something, Chuckles, or we're both going to have a shit time in a minute." He looked at me blankly, then smiled toothily. I sighed. "Your funeral."

There was no point dragging this out. The guy had nothing to say and probably had no real reason to do what he'd done except sheer desperation. The workers in the mines were half starved, beaten and bruised. I didn't know what Auger Enterprises was offering prospective employees on paper, but whatever they promised certainly wasn't this.

The mines were in the middle of butt-fucking-nowhere, so once they came in … well, safe to say it wasn't a party here. Anyone who somehow managed to escape the guards found themselves in a desert with monsters for company. Death by overworking and starvation, or death by teeth and claws? I couldn't decide what was worse.

At least I could give this guy a more dignified end. I lunged, covering his body with my own as I pretended to stab him. "Please," I whispered. "Just one small detail. A name. Even a fake name for fuck's sake, I don't know. I just need something."

Or else it'd be me getting tortured soon. For not getting answers, for failing my duty. Any number of bullshit reasons Victoria would report to my father later.

"Fuck. You."

I pulled back, shocked to hear the most lucid tone from the guy yet.

"Fuck you and your family. Fuck Auger Enterprises. Fuck every last one of the Auger bloodline. I hope you rot in hell."

I shrugged. Well, that was a no to my request then. "Wouldn't be the first time I've heard that," I said, clutching his shoulder with one hand. "But you know what? You can get in line."

I rammed my blade into his chest, twisting it up towards his heart to make it hurt. Painful, but swift. Enough to give my sick puppy of a sister the show she wanted. The guy sagged towards me, blood gurgling in his throat as the final breath escaped him.

"Happy?" I withdrew my dagger and turned, glaring at her. "I did my duty. Can I go home now, boss?" I saluted her mockingly, then folded my arms.

She sneered, looking the guy over. "A waste. But his body will serve as a warning when we string it up in the mines. A reminder that Augers don't forget, and we certainly don't forgive."

I flicked my blade, splattering a few drops of blood onto her face. "Oops, sorry."

Her gaze was murderous, but she only smiled, a promise of payback for later. Then she turned and stalked from the room.

I lingered a moment, looking back at my victim. One of many. Their deaths would haunt me forever, but I vowed to avenge each and every one of them, and I had just the plan to set the wheels in motion.

One more sleep and I'd be out of this city and in the House of Ascension, the famed academy where elite citizens from the most powerful Houses tried their luck at competing in a brutal round of trials to become the next king or queen of Terrulia.

The old king was dead, and it was my one chance at becoming powerful enough to tear my House down and wipe out my parents' empire. What I had yet to discover was how the business operated and, ultimately, how I could bring it down, but once I did, they would rue the day they'd been born.

I just had to survive the trials first, but after everything I'd endured so far, how bad could it be?

# A SKY OF STORMS

# FALLON

The current buffeted the feathers of my wings as I soared over the city, my brother laughing beside me as we raced around turrets and under archways, speeding along with minimal effort thanks to the aid of updrafts created from vents throughout Stormcrest. I shot over one of the larger vents and let it propel me, adrenaline pumping through my veins as I launched higher into the sky.

Fuck yes!

I laughed, tucking in my wings and letting myself freefall, my stomach dropping. I embraced the feeling, revelling in being airborne.

When I was with Ethan, my worries melted away and we could pretend we were free. Up here, no one could hurt us or force us to be or do anything. For a little while at least, I could forget the crimes my parents and Victoria made me commit.

I laughed as my powerful copper wings beat at my back, propelling me around and around as I circled my brother, teasing him, while my black hair rippled in the wind. He was fifteen, only five years younger than me, but his wings were smaller than mine and not yet fully developed. For now. With a bit of bulking up, he'd be stronger than me one day. Not that my parents could see his physical potential, nor did they value his quiet intelligence the way I did. Just another aspect of our fucked-up family. Everything my parents did was always a show of power, and if their children didn't live up to appearances and play their part, we were treated like the dirt beneath their feet.

"Last one to the summit has to be Victrus's shadow for a day." I winked at Ethan.

He grinned, his blond hair streaming back as he fell into a deep dive, tucking his wings in and gliding like a missile. I held back, watching my brother tear through the skies as he was born to, and only blazing after him once he'd got a good head start. We both knew I could beat him, but where was the fun in easy competition?

I caught up, reaching out to tap at his ankles, and he laughed. Seeing him and my little sister happy was one of my all-time favourite things. If I could bring a smile to their faces, I abso-freaking-lutely would.

Despite Ethan and I having the magical power to conjure our wings to sprout from our backs at will, it wasn't a common gifting. Our adaptations mostly stemmed from our bloodlines and our geographical locations. Those of us with wings could travel near anywhere and reach unobtainable heights, but the higher the climb, the greater the fall. Only the wealthiest families could travel by portabracelets—stupidly expensive jewellery that could portal the bearer anywhere they pleased—and of course, the wealthiest of these families were all members of House Jupiter. So basically, they were all assholes.

We still used regular vehicles and aircrafts like the rest of Terrulia, of course. My home was fully decked out with top-of-the-line cars, motorbikes, and even a helicopter, but down on the mainland, anything goes.

Rather than transporting, I liked to fly when I could, and being able to conjure my wings at will came in handy for exploring the city or finding good vantage points. The summit, as my brother and I liked to call it, had a view over the entire city. From here, the white buildings were a maze, with their golden domes glittering, and waterfalls roaring over the edge of the city in the sky. I scowled. It was a beautiful place if one could forget how sadistically House Jupiter ruled over it. Even the glittering decadence reminded me of the corruption paying for it all. Every home was gated, every street lined with trees, flowers, and white cobblestones. A pretty mask for an ugly underworld.

I swooped closer to Ethan, my wings blasting me forward until I was nose-to-nose with him. He glanced at me, brows pulling together as he gritted his teeth and exerted every muscle in his body to power up the column leading to our usual perch on the tallest building.

The monstrosity looked over the entirety of Stormcrest City, its stone symmetry and dainty arches inspired by Parisian architecture from Earth, where we'd originally come from. Like the house names that were a nod to gods of an ancient civilisation, the building was a showcase of power. Nothing awed and intimidated quite like wealth amassed over generations. Even though our civilisation on Terrulia was fairly new, we had kept to many of the old ways.

At the last second, Ethan's eyes widened, and his wings stalled. His body went limp as he plummeted to the city below. My heart stuttered as I dove to catch him, wings flapping furiously as sheer panic riled within. My fingers reached out for him and just as I was about to grab his arm, his eyes opened and he laughed, shooting upwards and leaving me staring disbelieving at his departing form.

At the top, he plopped himself on the rampart and grinned broadly.

The little shit.

Expelling one long breath, I shot him a wry look, flying up to sit beside him as we collapsed and magicked our wings away.

"Shifty," I said with a chuckle, ruffling his hair fondly.

"Sometimes you gotta use the tools at your disposal." He shrugged. "It's not my fault my safety is one of your biggest weaknesses."

"Since when did your cleverness evolve into the beginnings of an evil mastermind?"

He laughed and shot me a wry grin. "Since you stopped letting me win. So, are you still planning on raiding Victoria's room tonight? She's going to have your neck when she catches you."

I smirked and shook my head. "Don't you mean *if* she catches me? You underestimate my abilities, Ethan."

He studied me for a moment before his smile widened. "You've already done it."

"Yu*p*," I said, smacking the 'p'. I pulled my backpack off and opened it, my new spoils spilling out. Treasures I may or may not have borrowed from Victoria's secret stash. Okay, fine, stolen. Whatever. "A collection of daggers, an expensive-looking short sword, a crystal-powered proton gun, and some crystal stun balls. She'd also stashed some chocolate bars into the lining of her satchel."

"That's it?" he asked, looking a little disappointed.

"Well, I was going to mention the gigantic sparkling dildo in there, but I figured you wouldn't want to know about that," I said thoughtfully. Ethan blanched, and I burst out laughing. "I'm joking, but I did find this."

I wiggled the fingers of my right hand in his face where the House Jupiter ring—the same one as our parents'—glinted in the sunlight.

He gaped at me, shaking his head. "Holy shit Fallon. Put that back. If Victoria finds out…"

"She won't," I replied cheerfully. "Because you're taking it."

"Are you crazy? She'd kill me if she knew I had it."

I grinned, looking into his sea-green eyes, so like my mother's had been once upon a time. Only his were filled with all the kindness hers lack. He looked so much like her, with his blond hair, freckles, and bronzed skin.

I took after my father, with long, straight black hair, full lips and an athletic build. Of all our likenesses, I hated that we had the same eyes most—once hazel, they were now stained copper from being in proximity to the crystals farmed only in Stormcrest. So far, I'd managed to keep Victrus's filthy claws from sinking into Ethan and forcing him there, but my attempts would only last so long. I could foolishly hope he never visited that place and kept his green eyes forever.

"She won't find out because you're going to hide it. Here—" I jimmied a stone loose from the wall to reveal our little hidey-hole. No one would look for our stash here.

I placed the ring inside, along with our new finds. Over the years, we'd hidden many treasures in there, from toys to chocolates to money. Yeah, we had to hide sweets, because our parents were monsters like that and never let us have them. As for the money...

"This ring alone will get you enough credits to grab new papers and get the fuck out of here. This is your get-out-of-jail-free card, Ethan." The reference to the old Earth boardgame made his lips twitch but the seriousness in his eyes didn't budge. I sighed, resting my hand on his gently. "If something happens while I'm gone, I want you to take Hadley and run. Get the hell out of here and head to the Verdant Plateau."

My brother looked at me, his eyes clouding with worry. "I know why you're doing this."

I didn't respond, shielding my face with my hair and basking in the setting sun. The clouds looked like fairy floss today, swirling in front of peachy rays.

"You don't think you'll come back, do you?" he pressed. "I've researched the odds and, well..."

I pasted on a smile and turned to him, dangling my legs off

the edge. "Come on, you don't think I can take on some elitist assholes? If I can deal with Victoria and our stick-up-the-ass parents, this will be a piece of cake," I joked.

He smiled slightly, but Ethan was a hound on the scent. He always knew when I was lying and saw right through me, deep down to my core. He was my best friend, the only companion I had ever been able to rely on. I loved him with everything I had.

"Swear you'll come back," he said suddenly, with a fierceness to his gaze as he grabbed my arm. "Swear you'll win the Terrulian Trials to become queen."

"Ethan, I—"

"Swear it!"

His face was so stern, so serious, that I shifted, straightening. Fear swam in his big green eyes—not for himself, but at the very real idea that I could die in the competition. The unpredictable trials that decided the next ruler. I burned the visual into my brain, telling myself I would remember this moment every time I wanted to give up or roll over. I could do this for Ethan and Hadley. I would do this to keep them safe and away from our parents' clutches. The world needed it and frankly, so did I.

"I swear," I said, lifting my chin and clasping his hand in my own. The power of that promise seemed to reverberate through my very soul, and I knew there was nothing I wouldn't do to hold true to my word. My parents may have been some of the worst people in this world, but they had done one thing right, even if they wished Ethan was anything but himself.

All my life, I had been trained among the very best. A scholar, a gifted, a killer. My life had never been pretty or perfect like my parents wanted the world to believe. It was raw, gritty, and ugly. Most of all, it was real. If competing meant becoming the worst parts of myself, then so be it.

I *would* one day be queen … I just had to become a monster first.

"Come on," I said, nudging my brother. "We'd better get

home. Victrus will blow a lid if we're late to dinner."

Ethan grinned and in a sudden move, he shoved me over the edge. I fell with a surprised scream, my wings immediately beating on instinct and levelling me out. I gaped at him as he hovered beside me. Then we burst out laughing.

"Race ya." He grinned, shooting towards the hill overlooking the city where an enormous mansion sat. Our home. And our parents' lair.

———— ◆ ————

I pulled up on the landing balcony with Ethan by my side, both of us jogging along the marble floor and slipping into our seats at the dinner table without a word.

My father sat at the head of the table, Victoria on his right and my mother on his left. No one batted an eye, nor bothered to acknowledge us. Typical. Bastards.

"Are you ready for the Terrulian Trials?" Victrus asked as he sliced into a steak, his copper eyes directed at my sister.

Victoria smiled serenely at our father; her blond hair coiled perfectly into a tight bun. "I have been training all my life for this. I was born ready."

It took everything I had not to roll my eyes or jam my fork into her hand. She was like a mechanical doll. In fact, machines had more personality than she did. I bet if he commanded, she'd roll over and bark like the whipped dog she was.

Victrus nodded satisfactorily, swirling his wine goblet in hand. "You will make the Auger family proud when you take the crown." His eyes narrowed as he studied the slender curve of his knife. "Our enemies won't dare to cross us when you win the competition."

*When she wins*, I thought bitterly. Victoria was their shining star and prize pupil. Always had been. For Victrus and Eliana Auger, their eldest and first-born daughter was the crown jewel of this family and House Jupiter's most promising candidate. The rest of us were merely placeholders in the event our enemies ever displaced or dispatched my dearly beloved sister. Ethan, Hadley, and me? We meant *nothing* to our parents.

I used to cry over that, but my heart was shrivelled and blackened now. Years of bitterness and abuse had seen to that. Oh, they still found ways under my skin, but I'd learned to replace those little hurts with anger. My parents were ruthless, cruel, and unforgiving, and they ruled with an iron fist. Victrus and Eliana loved each other fiercely, which, in any other family, might have been a wonderful gift, but in ours, it was a curse. For each other, for their empire, they would do anything. Kill, torture, maim, and, as was their business, smuggle their goods to the highest bidder. Everything we owned, everything we had, they built off the backs of innocents or acquired through unforgivable crimes.

House Jupiter was the worst of them all. And because of it, the best. It made me sick, and one day I'd bring them to their knees and make them pay.

"When I win," Victoria added smugly, "I will dispose of them before they get the chance."

I scoffed, hiding my outburst behind my glass as I sipped my wine. Victrus's eyes narrowed, but he said nothing.

Victoria glared at me, but her lips curved into a coy smile before turning back to Victrus. "It's a shame they will pit me against Fallon in the finals," she continued, glancing meaningfully my way. Uh-huh. A crying shame. The bitchy once-over she gave me really screamed sorrow. If she had it her way, she'd be first in line to take me out. Well, two can play that game.

"House Jupiter weeds out the weak," Mother said in her lilting tone. "Only the strong survive."

My lip curled. "When I beat Victoria's ass into the ground, we'll know how true that is," I said sweetly, looking all three of them hard in the eyes. "And when I become queen, you will bend the knee as my loyal subjects."

Ethan kicked me under the table, warning me to shut up.

He shook his head ever so subtly as I frowned at him, but I understood. Victrus did not appreciate being baited, and Eliana, however lovely she pretended to be, was no better.

My father's hand clenched around his knife and, for a second, I thought it might be plunged into my chest. Instead, a sharp, piercing pain burrowed into my mind, lashing at my mental barriers. I cried out, doubling in my chair as my father pushed against my mind, inflicting pain for what I said, or simply because he could. A single tear trickled down my cheek as I fought him off, but this was an agony I could not defend against, no matter how hard I tried. Ethan's hands closed into fists, but I managed to shake my head just once, lest my father's wrath move to him instead. When I thought my brain might shatter or melt into a puddle of goo, my mother rested a hand above Victrus's until his grip relaxed—both on his dinner knife and my mind—and his posture eased.

This was the twisted game he liked to play to keep me in my place. It also served as a subtle reminder that he was more powerful than me and that my telekinesis abilities, however strong, were no match. Not many gifted held the kind of magic my father had. Someday, I would rip it from him, one way or another.

My mother cleared her throat, returning to her meal and cutting it up ever graceful and dainty.

"We wish both our children luck in the trials, of course," she said, as if I'd simply imagined my father's attack. I straightened, still panting from the lingering pain, but I caught the way she directed her gaze at her prized pony. "The trial is brutal, girls. It will take all your cunning to survive. You will be pitted against each other time and again, forced to make allies and to meet your greatest fears. When the time comes, you must be ruthless. Trust no one and offer no mercy."

I almost snorted. Right, brutal, because I hadn't learnt the true meaning of that by now. Nothing could be worse than being in this place—than Victrus and Eliana and their whole gods damned House. *Nothing.*

"I don't want you to go," Hadley said, clinging on my shirt sleeve. Her green eyes were wide and full of tears.

My little sister, still so pure and good-hearted. I had to win this, if only so she never had to learn how monstrous her parents really were, so she never felt the sting of my father's power.

"I'm not leaving until tomorrow and, when I do, it will only be for a little while, Ley-ley," I said gently, twisting one of her brown curls around my finger. "And just think, when I'm queen, I will be able to build a toy store and ice-creamery just for you."

Her little face brightened at that, but she cocked her head cautiously. "Will there be rainbow flavour?"

"And chocolate and strawberry." I winked. "Whatever you want."

Her eyes just about bugged out of her head at that, and I chuckled, but our little moment died as soon as I noticed the family watching me. We weren't allowed treats or toys. Hours outside of education or training were supposed to be spent bettering ourselves or the House. Honestly, they could go to hell. Maybe I'd force them to work in that ice cream shop one day, wearing cute little candy-striped uniforms and bobble ice-cream hats. I almost snorted at the imagery. It would be a satisfying sight, but I had more sinister plans in mind, starting with crumbling their empire.

"Sweets make you soft and complacent," Victrus growled, stabbing his knife into the table. "There will be no ice cream, Hadley, nor toys. Your sister knows that, and if she insists on ignoring that fact, I'll have her whipped for her insolence. Now, off to bed."

Hadley whimpered, and I shot up, lifting her into my arms before the servants could step in. "I'll take her."

He grunted but waved a dismissive hand. I left hurriedly, bolting for the door when his voice stopped me in my tracks before I managed to reach them.

"Fallon."

I gritted my teeth before turning slowly, raising a brow. "Yes, Victrus?"

"If you fail the trials, your place in this family will be forfeit. There is no room for weaklings in our House. I'd rather see you dead than look upon your failure."

His words slithered inside my gut, coiling into a long spool of bitterness and hatred. I didn't reply, turning my back on him and giving him the finger once I'd stalked down the corridor. As I put Hadley to bed, I snuggled in beside her, once again promising to buy her that ice cream one day.

*Pinkie swear it.*

I stayed with her for a long time, stroking her hair and watching her little chest rise and fall. Ethan appeared at the door sometime later, and I carefully untangled myself from Hadley. Silently creeping out of the bedroom, I found him in the hallway.

"You need to be more careful," Ethan whispered once I was out. "Provoking them isn't smart."

I sighed as we walked towards my room. "I know, but I can't help it. Victrus makes me so mad. It's like a reflex."

Ethan frowned. "That so-called reflex is going to get you killed."

"Luckily, I'm leaving tomorrow, so he will have to wait a while," I replied, pushing my door open. I could hear Ethan grumbling under his breath behind me as I grabbed a bag from my cupboard and started filling it with clothing.

"You're forgetting one tiny detail that other people will want you to fail instead," he said. I turned to see him flopping onto my bed, his eyes tracking my movements. "I looked up the past Terrulian Trials. Fallon, the stories people tell aren't exaggerations."

"I assumed as much."

"I'm talking trials that either drive you to insanity or literally rip you to shreds," he continued, eyes wide and hands waving dramatically. "According to a witness to the fourteenth trails, one guy was obliterated into nothing but a bloody mist. A. Bloody. Mist."

"Sounds painful," I replied dryly. I didn't want to think about all the ways my life could be ended. That shit was scary, and I didn't have time to be afraid, not when so much hung on the line. "Ethan, you could die tomorrow just walking down the street. Life is full of unknowns; I can't stay here and do nothing when this is such a golden opportunity for us."

Ethan ran a hand through his hair. "I get it, but please be careful. You're all Hadley and I have that matters, and you made a promise."

"I swore I'd come back." I nodded. "I never go back on my promises with you both, and I'm not about to start now."

"Good," Ethan replied, moving to help me pack for my journey tomorrow.

We talked for an hour, reminiscing on all the mischief we'd gotten up to and making more promises to each other that somehow, despite all the obstacles, we'd get through this together. That we would live a life free from all the bullshit at each other's side.

Once he left, I lay in bed and thought about the life I was leaving behind. Tomorrow I'd be done with Victrus and Eliana, but I'd be stepping into the belly of the beast instead. Many people wanted my family dead, and they'd make no exception for me. The Auger family had ruined many lives and stripped so many resources from other cities. I may as well have painted a freaking target on my back as well as packed my bags, because the other participants would sure as shit be coming for me.

I frowned, rolling over in my bed. The Terrulian Trials were going to make me or break me, but I knew one thing for sure, I would never give up. I was clever, and I was strong. I'd been beaten and bruised inside and out more times than I could count and seen things I'd never forget. The things I'd been forced to participate in were so fucked up, they would haunt me forever.

I wouldn't let Ethan and Hadley be subjected to the same fate. I would do anything it took to become queen, and if I had to claw my way to the top, then screw anyone who got in my way.

This could all go away. The exploitation of those under Auger Enterprises, and the incessant greed from my parents and those who orbit them. And Stormcrest City was just the tip of the iceberg of a whole host of problems in this country. If I wore the crown, I could do something about the bullshit squabbles among the great cities and the petty warmongering between Houses.

My enemies had better watch out because Fallon Auger was about to tear them apart.

# KAYDEN

I stared at the sun emerging above the horizon and felt a kinship to that burning orange ball in the sky. I would soon rise too and claim my rightful place in this world.

Kayden Hale, King of Terrulia.

It had a nice ring to it.

Old King Theodore the Blessed had finally croaked in his sleep one month ago after a long, drawn-out battle with old age. Bro had been losing the plot for years, his body and mind failing like an old battery. The last few years had him constantly shadowed by his advisor, Julian, who was a dead-set oddball.

"Reckon I'll have Julian breathing down my neck when I become king? Or can I fire his ass?" I asked Flynn. He was my second of sorts, but mostly my best friend. We grew up together here in the Crimson Steppes and instantly clicked thanks to our love of pulling pranks, weight training and boxing.

The stocky guy chuckled as he adjusted the tape around his knuckles. "Not a chance. I'm gonna be there to advise you. Unless you want him around to wipe your ass like I heard he was doing for old Theo?"

I punched him hard in the side, earning a barrel of a laugh

from him as he stumbled. The news may have said that King Theo had died from natural causes, but Chief Advisor Julian was way too shifty for that to be believable. The guy was suss and had probably been doing something dodgy to the king for years.

It's kind of sad because old Theo had been a top-notch king in his youth, but now it was time for a new reign … and I planned to be at the head of it. With the Terrulian Trials fast approaching, I would have the perfect opportunity to compete and secure my throne as the new king.

There were five ruling Houses in Terrulia. Jupiter in Stormcrest City, Neptune in Tritosa City, Mars in the Crimson Steppes, Ceres in the Verdant Plateau, and Pluto in Damascon Hollow. Each had its own specialised industries and people with geographical adaptations. Unfortunately, the divide between cities was only deepening in Terrulia, and it was bound to get worse without a fair leader.

Good luck to Julian if he thinks he will mess with me. He'll be out on his ass as soon as I stroll through the palace doors.

"You're a dick," I said to Flynn, huffing a laugh and curling my fingers. "Break's over. Ready, bro?"

He nodded, and we spread out again on the cliff edge overlooking the red sands of The Crimson Steppes in all its glory. There wasn't much room up here to spar, but nothing raised the stakes like a drop to your death. We circled each other in the limited space, the dusty red stones kicking up with the movement.

"No adaptations this time," Flynn declared, and I grinned. Being unable to turn my skin to rock meant I was more vulnerable. He wanted to draw blood.

"Fine by me," I said with the shrug of a shoulder. "You're the one who's gonna spend the night being patched up."

"We'll see about that."

I made the first move, darting towards him and throwing a fist at his chest. He grunted, but it didn't stop him from retaliating. We exchanged punches, blocking and absorbing blows. We were relatively equally matched, but that was to be expected. Having trained together for so long, we knew each other's strengths and weaknesses the way I knew each crevice on my rocky hand—at least when I let my adaptation cover my skin; otherwise, my tan was silky smooth.

"Couldn't let me get the first hit?" Flynn said with a grin as we stepped back, and he wiped his thumb over his split lower lip. "Impatient bastard."

I laughed, bouncing from one foot to the other and shaking out my shoulders. "If I had to wait around for you, I'd be long dead. We both know that I take the lead."

"Not like I ever get the chance to forget."

"It's going to be burned into your brain when you see me in the crown," I replied with a shit-eating grin. "And made worse when I make you bow."

"Fuck off," Flynn said, chuckling.

It wouldn't be easy winning the crown, but I didn't cower from a challenge. The trials were notoriously dangerous, and over the centuries, countless people had died in pursuit of becoming the kingdom's future ruler. The Terrulian Trials were renowned for its brutality. Consisting of three brutal tests, the trials were devised by a council of representatives from each of the five cities to ensure only the most powerful and cunning Terrulian was crowned in the end.

The throne had my name written all over it.

"Why do you think the first Terrulians thought trials to the death was a good way to find a ruler?" I asked.

Flynn shrugged. "It takes a special kind of person to survive the destruction of a planet. Maybe leaving Earth scrambled their brains."

"Damascians are still feeling the effects," I joked, earning a booming laugh from Flynn.

Damascon Hollow was like an illegal dogfight. They were just a bunch of psychos scheming to survive. From what I heard that place was a free for all.

"Go again?"

"Nah," Flynn replied. "I got called into city hall for a meeting scheduled soon."

"What for?"

"No idea, but maybe after I'll check in on your mum," he said with a sly grin. "She's been looking fine lately."

"Don't make me cut your eyes out," I said, shooting him a half-hearted glare. I knew he wouldn't touch my mum like that. He respected her too much. My dad too.

They were the heads of House Mars, making them the leaders of the Crimson Steppes. Our city in the sands had been crumbling to dust for a long time, our people struggling to survive with minimal resources, nothing to trade, and a failing council. My parents' seat was under threat, and House Mars was falling, but they were still respected despite it all. Especially since they nominated anyone who wanted to go to the trials.

They'd used the last of their credits to make sure anyone who wanted to compete could. Deeming it a worthy challenge to show who was the strongest of all from not only the Crimson Steppes but the entire country. The other Houses would be throwing as many young people as they could find at the trials in the hope they would win power, and they had enough credits to pay for it too. My parents weren't as rich, but they were resourceful and knew well enough that this was the Crimson Steppes' last chance to save itself.

Power was everything in Terrulia, and every House happily sacrificed its best candidates between the ages of twenty and twenty-five to compete, knowing only one would walk away the winner.

It was about time The Crimson Steppes had a win, and I would be the one to deliver it.

The people of Terrulia believed in modern advancement and technology, so what better way to start a new reign than with someone young and fresh and not so set in their ways?

"It'd make me look like a badass. King Flynn Stewart the Eyeless," he said, making his way down the cliff.

"More like second," I replied, catching up and dropping an arm over his shoulder. "The crown is mine, bro, there's no way you're gonna beat me, but maybe I can get you a little badge or something made." I tapped him on the chest. "'Badass Advisor.'"

Flynn laughed. "Might have to get rid of you in your sleep."

I grinned, thinking back to when we were kids, and my parents organised some camp for a bunch of us. We'd spent the week doing competitions, and of course, I won every single one of them. Not because my parents ran the thing but because I was, and always have been, the best. You couldn't call it favouritism when I was a league ahead of the rest in speed, skill and strength.

Flynn had been pissy about coming second, so he tried to eliminate the competition. One night he dragged me out of the tent and tried to bury me, sleeping bag and all, in the sand. He was surprisingly stealthy about it. But I played dead until I scared the shit out of him mid-bury.

We'd thrown a few fists, then slept out under the stars together.

"Remember how last time went?"

"I was six. This time would be different," he replied with a huff. "Though maybe I'll pack some stuff to make s'mores just in case."

"Beers too." I slapped him on the back and teleported home, leaving him and the cliffside behind.

"You're late," my father scolded as soon as I appeared in the house. Despite my parents being the head of House Mars, our home wasn't as glamorous as those I'd seen on TV in places like Stormcrest City or Tritosa. We didn't have the credits nor the resources here, but compared to everyone else in the sand bowl, we were living very comfortably. "All we ask is you have dinner with us one night a week, and you can't even make it on time."

"I was training with Flynn," I replied, dropping into a seat at the table. "Mum's not even here yet."

"Her meeting's running late," he said, returning to chopping the vegetables on the bench. He was a big guy, built like a boulder with muscles that could break skulls without a thought, not that he would ever do it. My dad was a walking contradiction. Hard and intimidating on the outside yet soft like a marshmallow on the inside. "It takes time to work out the logistics of supply distribution."

"Soon, we won't have to worry about that," I said. I leant forward, resting my muscled forearms on the table. "The Crimson Steppes won't be scraping around to make do much longer."

"We are sending our best."

I grinned. "I won't let you down."

"We know," my mum said as she strode into the room. Her long red hair was like a burning blaze that fell to her broad shoulders, and a warm smile graced her lips. She kissed my father before sitting beside me, squeezing my wrist in greeting. "You always do us proud."

I wasn't a soppy sucker, but I'd seen how shit some people's parents were, and I was glad I got these guys. In fact, the entirety of the Crimson Steppes was lucky to have my parents. It didn't matter the number of credits in your bank account or social standing, all that mattered was your strength and your drive to take what was yours. My parents cared about this city. Those opportunistic assholes that were trying to steal House Mars were going to fuck us all over if I didn't win the trials.

"House Mars is not going to bow any longer," I said, raising my chin. I looked from my mum to my dad and held my tone firm. "I'm going to save the city."

My parents beamed. The crown was mine.

———— ✦ ————

I woke to hands grabbing my wrists and ankles. I roared

as my senses kicked in and my skin turned to rock. It was pitch black, but that wouldn't stop me from beating the shit out of my best friend for this stunt. Then I'd eat about fifty s'mores.

"Fuck Flynn! You're so dead!" I shouted, pulling against his hold. "Payback is gonna be a bitch for you, bro, and whoever else you roped into this. Just you wait."

Flynn didn't reply. Bro must have been too busy trying to hold me down with whomever he convinced to help him.

"You're a sneaky shit," I huffed, kicking someone off my leg.

"Why isn't he out yet?" someone hissed, and I froze. That wasn't Flynn's voice. It wasn't a voice I recognised at all.

"Who—"

A gag was shoved between my lips, and I thrashed, putting all my strength into head-butting whoever the unlucky bastard was in front of me. A satisfying crack sounded as my temple connected with cartilage, and I tore my wrist free from someone's grip.

Snarling, I made to teleport and get the fuck out of there when something sharp pinched my neck, and my magic suddenly fizzled out, fading away into the deepest recesses of my mind.

I shouted through the gag, my words muffled, as I fought to rise from the bed. I threw a fist to my right, making contact with some asshole. A gruff curse echoed, and I smiled viciously.

"Restrain him," a man barked, and a bag was shoved over my head as I growled behind the gag.

These fuckers were going to beg for mercy when I got out of this.

I felt a weight on my chest and swung my arms, trying to knock whomever it was off, only to hit the air. They were using their powers on me. I pushed all my strength into fighting them off, but I felt myself fatiguing despite the rage inside me.

My body slackened against my will, and with one last surge of effort, I managed to kick someone before the world slipped away.

# ACE

The familiar metallic taste of blood coated my tongue and a thudding pain pulsed through my forehead as I slipped back into consciousness. Rough fabric rubbed against my cheek and nose, reminding me of the attack that brought me here. I'd been jumped in the streets, and even though I'd put up one hell of a fight, my opponents had gotten the better of me and shot me up with something to knock me out.

I remained still, my wrists tied behind my back and ankles strapped to the legs of the chair I was sitting on. I didn't want to alert whoever was speaking around me that I was awake. The bag over my head inhibited my view of whomever the fuck had the guts to kidnap me, but that didn't mean I couldn't memorise the sound of every voice in this room. You didn't need to see someone's face to recognise them; a person's voice was as distinct as a birthmark. Over the years, I'd learned to catalogue a scene down to the most minute detail. This wasn't my first kidnapping and in my line of work, I doubted it would be my last. Though I was rarely on this side of the game.

Those who ran the Terrulian Trials had accepted my nomination to compete which meant life was going to get really fucking interesting. Normally only candidates from House Pluto of Damascon Hollow—or DH—were allowed to compete, but seeing as my gang, The Drakes, now had the leaders under our payroll, things were a little different this time around.

I'd been on some unusual jobs, but I never balked at a challenge, and the trials were just another obstacle between me and my orders. First, I needed to get out of this mess. It wasn't lost on me that I had been jumped the night before I was supposed to leave for the trials. I was eager to learn what these thugs wanted, just so I could deny them and put them in their place.

I reached for my power to check for any electrical currents in the vicinity. In these modern times, there was always some current pulsing away. No one left the house without a phone or smartwatch, and hell, even the human body had currents sparking inside to manipulate if one had the gift to do so. My brows furrowed as I continued reaching for my power, but I felt nothing. Something was blocking me, and that knowledge tightened my chest with uneasiness. The bag was tugged from my head, and a light like something out of an old gangster movie illuminated the room. Whomever these people were, they were stuck in the olden days. No real criminal worked like this anymore. Why have a swinging globe when you could blind someone with the tap of a phone?

My eyes adjusted quickly to find three men in the uniforms of the Terrulian guard standing before me. There were no windows or decor of note in the room we were in, just smooth grey walls like an isolation cell. One guy stepped forward cockily and slapped me hard across the face. Hello to you too, asshole. He'd be the first one to go.

"Where is he?" the guard demanded; his brown eyes boring into mine. He was at least twice my age, judging by the wrinkles beside his eyes and the stormy colour of his hair. A scar cut through his right brow, giving me the impression that he had some experience in the darker side of his occupation. I smiled.

Reaching his age meant he was either very good at his trade or very green when it came to interrogations. My money was on the latter. I was no small fry and these scare tactics? This was foreplay. "Speak!"

The idiot was in way over his head. I was a Drake, and we didn't break, not for the DH cops or the knuckle draggers of rival gangs, and definitely not for any of the assholes standing before me. I assumed they were asking about my boss, Cormac, but if they didn't know his whereabouts, they'd get nothing out of me. Loyalty to my gang was stronger than any law and worth any torture they could deliver.

"Tell us!"

"Fuck off," I growled, receiving a hit to the side with a metal bar from the blond guy on the left, breaking at least one of my ribs. Son of a bitch. Scratch what I said before, that beanpole was first up.

"Speak now or it will only get worse," the guy in front of me said. He must have been the leader of this little trio as the other two waited by his side for direction like good little pups. "The choice is yours."

I smiled wider, reclining in my seat. I knew how this shit went down. They would kill me once I told them what they wanted to know, and if I didn't break, they'd still kill me—slowly. I wasn't interested in being tortured to death, but a man's got principles. Besides, I didn't plan to let them live long enough to try.

I jostled my tied wrists, testing the ropes only to find them tight and digging into my skin. I had no access to my power or my limbs. I couldn't even move the fingers on my bionic hand let alone use the weapons hidden in it. They must have disabled it too. Looked like I needed to get creative and luckily, I had a few tricks up my sleeve.

"You really gonna make me get my knuckles bloody, kid?" the leader continued, pacing before me with his hands behind his back. "You'll only drag out the pain. Is he worth dying for?"

The guy on the left slapped the metal bar in his hand in a shitty attempt at looking threatening. Had these people read the Idiot's Guide to Intimidation and Torture? The whole thing was so stereotypical it almost made me laugh. I didn't get the chance though as Beanpole slammed his bar against my chest. I grunted as it connected with my aching rib and rewarded him by spitting blood on his face. His eyes widened furiously, and I laughed as his leader held out a hand to stall the next hit.

"All we need is a location and this could be over."

"Say please," I said smugly. The leader waved his hand, and another blow snapped my skull to the side.

I hung my head. "You know what? I'll tell you," I croaked, dropping my voice.

"Speak up," the leader commanded. "What did you say?"

I mumbled under my breath and Beanpole took the bait, stepping closer, his ear hovering near my lips.

"I said I'm going to enjoy making you bleed," I drawled, then slammed my head into his.

The guy tumbled to the floor, crying out in pain. Blood dripped from my temple down the centre of my face, but I ignored it. The leader seethed, helping his lackey to his feet before punching me in the head.

"You're pathetic." I laughed, but the sound died in my throat when I spotted my favourite possession.

"Need a hand?" the guy on the right taunted, holding up my bionic limb. His long fingers curled around the metal like the talons of a bird.

Blocking my power was one thing, but stealing my hand was too far. They'd just signed their fucking death warrants.

"Did you really think we'd leave you with a weapon like that?" the leader asked.

Judging by their actions so far, I didn't need access to my power to know that they didn't have enough of a spark between them to power a phone, let alone the interrogation of a member of The Drakes. They had my hand, so whatever was currently stuck to the end of my right wrist had no value to me. I'd done this move before but knowing that I wouldn't damage my bionic hand was a bonus. In one well-practised movement, I tugged my wrist, pulling whatever was at the end into the rope loop, then twisted. It didn't budge on the first go, but on the second, it clicked, which I covered up with a shout.

"Give me back my fucking hand!"

"Answer my question, and it's all yours. Where is he?" the leader asked again, his patience dwindling. When I didn't reply, he sighed deeply. "You need to give us something."

Wrong. They weren't getting shit out of me. I stared down the trio of thugs. "There's nothing to say."

"Very well then."

Fuckwit on the left lifted the metal bar once more and strode towards me, a sadistic glint in his grey eyes. He hefted the weight of the bar in his hands, clearly anticipating the infliction of pain on me. The joke's on that fucker, because I was really going to have fun using that bar to paint the walls red in a minute. I jiggled my wrist and couldn't help my own shit-eating grin as whatever they'd swapped my bionic hand for fell to the floor with an audible thump. The rope loosened immediately, freeing both my arms.

The guard in my face frowned, but his eyes widened when I launched myself forward. I grabbed the bar with my left hand and slammed my right elbow into his ribs. Because nothing in my life came easy, my legs were still tied to the chair, and the thing fell on top of me as I collided with the guard. It wasn't ideal, but I was creative when I wanted to be and was going to make fucking do. I pulled the bar from the guard's grip and slammed it down repeatedly, rearranging his features.

"Enough!" the leader shouted as he kicked the chair I was still attached to and dragged me away. I didn't acknowledge him as I slammed the metal bar into the other guard a few more times before he was out of reach. "That's enough!"

I swung the bar in the leader's direction, a snarl ripping from my throat. You didn't get to my position in The Drakes without losing part of yourself to your inner beast. The man backed up; his hands raised in surrender as fear flashed through his eyes. My favourite kind of expression.

"You passed the initiation to the trials," he said hastily. "Drop the bar and I'll untie you. The Overseer will address you shortly."

"Are you fucking kidding me?" I asked, panting, the bar still firm in my grip. A billion questions filled my head, like why the hell Cormac hadn't known about this initiation bullshit when he was gathering intel? What was the point of it, and what information had they wanted from me?

"It's not my place to say more," he said, his voice shaking as he spoke. He glanced to where the blond guard lay motionless on the floor, blood pooling around his body. He was still breathing … barely, but he'd live. "Put down the weapon, and you'll see for yourself. The Overseer will tell you everything you need to know."

"Give me back my hand and then I'll drop it," I replied, because there was no way I was trusting him that easily.

"Yes, fine." He gestured for the remaining guard to hand it over.

The other grunt stood in the far corner of the room, his face pale and beaded with sweat. He dropped to his knees and slid my hand over to me cautiously. I scowled at the sound of metal scraping against the concrete. That tech was expensive, and the fucker was scratching it up while he refrained from pissing his pants. As much as I wanted to reattach it, I didn't trust the guards while I did. Fuck knows what they'd do in the few precious seconds it took for my brain's nerve endings to connect with the signals in my hand. I dropped the metal bar, quickly untying the ropes around my legs one-handed. I didn't want or need their help with that. I rose to my feet without a sound. My body ached, but I refused to give them the satisfaction of my pain.

"Open the door," the leader commanded, and the other guard punched a couple of buttons before the door slid open with a woosh. "Follow the hallway to the left."

I nodded, not giving them a second glance. They didn't deserve shit from me.

Stepping over the injured guard, I strode through and found myself in a hallway lined with doors. I leant back onto the wall and looked both ways before twisting my hand back on. My vision blurred as my brain reconnected to the metallic prosthetic. I hated this part; I was still there but lost control of my body and all awareness of my surroundings.

My vision cleared just as I was shouldered by a broad guy walking past me.

"Fucking asshole," I growled, my ribs smarting. The red-headed tool threw me a cocky smirk. He looked like someone had taken a bat to his face. Red and purple splotches covered his tanned skin and his right eye swelled to the point that it had closed entirely.

"They got you good," he said, giving me a shit-eating grin before turning and stomping away. "Beat you up and scribbled dicks all over your skin, that's rough."

"What?" I held my pale arms out before me and inspected my tattooed skin. Both were covered down to my wrists; my left inked with imagery that made my arm look bionic like my hand. My right was a contrast with swirls weaving through art or quotes that spoke to me .

Red's laugh boomed ahead of me. "Made you look."

"Flog," I grumbled under my breath as I followed him down the hallway, raising my bionic hand and moving each finger to make sure it was connected properly. If I had to take a guess, the guy was from the Crimson Steppes. He was built exactly like a boulder you'd expect to find in the desert, and he was about as funny as one too.

"Too easy, bro."

"I'm not your fucking bro." I punched him in the shoulder with my bionic hand and the man grunted, knocking into the wall beside him. Yep, it was working.

His split lips cracked even further as he snarled, turning on me. "Watch yourself, little twig. You don't want to get on my bad side." He wasn't much taller—maybe an inch or two—but his wide shoulders made him appear larger all around. I held my ground as he puffed his chest to intimidate me. It was almost laughable.

"Get out of my way," I said, holding his gaze. The man's muscles threatened to rip out of his linen shirt as he tensed. Dude clearly wasn't used to people standing up for themselves. "Do you understand me? If I knocked on your head, would it be hollow? Or perhaps it would rattle with rocks."

Red stepped back and laughed again. "You have big balls for a little twig."

"And yours must be shrivelled from all the shit you inject," I bit back, shoving past him.

Typical Steppes bullshit. All ego, no intelligence; no wonder they were at the bottom of the food chain. I had no time or desire to deal with meatheads like him. The initiation was over, and I had a job to do.

Thousands of years ago, when Earth became uninhabitable because of our destructive species, humans all moved here, to Initium Novum. The gold, jewels, and other priceless objects brought with them to Terrulia were stored in two places: The palace, and the House of Ascension.

There was no way into the palace without getting caught, which left the academy. Every sixty or so years, once the monarch either died or retired, those selected by each of the Houses aged between twenty and twenty-five were given the honour of competing in the trials, which meant temporarily living in the academy.

Cormac didn't want to waste the opportunity and as I'm the

best thief in the Drakes—scratch that, all of DH—he organised my nomination and a shot at making us rich.

So other than my job, I had no interest in making small talk or friends. Not that I'd ever be chummy with shit-for-brains here.

The corridor opened to a hall large enough to fit hundreds inside. Just as well there were only a handful of people, all in varying states of fucked up. I found a spot to lean against the wall and watch as newcomers entered through the two archways on either side of the room. I toyed with my hand, checking its wiring and ignoring the pain in my head and ribs. I'd had worse. None of my injuries were life-threatening but standing around wasn't ideal.

More people started filtering in. Some looked like they'd been dragged through glass and straight up whaled on. Bruised faces, broken noses, and bloodied clothing were the most common injuries, though many were limping or cradling broken limbs and digits. One guy had pissed himself but looked so shell-shocked, he didn't seem to care that people were staring. A few people formed small groups, but most stayed on their own, checking out the competition. I picked out the odd few who looked confident, and I shook my head at the delusional elitists who looked relieved, celebrating their wins. Poor fucks had no idea what was coming, but I knew things would only worsen for them. I just needed to get my loot and bail.

There was not a House in Terrulia that would let a gang member from DH become king. There would be an uproar and part of me wanted to actually compete just to watch them throw tantrums like children.

I rolled my eyes at the eager souls who stood before the stage at the opposite end of the room. They reminded me of groupies at a concert. No matter where you went in life, there were ass-kissers everywhere. The Crimson Steppes blockhead from the hallway had found himself a group mostly made up of people from his city. It was an easy pick seeing as they all wore cheap linen suited to the desert heat. Their attire would do them no good here, and their apparent leader would serve them even less. Red looked to have assumed command already. Domineering ass.

The room was filling up; there had to be easily a hundred people here. From what I could tell, there was an even spread of competitors from all over the country. Each city had different terrain and climates, and most people seemed to wear clothes suitable to their geographical location, so it was easy to tell where they came from. The Crimson Steppes crew all dressed like their douchebag leader, for the most part, though there were a few that had their own style. Many of the Tritosa City participants looked like they had just stepped off a beach. Then there were the snobs from Stormcrest City in their designer bullshit. Finally, the odd contestant from my home, Damascon Hollow, mostly wore jeans and t-shirts because we were normal and not like the other cities with their ridiculous clothes.

My eyes snagged on a woman walking through the crowd with confidence, her long black hair flowing down her back. I ran my gaze over her; she was clad in pants that cost more than a month's wage back in DH. I ran a thumb over my bottom lip. I'd bet she wasn't the only Potential with an expensive travel bag I could take and hock on the streets back home.

She turned and I hissed, seeing her copper eyes and a very recognisable, albeit bloodied, face.

Fallon Auger of House Jupiter. I should have fucking known.

Everyone in Terrulia knew of the Auger family. They were filthy rich and proud of it. People like her didn't have to lift a single finger whilst the rest of us fought for every scrap we had. The parents were like the damn godparents of the mafia, near untouchable in their pretty perch amongst the sky. That rich bitch and the rest of Stormcrest City were the worst of humanity. If there was one good thing that could come from Fallon being here, it was that she'd soon be dead. The world would be all the better for it.

In Damascon Hollow we fought and stole for scraps because of greedy people like her and her family who took more than they needed or deserved.

"Welcome Potentials! Welcome to the House of Ascension!" a voice called, hushing the crowd and drawing my attention away from the spoilt princess with a soul as black as her hair. "Wonderful, just wonderful!" A woman stood on the stage wearing a loose white gown with a brown belt tied around her waist. She clasped her hands together and looked over us all as though we were children. Those in the front row ate that shit up, the fucking brown-nosers. "I am Celeste, the Overseer of this esteemed academy, and I am thrilled to congratulate you on your first victory. You have passed the initiation and are set to walk a wonderous path towards unveiling our new monarch. Unlike the unworthy who failed today's task and have been sent home, all of you succeeded in keeping your secrets and defying your captors. A true leader must not buckle under pressure and you have all shown you can shoulder the burden."

A ripple of excited voices tore through the room. I felt nothing but anticipation for what was to come. The trials were just a game and oh, how I loved to play. There were at least one hundred people in the room, but only one could become the king.

"You stand within the hallowed halls of the House of Ascension, where greatness is forged and monarchs are made. Over centuries, kings and queens have walked these halls, trained on these grounds, and have been crowned upon this stage." She looked down to the floorboards at her feet and sighed lovingly, her shoulders sagging. "What a privilege it is for you to be on this journey. Nominated by your cities like knights of old.

"One of you will prove yourself worthy of the throne, and all of you will be guided by the best teachers in this country to ensure you are at peak mental and physical form." The woman waved her arm as though she were one of those chicks who revealed prizes on game shows. "There are three tasks you will undertake. One of physical strength, one of magic, and one of the mind. Each trial will test you and attempt to break you. Only the worthy will progress. This is not a journey for the faint of heart but a quest to uncover the worthiest to become our monarch."

I rolled my eyes at the way she spoke. We weren't in some fairy tale. It all sounded like an epic adventure, but this shit was real. The truth was most of these weaklings would leave these halls broken or in body bags. Many Potentials present were only here because of the blood running through their veins or the credits in their bank accounts. Privilege was a fine thing, but wealth was useless if you weren't around to spend it.

I would be sure to spend the money I made here well. I had my own ideas, as did Cormac. Lately, the Drakes had been making bank through some of Cormac's investments. He'd moved me from grunt work that got my hands dirty to prepare me for this job. Soon we would have more influence than ever before.

"Prior to each trial you will be allocated sessions for training," Celeste continued. "The Trial of Body is the first you must conquer, and so your training will be in combat, endurance, magic, and obstacles. The sessions aim to refine your skills and weigh your merit. Consider carefully in the coming weeks, whether you truly belong in this academy. Once you submit to the first trial, there is no going back.

"Each of you has been implanted with a chip that restricts your power for your safety and the safety of those around you. Your adaptive forms, should you have them, will not be affected," Celeste said in her annoying sing-song voice. "We will deactivate the chips when you require access to your power, so do not fear, the restriction isn't permanent."

The woman smiled broadly like some psychopath as she clapped. "Now, with all the admin out of the way, you can make your way to the guards at either side of the room, who will allocate you to a living quarter. Before you go, children, I must tell you this. Be sure you wish to continue down this path, for you may not come back from it. Only one is destined to wear the crown. The rest shall fall."

I chuckled, looking around at the Potentials. Sucked to be them. I was gonna be out of here before the first trial began.

# FALLON

The Overseer of the academy was a real peach. As if knowing we could all very well die during these trials wasn't enough, Celeste had ordered her cronies to grab us from our beds and beat us bloody.

Well, if they thought a few bruises and a split lip were going to break me, they were dead wrong. After being interrogated, I'd managed to knee one of the guards in the balls so hard he threw up, and I gave as many punches as I got once I'd hooked a blade from his belt and freed myself from the ropes.

Before I knew it was part of the initiation, they'd asked about my parents and their business, and I sure as shit wasn't going to tell them anything. Doing so put Ethan and Hadley in danger, and I'd die before I let anyone get to them, even if it meant protecting my psycho parents.

I looked around as the Overseer gave her grandiose speech, waffling on about knights and other rubbish as I studied my competition for the foreseeable future. Everyone was bruised and battered, and I swear I could smell someone's piss wafting through the hall. Some of the others were buying the sing-song, airy fairy bullshit Celeste was selling, but I wasn't signing a cheque. The whole charade made her actions worse in my books, like she was trying to hide the fact she was the one pulling the strings.

Near the front, Victoria caught my eye and sneered, already surrounded by a group of girls who were practically grovelling at her feet and cooing over my sister's beauty and her expensive clothes. I rolled my eyes and flipped the bird, turning my back on her to suss out the rest of my competition.

Three guys drew my gaze, and I assessed them curiously, trying not to linger on their easily distracting muscles and instead figure out where they came from. I knew we were in a competition, but I was only human. Besides, I needed to study them for … research. Yeah, that's why. A big redhead the size of a freaking house and bronzed and shredded like some roman god was laughing and jostling his peers. Everything about him screamed The Crimson Steppes. His brown eyes landed on me, and he sized me up like a predator eyeing its meal as he rolled his shirt sleeve up to reveal a large scorpion with boxing gloves hanging from its tail inked there. Yep, total fuck boy. I would have to be careful not to get on his bad side. He flexed his shoulders and gods dammit, I looked, because … research.

Moving on quickly before he could peacock about my wandering gaze, I looked to the next guy who had strolled onto my radar. He looked like a merman, his long blond hair as shiny as a shampoo commercial, with dreamy green eyes and tanned muscles which begged to be released from the tank top he wore. He caught my eye as he ran his hand through his long hair, which was shaved on one side. He winked, and I averted my gaze immediately, which unfortunately had me catch the eye of the guy who I knew had been shooting daggers at the back of my head the moment he'd seen me. Some things you can just feel without having to actually see them, ya know?

I didn't have to guess where he was from. Judging by the ink covering his very naked, muscled torso—and let's not forget the creepy bionic hand—he was a Damascian, and definitely a gang member. Though he was leaner than the other guys, he was all muscle, but the cold glint to those watchful grey eyes gave me the impression he was intelligent and observational, and probably ruthless as fuck. I spotted the two-headed dragon tatt over his heart, confirming my suspicions. Yep, he was a Drake—a member of one of the most brutal gangs in Damascon Hollow who also seemingly hated my guts. He spat on the ground when our eyes met, and I smirked, tossing my hair over my shoulder dismissively.

Fuck my life. Day one and I already had an enemy. Not to mention a couple of competitors that would take a little more effort to defeat than the rest. Oh, and apparently the Overseer had chipped us like damn dogs, blocking our magic. Peachy keen.

Celeste clapped her hands together, rubbing them gleefully like a fly spotting spoiling fruit. "Well then, chop chop, everyone. Form rows and the guards will call your name and direct you to your assigned dorms. Breakfast will be served in the cafeteria shortly, then you may take the day to recover. You will each be given a smart cuff to wear on your forearms. They will show your personalised timetables and notify you with updates from your tutors and me. Contact with the outside world is blocked, but we encourage you to use the Acadameet app on the cuff to socialise."

I scoffed. Sure, because becoming besties with your competition in a deadly game is a great idea.

"Lessons will begin promptly at 9 am tomorrow," Celeste finished with a broad smile. "Dismissed!"

A collected grumble filled the hall as everyone shuffled into lines. Yeah, I was pretty pissed about not being able to contact Ethan or Hadley. I didn't give a shit about anyone else—it's not like I'd ever been able to have any real friends. My parents had ensured we were locked away from the world so no one could use us for their gain or exploit our wealth. I was mostly fine with that fact, except for the few 'friends' they allowed to visit solely because they wanted to play nice with other important families. It was peak controlling behaviour, of course. The people they chose were insufferable, to put it nicely, and Ethan and I always managed to ditch them to hang out together. Except when I snuck off by myself to explore the city that is. *Especially* when 'exploring the city' was really exploring the body of whichever guy was currently eager to please a daughter of House Jupiter. A girl's gotta blow off some steam somehow. Getting off with some guys who thought they could gain influence by getting into my pants was one way to go about it. They thought they could use me, so I wouldn't feel bad about using them right back.

The secret missions were often made more exciting because of the danger involved, but it was kind of annoying too. Victoria was the only one our parents trusted wholeheartedly, which meant she was allowed into society and could hang with whomever she wanted. Probably because she'd cut anyone who tried anything. She was freaking terrifying like that.

"Fallon Auger," the guard yelled out, and the room hushed to whispers as I stalked forward, ignoring a hundred pairs of eyes on my body. "Follow him," he grunted, jerking his head to another guard who promptly turned around.

"Auger scum," someone roared behind me, and the room burst into laughter as everyone threw insults in his wake. I winced, but I didn't slow. My lack of a social circle meant I was a little short on backup, and my reputation was that of a spoilt snob who thought she was better than everyone else, but ... seriously? These people had no idea what was really going on and wouldn't believe me if I tried to convince them otherwise. Victoria didn't get off quite so easily either, but her reputation as a cold, hard bitch helped sway them to keep their mouths mostly shut. She also had rich, influential friends who loved to gossip and spread rumours. I didn't have the same influence, so everyone seemed set on hating me on her behalf as well.

Those mother fuckers could taunt me all they liked, but I

was the one who'd come out of this on top. And I had better tricks up my sleeve than a few tired insults.

The guard led my small group through a long corridor with numerous classrooms on either side before finally escorting us across the grounds towards a domed building on the other side of the courtyard—presumably where the dorms were. The academy was huge, dotted with numerous training arenas and tracks that seemed to match Terrulia's cities. A river snaked between the grassy fields, trees, and red rock jutting out from the ground, leading to a lake by the eastern edge of the academy surroundings. Another dome that appeared to be filled with fluffy clouds and lightning flashing inside sat propped up on a hill to the west. There was also a weird metal scrapyard set up like a maze to the north. The academy grounds was set up like a mini version of Terrulia, all innocent-looking and gleaming before it ate us alive.

We made it to the dorms and marched past several students chattering excitedly among themselves or watching cautiously as they waited to be let inside their rooms. I caught the eye of a tall, dark-skinned man with short-cropped hair and brown eyes. He looked at me curiously, and I got a glimpse of green shimmering out from his top. He shifted his shirt self-consciously but didn't drop his gaze from my face. So many yummy Potentials around. I winked at him, chuckling as his lips twitched with the faintest hint of a smile. So much confidence here, but the question was, who had the skills to back it up?

After climbing an endless set of stairs—seriously, have they not heard of elevators?—we finally made it to the top floor after multiple drop-offs until it was just the guard and me. He led me towards the room at the end of the corridor, jabbing his thumb at the door. "This one's yours," he grunted, handing over the smart cuff before he left without another word.

Grumpy, much? I sighed, fastening the cuff around my wrist. I tapped the screen and it blinked to life, showing a couple of basic apps; Timetable, Map, a couple of media apps, and Acadameet.

I'd check them out properly later, right now I wanted to see my room. I reached for the handle, squaring my shoulders. To my surprise, it opened with a bang and I stumbled forward into warm, muscled arms. It was actually kind of nice to be held and I allowed myself to stay there for an embarrassing smidge too long. Gods, how messed up was that? When the person cleared their throat, I looked up into glittering green eyes and sparkling white teeth and backed away quickly.

Well, what do you know? It was the guy with pretty blond hair. Up close, I could see he even had colourful shells and beads plaited in sections of it. He laughed.

"Hey babe. It's okay if you've got sea legs, you can cuddle in my arms anytime you like. All you have to do is ask."

I raised a brow. "Sea legs?"

"Yeah, you're clumsy, but it's okay, you're totally hot so it doesn't matter."

"I am not clumsy," I said indignantly. "You threw the door open and—"

"Shh," he said, placing a finger against my lips. "It's okay my little starfish, I've got you. Are you rooming here?"

I shrugged him off, glaring at his too handsome face. "No, I just came for the grand tour," I drawled, looking around the expansive room. There was enough space to stretch my wings if I ever conjured my adaptation form. Despite the size, there were only six beds, and judging by the belongings piled on each, all but one had already been claimed. Dammit. At least the guards had been kind enough to grab our bags when kidnapping us. How thoughtful.

The one positive was that everyone else appeared to have left already.

"You can bunk above me," the merman said with a wink. He strode over and patted the mattress above his.

I glanced down at his bed to see he'd already laid out his pyjamas, which just so happened to be a shorts and t-shirt combo featuring him riding two dolphins in various poses, with the words, 'surf's up' repeated everywhere. Interesting clothing choice...

"Yeah, sure," I said, not giving two shits where I bunked. He didn't give off vibes of being anything beyond a threat to fashion, so at least I could sleep without expecting to be knifed sometime in the night. Apparently, though, the gods were out to get me, because a big beefy bastard with dirty blond hair, squinty blue eyes and a sneer on his face chose that moment to storm into the room, eyeing me off like a piece of meat.

"Well, well, well," he said, his eyes raking over me. He stalked into my personal space. "I knew you were signing up to the tournament but I wasn't expecting such a fine piece of ass. The name's Mark." He put his arm around my waist and I flinched as his fingers slid under my waistband.

The merman stepped forward to intervene, but I shook my head. I fought my own battles.

The creeper clinging to me laughed. "Relax, baby, I'm going to show you a good time."

"Hard pass." I put one hand up, but he dug his finger into my waistband and pulled me closer, licking up the column of my neck.

"I like it when they fight back. Makes the catch all the sweeter."

The hairs on my arms stood on end and my skin crawled as I placed two hands on his chest and shoved him into the bunk bed. "The fuck is wrong with you? Get the fuck off me."

"Angel bitch," he spat. "You'll get what's coming to you."

The merman stepped forward and ushered me behind him, but I planted my hands on my hips and smiled sweetly. "I didn't expect to be rooming with a creepy lowlife like you, but alas, here we are."

"Your reputation doesn't do you justice," he snapped. "You're more of a cow than everyone says and trust me, there is a lot said about you. I'm from the Verdant Plateau and even there we've heard of the spoilt brat from the clouds."

Of course he'd call me that *after* I rejected him.

"Ah, but you have heard of me," I said, tapping my nose before turning away from him. "I, on the other hand, have no idea who you are. I don't waste my time with petty gossip or those who believe it."

"Nobody turns their back on me like that!"

He reached out to grab my wrist and I twisted. "Touch me again with your greasy paw and I'll break all your fingers so bad you won't be able to wipe your own ass."

He growled, charging at me like a bull, and the dolphin dude just stepped out of the way, leaning on the other bunk like it was the best show ever.

I conjured my wings, flapping right above the asshole attacking me so that he collided with the metal post of the bunk. "Hey dipshit," I called from my perch on another bed. "Come and get me."

"Bitch," he hissed. "You're going to pay for that. You House Jupiter cunts are all the same, with your expensive houses and your fucking wings. Let's see how well you fly when I rip those pretty little feathers out."

He slipped a knife from his pants, and I narrowed my eyes, dropping to the floor in a crouch. What the hell? I didn't think weapons were allowed in the academy, but it didn't matter. I sure as shit could finish him with my fists. He lunged, and I dropped beneath him and drove my fist into his groin as hard as I could, following through with a punch to his nose. He dropped the knife to cup his appendage as he fell to the floor where the blade clanged beside him.

Blood streamed from his nose, and I leaned back with a smug grin on my face. "Next time you run your mouth, you better back it up with a real fight. And if you try to shank me in my sleep, I'll spank you so bad you'll be calling for your mummy."

"Less brains than a jellyfish," the merman said as he looked down at Mark in disgust. "Your attitude messes with my vibe. Learn to chill in the communal space, yeah?"

Mark glared between us but seemed to have enough sense to know when he'd lost. He exited the room with a few grumbles and his tail tucked between his legs. Mentally, I added a strike to my enemy list. That wouldn't be the end of it.

"Holy shit," a small voice squeaked. We both turned around, finding a petite girl with dark brown hair in space buns standing in the bathroom doorway. She was dressed in a hot pink crop top and tight black pants with a silver chain dangling from the hip to pocket. Honestly, she was cute as a button. "You just decked Mark Leroy without breaking a sweat."

"You can never trust a Mark," the merman said in a conspiring tone, slinging an arm around my shoulders. "Especially one with a fragile ego. But he's old news. I'm Zane Loch, from Tritosa."

"From—from the Loch family?" the girl breathed. I didn't blame her, his dad was the head of House Neptune and had one of the wealthiest, most respected families in Tritosa City—the water world built under the sea. I swear I just about saw stars in her eyes as she looked at him and had to visibly shake herself out of whatever mesmeric trance she fell into. "I'm Kendra Reynolds, from The Crimson Steppes. No big name, just … just me. And you're Fallon Auger," she said in awe.

I smiled. "Well, just Kendra, it's nice to meet you." I held out my hand and was pleasantly surprised when she took it, smiling back. Maybe the trials wouldn't be so bad after all, and perhaps I was wrong about the whole not socialising with my competition. Maybe friends were off the cards, but a few allies couldn't hurt.

# FALLON

Okay, maybe I was jumping the gun at thinking things might go well. After having the crappiest sleep of my life thanks to keeping one eye on Mad Mike—or Mark or whatever his name was—most of the night, I'd been thrust straight into combat training as my first lesson.

And guess who I was up against. Kayden freaking Hale, the huge unit from the Crimson Steppes. I mean, it should have been illegal to have muscles that big. He was practically the size of a bus … not that I was complaining about the view.

The sun glimmered obnoxiously happily above as I stretched out my muscles. I groaned, wishing I could drown my bad mood in coffee. Instead, a few unfortunate souls had suffered it already this morning. I didn't feel bad about it—this was a competition after all—and they were throwing just as many punches my way. It just sucked for them that none landed like mine did.

I stretched, ignoring the groans of students getting the shit kicked out of them. Ah, just another day in the life. Combat training class took place outdoors, but of course we didn't get to practice on the soft, spongey grass lining the hills nearby, or on the glittering sands by the lake. No, we were in an area with red compact earth that hurt like a bitch to land on. A fact my new opponent had indulged in after driving everyone into it with his damn rock hands.

Kayden's bronzed skin gleamed with sweat, tracking down his pecks all the way to the vee at his navy sweatpants. He caught me staring, and I did my best to paste on a 'fuck off' expression which caused his brown eyes to crinkle with amusement as he smirked.

"Like what you see, angel? I can show you more in my room later—show you how men from The Crimson Steppes handle their women."

I shrugged, smiling like a cat. "No thanks, I'm afraid your size has gone everywhere except where it really matters."

Kayden bristled, and I bounced on my toes, anticipating the fight. Bullies with as much brawn as him didn't have the brain power to do anything but swing their fists.

He lifted a gigantic arm inked with a scorpion lifting a pair of boxing gloves, flicking his fingers for me to advance. "Don't feel too bad when I drop you on your ass, gorgeous. Wouldn't want you to chip one of your pretty nails."

I feigned indifference, studying my black nails as they sparkled in the sunlight. "Actually, I had them sharpened just before I came. Never know when a girl might need to draw blood."

"She fights dirty," he purred, licking his lips. "I like that."

"Enough chatter," the combat trainer barked from across the ring. Master Nolan, one of the Overseer's three musketeers and a total asshole. Apparently, he enjoyed pairing fighters with impossible odds, because Kayden had already taken out half the group and left them groaning on the ground, cradling broken bones and nursing new bruises.

Nolan didn't seem to care about the injured, ignoring them as they moaned about their wounds. I would have been concerned for them if it wasn't for two things; the giant rock currently trying to knock me out, and the fact that we were in a competition. If those students had to go home because they couldn't cut it, I wouldn't be the one standing in their way. I seized my moment while Kayden was distracted, tearing across the dusty red arena and flicking dirt in his eyes to blind him. He grunted, clawing at his eyes, and I climbed his back like a ninja and wrapped my legs around his neck, squeezing my thighs tightly. The muscles in his neck corded with effort as a snarl ripped from his throat.

He reached up and grabbed my shirt to toss me forwards, then gasped for air while simultaneously stomping the ground with his crushing feet. I rolled across the dirt quickly, his foot missing me by an inch, then rose into a crouch, swiping my leg at his feet while he was unbalanced so he would fall on his ass. But he flung out an arm, grabbing my shirt again and taking me with him as we hit the red dirt.

The momentum of his fall and my countering his hold on me caused us to roll across the training grounds, his weight damn near flattening me until we came to a stop. I punched him in the jaw as soon as we stopped, hissing in pain as the skin over my knuckles split. It was like punching an actual rock. Apparently, his strength and size were accompanied by some sort of magical barrier that hardened his skin—a trait I'd heard was an uncommon gift, even for those born in the Crimson Steppes. Either way, boulder brain was gonna pay.

His laughter boomed in my ear as he rolled us once more and pinned me down, securing my wrists and sliding his leg between mine so his dick—which was either suspiciously happy to see me or was just way bigger than I'd given him credit for—pressed against me.

Hunger swirled in his gaze, and I had to admit, it was pretty freaking hot being overpowered by this guy. But I wasn't exactly the submissive type and the look in his eyes said he knew that too. I writhed against him, and a soft groan pulled from his chest.

"Keep doing that, angel, and we're going to give the audience a real show in a minute," he said huskily.

I looked around to find everyone watching. Did this guy really think I'd submit to this dominant bullshit? It took a lot more than some muscles and a big dick to get me going—well, okay, sometimes that worked, but not with high stakes like these. Besides, someone had to teach this misogynistic prick a lesson sometime soon.

I snarled. "Get off me you big brute."

He grinned, slamming my wrists into the ground so hard that pain flared up my arms, the bones in my wrists jolting. "The next time you take me on, I won't be so kind," he hissed in my ear before getting up and walking away.

"Jerk," I muttered, getting to my feet and dusting off my shorts.

Kayden shouldered the guy with the bionic hand on his way past. "Woops, sorry twiggy, didn't see you there."

"It's Ace."

The guy flung his hand out, cracking his bionic fist so hard and fast into Kayden's gut that everyone gasped as the big guy stumbled back a step. I laughed, and everyone looked at me like I was going to get my head ripped off, but fuck if I wasn't going to enjoy the show. Where was the popcorn when I needed it? If this guy wanted to take Kayden on, I'd get my pom poms out and do a little dance.

Master Nolan appeared to be as eager as I was to see how this thing would play out, despite the constant scowl on his face. He stood with his arms folded over his wiry chest, his brown eyes fixated on the two men who clearly hated each other. For what reason, I had no clue, and I didn't particularly care. Let them destroy each other, more's the victory for me.

Kayden blinked, his eyes narrowing into dangerous slits at Ace's back as the smaller Damascian strode away.

I hadn't heard much about Damascon Hollow, but everyone knew it was rough. The city was famous for its gang rivalry and high crime. Drugs, trafficking, theft, you name it. Unlike the rest of Terrulia, however, that city didn't bother to hide it. People born there could never really afford to get out, and those that entered into gangs … they were in them for life.

"Catch up with him," Master Nolan barked at Kayden and pointed at Ace. The guy clearly wasn't happy about how the tiff had de-escalated. "He's your next sparring partner."

Kayden grinned, hulking off to where the guy from DH stood, tapping away at his cuff. Ace's shoulder's slumped at Kayden's approach and he tossed his cuff onto the dirt irritably before moving into a stance opposite Kayden.

Kayden roared, racing towards Ace, picking him up, then slamming him to the dirt. They ended up rolling in a scrabble of fisticuffs, and even Nolan's eyes widened delightedly as they threw wild punches, blood misting everywhere as they fought. He'd gotten the raw fight he was hoping for.

Eventually the trainer seemed to tire of it though, blowing a whistle that had us all holding our hands to our ears. "Enough," he roared as his scowl deepened. "Both of you, go find other people to hit. As for the rest of you, get back to work or I'll partner you with one of these assholes."

I chuckled, lingering a little longer to enjoy the sight of the guys glaring daggers at each other before heading off in opposite directions. I noticed another guy hanging back, being verbally assaulted by the over-enthusiastic and animated merman, Zane, while they sparred together. I recognised him from the dorm hallway—the cutie with dark skin and green shimmer. He was quiet as a mouse as Zane did enough talking for both of them.

Zane noticed me standing there and waved as I moved to spar with Kendra, a stupid grin on his face. Day two and my assessment of the competition was proving more intriguing than expected as some obvious tensions were heating up, but at least I had made two potential allies.

Things sure were getting real interesting, real quick.

# ZANE

If Zara could see me now, she'd be choking on a tentacle. My sister didn't believe me when I said I'd been nominated for the trials, but the joke was on her. Sure, technically I'd had to do a bit of a work around to get my nomination through because my dad had other bright ideas for me and House Neptune, but that was beside the point. Once I won this little set of trials, I'd have a parade that visited every city of Terrulia with a marching band, confetti, and fireworks. Yeah, fucking fireworks that spelled out my name in sparkly letters that glowed so bright my dad could see them through the surf.

A fist hit my jaw and I was literally smacked back to reality by my sparring partner. I'd gotten distracted planning my victory parade and forgot all about the dude opposite me. Noah was quiet. Like … he barely said shit all, which was weird because I loved a good chat and I may have liked to hear my own voice but a little back and forth was always good for the soul, you know? I was determined to get him to warm to me, like two marshmallows roasting over a fire warm. There was something about this dude that just screamed lonely, and I wanted to fill that obvious void in him that begged for a cuddle and friendly ear.

We stood a few feet apart in our section of the outdoor training area. It could best be described as a dust bowl, which wasn't great for my gills. Fine sand and hard dirt dried them out quickly and made my neck itch. Around me, the other Potentials looked a little worse for wear. The dude from The Crimson Steppes had laid into a few before he was partnered up with Fallon. They'd put on a bit of a show, but the main event had been between Kayden and the broody guy from Damascon Hollow. How that skinny dude had held his own against the giant boulder was a mystery to me. Then again, Ace was a member of the Drakes.

"Shit in a sailor's hat!" I hissed after Noah landed another fist to my head.

"You're really good at this," he deadpanned. "Your focus is impeccable."

I wiped a hand over my face. I needed to concentrate on the dude who needed my help, not the drama going on around the place. His sarcasm couldn't hide what I knew dwelled deep beneath the surface.

"So how do you like your roomies?" I asked, trying to start a conversation once more while rubbing my jaw.

"I don't really know them," he replied with a shrug of his dark, muscular shoulders.

I groaned at his basic reply. I wish they hadn't put stupid chips in us to block our magic. I could have used my power to relax the shit out of him and loosen his tongue.

"There's an absolute babe in my room." I grinned, thinking of Fallon's sweet body and how she slept on the bunk above me. I reckon I could convince her to dive down to my reef in no time. "Gonna have to ride that wave before the first trial."

Noah didn't reply, instead bouncing on his feet as we circled each other. I was starting to think the dude had the personality of a sea sponge—and I'd tried conversing with a few of those. Nothing but a waste of time.

I sighed. I'd persist with Noah until he was sharing all his deep-seeded feelings with me in no time. There had to be more to him, I just knew it.

We continued moving around, but then I saw an opening and went for it. I was an opportunist, what can I say? I lunged for Noah, throwing a fist into his side. He grunted, following my blow with a retaliating uppercut to my jaw. He was really working over my face which was a huge no-no in my books. I leant my weight into my next punch then tackled him to the ground, landing on top of him, straddling his hips and pinning his wrists. He flopped around like a beached tuna fish, which was weirdly endearing.

I laughed, my muscles straining as I held him down and basked in my win. I was destined to be the king of Terrulia. No one could get in my way, no one could defeat me. I was going to prove to everyone that I was meant for great things. A king among peasants. I was—

"Oh fuck!"

Noah flipped me then slammed his fists into my ribs repeatedly. For someone who didn't like to use his words, he sure knew how to use his fists. I blocked most of his hits, only to get one to the neck. Pain shot up my throat and I growled, throwing him off me. Getting hit in the gills was second only to a kick to the balls. It was excruciating. He fell somewhere to my left whilst I lay there, puffing, my hand wrapped around my throat and my eyes squeezed shut.

Last time I'd been hit in the gills like this was because my brother Zeke had been pissed that I'd eaten his chocolate brownie, but look, he shouldn't have left it lying around unprotected. As I said, I was an opportunist and leaving a brownie all alone on a plate while he got up to answer his phone was a rookie error. Never mind that I had been the one on the other end of the line. Zeke obviously should have known better. It's why I was the only person from my family competing in the trials. My siblings weren't fit to protect dessert, let alone a country.

"Your problem is that you don't shut up," Noah said from somewhere nearby, and I opened my eyes to see him lying on his back with an arm over his face. "Even when you're not talking, I can tell you're talking."

"That's oddly insightful," I replied, turning onto my side and propping my head on my hand. "Tell me more."

He dropped his arm to look in my direction, rolling his brown eyes. Without a word, he got to his feet then offered his hand to me. "Okay."

"Really?"

"Nope."

"Why not?" I asked, letting him help me up. "Friends help each other."

"Then I suggest you go find them," he said simply.

My little fighting fish, being all cute and hard to catch. "You're my friend," I replied with a knowing wink.

"Not possible," he said, his face blank. "It's illegal."

"To be friends?"

"Yep. Unfortunate, I know, but the law is the law."

"You're lying," I said, adding another wink for good measure. "Am I?"

He turned away from me, but not before I saw his lips quirk. 1-0 to Zane. Not only had he given me some insightful commentary, but he'd offered me his hand! I'd finally cracked the dude's exterior and was ready to dive in and explore the treasures within. We were each other's competition, I wasn't delusional, but there were multiple trials which would mean weeks at the academy. Being a loner just didn't suit me. I was collecting friends like a pirate collected jewels. Might as well add my fighting fish to my loot.

Looking around the training area, I spotted the other person I wanted to enjoy my time with. Fallon was sparring with Kendra, seeing as Kayden had been told to use some other Potential as a punching bag. I had to admit, I was pretty relieved when he'd walked the other way and chosen some other poor dude to spar with. Kayden was one massive unit and I didn't like the way he had been crushing my little starfish, Fallon, beneath him. She could have gotten seriously hurt. Kendra was holding her own, but she was no match for Fallon, who had her on the ground within seconds. It was fucking hot watching her move like that. Confidence and skill were such a turn on.

I retied my long golden hair, watching Kendra get a few good hits in. The girl struck as quick as a snake. Grabbing Noah by the bicep, I tried to drag him along with me to where the women stood.

"No way," he said, shaking me off and striding away. "Give it a rest, man."

I sighed. The poor dude really needed a shoulder to lean on. I looked back at the girls, who were now sitting on the ground casually chatting like old friends. Why wouldn't Noah give in and chill with me? Couldn't he see that we were surfing a wave towards the shore that was our friendship?

A whistle sounded, the noise shrill in my ears.

"Time's up!" Master Nolan declared, blowing the whistle once more. He stood in the middle of the training area, hands on his hips. He looked like a high school PE teacher with his matching tracksuit, rounded stomach, and a look of fallen dreams in his eyes. Nolan was definitely the type to mope about *almost* being someone special if it hadn't been for blowing out his knee or something like that. I guessed that was the reason for the constipated look on his face all the time. "You're dismissed!"

I headed towards my room, grabbing my hoodie and cuff on the way. I passed a few familiar faces from Tritosa City as they made their way from the training area. My father had nominated a few people from Neptune House, and I smiled at each of them when I caught their eyes. There were a lot of people here, so I didn't blame them for not noticing me. I'd have to send them a text through Acadameet and organise a catch-up. They'd be part of my pod in no time.

My dorm was on the top floor of the residential building, which was probably the fanciest part of it. The room was nothing to text my brothers or sisters about, not that I could anyway. There would be no bragging coming from me in that department, which was bogus because you'd think they could have organised some lux rooms for the possible future ruler of this country. Unfortunately, we were stuck with plain walls, bunk beds, and a communal bathroom.

After a hot shower and a good clean of my dusty gills, I dropped onto my bed and slid on my cuff. I tapped the screen on my wrist, sending a couple of texts to those from the water city, before drafting one to Fallon. I hit send then stretched my arms behind my head just as my little starfish strolled in.

I waved her over and she smiled. She was so cute in her little black short-shorts and tank top, and I bet she had no idea. Maybe it had something to do with how most people kept looking at her like she was some evil bitch. Sure, her parents were the owners of one of the most successful companies in Terrulian history and usually where there was a huge profit margin there was some form of exploitation, but could Fallon really be to blame? I was pretty sure she was younger than me and I hadn't had the time to build a trillion-dollar company. My plan had always been to make my mark on the world by becoming king, so other than learning what I could do to make that happen, I spent most of my free time surfing with my dolphins. Pip and Delilah were the best friends a dude like me could ever have.

"Hey Merman," Fallon said with a smirk, coming to stand beside our bunk. She waved her cuff at me. "Were you feeling lonely here all by yourself?"

"Maybe." I shrugged. "Get into any more fights today?"

"Nope," she replied, popping the 'p'. "Though I haven't seen our friendliest of roommates."

"He's probably avoiding you after you totally showed him up

and bruised his giant ego," Kendra said with a smile as she strode in and headed for her bunk.

"Ha! What a blowfish." I chuckled, rolling onto my side and patting my bed. "Sit for a bit."

"Why?"

"Because it's early afternoon and we're stuck here with nothing to do until dinner," I replied with a grin. "What else is there to do with our down time?"

"How about we go exploring instead?" she asked, tapping her plump bottom lip. "I wanna check out the rest of the grounds."

Aw, how cute, my little starfish playing all hard to get. I did want to check out the lake though and get all deep and personal in it. "Fine," I said with a sigh. "But next time, I get to choose our activity."

"What makes you think there will be a next time?" she asked, raising a brow at me.

I grinned. "You'll see."

"Indeed we will," she said, her lips quirking. "I'm going to shower and change. Give me a minute."

While Fallon collected her things from her bunk and showered, I grabbed myself a t-shirt, shoes, and brushed my hair. I hated when it got knotted, so I made sure that it was brushed properly before I tied it up. By the time Fallon stepped out of the bathroom, I was leaning against my bunk and ready to go.

"Want to join us, Kendra?" Fallon asked.

Her friend waved her off with a lazy yawn. "Nah, I'm good. Time for a nap." She winked at Fallon. "But you two have fun."

I was pretty sure Kendra was all cosied up and asleep in her reef before we'd even gotten past the door.

"Where should we start?" I asked once we made our way down the million stairs to the courtyard. There were a few Potentials out and about, enjoying the cooler part of the day.

"Let's look at the training areas that are modelled on our cities," she said, walking towards the nearest setup that looked like the Verdant Plateau. The training area had tall trees, lush green grass and even little ponds scattered around.

Crouching beside one of the ponds, I stuck a finger into the water and tickled a tadpole. "Hey cutie."

"What are you doing?" Fallon asked, a smile on her lips.

"Making friends."

"Of course you are." Fallon chuckled, sitting on the grass. "I'd love to live in the Verdant Plateau."

I dropped down, lying next to her and propping my head up on my wrists. "It's pretty nice. I reckon it'd be hella peaceful, but why would you want to leave Stormcrest City?"

"The city itself is beautiful. I mean, who wouldn't want to live in the clouds?" she said, laying down on her back. "The problem isn't the place though, it's the people."

"Home life that bad?" I asked as we stared up at the amber sky.

"It's not great." She huffed a laugh. "Couldn't you tell? Anyway, I'm here now and hopefully, that will change things."

"You think you have what it takes to become queen?"

She turned to face me, her brows furrowed and jaw set. I had to fight the urge to tickle her and turn that frown upside down, but one of my sisters told me some people don't like that. Strange, I know. Luckily, a smile spread on Fallon's lips, so I didn't have to resort to desperate measures.

"I have to."

"Me too."

"Do I have some competition on my hands?" she asked, her smile slipping up on one side, along with an eyebrow. "You gonna beat me to the throne?"

She looked like a sly fox. A sexy sly fox to be exact.

"Of course I am," I replied with a firm nod. It was my destiny, and you can't fight that shit. "I'm king material and you know it."

"Okay, king material," she said with a laugh as she rose to her feet, dusting off her pants. "Let's see what the other areas are like."

We strode along the path until we found ourselves in a mini Damascon Hollow. It was basically gnarly metal scrap in a concrete city, though it was kinda spooky because there were a lot of empty buildings, like some sort of apocalypse. Gave me the heebee jeebees, not that I let my starfish see that.

"I've never been to Damascon Hollow before," I told her, jumping up to grip a steel bar and swinging from it. "But the stuff I've seen on TV and the web don't look like this."

"Same," Fallon replied, watching me swing back and forth. "If there are places like this, I also haven't seen them."

I jumped, landing in front of her and smiling. "I bet if you had, you wouldn't have set foot in a place like this anyway. Probably a fancy hotel more like ... if they even have those there." I frowned. "Do they?"

Fallon rolled her eyes and walked away from me. "Maybe you should do some more research, seeing as you think you're going to be king."

"I don't think, *I know*," I said, catching up to her.

The next area was modelled on the Crimson Steppes and turned out to be an enormous sand pit with a few red rocks thrown around the place like some giant got drunk and dropped them.

"I've never been to the Crimson Steppes before either," I told her, leaning up against one of the boulders, only to have it move. "Shit!" I jumped back with a scream. "Not a rock!"

"No, you fuckhead," Kayden growled, turning around. He rolled his shoulders, the rocky surface of his skin smoothing out into its usual tan. "Could you not see my shorts?"

"I wasn't exactly looking," I replied, raising my hands as I stepped towards Fallon, my gaze running up and down her figure. She was gorgeous. Like, could dry up all the oceans hot. "Who notices anything when there are babes around?"

"She must have been really impressed with that high-pitched

squeal of yours," he said, snickering.

"I did not squeal." I placed a hand on my chest. "But you are right. I am super impressive."

"Oh yeah?"

"Yeah."

"Prove it," Kayden said, folding his arms over his broad chest. "Lift that rock over there."

I looked to where he angled his head. It was about the size of a basketball, but nothing I couldn't handle. "Piece of fish cake."

"I don't think this is really necessary," Fallon stated, though she sat her perfect ass on the sand anyway, clearly happy to enjoy the show. All she needed was some snacks and she'd be set because I was about to impress her so bad.

It occurred to me that our little game was a bit childish, but then, those were my favourite kind. Back home, I'd compete with my siblings over the most bogus stuff. Who could swim the furthest, how many calamari rings I could balance on my head... you name it, we did it. Being in the trials hadn't dampened my competitive streak no matter how bogus the contest.

I moved over to the rock and picked it up easily, lifting it over my head to show them just how strong I was. I made sure to really flex my muscles and, judging by the glint in Fallon's eyes, she appreciated it.

"Too easy, dude," I said, dropping the rock to the sand.

"No shit." Kayden picked up another rock, this one the size of a backpack. He did a few biceps reps, throwing me a shit-eating grin. I got the feeling the guy was having too much fun toying with me. I also couldn't help but notice Fallon's copper eyes were moving up and down with each movement.

"My turn!" I announced when she bit her lower lip. I scowled, not at all pleased with the way she was eyeing him up. Starfish was *my* date tonight.

"Here," Kayden said, grinning as he dumped it at my feet. "Be my guest."

"You joined us, so you are actually *our* guest," I replied, lifting the rock. My muscles strained a little, but only because they weren't used to this sort of impromptu weightlifting. They could totally handle it though, even without a warmup. I did a few quick reps, just so Kayden didn't feel left out, then dropped the rock. "Easy peasy. Are you going to give me a real challenge or what?"

"You asked for it." Kayden strode over to a rock—no, scratch that, a literal boulder the size of a baby dolphin—and lifted it into the air. Dude barely broke a sweat. He even had the audacity to wink at Starfish.

"Give it here." I swallowed hard as he strode over and dropped it at my feet. I reached for the rock and lifted it from the sand. I mean, I couldn't see if I *was* lifting it, but I was pretty sure it was at least a few inches in the air.

"Are you okay, Merman?" Fallon asked, getting to her feet. She stood beside Kayden, her brows scrunched, which was the exact opposite look of what was on Kayden's face. The dude was grinning like a shark about to eat a slippery seal.

"No problemo," I managed to get out. My arms and legs were shaking, and not in a good way. Actually, I'm not sure there was a good way. I was out of my depth and in my rush to get back to shallow waters I almost fell flat on my ass.

"Zane—"

"Woo! I'm pumped!" I jumped up and down, shaking out my limbs.

Kayden rolled his eyes. "Are you going to lift it now?"

"I already did," I replied, tilting my head to the side. Silly rock boy.

"No—"

"I have a better idea before someone gets hurt." Fallon jumped up, a mischievous glint in her eyes. "Race you both to the cafeteria! Last one has to tell Ace they love him!"

With that, she spread her copper wings and shot into the

air. She'd definitely get to the cafeteria first with her speedy angel feathers, especially as I had no idea where it was from here. Kayden shoved me hard in the side, knocking me to the sandy ground before bolting away, laughing like a mad man.

He could laugh for now, but the dude would be crying soon. I jumped up and took off into a sprint. He may have gotten a head start but it wouldn't help him in the long run. *Ha! I'm punny without even trying*. Kayden may have been strong, but I was as quick as a sailfish. Let him come up with some way to tell Ace he loved him without getting a bionic fist to the face.

# KAYDEN

I lifted the 300kg bar without breaking a sweat, my muscles bunching together as I pumped out my reps. Bench presses were my bread and butter, and right now it was just another way for me to intimidate the fuck out of my competition. If they could be even called that.

Most Potentials were only here on mummy and daddy's money or reputations, but they'd be lucky to last the first trial. The others were just running on borrowed time. Grains of sand for me to squeeze between my fists.

It paid to know one's opponents though, so I'd had Flynn start investigating any Potentials of note, including their adaptations and habits. Better to know what I was up against to prevent any unwanted surprises from the likes of Twiggy or Victoria Auger.

"Tell me about the loner," I said to Flynn while he spotted me. Not that I needed it. I could lift boulders without breaking a sweat, so weight training was just muscle memory at this point. The other night proved that. Zane was lucky the pretty little Auger girl ended our competition early.

Flynn and I always had each other's backs in every aspect of life, so it made sense for us both to be here. At the final trial, we would be true competitors and battle it out once and for all. I was amped for us to put everything we'd trained for to the test—Flynn and I being the final two would be something for the history books. He was the only worthy opponent in this place. When I won and became king he'd be my right-hand man, just with a few more responsibilities and a higher pay.

I didn't just want to become king. I needed to—for my family and for my home. And I would because I was Kayden fucking Hale. Failure wasn't a word I was familiar with.

"Noah Hawthorn. From the Verdant Plateau," Flynn replied. "He's yet to show an adaptation or magical ability, though judging by the way he lurks in the shadows I doubt either are all that powerful. Caught him with a book, so probably smart."

"And the merman?" I already knew a bit about him but was keen to hear if Flynn had anything else of note to tell me.

"He's got gills, so he's from Tritosa City," Flynn said. "Dude's annoying as hell, so he won't make many allies, if any."

I scowled. "I wouldn't be too sure about that. Fallon seems to have taken a liking to him."

"Beggars can't be choosers. Everyone else hates her. Guess she doesn't wanna be alone so is settling for the talking fish."

I huffed a laugh, lifting the bar and dropping it on the rack before sitting up and glancing around the room. It was full of other Potentials utilising treadmills, weight racks and other contraptions to keep their fitness up. Some of the Potentials had their work cut out for them. It was almost comical watching the scrawny ones shake with just a little weight.

I spotted the guy from Damascon Hollow over by the squat rack. Everyone gave him a wide berth, his attitude enough to scare most of the Potentials away. He didn't scare me though. Damascon Hollow wasn't that different from the Crimson Steppes, and I knew his type. Sure, we were the poorest of the four cities—our lack of resources and credits making it hard for us to compete—but that just meant we were survivors. Whilst the richer cities used credits to get what they wanted, we earned it with our strength, sheer determination, and true grit.

Wealth may make you popular, but it didn't make you worthy of being a ruler. Just one look at Victoria Auger was proof of that. The woman's personality was as appealing as a cactus. Without credits and her family's reputation, she'd be a nobody.

"Nevertheless, the Auger girls could be a problem. The younger one is a wild card," I responded, my blood heating at the memory of pinning Fallon down when we'd be training. The girl had fire ... I liked that. Most women fell at my feet, but that one would give back as well as she got. A nice change—one that shouldn't interest me but absolutely did.

I scanned the gym, spotting her running on the treadmill, her little friend with the funky hair sprinting on the one beside her. Fallon's tight black shorts shaped her ass perfectly, and I stared, transfixed as her long black hair bounced in a high ponytail.

A ponytail I could imagine wrapping my hand around once I clipped that angel's wings and reminded her who was boss.

"I don't like unknowns," Flynn said, swapping places with me as I slid off the bench. I moved around to spot him as he lay down beneath the bar. "We'll need to get to know them better."

"Already on it." I grinned.

"You look pleased with yourself, Kayden," Victoria purred as she strode over to us, her chest pushed out like her tits were trying to escape. Didn't blame them, I wouldn't want to be that close to her either. She'd been working at the squat rack nearby, but I hadn't thought she could hear my conversation with Flynn. I wouldn't be making that mistake again. "You managed to count your reps without assistance. Double digits can be so tricky."

"What do you want?" I returned my gaze to Flynn as he continued lifting. I wasn't gonna give the bitch my full attention, that was for sure.

Victoria stepped close enough that I could feel her breath on my skin. She traced a finger up my arm, the sensation making my stomach curl. "Actually I'm here to offer you some advice."

"I don't remember asking for it," I growled, shaking her off.

"All the more reason to give it." She smirked. "Stay away from my little bitch of a sister."

I raised a brow. "Feeling protective?"

"Hardly," she replied, shooting daggers to where Fallon was working out. "She's going to die here and I couldn't be happier. Might even throw a party."

Her groupies giggled like fucking psychos where they stood back, watching. My shoulders tensed at her words, the urge to eliminate her where she stood rising to the surface. Was I feeling protective? I shook my head because there was no fucking way. It was her heartless attitude that got a rise out of me. Yeah, that was it. We were all here to win and that might involve killing a few people, but to be planning a celebration after murdering your own blood? Victoria was one messed up bitch.

"Well, fuck," Flynn said as he lifted the bar and sat up. "Ice queen."

"Exactly," she said, flicking her long blond ponytail. "You look like you're hard to kill, Kayden, but that doesn't mean you'll wear the crown in the end." She stood taller, lifting her chin. "I will be queen. The throne is mine."

I rolled my eyes. This woman and her cronies were wasting my time with her delusions. "Hurry up and get to the point of why you're here."

She trailed her perfect nails along my biceps and I had to stop myself from grabbing that hand and snapping her fingers. "Your time here is limited, but I can't deny you'd be a useful ally. Why not work with me?"

"How does that benefit me?" I asked, laughing as I shook my head. She had to be joking. "If you're looking for a free ride, you won't find one here."

Victoria narrowed her copper eyes at me. "You are going

to die, Kayden. You won't win this. Don't you care about your parents?"

I stiffened. "Don't talk about them."

"Ally with me and once I'm queen I will make sure they are comfortable. Send them a few credits and lift them out of the poverty they currently dwell in."

"Like I can trust your word on that."

"Ruling is all about negotiation."

"How about this offer then?" I prowled closer, folding my arms over my chest and grinning as she was forced to look up at me. "You die, and I become king and raise the entire Crimson Steppes up to glory."

"Be realistic. I know it's hard to see facts when there's not much going on up there in that head of yours, but the Crimson Steppes will always be at the bottom. Someone has to be there and it's always going to be your city. That's just how the world works, but I could at least make it more comfortable for you."

"Fuck the world and your offer." I sneered at her. She'd be pretty if it weren't for that cutthroat look in her eyes that said she'd happily kill you in your sleep. "You and I will never be allies."

"You've just made a big mistake," she spat.

Victoria spun on her heel and stormed away, her minions following closely behind. I chuckled, enjoying winning that little verbal bout.

"She's gonna have it out for you," Flynn said. He was sitting on the bench wiping the sweat from his chest with a towel. The guy was ripped, but not as big as me. "You better watch your back."

"She already wanted to kill me before her measly offer," I replied with a smirk. "And I have you watching my back. Don't think you can best her?"

He scoffed. "Don't insult me."

"Wouldn't dream of it," I said, slapping him on the back.

Victoria Auger had always been my competition, but Flynn

was right. I'd have to keep an eye on her. Someone of her station didn't let rejection slide. She'd be out for my blood.

———— ✦ ————

I looked at my prospective minions, assessing them all with a keen eye. Some were decent, but most were passing at best. I shook my head. Nope, this would not do. These people needed a lot of work.

"You'd think none of them had done burpees before today," Flynn said, sneering as he came to stand at my side. "I'm embarrassed some of these people are from home."

"We'll have to work them harder," I replied. I put my hands on my hips and barked at the Potentials sweating before me. "You all need to put in more hours. Sleep is off the cards until you can do two hundred without breaking a sweat."

The Potentials groaned, the sound like music to my ears. What was the saying? 'No pain, no gain'. If they wanted to be on my team and stand a chance of surviving until the final trial, they had to put in the work. Nothing in life was free, and it was time for them to start paying.

"Trying to kill your minions?"

I turned to see Kendra striding towards us. She was a tiny little thing but letting her size fool you was a mistake. She was from the Crimson Steppes too, and though she looked like a fennec fox pup, she could sting like a scorpion.

"Want to help?" I asked, throwing her a grin. I could use her on my team, not that I'd tell her that.

Kendra shook her head, her long brown plaits swaying with the movement. "Just enjoying the show."

"Sure." I folded my arms. "I know it's survival of the fittest in the Crimson Steppes, but there's no shame in working together here. You'd be smart to hook up with the team with the best odds."

She surveyed my weakling minions with an amused grin.

"I'll keep that in mind."

"We're all from House Mars," Flynn said. "We should be working together. We have the same goal."

"To a degree," Kendra replied. "I want to help our city, but brute force isn't the answer."

"And what?" I scoffed, looking down at her scrawny figure. "You think you are the better choice?"

"It takes more than muscle to rule Terrulia," she said, poking me in the bicep. "If your parents thought you were a guaranteed win, they wouldn't have nominated the rest of us."

"The nominations were a matter of fairness."

Kendra smirked and patted my arm. "Okay, big boy. You keep telling yourself that."

She spun on her heel and practically skipped away, leaving me clenching my fists. Kendra had always known how to push my buttons. The chick was a shit-stirrer and had been since we were kids.

"Bro, don't listen—"

"I want fifty more!" I barked at my minions, cutting Flynn off.

A communal groan rose from the Potentials, but I ignored it. I'd show Kendra and the rest of them that I was made to be king. My parents nominated me because they knew that, and soon the rest of the world would too.

# NOAH

It was easy to remain hidden when you had the ability to camouflage with your environment. The green shimmer coating my shoulders and back helped me to blend in, but the downside was that I had to be butt naked for full concealment. The people I passed couldn't see me, but that didn't make it any weirder to have my dick out in public. I've had the ability my whole life but it didn't change the fact that stripping to my birthday suit with a bunch of people around felt pervy as heck.

Adaptations were common in Terrulia, though not universal the way powers were. Each city tended to have residents with similar adaptations, which was usually why they lived where they did. Stormcrest City inhabitants were more likely to have wings or gliding membranes, while Tritosa City was home to those who had gills or fins so they could swim unhindered in the ocean. There were also adaptations that were entirely random, like mine, and then there were people who didn't have one at all. Our gifts were weird like that.

Our magic was similar to adaptations in that locations tended to have clusters of similar abilities. Unlike adaptations though, magic could be easily concealed and was more diverse.

Think of any possible power and you'd find someone in Terrulia who could wield it to some degree.

I rubbed my side and frowned, irritated by the bruise Zane had given me from sparring. It was frustrating not to have access to my restorative power. Not being able to heal meant I had to rely on the doctors here and they refused to heal anything that wasn't serious. Really nice people, you know?

A shudder ran through me. If not being able to heal quickly wasn't enough, the air-con was amped in this place, the hallways consistently frosty, which was just dandy when I had no clothing. I cupped my junk and refocused on my target.

Mark Leroy.

I'd followed him back to his room after dinner in the caff, which my growling stomach wasn't too pleased about. I'd skipped eating just so I could lurk near his table and listen in on his conversation with his friends. They'd mostly talked about training and the upcoming trial, but then he made a flippant comment about meeting someone and now here I was; standing butt naked outside his room like a creeper, waiting for him to re-emerge.

Mark was from the Verdant Plateau like me, though he was from a family that had only come into wealth and influence in the last few years. One day no one had heard of the Leroys and the next they were attending the most exclusive events and spending credits like an oak tree dropping leaves in Autumn. The Leroy family's rise to fortune wouldn't have bothered me normally, but the sudden wealth coincided with a string of robberies concerning precious minerals and an increase of missing people around the Verdant Plateau.

Missing people like the Robinson twins, whom I'd grown up with and loved. They were orphans but they were as much family to me as my own blood. My mums had all but taken them in when I was younger, feeding them, giving them a bed to sleep in when times had gotten tough … they were sick with worry for the girls and so was I.

Katie and Rena weren't the only ones missing either. It's like someone was targeting our people from the Verdant Plateau city on purpose, picking out isolated members of the community and kidnapping those too weak to defend themselves.

The local police said they were looking into it. I called bullshit. Something wasn't adding up, and my instincts were pointing to Mark and his flourishing little family.

Unfortunately, I had no evidence of their involvement, which is why I'd decided to join the Terrulian Trials. Once I found out Mark had been nominated, I was all in.

I didn't want to become king. There was nothing about the role that interested me in the slightest. The Verdant Plateau was self-sufficient and the land was bountiful. We traded amongst ourselves and only reached out for things our citizens didn't produce, like phones and porta-bracelets. We were part of this country, but for the most part, we kept out of its affairs. House Ceres—my house—was known for its fair and honest leadership. My mums cared for the people of Verdant Plateau as though we were all one big family. My older brother, Wren, would follow in their footsteps and was already adored by the people, whom he loved in return. We were a respected family not because we were wealthy, but because we earned everything we had. The people trusted House Ceres to look out for their best interests, so that's why I was here trying to do just that and keep them safe.

Footsteps sounded down the hall and I pushed myself backwards, sucking in a breath when my ass cheeks touched the cold wall. A lean tattooed guy came swaggering towards me, his gaze focused on his smart cuff. Ace didn't look too pleased about whatever he was reading, though the guy rarely looked happy in general from what I'd seen of him. I bet he was a real treat to be around. They must have healed the worst of his injuries after the fight he had earlier with Kayden. Surprisingly, he was able to trade the big guy blow for blow, but he'd still walked away with a split lip and bruising cheek. Ace stopped a few feet away, grumbled incoherently, then took a quick scan of the hallway and slipped into one of the rooms. Suspicious, but not my problem. I had my city to watch out for and had no interest in dissecting whatever the Drakes had him up to within the academy's halls. The Damascon Hollow gangs were always doing dodgy stuff and that was a rabbit hole I would not be travelling down.

I waited a few more minutes, wondering whether I'd misheard Mark at dinner and I was wasting my time. I thought about packing it in for the night, but then the jerk showed his sneering face. Mark slipped from a room at the end of the corridor and once he passed me, I followed close on his tail. He led me down from the top floor and out into the courtyard, his steps making more noise than I think he'd like thanks to his bulky size. Moving with grace was not one of his talents.

There were a few lights around the place but mostly the grounds of the House of Ascension were cast in shadow. If I'd thought I'd been cold inside, it was nothing on the cool breeze out there. Mark bypassed the training areas modelled on the five main Terrulian cities and made a beeline for the caff. My stomach growled and I froze, praying to the gods that he didn't notice. When he showed no sign of hearing, I continued to follow, contemplating sneaking a bite to eat once I'd gotten an idea of what the guy was up to.

There were still groups of people in the caff, sitting around tables chatting like they were in high school and not in a deadly set of trials for a crown. It amazed me how even in circumstances where your life was at risk, there were still people who could act like it was just another day. As if all this was normal. The Terrulian Trials were known for their brutality. At best, you returned home shamed and sporting a couple of broken bones, at worst, you were given a one-way ticket to the grave. Turns out people liked to ignore such alarming details like the high probability of imminent death.

I, for one, thought contemplating my demise was an uplifting topic, like swallowing nails or cutting the bottom of my feet with razor blades. Really enjoyable shit.

Mark strode through the caff as though he owned the place, and I had to give him credit. There was something about his confidence that made him immune to attracting attention. If you acted like you belonged, people tended to believe you, and he sure as heck was acting as though he should be opening a door that clearly stated, "No Access".

Without looking to see if anyone was watching him, Mark stepped into the room and it took all my finesse to slip in after him without getting caught, my dick grazing the closing door as it shut. The place was dimly lit. We were in a storeroom, judging by the boxes and bottles that filled the tall shelves. I leaned in close to read that they were just cleaning supplies and nothing of note.

"It's me," Mark whispered, and a moment later the scrape of shoes had me turning around to find a hooded figure behind me.

I quickly sidestepped out of the way but not without trying to sneak a look under the mysterious guy's hood. Unfortunately, all I got was a stubbled chin.

Excellent investigating skills if I do say so myself.

"You're late," the hooded guy snapped. "Do you think I have copious amounts of time to waste waiting in a storeroom for you to grace me with your presence?"

"I'm here now, old man," Mark replied. "You're lucky I came at all."

The hooded figure rushed forward, grabbing Mark by his shirt and pinning him against the wall with an arm. "You're lucky I decided to cut your family in on this at all. Remember who you are speaking to."

"Alright, alright," Mark said, raising his hands. "Settle, all's good."

The guy scoffed, releasing him. "Just shut up and listen.

House Jupiter is expecting the next shipment to go out during the first trial. I want no problems, you hear me? If anything goes wrong your family will pay the price. Is that clear?"

"Crystal."

"Good, now get out," the hooded guy ordered before rounding the shelf. I crept after, only to see no sign of him. It was as though he'd disappeared into thin air. Behind me, Mark sighed, muttering 'bastard' under his breath as he shoved the door open. I quickly followed out the door but didn't go any further. Mark found a seat at one of the tables, lifted his sleeve, and started tapping on the screen of his smart cuff. The thing beeped a few times in quick succession and he scowled at it before stuffing his hand into his pocket.

I stood frozen in front of the closed storeroom door, watching Mark while going over what I'd heard. Mark was overseeing a shipment meant for delivery to House Jupiter during the first trial, but what would be on it? I ran a hand over my shaved head, pursing my lips. Would it have something to do with the disappearances? Stolen goods? Or something else entirely?

Then there was House Jupiter's involvement. How had Mark gotten wrapped up with them? Were Victoria and Fallon Auger somehow involved? And who was the hooded guy he was talking to? I had so many questions, but at least my suspicions were now confirmed. Mark and his family were involved in some shady shit with some very powerful people. House Jupiter was one of the wealthiest families in the entire country and I was certain that whoever the hooded guy was, he was either powerful in his own right or extremely well-connected.

Laughter filled the room and Mark's groupies scurried over to him, offering ridiculous compliments that made me want to gag. I was getting second-hand embarrassment just listening. Deciding that there was nothing more I could learn for the night, I went over to the snack bar for some fruit and found only grapefruits left. Ugh, not ideal but it would have to do. Grabbing the fruit, I strolled towards the exit. I was cold and drained after using my ability for so long, not to mention being exposed the whole time. Unlike my restorative power, which drained me quickly with more complicated injuries to heal, using my camouflage felt like going for a long run and getting that physical exhaustion that only a hot shower and a good night's rest could heal.

I was looking forward to both.

"That angel bitch is going down," a woman said as I passed the chattering group. "I can't wait to see her stuck-up face get what's coming to her."

Mark snorted like the piggy he was. "I'm going to film it on my cuff, then replay it over and over again for a laugh."

"Yes! You'll have to send copies to everyone," another woman giggled. "She is so pathetic it's almost sad. Did you see how Victoria snobbed her off? Like if your sister can't stand you, why would anyone else?"

"I know right!" the first woman exclaimed. "Victoria is so freaking cool and Fallon is just... blegh. I still can't believe she attacked you, Markie, she's such a hoe bag."

"She didn't attack me," Mark snapped. "I told you I tripped after I gave her a piece of my mind. The two things are completely unrelated. Fuck, Britney, you can be such an air head sometimes."

I didn't wait around for Britney's mumbled reply. Their conversation wasn't overly interesting, especially when most people around here spoke about Fallon in a similar way. It didn't help that Victoria shunned her sister. She'd probably invented a lot of the rumours too. The way Mark and the others spoke about Fallon gave me the impression that she wasn't involved in whatever the Leroy family and House Jupiter had going on.

Then again... Perhaps their hatred was a ruse, a sleight of hand that wanted us to look the other way and think that they hated her when in fact they were all working together. No, something about that conclusion didn't sit right with me. There was something about Fallon that was different to her sister. I just didn't know what it was yet.

I sighed heavily, opening the door to jog back to my room, only to slam into a hard chest and fall on my ass. My camouflage disappeared instantly and I stared up to find Kayden with a giant grin on his face. Moving faster than I thought the big guy could, he angled his cuff and snapped a shot of me in all my glory.

"Ewww, why is he naked?" one of his friends asked the woman next to her.

"Probably fucking the grapefruit," the other snickered, pointing at the fruit in question. "I hope he wasn't planning on doing it in here."

"Why else would he already be in the nude?" Kayden smirked.

Laughter rang around as cuffs buzzed and my cheeks heated. For fuck's sake. I rose to my feet, trying to cover my junk with one hand whilst holding the grapefruit in the other. Shit, why was I still holding it? I dropped the fruit then shoved passed Kayden and co, not bothering to get into a verbal sparring. What was the point when he'd already got a photo and had clearly captioned it with whatever story he wanted people to hear?

"Bro!" Kayden called to my back, chuckling as he shouted. "If you can't pull the ladies, there are other options! No need to assault the fruit!"

The door slammed behind me and I breathed in the cool night air, trying to forget about Kayden and his idiotic cronies. I refused to let him get to me, even if he sent a naked photo of me around the academy, insinuating that I fucked grapefruits. I had bigger problems to deal with.

Tomorrow I'd have to start looking into House Jupiter. Once I found out what they were after I'd be closer to knowing more on how Mark was exploiting the Verdant Plateau. The two Auger sisters would be the likely choices for my next spying session, though one stood out over the other, and not in a good way. Victoria Auger had the working of an evil mastermind. If anyone was dealing with Mark, it'd be her.

# FALLON

I headed towards the meadow with a smile on my face and a little pep in my step. My first magic class was this afternoon, and I was beyond ready for the chip to be deactivated so I could stretch my telekinesis muscles and kick some serious butt.

As much as I despised my parents and my family name, being the daughter of an Auger did have its perks. Victrus and Eliana had powerful telekinesis magic, and that gift had passed to me too. Of course, their brutal teaching had honed it, but I wasn't about to give them credit for that. I was strong because I refused to let them break me.

"Fallon, wait up," someone called from behind, and I turned to see Kendra jogging up the path, her long brown hair swaying with each step. She was wearing a white crop top with the words 'eat my dust' in bright pink on the front, paired with loose black pants slung low over her hips and a gold body chain looped over her slender waist.

Her style was super cute. It matched her sassy attitude.

I smiled warmly as she pulled up behind me. "Hey girl. What's up?"

"Oh, you know." She shrugged. "I'm enrolled at an academy

with a bunch of Potentials ready to stab me in the back so, just another day, really."

I snorted, thinking of my own ruthless family and how readily they'd put down anyone who got in their way. "Yeah, I can't say much has changed since I got here."

She put her hands in her pockets and tilted her head back to the sun, her high cheekbones glowing a soft pink over her glassy skin. "I'd rather not be pitted against everyone like this, but things have gotta change. I grew up in an orphanage back home and there're a lot of kids who don't make it. Where I'm from, you grow up fast or you don't grow up at all. I don't want to see that happen anymore. I don't want to pretend all those kids don't exist. This whole divide between the wealthy and the poor has gotta give."

I would have had no idea she'd gone through all that if she hadn't offered that information up so readily. She hid it well, but I liked her honesty. It was kind of jarring, but surprisingly refreshing. Plus, I had to give her credit for why she was here. She actually wanted to do some good. I'd bet many of the other Potentials here had less noble intentions.

"I couldn't agree with you more," I said. "It's why I want to be queen. To make things better. Not just for the country but for my siblings too."

"Plural? You have others besides Victoria?" Kendra asked, her eyes darting around for my wretched sister as she spoke.

I laughed. "Yes, but don't worry. My parents haven't corrupted them yet—or ever will if I have my way. I have a brother, Ethan, and a little sister, Hadley." I smiled, wondering what both were doing that very minute. "They're my everything."

Kendra nodded. "It must be special," she said softly, but not unkindly. "To have people who love you and look out for you. Not all of us are so lucky."

My heart did a sad little sigh at her downcast face. She was right, I was lucky to have my siblings. To have Ethan in my corner. Everyone deserved to have someone to love. Especially someone like Kendra.

"Hey," I said suddenly, grabbing her wrist and pulling her to a stop. "Let's make a deal to watch each other's backs while we're here. To make it to the end together. And whoever wins? We can cheer the other on when we're done with this place."

Kendra's eyes narrowed, even as a hopeful curiosity lit those dark brown eyes. "Why would you offer such a thing?"

I didn't blame her for being sceptical. Honestly, striking such a deal could bite me in the ass during the trials, but hell, I felt like I could trust this girl. She was clearly smart and strong, having survived in this fucked-up world despite all the obstacles against her. Besides, I'd be lying if I didn't want to see her succeed ... if not by gaining the crown, then by some other means.

I shrugged, smiling as I cocked my head. "I know what it's like to be on your own. To feel like every day you're just fighting to survive. My parents are—" I swallowed, shaking my head. I may have wanted a friend, but I wasn't ready to talk about *them* yet. "I just think it'd be nice. To have someone in our corners. Someone who we can rely on."

She looked at me long and hard, and I knew she could tell that maybe I wasn't as put-together as I pretended. But after a while she shot me a broad grin and held out her hand. "It's a deal, sky girl. And whoever wins can ensure the other is comfortable— their loved ones too. Let's show these other Potentials what we're made of."

I blew out a breath and matched her smile as I slid my palm against hers. "Now that I can do." We continued walking, and I felt a weight I hadn't realised I'd been carrying ease from my shoulders. "You headed to magic class?"

"Yeah, I can't wait to put Kayden in his place," she said, crinkling her small nose in amusement. "It's like toying with a mouse. The guy makes it too easy to rile him up."

My brows shot up as I looked her tiny frame up and

down. "You're taking on Kayden? Do you have a death wish or something?"

She laughed. "I'm stronger than I look. I'm from the Crimson Steppes, remember? Not all of us need to be the size of a mountain to be as powerful as one."

I followed her eyes as the man in question walked into view, shouldering people in his path until students started scrambling out of the way before he reached them. I didn't miss the way she appraised those muscles though.

I grinned. "A mountain you would have no problem scaling though, right?"

Kendra pouted. "He might be an asshole, but I can still appreciate the view."

"I see your point." He was wearing a black tank top that barely contained his muscles and a pair of tight grey sweatpants that ever so slightly showed the outline of his dick. Goddess have mercy. It was unfair that assholes like him looked so good.

"Hey sweet cheeks," Kayden said. I rolled my eyes, trying to cover up that I'd been staring, but that damn smirk of his said he knew. "Did you pick out that little number just for me? I bet you can't wait for me to rip it off you before the end of this."

I smirked, tossing my braided high ponytail. I did dress hot today, but certainly not for his benefit. I was wearing black short-shorts and a tight blue crop today, with cute black and gold sneakers that had little wings on the back.

"In your dreams, caveman. But you're welcome to salivate all you like once Kendra kicks your face in."

A muscle pulsed in his jaw, but as he opened his mouth to speak a feminine voice beat him to it.

"Quiet everyone," the woman in her late thirties called out, gesturing for us to gather closer. She had long brown hair, brown eyes, and was a complete bombshell. And I was guessing she was Master Luna Jenkins, our magic tutor.

She steepled her fingers as she paced in front of the class in a skin-tight black top and pants combo, which I bet half the guys would be ogling right now. I looked around suspiciously. Yup, there were quite a few eyes glued to her ass.

"In less than two weeks you'll be fighting for your life in the first trial. You won't have access to your magic there, but believe me when I say, your survival in the tests beyond will require a sharp mind and even sharper magic skills." She paused, a creepy smile spreading over her face. "Of course, most of you will be hard-pressed to get to the second trial at all. I don't teach weaklings. If you aren't in this with everything you've got, you may as well pack your bags and go home."

Everyone looked at each other with wide eyes—everyone except Kayden, Ace, and Victoria that is. I saw them weighing each other up, and then their eyes swivelled to me, a challenge. I lifted my chin and clenched my fists, letting them see I wasn't afraid. I'd faced worse monsters than them. Much, much worse.

"You there," Luna snapped, pointing a deadly finger at a smaller student. "What's your power?"

The poor kid shrivelled under her stare. He looked around twenty but was scrawny as a rake. He'd be lucky to last a few days in the first trial. "P-p-persuasion, Ms Jenkins," he stammered.

"Ah, a Tritosian then." She nodded, seeming satisfied. "A magic most common to the water dwellers of Tritosa City. A handy gift to have when facing opponents of varying magics. Tell me, Mister...?"

"Dick. Dick Jobs."

Kayden burst out laughing, and I had to admit, it was pretty freaking hard to contain my chuckle. That poor, sweet, innocent child was going to be picked on all his life. What kind of heartless parents would do that to their son!?

Luna cleared her throat. "Mister Jobs. When faced against someone with nullifying magic, what are your options?"

"Ummm." Dick looked around nervously, panic setting in as he realised no one would help him.

"Get on your knees and beg for forgiveness," Kayden shouted. A chorus of laughter from his followers echoed after him.

"I asked what Mister Jobs would do, not you," Luna said, sighing heavily.

"I'd get on my knees for the right girl," Kayden replied, ignoring the instructor and looking at me, wiggling his brows. "And I wouldn't be the one begging."

My cheeks flushed, though they weren't the only part of my body that heated. Luna began to give an explanation but my mind was too focused on imagining Kayden's words to hear a single thing she said. Fuck. I couldn't let him do this to me. *Focus Fallon, for gods' sake!*

"Right. I want you to pair up with someone who has magic in the same vein. Mr Warner, work with Mr Jobs here. Dick needs an experienced hand and I'm sure if you show him your skills, you'll help him release his magic." I snorted, and a few other snickers circled the room, but the teacher didn't appear to notice. "Your power is too dangerous, Ace, and I can't risk someone getting zapped in the eye."

Ace scowled, his slate gaze moving to Dick. The kid just about melted from fright as that scary mofo approached him with a dangerous glint in his eye. I sighed, looking around the group for potential opponents. There were only four students in this class from Stormcrest City, and as two of them paired off with each other, my heart sank.

"Looks like you're stuck with me, little sis," Victoria sneered as she led us over to an arena with miscellaneous items, presumably to use for telekinesis. "I promise not to go too hard on you."

I positioned myself opposite her, finding her smiling smugly like she'd already won the match. "That would be a first," I said with a click of the tongue, shaking my head. "It must be so tiring."

"What is?"

I smiled sweetly. "Being such a bitch all the time."

Her eyes simmered with rage, and she swung her hands up,

her irises flashing a vibrant copper as she flung two sacks at me, but I was ready. I grinned, cartwheeling as one of the sacks sailed past me and took out a group of students. I jerked my head to send the other one surging back to Victoria. It hit her in the stomach and she went flying, her blond hair streaming out from its ponytail.

"Holy shit," Kayden boomed from somewhere behind me. I turned to see him take out his cuff and begin recording. "Cat fight between the Auger girls."

I heard the clamour of students gathering behind me, but I didn't have time to pay them heed as Victoria picked up a student—a freaking student—and sent them careening into my side. I slammed to the ground with an oomph, thankful for the grass cushioning my fall. I couldn't say the same for the student though. Oh, shit, it had to be Dick, too. The guy whimpered, clutching his arm to his chest.

"Sorry about that," I muttered, patting him awkwardly on the back before racing back to my sister.

We stared each other down and she flicked her hair from her face, shooting me daggers with her eyes. "You're nothing," she spat. "Just a backup in case anything happens to the real heir of House Jupiter."

"If you're so special, Victoria, why would our parents feel the need to have me at all?" I remarked casually. "You're expendable, just like the rest of us. Replaceable. Ordinary."

She screeched, and a barrage of sacks, balls, punching bags and other odd assortments came rushing at my face. I ducked and sprinted between them, conjuring my wings to give me a burst of speed, halting at the last second before I could collide with her and instead surging into the sky. She blinked, and I knew I had her.

A torrent of sacks belted her back and she tumbled forwards, crushed beneath their weight. The class laughed, and I couldn't help the victory grin which pulled my lips. I bet Daddy Dearest would have a few things to say about her failure if he saw the video.

"Well done, Miss Auger," Luna said, appearing beside me, that awful grin back on her face again. I just about jumped out of my skin. Stunning as she was, she was damn creepy. "You can take five, then I want you to practice keeping five of those items suspended for as long as you can. Sheer strength is one thing, but maintaining focus is another." She shot a sharp look at the audience, who quickly returned to sparring with their own partners.

I grinned, feeling my chest puff with pride. It felt good to get a win for once. Not to mention being praised for doing something well. I couldn't remember the last time my parents had ever done that … *if* they'd ever done that. That sudden realisation sent that floating feeling plummeting in my stomach. I glanced at Victoria, who was only now crawling out of the sack pile, shaking off her friends and barking at them to back off.

I took a slow breath as she shot me a death glare. There would be repercussions for what I'd done—for the video that was now pinging on everyone's cuffs on the Acadameet app. Shit.

Oh well, that was tomorrow's problem, and right now I was more than content to bask in the sun and watch Kendra take on Kayden and his beefy biceps. My new friend was a little badass, I had a feeling she could handle herself.

My attention drifted to the battles taking place around the meadow, and I couldn't help but smile as I caught sight of Zane practicing with a group of other Tritosians, his long hair rippling in the breeze and shirt off. His tanned skin glimmered in the sun, and I took a minute to appreciate the vee dipping below his pants. For someone as gorgeous as him, his mellow attitude was refreshing as fuck. I wasn't sure if pairing Tritosians together made much sense because they were all sitting in a circle as if meditating, appearing completely Zen and at ease as they nulled each other's powers and just chilled out.

After practising for a while, I jogged towards the shower block, heading towards the entrance of the ladies' changeroom when I noticed Ace in the distance, stepping out of a side door. He shut it, then tapped the keypad next to it, making it flash red.

"What are you doing?" I asked, my curiosity getting the better of me as I stepped towards him.

He looked up, narrowing his gaze at me. "None of your business."

"Sneaking past locked doors, huh?" My lips curved. "Not suss at all."

He cocked his head predatorially, the sharp angle of his cheekbones and jaw as cutting as the eyes raking over me. I couldn't help but notice the tattoos covering his exposed arms and neck, swirling over the hardness of his body. The subtle spark of electricity running over his hand damn well made me pause though. I was not in the mood to be on the receiving end of that shit.

"You gonna tell on me, Princess?" I paused, folding my arms. Nah, I wasn't a teacher's pet, and it wouldn't serve me anyway. He must have taken my silence as fear because he smirked. "Run along."

"To be anywhere away from you? Happily." I flicked my hand, using my telekinesis to send a whirlwind of leaf litter crashing into his face. To his credit, he glared throughout it all and I laughed. Before he could retaliate, I flicked my hair and jogged away back to the shower block, silently scolding myself for approaching him to begin with.

As I glanced over my shoulder, I saw his fingers curl into fists when the whirlwind died down, then he swore viciously, sending a spark up another Potential's ass which had the poor guy yelping and literally ducking for cover, losing the fight he had been winning.

I shook my head, strolling into the building and towards the first shower stall closest to the door, only to find someone already there, butt naked in all his glory.

"How did you get here so quickly?" I leaned against the turquoise tiled wall of a stall in the opposite row and folded my arms, appraising the merman from head to toe. "And in the ladies' room no less."

He turned, a wicked smile on his face as I copped an eyeful of his junk. Nope, there could be no denying he was one hundred percent pure male and *not* meant to be in here.

"A siren called and I had to answer," he replied, his green eyes glimmering.

"Oh?" I stalked towards him, licking my lips. "And what were you planning to do with her?"

He ran a hand through his long hair, shampoo trickling through the shaved side and down the blond strands. "Come closer and find out."

Oh, shit, this was a bad idea. But how could I say no to the bronzed god before me? I eyed his abs greedily, feeling heat swell between my legs as he fisted his cock and began stroking it lazily, not taking his eyes off me for a second.

"Don't be afraid, Starfish. I don't bite… much."

I stood there, hesitating for the briefest second before my hands seemed to move against my will. I peeled my top off, shrugging out of my shorts and panties, then ever so slowly unclasping my bra and letting it fall to the floor.

Zane's eyes drank me in, his cock twitching as I swished my hips, walking confidently into the water beside him. He took my neck and pulled me forward, claiming my lips, his tongue swirling against mine as he pressed himself into my stomach.

"You're fucking perfect," he breathed when we broke apart. His fingers trailed over my skin, leaving burning trails in their wake, and I sighed as he kissed down my neck, then pressed his lips over my nipple, sucking in teasing little bursts.

"Zane," I said in a half moan, rubbing my thighs together to ease some of the ache. "The class will be over any second.

Someone will see us."

"Then let them," he growled against my skin, grabbing my arms and shoving me against the wall, shoving his cock between my legs and just shy of where I so desperately wanted him to go. "I know you like the danger."

Oh gods, he was so right. The thought of him fucking me in full view of anyone who might step in here only made me wetter, and I jumped up, wrapping my legs around him and groaning as he squeezed my ass.

I kissed him deeply, raking my nails through his hair and down his back, starved for his every touch, needing this so badly.

Laughter bounced off the walls and I squeaked, flattening myself under his weight, like that might disguise the position we were in. "Quick, pull back the curtain."

He lifted me easily, hiding us behind the flimsy material of the stall right as a bunch of girls wandered in, chatting about the session.

Zane and I stood rigidly still, our lips curling with the sudden urge to burst out laughing. Oh, but I had a better idea.

I sank to my knees, a smirk on my face as I took his considerable length in my hand and began pumping him. He rolled his head back against the wall, sighing softly, his breath hitching as I wrapped my lips over his cock and began to move.

I looked up at him innocently, fluttering my lashes as he stared at me in surprise, his mouth parting with pleasure.

Forcing my throat to relax, I took him deeper still, his hand wrapping in my hair and grasping at the roots, moving my head back and forth as he plunged into me. The girls in the bathroom giggled and chatted, none the wiser, and I felt my slickness trickle down my thighs along with the water swirling down the drain.

I could fuck him right now and no one would know. It sent a delicious wave of pleasure racking through my body. When Zane moaned a little louder, I grinned around his length, running my tongue up the shaft and over the head.

The muscles in his abs contracted as he sucked in a gasp, and I could tell he was close as he took total control of my head, bobbing me up and down on his dick. His breaths came quicker, his chest heaving as he tipped his head back and stifled a groan, his cum sliding down my throat.

I lapped it up greedily, swallowing every last drop until he heaved me up and plunged two fingers into my pussy. I gasped, riding his hand as he worked the pleasure out of me, a crooked smirk on his face as I struggled to bite back the noises escaping me.

"Quiet, Starfish," he demanded breathily in my ear, before sinking his teeth into my shoulder. *"They'll hear."*

His mocking tone didn't escape me. I'd have to punish him for his teasing later. Or maybe…

An idea formed in my head and I grinned to myself before pulling my head back, letting him lick my nipples as his hand shifted, circling my clit. "Fuck, Zane," I said between pants. I was close now, my body hot and my breasts heavy as he drove me wild with his hand.

He slipped a finger into my mouth and I moaned around it, feeling the muscles in my pussy contract as an orgasm ripped out of me, making my bones sag.

"What's that sound?" a girl said.

I couldn't help but giggle, the sound muffled around Zane's finger as he snickered quietly. His fingers continued to move over my clit as my pleasure soared higher. When I was done shaking, he gripped me to him, kissing me deeply before lathering me up with the soap. I let him clean me thoroughly, then kissed him once more, brief and teasing. He growled as I moved out of reach, cocking his head at the wicked glint I knew he'd find in my eye.

"Thanks Merman," I whispered, patting his chest. "This was just what I needed."

"Starfish," he asked, his eyes narrowing as I backed up. "What are you—?" I took another step back and his eyes widened with realisation. "Starfish, don't you dare."

"Let's do this again," I said, then blew him a kiss before I stepped out of the shower, smiling to myself. The other girls looked at me in surprise, and I saluted them lazily before grabbing a towel and slipping on my things.

"Fallon," Kendra said with a knowing grin, jerking her chin subtly at the pile of men's clothing near the stall, then towards the door, her eyes mischievous.

Great minds think alike.

I edged my way over, grabbing the pile and barely managing to contain my grin as I dipped my head. "Ladies," I said, then hurried on out of the shower block, leaving poor Zane stark naked and hiding behind a shower curtain in the increasingly filling ladies' room.

Shrugging to myself, I burst into laughter as I spread my wings and took flight.

There were worse places he could be.

# FALLON

I massaged my temple, rolling my neck as I walked along the path surrounding the academy grounds, figuring I'd enjoy a peaceful evening stroll. My earphones smashed out a rock beat, and I grinned, relishing in the freedom of not having Victrus or Eliana watching my every move for the first time in my life.

My body was pleasantly sore from Physical, and my brain was the comfortable kind of sluggish that came from pushing my magic … and maybe having a certain someone pushing all the right buttons too.

I'd sleep well tonight, that was for sure, but not until I'd feasted at the cafeteria. I just hoped there'd be some dessert left over by the time I made it back. Gods, if this place was good for anything, it was dessert. My mouth was salivating at the mere thought of all that sweetness just waiting for me to stash away in my room. Actually, fuck the walk, I needed that goodness in my belly right now.

As I rounded the path by a wooded area, someone jumped me, pulling me back into the cover of the trees. I tried to scream, but a dainty hand slapped over my mouth, and as much as I kicked and flailed, my surprisingly strong attacker wouldn't let go.

When we were well and truly within the woods, I was shoved to the ground. "What the hell?" I demanded, pushing to my feet.

Victoria flashed a cruel grin, two of her cronies sneering down their noses at me beside her. "Did you think you'd get away with that little stunt today?"

"Aw, what's the matter? Did I embarrass you in front of all your friends?" I jeered.

Her smile only deepened, her eyes glinting with malice. "Nobody disrespects me like that without facing the consequences. Especially a poor excuse of an Auger like you."

"Oh, don't be like that Victoria," I said with a grin. "Our parents were just trying to make me into a carbon copy of you, right? Only … an improved version."

"Teach her a lesson, Victoria," a girl with long blond hair and a cake face trilled beside her.

The other girl giggled, getting her cuff out. Right. Another video to be posted online. I sighed. "Get on with it then."

Something shuffled in the dark, and my eyes widened as I saw Ace leaning against a nearby tree. Too caught up in the moment, apparently no one had heard him coming.

"What do you want, Drake?" Victoria frowned. "If you have heroic plans to save her, you've got another thing coming."

His lips curved into a thin smile. "Whatever gave you that impression? I'm just here for the show."

My stomach twisted violently. "You're a psycho," I hissed. "You all are."

Victoria smiled coldly as she turned her gaze back on me, her fist shooting so fast towards my face it only missed by an inch as I dodged it. The girl with short black hair, let's call her Black Bob, stepped forward and jabbed me in the gut, followed by the blond one, Cake Face, yanking my ponytail and holding me there while Victoria kicked me in the ribs.

The breath whooshed out of me and I sagged, the hair pulling painfully at my scalp in Cake Face's talons. But I managed to elbow her in the throat, causing her to let go, and I staggered forward with a smirk. Right on time, Victoria clocked me in the face, my jaw cracking to the side and blood oozing out my lip and where I'd bitten my tongue.

"Is this what it is to be an Auger, Victoria?" I spat, glaring my contempt at her as my vision spun. "Jumping your mark with three against one?"

"Oh, them?" She laughed, cocking her head to the side and punching me in the stomach again. "They're just along for the ride. I wanted the Potentials to see that smirk wiped off your face and for you to be humiliated." She looked me up and down, slipping a small knife from her pocket and taking the cuff from her friend. "I think we can do better though, right girls?"

My heart leapt into my throat, confusion boggling my senses. Another student with a weapon ... but how? I didn't have time to contemplate as Black Bob sniggered, grabbing my arm while Cake Face restrained my left. Any other time I would have fought them off, but my body was already aching from the week, and my vision blurred from the pain in my jaw. Before me, Victoria's face wavered into two sneers. Then my top was being sliced, bra on full display, as my sister shredded my dignity before kicking me to the dirt.

I glared as Victoria checked her crony got it all on camera. The three girls' laughter reverberated through the trees as they left. In the real world, Victoria wouldn't dare do something like this. Father would whip her for allowing the world to see an Auger in such a state, and he would have beaten me for appearing weak. In the real world, I could have killed Victoria's friends and gotten away with it. But I wasn't like her. I didn't thrive on hurting others.

My own sister, dropping to an all-time low. I always knew she was a Grade A bitch, but I hadn't expected her to stoop to this level. This wasn't the behaviour of someone worthy of ascension, or even a respectable heir. Her actions told me she was afraid. In Victoria Auger's eyes, I was a threat. To her ascension, to her place in our family, and to her reputation. Well buckle up, big sis, because it would take more than a stupid video and a beatdown to stop me, even if my pride was wounded and the humiliation made my eyes water.

I huffed, spitting a mouthful of blood on the ground as a shadow loomed over me. I looked up to glare defiantly at Ace. "Stuck around to gloat?"

He shrugged, looking entirely unapologetic. "After your little trick today?" The slightest hint of a smile carved those cruel lips. "Maybe I didn't mind watching a little violence tonight."

"You just stood there when you could've evened the score. What the fuck is wrong with you?"

"You and your sister have bad blood. That's your business." He shrugged again, his tattoos contrasting to his pale skin as he held an arm out. Warily, I reached my palm towards his, but he pulled back at the last second, sneering. "On the other hand, it was quite satisfying to watch an Auger get what they deserved. You can all go to hell as far as I'm concerned." He turned away, following the path out of the woods.

"Coming from a member of a gang notorious for violence and smuggling," I hissed, staggering to my feet, refusing to give in to my emotions even as the tears blurred my eyes. I was not going to crumple at the first sign of hardship, I was not going to cry over Victoria Auger, and I was *definitely not* going to let this asshole turn his back on me. "I'm talking to you!"

He laughed, continuing to ignore me as he walked away. I looked around me in frustration, spotting a pebble and tossing it at his head before I could think better of it. The stone sailed through the air, but right before it could hit him, he turned and grabbed it with his bionic hand, squeezing so hard the freaking pebble crumbled to a soft powder. Holy shit.

"You threw a rock at my head," he said sharply, his eyes

narrowed to slits. "Are you serious?"

I huffed, thrusting my chin up. "It's the least you deserve after letting them humiliate me like that. If you want to get off by watching someone get beaten up, do it as far away from me as possible."

He stalked towards me until he was barely an inch from my face, his chest pressing against mine. I sucked in a breath at his proximity. Both of us were breathing hard as I waited of him to speak or strike me. "You think watching you turns me on, Princess?" He grabbed my throat, just enough to hurt without blocking my airflow. He pulled me closer—so close I wondered if he wanted to kiss me or kick me. "It takes a lot more than that to get me hard."

His hateful eyes raked over me, and I glared at him, challenging him to do his worst. We stood there in silence, his breath trailing over my neck. Something deep inside me thrilled at the danger oozing off this man. If only he wasn't a fucking psycho.

After what felt like the standard pause after a threat had well and truly passed, I punched him in the stomach so hard he released his hold on my throat. "You can watch all you like," I snarled, backing away several steps. "But you'll never get the real thing."

He stared at me for a moment and laughed coldly. "As if I would ever reduce myself to an Auger. Fly along little bird, before the other monsters come out at night."

I gaped after him as he left. I needed a moment to calm my racing heart and collect myself. Who the hell did he think he was? And why had he been out here in the first place? I raked my hands through my dishevelled hair, cradling my arms as I crouched back on my heels for a moment. More importantly, how did Victoria have a knife on her? Any weapons I'd stashed in my luggage had been taken, presumably by the guards who'd kidnapped us.

Something wasn't right here … and I planned to find out what.

My stomach grumbled and I rose, checking my cuff. The caff would be closing soon, and I wasn't exactly dressed appropriately anymore. "Just fucking great," I grumbled. They could mess with my mind but getting in the way of dinner and dessert was just plain rude. With a sigh, I picked up my sorry ass and my earphones and headed down the path towards the dorms.

I was almost to the building when someone laid a hand on my shoulder and I snarled, spinning around and putting my elbow to their throat.

"Holy shit, Starfish, chill," Zane said, his green eyes widening as he cradled an assortment of edible goods to his chest, a rogue donut spilling from his palm. I sagged, only managing to grunt in reply. His beautiful face shifted into a frown. "Are you okay? I saw the video. Well, everyone did. It was playing ALL over the cafeteria, and everyone had their cuffs turned up really loud, and—"

"Zane," I snapped. "Not helping. Go be a dick somewhere else, I'm really not in the mood."

He looked at me intently, leaning forward and getting in my face. "Oh, shit. You're hangry."

I frowned. "Excuse me?"

"You know, when you're so hungry that you start getting mad and turn into raging—"

"No, no, I know what it means." I rolled my eyes.

"Well, it's your lucky day because we're going to ride this wave out in our room. With snacks. Everything is better with snacks. Come on, you know you want some. You want them all up in your mouth like something else earlier today." He wagged his brows. "Naughty Starfish, pulling that prank in the showers. You're lucky I like you. I don't share my snacks with just any clothes thief."

I couldn't help but break a smile. He was like a puppy dog

that didn't know when to quit. "Are you sure you have enough to last the night there?" I teased. He'd scooped up a huge armful of supplies—enough to stash for a while.

He smiled broadly. "I got some for you. You weren't at dinner, and when I saw the video, I knew you wouldn't be joining."

My insides warmed, feeling all fluffy. "You brought these for me?" It was such a thoughtful gesture, and so very alien to me, I just wanted to give him a big hug.

"Yup, anything for my starfish," he replied happily, leading the way up the stairs.

When we got to the room, I opened the door and he emptied his goods onto his bed, patting the space beside him. "Let's watch a movie on the Acadameet app while we eat. And then I can give you a massage if you like, get allllll that tension out."

I laughed, shaking my head at how comfortable it felt to be around this weirdo in such a short amount of time. "Movie, yes, massage, maybe."

He removed his shirt, lay out on the bed and fluffed his long blond hair like an actual mermaid. All he needed was the flipping tail. "Are you sure? I'm very good with my hands."

There was no denying that. I bit my lip, running my eyes over his chiselled abs. He'd surprised me today, which was new for me. I'd surprised myself. Obviously, it wasn't a good idea to get close him, but I certainly wouldn't mind continuing what we'd started. Not one bit. His eyes simmered as he watched me rummage through my bag, a small smile curving his lips up as if he knew what I was thinking.

"I'm going to have a shower first. And before you ask, no, you can't join me. Once a day is enough." I laughed, watching his mouth snap shut as he flashed me the puppy dog eyes.

"Once a day?" he asked hopefully, then folded his arms behind his head, looking like a king as he grinned. "Once a day," I heard him whisper to himself, almost like a prayer.

I smiled as I padded into the shower and sighed when the

water kissed my skin and washed away the blood and dirt from Victoria's little attack. The heat worked into my sore muscles, taking away some of the aches and the tension behind my eyes.

Today had been a royal shitshow of a day. Probably the first of many to come, but at least I'd found some positives. I hung my head beneath the stream, thinking of the hot as heck man on the other side of the bathroom wall, and the promise of his hands touching me in all the best places.

Down girl. I'd already done things I shouldn't have. A quick blowjob in the bathroom was harmless enough, but I had to keep my guard up, especially when these trials could bring anything. Having fun with Zane—or any of the other delectable guys I had my eye on—was only likely to bring trouble. I sighed. No. No more touching for today.

There was no rule about fantasising though…

# A SKY OF STORMS

# ACE

Yesterday had been the gift that kept on giving. First, I'd hacked into the closed security system and had a look around. I wasn't able to make changes yet, but I could at least see what I was up against. It would take time to rifle through the codes to open doors and turn off cameras and alarms, but I wasn't so much in the dark anymore.

Second, I'd gotten a front row seat to not one but two Auger fights, and they had been glorious. There was nothing better than watching spoilt brats get their asses handed to them. Those Auger girls had some seriously bad blood and I could only hope that I got to be there when one finally killed the other.

If I haven't managed to break into the vault before the first trial starts in another week, I may just get the chance.

I turned a corner, bumping into a Potential with dark skin and brown eyes. Noah, if my memory served me correctly. "Shit, sorry," he said quietly.

"Watch where you're fucking going," I snapped. Everyone kept bumping into me in this place, like it was some kind of joke I wasn't in on.

"Yeah…" he mumbled with his gaze focused on something

in the distance. I squinted in the same direction, spotting Mark Leroy's bulky form stalking after a group of Potentials.

The slimy bastard looked at his cuff and hurriedly passed them, but not before groping one on the ass as he went. Mark had made an appearance in Damascon Hollow a few months back, but I hadn't seen him since. Lots of rich boys came to DH to gamble their credits, and Mark was no exception to the rule. The guy thought he was entitled to every woman and had assaulted a few dancers one too many times, getting him blacklisted from many of the DH strip clubs. He was always popping up acting as if he owned the place and wanting to dance with the gangs like it was some rite of fucking passage. The blondie wouldn't last a day with the Drakes, and if Cormac didn't eat him alive, then I damn well would.

As leader of the Drakes, Cormac didn't take new recruits often. He liked training them from a young age—said it made them more pliable and trustworthy—which I supposed was why he took me in when he did. Those good-for-nothing people who'd brought me into this shitty world had left me to rot in Damascon Hollow when I was just a few years old. I hadn't asked to be born, hadn't asked for anything at all, and they'd given me up like I was little more than trash. They'd shown me what people were capable of that day. Cruel, heartless, careless creatures. I never bothered to try and be anything different. Ace Warner didn't have a heart. I was ruthless, and that's the way I liked it. No one could hurt you if you never let them in.

Cormac was the closest thing I had to a father, but he would never be that. Would probably beat me half to death if I ever suggested it. We worked better keeping things strictly business, and if I played my cards right, I'd one day be running it.

But first, I had to deal with this job he'd given me. I glanced at Noah with interest, watching the way his eyes narrowed as he gazed after Mark.

"You two aren't friends then?" I asked.

"Best buddies."

I chuckled. Noah's family were the leaders of the Verdant Plateau and their reputation for living firmly on the moral high ground was well known throughout Terrulia. Cormac had tried making deals between them and the Drakes before—unsuccessfully. They stuck to their metaphorical guns.

"I see you've made a tonne of friends. Quite the socialite," he said, looking me up and down.

I shrugged. "Friendships here are a waste of time."

"Never thought I'd find myself agreeing with a Drake," Noah said with a shake of his head.

"Stranger fucking things have happened."

I strode away, heading towards the training arena in the miniature DH for another so-called lesson in physical combat. In my opinion, it was less of a lesson and more of an opportunity for Master Nolan to watch the Potentials beat the shit out of each other. There were no rules and the boulder of a guy, Kayden, took advantage of that.

"Today we are going to up the odds!" Nolan shouted, starting the lesson. "Two on one. Let's see which of you can come out on top when the odds are against you. Consider this a game of cat and mouse. You will be allocated a city area and for two of you, your job is to catch and secure the mouse."

The Potentials were put into groups and I soon found myself standing side-by-side with Noah again, with the princess from Stormcrest City opposite. I watched Fallon as she bent over and stretched out her muscles, her face neutral as though she didn't give a fuck about who she was up against.

"Ready boys?" she asked with a wicked grin on her face, then took off before either of us could answer.

I didn't wait for Noah, sprinting after the spoilt princess. She was quick, but there was no way she'd get too far from me. She darted off the street and into one of the buildings but I stayed on her tail as she raced up a set of stairs. Our footsteps pounded on the metal steps, the sound echoing around the empty space. I couldn't hear Noah behind me, and a quick glance confirmed my suspicion. What was he fucking playing at? I shook my head. What had I expected? Couldn't fucking rely on anyone.

Fallon turned sharply into one of the open doorways and I continued my pursuit. I loved the chase. From experience, it only made the victory sweeter. Sprinting through the doorway, I came to a stop in the middle of the room and spun around slowly. Sunlight shone brightly through the floor-to-ceiling broken windows, light glinting off the broken shards. Rusted metal crates were thrown about the place, though for what reason, I had no fucking idea.

This place was nothing like DH. Where was the graffiti? The stench of fumes? The homeless person huddled in a corner? It was like a shitty knockoff from the night market.

"Drawing this out will only make it worse for you," I drawled, moving on silent feet between the crates in search of her. My heart raced in my chest with the thrill of the chase making me feel alive.

I started on the left side of the room, creeping slowly and listening out for the smallest sound—a scrape of a shoe, a breath. Something clattered loudly and my gaze snapped to the opposite end of the room. I smirked, spotting her running behind a crate. She was good, but I was fucking better. That little trick was the oldest one in the book.

Without giving away that I'd seen her, I crept around the perimeter of the room, ducking low and keeping myself hidden. I spotted her crouched behind another crate. I sprinted at her, readying myself to tackle her to the ground. At my unexpected advance, her eyes widened before she smiled broadly, letting out a laugh as she launched to her feet to escape me.

I was close on her heels as she ran towards a broken window. This was it. "You're mine, Princess!"

"Not today, asshole!" she shouted back, her wings breaking

free from her back ready to carry her.

"Fuck," I swore under my breath, my gaze flicking to the open window. I gritted my teeth, pushing myself to run faster, but even I was smart enough to know when someone else had the upper hand.

She laughed, clearly enjoying the shit out of the whole thing.

Suddenly, she was knocked to the ground by someone, surprising even me. I'd considered Noah a flake and yet here he was, wrestling with Fallon on the dusty floor. She threw a fist into his jaw, knocking him sideways and giving her an opening to scramble away. Problem was, she scurried towards me. I dropped on top of her, straddling her hips and pinning her arms on either side of her head.

The twisted side of me liked the feel of her wriggling beneath me and the anger in her eyes only made it hotter. The wilder she became, the more I wanted to tame her, bend her to my will.

"Fine," she panted, going limp beneath me. "You won. Now get the fuck off me."

I leant towards her, my face inches from hers. "Will you behave?"

Her eyes darted to my lips and I couldn't help but smirk. It felt good to have the upper hand over her, to dominate her like this … not that I wanted anything to come of it. I still fucking hated her.

"You wouldn't know what to do with me if I did," she replied breathily, then slammed her forehead into mine. I reeled back and my grip loosened on her arms, allowing her to punch me in the ribs.

I reached for her again, a growl slipping from my throat as I tried to contain her once more. Noah dove in to help and between us we managed to restrain her again.

"Give it up. Your odds are shit-house," I said through

CHLOE HODGE & REBECCA CAMM

gritted teeth. Blood dripped down my face, and I assumed it held the expression that was a mirror of how she looked. The determined set of her jaw and the stubbornness in her eyes called to the dark in me. It was fucking tempting to imagine all the ways I could cage her, bend that wildness to my will.

"Alright, alright," she panted, looking between me and Noah, and bringing me back to reality. Entertaining those kinds of thoughts was like stepping into another gang's territory without permission. Really fucking stupid. "Let me the fuck go, assholes."

"We will when Nolan blows his whistle," Noah replied from where he looked down on her. He was crouched above her head, his hands holding her wrists firmly in place.

As if on cue, a whistle sounded from outside, signalling the end of training. I grinned like a mad mother fucker down at her. I'd beat her and it wasn't going to be the last time I'd get one up on Auger royalty.

"You lose, Princess."

# KAYDEN

I rolled over to find one of my followers had decided to stay the night. Ugh, I hated when they got clingy like that. I didn't do sleepovers, especially in beds the size of a weight bench. She felt me move and tried to tangle me in her arms, but I was not about to let that happen. She was a means to an end. A way to get Fallon out of my head and free me from the angel's tempting clutches. I wasn't the only guy Fallon flirted with but at least I wasn't dumb enough to be lured into her trap. I gave the chick next to me a not so gentle shove and she fell out of the bed onto her naked ass with a squeal.

"Kaydi, baby." She pouted, holding her hand up at me like my shove had been some sort of accident. "I fell out."

When I didn't reach out to take it, her eyes widened and her mouth opened even wider. I was tempted to let her back under the covers, only to help sort out my morning wood situation. I ran a hand through my red hair and decided to think with my head and not my dick.

"Nope," I sighed, rolling onto my back and stretching my arms with a yawn. If I gave her an inch, she'd take a fucking mile. I didn't remember her name, but by the time I sat up she got the not-so-subtle hint and scurried away to wherever her own bed was located. My treatment may have seemed harsh to some. I got it, who treated someone like that after sleeping with them? The thing was, I couldn't show favouritism or she'd think she had sway over me or a higher ranking over my other followers, which she in no way did. The only person that had any kind of power in that department was Flynn, and that was only because we'd been friends for so long.

It was important to maintain the authority I had established since arriving at the House of Ascension. My rules kept my followers in line. I had no time for disobedience. Running a group was like a good gym regime, strict and organised, and it was one of the many lessons I had learnt from my parents from watching them lead House Mars in the Crimson Steppes.

The place was a literal desert. Red sand, hot days, and cold nights. The climate was tough, but the people were tougher. Above all, we favoured strength and the survival of the fittest— and I was the fittest of them all. My nomination to the Terrulian Trials had been a no brainer, as my parents had trained me for exactly this. It was time the world remembered what the Crimson Steppes was capable of, and I would do so proudly. The past rulers had forgotten about our city in the sand, leaving us to starve and scrounge for credits, but it had only made us stronger. Soon the fate of my city and my people would be changed. We would no longer be the forgotten city or the bottom of the sand pit. And when we took our place at the top I would be at the very peak.

I rested my forearms on my thighs and yawned again, rubbing my hand firmly over my face. Waking up was the worst part of the day. If I could have stayed in bed until noon, I would have happily done it, not that I was ever given the luxury. Workouts had always been scheduled first thing in the morning growing up, and if I hadn't known my parents adored me, I would have thought they were doing it just to torture me.

I finally got my ass up, showered, and headed to the cafeteria where my followers hurried to put my breakfast on the table before my ass hit the seat. It hadn't taken too much to train them. There were a few Potentials from my home city that had been nominated by House Mars too. They knew how to fall in line, and it hadn't taken the others much to do the same. The best way to get through these trials was with a team, Victoria had been right about that. Only, once I was near the finish line, I'd cut my team loose and claim my victory. Those from the Crimson Steppes wouldn't hold a grudge about it because it was how things were done. If anything, they'd respect me more.

"Hey bro," I said to Flynn, who was sitting opposite me and ignoring everyone else at the table.

"Morning," he replied, taking a sip of his coffee.

"What news do you have?" I asked. "Any Potentials looking to be recruited?"

"A few possibilities," Flynn replied. He spent about as much time as I did working out, though with a very different outcome. Where I was tall and broad-shouldered, he was short and bulky all over, making him look like a walking cube. I made sure to give him shit about it on the regular, because what were friends for?

I devoured my bacon and eggs, eyeing my minions, "Sit up straight," I barked at one, snatching a piece of toast from his plate. "You're not in this team if you have no discipline."

The guy beside him snickered so I shot him a glare for good measure.

"For that, you can drop and give me twenty, smart ass, or you're out."

That wiped the smile from his face. He pushed back from the table and dropped to the caff floor. I leaned back in my chair and gave Flynn a nod to continue as I watched the minion do push-ups.

Flynn raised a brow, shaking his blond head in amusement. "The tiff between the Augers the other day has had the reluctant Potentials looking for allies. No one wants to end up like little

Auger in her solitary position, not that I blame them."

I smiled, fondly recalling the show the sisters put on in magic class. The video that came through on Acadameet later that night of Fallon Auger looking all kinds of messy, however, was even better. There was something about smudged lipstick and hair long enough to pull. It also helped that Fallon was hot as fuck. What I wouldn't give to wrap her hair in my hand and take her for a ride. *Shit.* I needed to stop that train of thought. Obviously that chick from last night didn't get the job done. But no more dwelling on Fallon Auger.

"Like you'd ever find yourself in the same position as her," I told Flynn.

He smiled. "Maybe if you decided to one day drop me as a friend I might."

"Like I'd do that," I said, stretching my arms over my head. "So hard to train good help these days."

"Asshole," he said with a chuckle.

"So why do we only have a few possibilities from the stragglers?" I grabbed a croissant off a girl's plate on the table, biting into it thoughtfully as our conversation turned back to business. Who were the last few Potentials choosing to ally with if not me? I'd proven that I was a big player in this game; I should have had people begging to join me.

I glanced around the room, eyes snagging on Twig. His grey eyes were narrowed to slits as he ate, watching everyone carefully, his tattoo sleeves on full display. The guy thought because he was in The Drakes and had a hand made of soda cans that he was tough shit. He was just lucky that messing with him was one of my favourite things to do in this place. As much as I loved to train, everything else was as dull as a sandstorm.

Twig made for some great entertainment, and I was man enough to admit that he was a decent opponent. Better than the rest of the riffraff around here at any rate. I'd have to watch out for him during the trials. I wasn't worried that he'd best me, but I wouldn't put it past him to pull some sneaky shit. I wasn't going to be blindsided by him. You always had to watch your back when gang members were around.

The filthy rich too, I thought, turning my attention to where Victoria Auger sat amongst her little worshippers. The woman didn't even try to look endearing. She was hot, but in the 'I'm going to fuck you then dismember you and sell your body parts on the black market' sort of way. Not my type at all. Her sister on the other hand ... I was definitely going to be rewatching that video again very soon.

Dammit. I blew out a breath. I needed to delete it.

Victoria made some comment I couldn't hear and the Potentials huddled around her laughed like she was a comedian. I ground my teeth. Her numbers made her another threat I needed to keep an eye on, especially after I rejected her the other day. The woman was wealthy in credits and followers, and if I wasn't careful, she'd crown herself queen before the trials were even over.

"Hi, err, Kayden ... s-sir," Dick Jobs said, appearing at my side. His breakfast trembled on the tray he held. "I want to ally with you."

I grinned at the nervous little rabbit. "You do, huh? What do you bring to the table?"

"I'm smart and I've been told I've got good survival skills," he replied with a firm nod, or at least the best attempt at 'firm' he was capable of.

"I'm not sure how smart you are seeing as you're here," I said, looking him up and down.

"Give him a go, bro," Flynn said with a chuckle. "Might surprise you."

"Fine." I sighed, shaking my head. What was I getting myself into? The little dude was going to need a lot of work to be whipped into shape.

Dick rushed into the seat beside me, a wide smile on his face. He placed his tray in front of him, his rainbow cereal swirling around his bowl. Fucking fantastic, I was adopting a child.

"You won't regret it. I promise."

"I think I already am," I groaned to Flynn, earning another laugh from my second. I turned to Dick. "You're not eating this. Go back and get real food."

He rose slowly from his seat. "But I like—"

"Protein. Good fats. Now," I ordered, startling the guy.

"Leave him alone," a voice said behind me, and I turned to see Fallon looking all kinds of hot with her hands on her hips and her copper eyes flaring. The younger Auger was a force. It had been so hot to spar with her in training the other day and she'd managed to hold her own surprisingly well.

Around us, the cafeteria had gone quiet, all eyes on our little interaction. I wasn't gonna waste this opportunity to get her out of my fucking head. The people loved a good show, and I was about to give them one. It didn't matter whether I wanted to bed the angel or not, she needed to learn her place—and that place was beneath me. From now on, she no longer commanded my thoughts.

I rose from my seat and placed a hand on Dick's shoulder, giving it a squeeze. "This is between me and Dick, isn't it?"

"Err." His eyes blinked nervously. "Ye-yes."

Fallon didn't back down though. She stormed towards me, shoving me in the chest. It was cute watching her attempt to overpower me. I couldn't help but add this little part of our interaction to the wank bank. I liked her strong will, but as much as I wanted the memories for later, having her question my actions in front of all the Potentials, especially those under me, wasn't going to slide. I dropped my hand from Dick's shoulder.

"Fallon, Fallon, Fallon," I tsked, shaking my head slowly. "Looks like you didn't learn anything from your sister's video."

Fallon sneered. "There was nothing to learn. I already knew she was a coward and a bully."

Someone gasped behind me and it was followed up by

Victoria shouting that her sister was a lying bitch. I chuckled, grinning at Fallon like an idiot because she was about to find out that though I found her hot, she had no control over me. She could focus her attention on flirting with the other guys because I was done.

If there was one thing I knew about rich kids in high society, it was that they thrived on petty humiliation. If I was going to survive here, I'd stoop to their level, even if it made me a prick.

"Hey Flynn," I said, my hand dropping to the table behind me. "Got my back?"

"Always, bro," he replied, and I quickly grabbed Dick's rainbow cereal and dumped it onto Fallon's head.

Laughter filled the cafeteria. I smirked, too enthralled with the look of vengeance on Fallon's face as she stood there before me, drenched in a milky rainbow, to laugh. It did nothing to dampen the spark in her eyes though. If anything, it ignited as hot as the surface of the sun. She slowly lifted the bowl off her head, dropping it to the floor where it smashed into jagged pieces. Then in a move that was sexually charged with how much she wanted me, she wiped the milk and cereal from her face, holding eye contact with me. Even humiliated and covered in breakfast, she was a formidable force. Just like her sister, she was competition for my crown, but unlike Victoria, she was still strong on her own and that made her a bigger threat.

"Real fucking mature," Fallon said, stepping closer so that her next words were for me alone. "You must be really scared of me if you're resorting to childish pranks like this."

My grin faltered and I narrowed my eyes. "I'm not afraid of anything."

Fallon laughed, stepping back. "I'm sure you'll eventually convince yourself of that if you repeat it often enough. Isn't that what mantras are for? Brainwashing yourself into believing something?"

She spun on her heel, her hair flinging soggy rainbow puffs

onto my shirt as she whirled off. Potentials continued to laugh and point at Fallon as she strode out of the cafeteria. I wanted to revel in it, but there was a small sinking feeling in the pit of my stomach that hinted maybe I didn't win that one. I quickly tried to shove that shit down; I'd won. Just one look at everyone around me and it was obvious I had taught her a lesson.

I forced a smirk to my face, going around the table to sit next to Flynn where he waited with a high five. Fallon had lost this one, so why did I feel like the loser?

# NOAH

I leaned against the shelves in the darkened storeroom where I'd first seen Mark meet with the mysterious hooded figure. It was an effort to keep myself from nodding off where I stood camouflaged. With each night I came back I increasingly grew bored. I would have brought a book but there was no point trying to read in the dark, plus it's not like I was wearing anything to smuggle one in.

Neither Mark nor the hooded guy had returned and there was every chance they wouldn't come back at all, but I had no lead as to where else they might meet. I'd followed Mark in my free time, waiting to catch his next meeting, only to find him being a jerk or a straight-up sleazeball to the other Potentials. So, after he went to bed, I'd venture here and wait it out a few hours just in case either one of them came when everyone else was asleep.

I made sure to be hyper-vigilant of my surroundings when spying now. I wasn't keen on getting caught wandering around with my birthday suit on like I had last time.

I'd stashed my clothes in a box on the highest shelf so I could get changed before leaving the room. That damn picture of me with the grapefruit was still making the rounds. I'd like to say it wasn't my proudest moment, but my teen years were filled with many embarrassing stints when I was still practicing with my invisibility. All I want known is that the grapefruit remains a virgin.

I wasn't the only target of such jokes. There were images and videos of other Potentials being circulated too. Celeste was a genius for giving everyone a means to capture their competition in their worst moments. Evil, but a genius nonetheless.

I rubbed my eyes. All this spying was exhausting both my magic and me physically, not to mention how it ate into my sleep. I couldn't give up, though. Katie, Rena, and so many others were relying on me.

Light bled through the crack of the door where it opened, and hope surged in my chest that the night had not been a total waste. I quickly became invisible and leant forward to see Victoria Auger strolling in with her chin high. She passed a shelf then stopped, placing her hands on her hips as she tapped her foot. Apparently, she was already pissed off about arriving before whoever she was meeting.

I wondered whether it was Mark or if she, too, was meeting the hooded guy. He'd mentioned House Jupiter accepting a shipment, so I knew they were involved with Mark, just not to what extent yet.

Victoria was ruthless and thirsty for power. I'd seen enough of her to know that she thought she had already been crowned queen. How her sister managed to continue to get back up and face Victoria was a mystery to me.

Fallon Auger had a strong will, that was obvious. I wondered whether her competing against her sister was about saving her pride or something else entirely, though I had a hunch. I'd seen how Fallon had made friends where her sister had made subordinates. The siblings were night and day.

Something about Fallon drew my interest, but I couldn't put

my finger on it. She caught my eye, sure, and judging by the attention she was getting, she caught others' too, but it wasn't her physical appearance that intrigued me. There were those who, like Victoria, wished Fallon harm, and then there were others who sought her out for another reason. It was obvious she had admirers, despite how many sneered at and taunted her. If I had been here for any other reason, I might have thrown my hat in the ring and shown her how she should be treated. Not the crude words or the lusty looks. Unfortunately, that wasn't the case, and I needed to keep my mind focused on the end goal.

Soft steps sounded and the hooded guy appeared as though out of thin air once again. I inched forward, hoping to get a good look under the hood, only to have Victoria cut dangerously close in front of me. Fuck.

"Well, do you have them?" she snapped, pointing a finger at the guy's chest.

"Yes," he replied, taking out a bundle from inside his cloak and handing it to her. "Everything you asked for."

She looked at the bundle, testing the weight of what he had given her, then unravelled the fabric and held up pulse gun. "It's Sylvetti made?"

"Of course, only the best for you."

Whoever the hooded guy was, he seemed to defer to Victoria. The conversation was already vastly different to the one he'd had with Mark, who was clearly at the bottom of the food chain.

"Fallon?" he asked.

"I'm dealing with the bitch," Victoria said, turning the gun over in her hands. I couldn't help the jolt of disgust that went through me at the way she spoke. There was no love there and it was clear Fallon's life was under threat. "What about your side of the plan?"

"In motion."

Victoria smiled. The image was sinister in the low light. "Perfect."

"Good." The guy nodded, stepping back a few paces. "I'll report back."

"Whatever," Victoria replied, flicking her ponytail and turning around.

She reefed the door wide open, flooding the room with sudden blinding light. I blinked furiously, retreating into the dark. By the time my eyes readjusted, the hooded guy was gone.

"Shit," I swore under my breath.

I shook my head, pissed with myself for not being any closer to knowing who the mysterious hooded person was once again. I quickly grabbed my clothes and changed, allowing myself to become visible.

Pieces were coming together, but there were so many more I needed to uncover before I could try to put them into one whole coherent image. It was infuriating. I strode from the room, my mood evident with each stomp of my shoes. Despite the trials only beginning, I felt like time was running out.

At this time of night, the academy was quiet. Most Potentials were fast asleep, unaware of those sneaking around and scheming in the halls. As I passed the training areas I spotted Ace sitting with his back against a wall. His head was bowed, his shoulders rising in an even rhythm. The guy had serious trust issues and the fact that he chose to sleep out here alone was beyond sad. It must be lonely, feeling like you only have yourself to rely on.

I couldn't imagine a life like that. My family meant everything to me and without a doubt, I knew they would be there for me no matter what, just as I was for them.

Reaching the dorms, I opened the door to find Kayden storming up the steps. He disappeared for a few seconds, the sound of his feet still audible, as well as the words he was muttering between breaths. Something about keeping her out of his head, whomever that was. He reappeared, descending and pulling to a stop at the bottom, his eyes widening as he saw me. He quickly recovered, replacing his look of shock with a smirk.

"Lurking in the night?" he asked, raising a brow. His words came out puffed. He must have been pacing for a while.

"That's what all good vampires do," I said with a shrug as I made to stride past him up the stairs.

He grabbed my upper arm. Kayden was huge, but up close it was hard to ignore just how big of a guy he was. Pure muscle too. "Aren't you gonna ask why I'm awake, smart ass?"

"Safety-testing the steps?" I replied, tugging free.

Kayden huffed a laugh. "You're a funny guy."

"I'm a real barrel of laughs," I deadpanned.

"You're from the Verdant Plateau, right? What's it like?"

"Green," I said, then decided to be straight with him. "Peaceful. The people are happy, the city is thriving—at least they were until…" A thought popped into my head and I looked at him curiously. "Anything strange happen in the Crimson Steppes lately?"

"Huh?" Kayden tilted his head. "Like what?"

"I don't know, anything out of the normal?"

He smirked. "What's your definition of normal?"

I shook my head. It was too late in the night to be dealing with Kayden's idea of fun. I shouldn't have thought he'd answer my questions properly. Guess I deserved that. "Never mind."

"You should join me—my team," he called after me. I turned halfway up the stairs, looking down at him. "You have skills that I could use and, in return, I'll protect you from dying too early."

*Too early.* I rolled my eyes and huffed a laugh. "What a kind offer. Unfortunately, I must decline."

"You're making a mistake."

"Maybe, but I guess I'll have to live with it."

I barely had enough time to eat and sleep, let alone be someone's lackey. Not that I would ever be bossed around like that. I may have been quiet, but my life belonged to me, not for someone else to wield as they saw fit. I wasn't here because anyone else wanted me to be. Not my family, a boss, a friend, or even the pressure of societal expectations. Nothing made me participate in the trials against my will. I was raised to set my own path and right now it was leading me to find out what was happening to the people of the Verdant Plateau.

Kayden would have to try his luck with someone else to strengthen his position in the trials because he had no chance of recruiting me.

"Hey!"

I froze at the top of the stairs but didn't look his way. "Yeah?"

"You didn't hear me before? When you first came in, I mean." Kayden's voice had lost its strength. If anything, he almost sounded worried.

"Nah," I lied. I wasn't interested in getting involved in anyone else's drama.

I continued up the stairs to the second floor where my room was located, silently opening the door and making my way over to my bed. It was beneath some guy who liked to mumble in his sleep about video games. I didn't mind playing the odd game, but back home I liked to spend my spare time playing guitar or reading a good book. Both didn't require me leaving the house, which I loved, because after socialising with my family I liked to recharge by being alone. The only other thing that got me out the house was being in nature and going for a hike.

I quickly got ready for bed, yawning louder than I expected before sliding between my sheets.

"Get on top of him. Push a bit harder forward," the guy muttered.

I cocked my head. Maybe his dreams were drifting to a different topic tonight?

"Shoot, shoot. What a noob."

Nope. Still the video games. Shit, gamer talk could sound so suggestive when hearing it out of context. With another yawn, I stretched my arms before closing my eyes. Tonight had been full of information, but I was still in the dark. Time was ticking and

I just hoped I wasn't too late.

# FALLON

Sunlight streamed through the window to touch my face. I grumbled, burrowing deeper beneath the covers to hide away from the world. Yawning, I stretched my arms and legs and winced at the aching muscles all over.

I'd survived the first week which felt like it was inspired by hell and we hadn't even reached the first trial yet. Who knew what horrors awaited? The first was a trial of the body, which meant we'd have no magic to rely on—just our strength and our wits.

Given the injuries I was already sporting, I didn't like my chances, especially when I was quickly gathering more enemies each day. Apart from Zane and Kendra, I was a walking target to just about everyone here. In the last few days, I'd been beaten and bruised bloody, and humiliated twice now by both Victoria and Kayden.

My skin heated as I thought of them. There were videos all over Acadameet of Kayden spilling Dick's god damned cereal all over my head and the fight between me and Victoria with her twit friends. I sighed. At least some students were on my side. Many had commented saying it wasn't a fair fight and that

Victoria wasn't strong enough to fight fairly on her own. I smiled smugly at that thought. It would have infuriated her to no end to realise not everyone wanted to grovel at her feet.

Deciding to go for a fly to stretch my wings and clear my head, I threw off the covers, rolled over, and yelped.

Green eyes stared at me an inch from my face and I scrambled back in fright. "Fucking hell, Zane," I panted. "You gave me a heart attack. What are you doing?"

"I thought you might want some cuddles." He smiled, his eyes lingering on the tight tank top I was wearing. "You were having bad dreams."

"Eyes up here, Merman." I grinned. "Are you sure you don't want to cuddle Mark? He looks like he needs some emotional support."

I looked pointedly at the finger Mark had jammed in his mouth and Zane laughed like a freaking dolphin. "Nah, guy's got mummy issues. I'd rather cosy up in your coral reef."

"You are so strange," I said, laughing. "Unfortunately for you, this angel fish is going for a fly."

I blinked. Oh gods, I was speaking like him now.

Zane shrugged as I hopped out of my bunk. I grabbed my things and padded to the bathroom where I could feel his eyes glued to my ass as I went, then realised he had followed. He stood leaning against the door.

I chuckled. "Uh, a little privacy, Zane?"

"It's just skin." He grinned mischievously. "We all have a birthday suit and yours is really nice."

I smirked, sashaying towards him and hooking a finger in the waistband of his sweats. He wasn't wearing a shirt, and damn, he looked edible today with his hair tied into a top knot and his tanned muscles on display.

"Yeah? You like what you see?" I teased, nipping his ear and running my hands around his neck.

"I'd like it better with those clothes off," he replied softly, leaning in for a kiss.

I offered him my cheek at the last second, raking my nails gently down his stomach and lightly passing over his junk with a giggle.

He groaned, allowing me to push him away. "You're such a tease, Starfish."

I bit my lip, loving that sound coming from his lips. There was no denying the attraction between us, but it wouldn't be as fun if I didn't make him work for it. With a wink, I shut the door in his face and stripped out of my clothes. "I'm naked now," I called lightly.

Another groan answered me. "You're such a bad girl, you know that?"

"I know," I called cheerfully, stepping under the shower. "Guess you'll just have to wait and see how bad I can be."

"Oh, I have a pretty good idea," he said through the door. "But it's fine. I'll play your game, Starfish. It'll only be all the sweeter when I win."

I smirked, stepping into the shower and turning the handle. "Maybe 'sweet' isn't my style, Zane."

There was a pause and for a moment I had to wonder what he was doing on the other side of that door. "I'm off to get breakfast, but don't think I'm going to forget this."

I laughed, feeling lighter since waking. Zane was just so refreshingly down to earth and upbeat all the time. He didn't seem to have any worries in the world and didn't give a shit what people thought of him—or of me, for that matter. He was just … fun.

And hot. So flipping hot.

I sighed, letting the hot water ease into my bones as I washed my hair and scrubbed my body. It was so pleasant that I just stood there for long minutes and soaked in the peace and quiet. Right up until dickwad Mark banged on the door.

"Hurry the fuck up," he growled. "Some of us have things to

do with our free time."

*Well, there goes that.* "Like what? Finding your next victim to torment? Yeah, you can just wait your turn like a good little boy." I turned off the tap, drying myself slowly and running a brush through my hair.

His snarl seemed to echo through the bathroom, and I rolled my eyes as I donned a pair of navy leggings and a white hoodie that had wide slits in the back to make room for my wings.

"I swear, if you don't get your ass out of there, I'm going to knock this door down and drag you out by your hair."

So dramatic. I turned towards the door and paused, a better idea coming to mind. With a grin, I slid the bathroom window open. It was wide enough for me to climb out, and I did so eagerly, launching myself into the air and unfurling my wings.

Little Marky could waste his time yelling at me for a little while longer. Suck on that, asshole.

I twirled through the air, enjoying the way the breeze caressed my feathers as the warm sun beamed down on my face. It was a gorgeous day, and I soared into the skies, flapping high enough to find myself sailing through fluffy clouds before tucking my wings in and letting myself fall.

My stomach dropped and I laughed giddily as I plummeted through the air before banking into a glide over the grounds.

It felt so good to stretch my wings and feel the sun soaking into my copper feathers. In the distance I saw another guy doing the same, but I wouldn't encroach on his space. Most residents of Stormcrest City preferred to fly in solitude. I wondered if it was the same for the swimmers of Tritosa City.

Being able to summon gills at will, many Tritosians could comfortably swim underwater for as long as they wished, and if Zane and his beloved dolphins were any example to go by, I'm betting that meant Tritosians had a natural affinity with sea life too.

If I was being honest, swimming with dolphins and sea

turtles sounded like a hell of a good time. No wonder Zane was so laid back. His power was persuasion, calming, and nullifying other magics, so it made sense, but just how far would that get him when pitted against magic like Ace's or my own?

Ace could manipulate electrical currents, which was equally badass and terrifying. He could short circuit someone's brain, break into high tech security—who knew what his limits were? I shuddered. He was not someone I wanted to be around when our chips were deactivated in the magic trial … if I made it that far.

I glided around the academy grounds, trying to leave these worries behind and clear my head. The grounds were beautiful from above. The lake shimmered in the sunlight, students laughing and messing around as they swam. Others lounged around the meadow, some reading books while others sat with friends.

It all seemed so normal, seeing everyone from all backgrounds coming together. But everything would change in a week. Many of these students had found their groups, but would that change when the first trial began? Survival of the fittest, Celeste had said. And not all of us would come out of it alive.

My mind drifted to Ethan. I had to survive for him and Hadley. There was no alternative. I flapped my wings, descending towards the ground when I spotted Noah running along the path through the woods.

He had his shirt off, the beautiful green pattern snaking around his collarbone and down his chest and back, glittering over his dark skin. The guy was sleek over his muscles. Sweat dripped down his chest toward the vee above his hips, his powerful thighs pounding beneath loose shorts.

I changed course, gliding after him thoughtfully. Noah was mysterious and quiet, always lingering in the background observing others. The pattern on his skin meant he could camouflage, which made him the perfect fly on the wall to gather information around this place, so if anyone would know about how students were getting weapons and who knew what else into the academy, Noah would.

If my sister had access to information or smuggled goods from outside the House of Ascension, she had a serious advantage over me, not to mention she could have some ulterior motives. And if a troll like Mark had access to the same, it didn't bode well for anyone. Come to think of it, Ace had seen Victoria take that weapon out and hadn't batted an eye either.

Screw it. Noah and I were going to have a little chat. Zane seemed to like him, so how bad could he be?

I tucked my wings in tight and zoomed towards the guy, landing just in front of him so he had to skid along the dirt, stopping right in front of my face.

I grinned. "Hi."

"Uh … hi?" He blinked, running a hand over his eyes as if that might make me disappear.

"Yup, still here. So, I was hoping we could have a little chat." I looped my arm through his, ignoring the sweat and appreciating the hardness of his bicep as I pulled him along. He allowed me, looking thoroughly baffled and flustered.

"And here I thought you flew in front of people for sport."

"Look, I'll be straight with you. I've noticed you around. You observe people, and you're so quiet nobody really notices until they've already run their mouth. Probably doesn't hurt that you can camouflage too, right?" I winked at him.

He looked at me oddly, and I couldn't help but notice his honey-brown eyes had little flecks that looked like gold around the iris, so small you'd only see them up close. He was very attractive, with full lips, a strong jaw and nose, and … dare I hope for a dimple if he actually smiled?

"What?" I said, tucking a strand of hair behind my ear. It probably looked like a crow's nest after flying with it wet, and I suddenly felt self-conscious.

"Nothing," he said quietly.

It was definitely not nothing, but I'd let him keep some

secrets. The way he looked at me was a little uncomfortable—like he could see right into my soul—but it was a damn sight better than the way everyone else turned their noses up at me. His quiet yet commanding presence was actually kinda nice. I could see why Zane was so drawn to him.

"So … I'm an observer too, buuut I could see how you might not think that when I've been busy getting the shit kicked out of me and being humiliated in front of the whole academy."

A slight smile curved over his lips, the hint of a dimple popping into view. Bingo.

"So that's it then. You came here to ask about your sister," he said.

I cocked my head. No beating around the bush then. "That's right. And given you know that much I suspect you know why."

Noah beckoned us to continue walking, looking around in case anyone was listening. We headed deeper into the woods and he stopped, leaning against a tree and crossing his arms over his chest.

"It'll cost you."

I raised a brow. "Credits? Name your price."

Noah shook his head. "I don't want money. I want a favour. You'll owe me when I'm ready to call it in."

"How mysterious." I tapped my pursed lips, contemplating his terms. It seemed harmless enough, but to be honest, I was too curious to say anything but yes. "Okay, I'm in. As long as you're not asking me to forfeit the crown, you've got a deal."

He nodded, his posture relaxing. "I've been keeping tabs on a few people … for obvious reasons. The other night I saw your sister meeting with a hooded guy. They didn't reveal much during their meeting, though I know House Jupiter is heavily involved in whatever they're up to." He shook his head. "Your sister also had a pulse gun smuggled in."

I bit my lip, chewing over this information. Not only did she have a blade but a pulse gun too. If Victoria had weapons coming in, there was no reason others wouldn't have them too. The trials were rigged.

"If House Jupiter is involved," I said slowly, "it must mean my parents are aiding my sister. Either that, or she has some very powerful friends backing her for their own gain. Maybe she made a deal before coming here."

Noah shrugged. "Whatever the case, it means you'll have to watch your back. Many students have it out for you, if only because of where you come from. There are no rules in the first trial."

I heard him loud and clear. It was a trial of strength, and though I didn't know what it entailed yet, I knew Victoria would have no problems bringing weapons to a fistfight. Things could get really bloody, real fast.

"There's something else you should know," he said darkly. "I saw Mark meet someone hooded too. I'm not sure if it was the same person or whether he's working with Victoria. But he used the same meeting place."

"Why are you telling me this?" I asked curiously. He'd already given me what I wanted, why was he offering more? We weren't friends, and if he were strategic, keeping this information to himself could be beneficial down the line.

He studied me, his face betraying nothing. "Maybe I'm sick of people like them getting everything they want. Maybe I want things to change."

*Them.* Interesting that he didn't count me in that basket. I turned around, pacing thoughtfully along the dappled ground. I turned back to speak with him and blinked.

He was already gone.

———— ◆ ————

It didn't happen often, but sometimes the guys and gals upstairs smiled down on me. Thankfully, Mark was nowhere to be seen when I returned to my room, though the bathroom door was sporting a new gouge in the wood. I smirked. I hope he pissed himself before he made it in there.

I walked over to the lump in Kendra's bed and prodded it, earning a grumble. "Wake up sleepy head."

Another grumble.

"I've got coffee," I sang, waving the takeaway cup in my hand.

Her head popped out of the covers, her long black hair all tousled. I waved the cup near her face and she followed it with her nose, eyes still shut. When she got a good whiff of the caffeine, she snapped them open and threw me a crooked grin before snatching it from my hand. "I knew there was a reason I liked you," she teased.

I rolled my eyes. "Glad to know it's because of my winning personality. Wanna get some brekkie at the caff before class?"

She threw the covers off and stretched like a cat. "Am I a monkey's uncle? Yes, of course. Right after I put my warpaint on."

"Should I grab my sword and shield?" I asked with a smirk.

Kendra raised a brow as she gathered her things. "Always. Give me a moment to shower, I still feel like an exhausted pigeon."

I laughed as I saw the nest of hair at the back of her head. "You look like one too. Hurry up, I'm starving."

She got to the doorknob, hanging a little pathetically, and turned. "Do I even want to know?"

I laughed. "I'll tell you on the way."

She shrugged, tried to close the door, then gave up when it wouldn't click shut. I cringed. Maybe it was a bad idea to let Mark break the lock. I wouldn't trust him not to sneak a perve at whoever was in there. After making a mental note to tell the repairman—janitor, whoever—to fix it, I decided to change and put a little paint on myself. It was a tank top and jeans kind of day, so I slipped on some ripped black jeans, combat boots, and donned a black cropped tank. Then I set to work on some graphic eyeliner, mascara, and a little blush.

Kendra stepped out decked in a check mini skirt, knee-high boots and a black top with cut-outs, her hair in those trademark space buns and her eyes drawn like mine. "Time to slay," she remarked, looping her arm in mine.

"The breakfast foods don't stand a chance," I agreed. "To the caff!"

I told her about my incident with Mark along the way and filled her in on what had happened with Noah and me, but before she could respond, a sound coming from around the corner of the caff met our ears.

We exchanged glances, wordlessly deciding to check it out. My stomach instantly dropped.

*Mark.* And he wasn't alone. "Stop being such a tease," he was saying as he pressed a girl against the wall. "I know you want me."

"Please," the girl said, wriggling her wrists where he'd pinned them both beside her head.

In the shade, I couldn't see her face enough to tell what she was thinking, but the tone of her voice wasn't promising. We crept closer.

"It won't take long. Just a quickie," Mark replied, kissing up her neck.

The girl just squeezed her eyes shut. "No," she breathed.

"Don't be such a bitch, Jemma. You can't lead me on and leave me hanging. Just close your eyes." One hand slid down her body, to her thigh, then began creeping up again.

I swallowed the bile rising in my throat. *Enough.*

"She said no, Mark."

Kendra and I advanced, stomping towards him. He looked over his shoulder, sneering. "If it isn't the angel bitch and her little sidekick. This doesn't concern you. Run along before you get yourself into trouble."

"You're not going to lay another hand on that girl," Kendra said, stepping forward.

"And what are you going to do about it?" Mark said, looking

her up and down as he let the girl go and turned. Clearly, the guy had no idea what kind of strength Kendra was packing.

The girl looked between us all, and I jerked my head for her to escape. Her features smoothed out in relief. She mouthed a 'thank you' and scurried away before he could notice.

I shifted my stance as I looked at Mark, then back to Kendra. "I recall you saying something about war?"

The grin she gave me was pure viciousness. Then she advanced. Before I could blink her leg whipped out and she smashed little Marky's chest with her chunky boot. His back slammed into the wall with a satisfying thud.

"You little bitch," he roared. "You're going to regret that. I have no trouble beating down a woman."

"A statement that surprises exactly no one," I drawled.

Kendra's fists moved like lightning as she punched him once, twice, three times in the gut. Then she kneed him in the balls so hard he gasped, doubled over, and vomited into the bush.

Happy to watch my badass bitch of a friend whoop his ass, I stepped closer, flicking his chin up with my fingers. Then I waited for Kendra to impart some final wisdom. She knelt as I held him, then cocked her head.

"Consider this a warning, Mark. If we see you even look at a girl the wrong way, we'll find you. If we hear about you touching someone without their consent, we'll tear your fucking balls off. Play nice or suffer the consequences, kay?"

He didn't answer but his eyes glared murderous hell at us both.

"Kay. Good chat," I said cheerily as I pulled away.

Kendra just grinned. "See ya, roomie."

We relinked our arms and headed to the caff. I had the feeling breakfast was going to taste all the sweeter now.

# ZANE

Nothing beat the slippery wet embrace of submerging myself in the lake. The water had a way of calming my thoughts and relaxing my entire body. I hadn't realised how badly I missed it—especially against my gills. I sighed at the cooling sensation of the water against my neck. It was never ideal to spend so much time on land. I hated when my gills got too dry and showering just didn't lubricate them like I was used to.

I kicked my legs, propelling myself up until I popped my head through the surface and moved to float on my back. The sun warmed my tanned chest as tiny ripples tickled my sides. I ignored the far away sounds of the other Potentials, most of whom were either on shore or swimming close to it. All I needed now was Pip and Delilah and my day would have been made.

The lake was part of mini Tritosa City and was surrounded by sandy shores and green shrubs, a pier running out from the edge closest to the centre of the House of Ascension. After diving in, I'd swum down to check the lake's depth, but the thing went on and on and on and I wasn't a fan of getting lost in the dark on my own. Especially when I wasn't entirely sure what lived down there. As the lake was made by humans for the purpose of testing potential rulers, I had a feeling there would be some gnarly stuff swimming around in its depths.

A splash landed on my warm belly, followed by a succession of small waves through the water that wobbled my calm floating. I turned my head to see Kayden thrashing as he swam back and forth from one end of the lake to the other like it personally offended him. He had zero technique. He just used brute force to make his way through it like he apparently did in every other aspect of his life. The dude was using his energy to splash rather than push himself forward, and it was embarrassing to watch.

"Hey Kayden!" I shouted, grabbing his ankle and pulling him to a stop in the middle of the lake.

Kayden kicked furiously but I didn't let go. I had some very important pointers the dude needed to hear and I couldn't in good conscience let him keep swimming like that. He'd terrify all the poor lake creatures if he kept up that nonsense. Kayden rounded on me, throwing a punch towards my face, but I dropped his foot and pushed backwards before he could make contact. He dropped face first into the water, coming back up and sputtering before his red head went diving back down again.

"Tread water, man!" I told him, swimming closer. I gripped him under his huge, tattooed arm, holding him up above the water. "Doggy paddle at the very least."

"What?" he grumbled, wiping a hand over his face to clear the water. He didn't push me away from him, instead leaning into my hold.

"You know, kick your legs on the spot," I said, letting go of him so that I could do the action with my hands. He sank like a rock as I did. "Oh, sea cucumber!" I reached down for Kayden, pulling him back up. "Sorry, dude. Shouldn't have let go. As I was saying, tread water so I can help fix your stroke."

"I don't need you to fix anything," he said, placing a big hand on my shoulder to keep himself afloat.

I sent him a sly grin. Sure, sure, Kayden. It wasn't his fault he lived in a desert and couldn't dive into the water's sweet embrace whenever he wished.

He looked at something behind me, and I followed his line of sight to see Mark Leroy getting smacked by some chick whilst she yelled at him about keeping his hands to himself.

"Bro's a pervy dick," Kayden said.

"Yep," I agreed. Mark had tried to get all handsy with my Starfish. Dude didn't know a thing about boundaries. "Now, back to you. Kayden, you swim like a cat in a bathtub," I explained. "Zero technique and I can see the fear in your eyes a mile away. The water is here to support you, it's not cool to slap her like that."

"Are you high?" he asked, giving me a quizzical look.

The dude obviously had more brawn than brain if he was struggling to keep up with such a simple concept.

"Smooth out your arm strokes," I told him, slowing my voice down and nodding at him at the same time. He kept looking at me like I had swallowed too much salt water, and I was starting to worry that his biceps had stolen the blood from his brain. "Dude, the water is your friend. Be kind."

Kayden arched his brow.

"Like this," I said, raising the arm furthest from him and making a stroke movement. My technique was top-notch, he was lucky I was giving him this little tutoring session. "See how my arm—"

A red swimsuit stole my focus, like a rip had entered the ocean of my brain and drew me far away from my demonstration. My eyes found Fallon like a shark following the scent of blood. Starfish was walking into the water in a very red swimsuit that made her tits look like absolute perfection, showing off her sexy figure.

"Damn," Kayden breathed, then suddenly I was being dragged underwater.

I looked down to where Kayden was holding my wrist in his

rock-hard grip, and I meant that literally. The dude had turned to stone. His skin flushed a reddish brown and was all stony, kind of like a man-shaped version of the boulders in the miniature Crimson Steppes training area.

"What the fuck?" I shouted at him under the water, then silly me remembered he couldn't understand me through the water like I could. I rolled my eyes at his subpar adaptation and tried to tug him to the surface. He was so heavy. I was starting to think I'd have to leave him to become a decoration, like what you'd put in a fish tank. Kayden's rocky eyes widened and he shook his head like he was able to read my mind.

Could rocks drown?

I had a feeling I was about to find out, but then Noah appeared, his torso all sparkly green and looking gnarly beneath the surface. He looked a bit like a merman and the sight warmed my little aquatic heart. Another sign that we were destined to be besties. Together, we dragged Kayden to the surface and towards the shore. Once we reached land, we dumped him on his back at the edge of the lake for his friends to help him out. With Kayden saved, I slung my arm over Noah's shoulder and grinned. We were a dynamic duo.

"I'm not getting in," an angry voice grumbled along the shore, spoiling my happy mood.

"Mr Warner," Master Nolan said. "This is part of physical training. You will need to get in the water once I've explained the objective."

"Not a fucking chance," Ace replied, wiggling the fingers of his bionic hand. "Water and electricity don't mix."

"Can't you just take it off?" I asked, moving closer and pointing at the limb in question.

"No."

"How'd you get it anyway?"

"I could show you." Ace smirked, a dark gleam in his eyes.

"Nah." I shook my head. "How many terabytes of data can

you store on it? Can you replace the fingers with other things, like forks?"

"Why would he want to swap his fingers out for forks?" Fallon asked, coming to my side.

"Why wouldn't he?" I asked, my brows raised. "Think of how convenient that would be. Honestly, Starfish."

"Alright everyone!" Nolan called, gesturing for everyone to come closer. "Your training for the day will involve water assaults. Your task is simple. A race across the lake."

I bumped my side into Starfish. "Easy peasy, Fallon squeezy."

"Real cute." She smirked, walking to where a line was forming around the edge of the lake.

"At the siren, you may begin!" Nolan shouted.

A loud wailing sounded then everyone was running into the lake, making water fly all over the place. Well, not everyone. Noah was nowhere in sight, which I could only assume meant he was naked and invisible somewhere, trying to avoid the task. Ace stood with his tattooed arms folded over his chest and his trademark frown spread on his face. He saw me looking at him so I waved, hoping to cheer him up because he must have been so disappointed at not being able to go for a swim. I know I would be. Ace lifted his hand to wave back, but it must have glitched last minute because only his shiny middle finger popped up. Technology could be so unreliable.

Now that the splashing was all over, I raced into the lake. Unlike the chaos of everyone else, my feet slid perfectly into the water with each step I took, like slipping on the silky socks I'd bought the other month. Turned out they weren't great for walking in, but I'd found other uses for them. Ahead of me, people were being caught in rips and thrown under waves made with magic. It was weird seeing this sort of activity in a lake and I hoped the little fishies had swum to safety and didn't get caught up in it. When the water reached my hips I dove, narrowly missing getting hit by a jet of water.

Below the surface, I swam through the tumbling bodies and kaleidoscope of legs. They looked so funny, wiggling in the water like giant worms. I paused, tilting my head to the side. I wondered whether they'd let anything loose to nimble on those limbs. Piranha perhaps?

Something touched my foot and I jumped out of my skin, my heart pounding like a drum. I whirled around but there was nothing there. No more piranha talk, Zaney. I was freaking myself out.

I swam through the sea of legs, pinching a few as I went by and searching for my little Starfish. I spotted an ass in a red swimsuit and kicked towards it, giving it a squeeze before popping my head above the surface. I frowned at the blond who stared down at me.

"You're not Starfish," I said, pouting, just before we both got pummelled with a giant wave.

The water threw me back down and I laughed as bubbles drifted around me, enjoying the ride as I tumbled around. When I finally stilled, I swam through the water as fast as I could to the shore.

"Winner, winner, squid for dinner." I grinned, finding no one else on the other side of the lake but me. I raised my arms in the air, basking in my victory.

I turned, watching the chaos in the water. Potentials were being thrown around whilst others were chopping through the waves, Kayden among them. It turned out his aggressive strokes were good for something. He was hurtling towards me with the ferocity of a jet boat. I searched for Fallon, spotting her in the centre, rising with the swells with Kendra close by.

Starfish liked to make everyone think she was independent, but I sensed she needed me. Even without my power, I still had an uncanny ability to read others. Like how I knew Noah wanted to be my bestie. He was just afraid to make the dive. Fallon may have looked like she was chilling in the water, but I knew she needed her knight in shining armour—or boardies—to help her tame the waves. I puffed out my chest.

"I'm coming, Starfish," I declared like the righteous knight I was.

Diving back into the water, I swam towards them deeper down. It was chaos above the surface and I didn't want to get thrown around for no reason. When I'd reached about the middle, I shot up and popped my head into the air with a grin. I was so good at calculating distances.

I slipped between Fallon and her gal pal, dropping an arm around Starfish's waist and tugging her close. Kendra giggled, trying to cover it up with a cough. Not quick enough though.

Sneaky seal.

"Where did you disappear to?" Fallon asked, unclasping my fingers and pushing backwards just out of my reach. "I thought you'd be finished by now."

"I won ages ago." I grinned.

"Of course you did," Kendra said, rolling her eyes. "Why are you back here then?"

"I thought I'd better get you two. Hold your breath," I said, ducking under as a large wave crashed over us.

Once the bubbles cleared, Fallon came into my line of sight, her dark hair splayed out around her and the imprints of her wings on her bare back. They looked like tattoos done in a pearly white sort of ink. She kicked her legs, swimming for the surface, and I was hot on her sexy tail. We broke the water and she gasped as I took hold of her and Kendra again and swam for the edge of the lake.

"I can swim, you know," Fallon said, holding onto my shoulders and wrapping her legs around my waist. I smiled, then got hit in the head by a powerful jet of water.

Fallon and Kendra let go just as I was thrown away from them across the lake in the most unflattering way. My hair came undone and was plastered over my face as though someone had dropped an octopus on my head. Why was the water against me? We'd always been such good friends.

Fallon had been barely knocked around and was continuing towards the lake's edge. She was a talented swimmer—a great sign that she was a prize catch. I just needed her to bite my line and let me reel her in. Sure, we did the naked dance, but Starfish could be aloof and I wanted her all to myself. I swam towards her, finding Kendra beside me. We dodged the obstacles together, and finally caught a wave that we rode towards the shore.

"Took your time," Fallon said as she stood on the yellow sand, her hands on her hips.

"Couldn't leave your gal pal behind," I told her, slapping Kendra on the back. I quickly caught her as she stumbled forward, her sea legs all wobbly on the sand.

We sat on a dune, watching as the remaining competitors either made it to our side or found themselves back where they started, bruised or in some cases unconscious.

"Can either of you see my sister?" Fallon asked. "I want to keep track of who she's hanging out with."

I scanned the water but couldn't see Victoria anywhere.

"Why do you want to know who she is with?" Kendra asked.

"She's up to something," Fallon said, looking at her hands. She was playing with a small stick, twirling it around her fingers. "I need to know what it is."

"I could follow her, search her room when she's not there?" Kendra offered. My eyes almost bugged out of my head. "I'll let you know what I find."

"Wait, wait, wait," I said, raising my hands before me. "I am shocked at your gutsiness little Kendra, but I think I should be the one assisting Starfish with this investigation."

I gave them my most serious look but was met with Fallon's mischievous grin. Kendra just shook her head.

"No one is going to be spying on Victoria or searching her stuff," Fallon said, tossing the stick to the sand. "It's too dangerous, but I appreciate both of you offering."

"You don't think I can handle a little danger?" I pushed, puffing out my chest. I wasn't afraid of anything. Okay, maybe sea slugs, but other than those slimy suckers, there was nothing.

"Mark and Victoria have been meeting someone in secret. This person—or people—have been keeping their identity hidden," Fallon said. "Mark and my sister both have weapons now as well."

Kendra sighed, her shoulders slumping. "These trials are not above board."

"Wait, how do you know all this?" I asked.

"Noah."

"Well fuck me in the blow hole," I said, then looked around for the invisible bastard. There was still no sign of him. "What made him think to spy on them? Is he spying on everyone? Does he spy on me?"

"I don't think he spies on you," Fallon replied as a dude leapt out of the water and crashed into the sand before us.

"Why not?" I reached past Fallon and slapped him on the chest. "Doesn't he think I'm interesting?" Fallon and Kendra started laughing, the sound almost muffled by the dude groaning in front of us. I glared at him. "We get it dude, you're injured, but we are having an important conversation."

"Trust me, no one would accuse you of that, though you do pose a good question," Fallon replied, ignoring our unwanted guest. "Why was he spying on Mark and Victoria in the first place?"

"Please," the dude on the sand pleaded, reaching out a hand. "Help me."

"Maybe he's trying to get intel on all the major contenders? Know his competition and all that?" Kendra suggested.

"That's a good point," Fallon said, pointing out across the lake to where the trainer stood, waving his arms around. "I think Nolan is calling us over. We'd better get back."

"Take me with you," the dude begged.

"I wonder what he found out about me?" I mused, jumping up. I grabbed the hand of the dude in the sand and started to drag him back towards the lake. "I'm obviously high on his competition list."

"Of course." Fallon grinned at Kendra. "You'd be close to the top."

"Close?" I asked, looking between them.

"Well, there are others to consider," Kendra said, following us into the water. "Ace, Flynn, Kayden—"

"Wash your mouth out, Kendra," I replied, hauling the injured dude onto my back. He looped his arms around my neck and started breathing heavily into my ear. "As if they would be more of a worry than me. Sure, they look mean, but that's about all you need to worry about."

We swam back to the other side of the lake and I dumped the dude onto the sand for someone else to deal with. I had more important things to worry about, like the fact my new friends didn't even see me as a threat.

# A SKY OF STORMS

# ACE

"**A**tti the Ant," a slimy voice said from behind me. I spun, grabbing the jerk by the collar and slamming him against the outside wall of the dorm building. He was shorter than me, albeit stockier, his feet scraping the ground as I got into his face.

"Utter those words again and I'll cut your tongue off and feed it to you," I growled, raising my bionic hand and flicking my finger to reveal a blade. The metal shone in the moonlight and the guy's green eyes darted back and forth between my face and it. "Do you understand?"

"Chill, mate," he replied with a light laugh, though it was strained and nervous. "Just a fucking joke, yeah?"

I released his collar, gave him another shove against the brick wall, then continued walking towards the entrance of the auditorium for the announcement I was already running late for. My room was full of annoying Potentials who were just asking for me to slit their throats in their sleep, so I'd been hanging out around the dorms. They all spat so much bullshit about how tough they were, how educated and worldly, when really they were just privileged assholes hooked up to the family bank account. Rather than murder everyone in my room, I'd decided to take a breather outside.

Cormac, as leader of the Drakes, would be pissed if I drew attention to myself like that when it could easily get out to the masses. It was bad enough that the brick head from the Crimson Steppes kept getting in my face. Fighting with him was not a good call, but he just rubbed me up the wrong fucking way. There was a time and a place to make a scene and as I needed to break into the House of Ascension, this wasn't it.

"You don't remember me then?" the guy said, jogging to catch up. He fell into step beside me, careful not to touch me. "I'm a—"

"Hallow's Griff."

"So you do know me then," he said, chuckling nervously. He should be nervous. Hallow's Griff was a bottom of the barrel gang, full of the scraps no one else dared touch. They'd sell their own mothers for a couple of credits.

"What do you want?" I asked, rounding a corner. Potentials were still making their way over to the hall so I mustn't have been so late after all.

"Just thought, us both being from DH, maybe we could team up? Looks like the people from other cities are. Might not be a bad idea."

"No."

"Not even going to think about it?"

I turned, his eyes widening as I stepped into his path. Potentials streamed around us, getting a quick look before hurrying away.

"You and I will never work together," I said, pointing a finger back and forth between his chest and mine. "Coming from the same city doesn't mean shit. You are a fucking Griff. You're lucky I'm deigning to speak with you and haven't sliced you up and chucked you in the lake. Now fuck right off."

I left him and made my way into the hall, shoulder-checking anyone who got in my way. The Overseer was nowhere in sight, so I found a spot at the back and flicked through the Acadameet app as I waited for her to arrive. I didn't have any private messages, so I scrolled through the public feed. The app was filled with shitty gossip and humiliating shots of Potentials captured mostly by those in one of two camps—Kayden's little gang or Victoria's. The people here had this holier than thou attitude, yet when it came down to the crunch, they were just like everyone else. Sheep loved to group together under a powerful leader and abuse everyone else to make themselves look better. I'd seen it all before and it was always the same shit. Just a different day and a different bunch of assholes.

I thought of the little rat from Hallow's Griff and scowled. The fucker no doubt assumed that befriending me would be his ticket into the Drakes. The guy was delusional.

From memory, his name was something childish like 'Danger Dog'. The guy had the face of a ferret—including the hair—and he was far from dangerous. Word on the street was his loyalty was shaky and he was always scheming to move up in the ranks. He'd pulled a couple of low-level jobs, resulting in several suspicious arrests of those he'd been working with. With a rap like that, there was no way Cormac would ever initiate him into the Drakes.

The thing that set my gang apart from others—including the two that had formed here at the House of Ascension—was that loyalty meant more than your life and we didn't go after small players. Torture was endured and we'd die before betraying another Drake. When we made a move, we struck at the top and if we wanted to make a point, we made sure it was loud and clear. Only cowards struck out at those who couldn't defend themselves.

Kayden and Victoria's little gangs were pathetic and only reaffirmed what I already knew. None of them knew what real bloodshed meant. None of them had seen the things I'd seen.

The rat had been the only one from my home city stupid

enough to proposition me. There were others at the House of Ascension, all coming from smaller gangs, but they'd been drawn to the mean-spirited power that Kayden and Victoria were flaunting. I was almost embarrassed to think there were Potentials that came from my city, but then I remembered the dragon tattoo inked across my chest. We may have been from Damascon Hollow, but other than sharing the same streets, I was nothing like them.

I hadn't bothered to make nice with anyone. I didn't see the point in subjecting myself to small talk with people when I wasn't here for the same reason as them. They were all here to be crowned ruler of Terrulia and I was here to steal some shit. I saw no point in deceiving anyone with niceties without some sort of payoff at the end. I'd done my research and the past trials had a reputation for being fucking savage. The aim was to make them prove that they were worthy of the crown. I figured that meant a large percentage of the people in this room would end up dead. Why waste my time with odds like that when they most likely wouldn't be around to benefit me in the future?

The room fell quiet as the Overseer walked onto the stage and tapped the microphone, the sound echoing in the vast hall. I tapped the screen on my cuff, turning it off before I folded my arms over my chest and waited for another of the woman's over-the-top speeches. I hadn't planned on being here when the trials kicked off, but it was proving difficult to hack the security systems. I was in, but making changes and clearing a path was a whole other ball game. Much to my disdain, I needed to listen to the Overseer because it looked like I was competing in the first trial.

"Good evening, Potentials," Overseer Celeste said, smiling broadly. I swear she got some sick enjoyment out of this whole thing. Her hippy-dippy shit was the icing on the cake … Fucking psycho. "I hope these last few weeks of training have aided you on your quest for greatness, as tomorrow, your first trial will be thrust upon you!"

Murmurs rippled around the room and I couldn't help myself as I searched for the reactions of a few particular individuals. I spotted Kayden first, the biggest shit-eating grin on his face as he spoke to his stocky sidekick. Victoria was sitting a few rows away, his mirror image as she whispered to her friends. Those two were some of the cockiest bastards I'd ever known and I'd spent my life around gangsters who thought they were the baddest motherfuckers to exist.

"The Trial of Body will test your physical strength and stamina. It will force you to reach deep down inside yourself, and I pray that you are able to discover someone worthy within the depths of your soul. As many of you most likely already know, there is but one rule; you will not be allowed to use your magic." The Overseer glanced around, her voice lowering in warning. "You won't all return, for this trial will weed out the weak in this garden of would-be royals. I advise you to use whatever is at your disposal and push yourself harder than you ever have before. You are to survive a single month and survive you must, for the alternative is a grave."

I smirked. And there it was. They were culling numbers and they weren't dragging it out by waiting for the later trials.

Celeste waved her hand in the air, gesturing towards the exit that led to the courtyard. "Now is the time to whisk yourself away if bravery has not been blessed upon you, for once you're in the trial there will only be one way to leave before the time is up. Death."

A few nervous glances passed between people, but no one moved. It was one thing to fail the trials and another entirely to return home with the shame of not competing at all. It didn't help that she was offering a way out that meant announcing you had no balls in front of ninety-nine of your peers. Fucking brutal.

"There is much courage in these halls tonight," the Overseer said, smiling broadly and clapping her hands in a quick rhythm.

"Dinner will be served shortly, then I encourage you all to rest well, for your trial is but a few hours away."

Everyone started filing out, the hall echoing with the sound of cocky remarks and predictions of the trial's location and who would survive. I swore I even heard a whimper. Whoever it was should fucking leave while they still had the chance.

I waited for the crowd to shrink, not wanting to rub shoulders with anyone on my way to the cafeteria. I noticed Fallon Auger and Zane Loch were standing around too. The guy was talking quickly, his face switching from one expression to another, and I was feeling drained just watching him, let alone being in the conversation. Fallon was taking it in her stride and I had to wonder what she was playing at. What advantage was she getting from befriending the surfer? Last I'd heard, House Neptune and House Jupiter didn't get along, but anything was possible with the elite class. Money and power could easily turn the biggest enemies into friends. There definitely had to be an incentive, as Augers didn't do anything without a payoff. They extorted or manipulated to get what they wanted.

My cuff buzzed and I dropped my gaze to check it, finding a message from an unknown number on my Acadameet app. I knew exactly who it was though. The Overseer may have stopped me from using my power to manipulate electricity, but they couldn't take away the other skills I'd acquired over the years. I tapped on the screen, opening the message from my boss.

Cormac had sent a single sentence cutting straight to the point.

*I want the sky ring.*

There was only one thing Cormac could possibly mean by that and it was the ring high-ranking members of House Jupiter wore. What he needed it for, I had no idea, but I never failed a job. I added it to the list of things I would take from this place.

Removing incriminating evidence was a habit, so I quickly deleted the message from my cuff then pushed off the wall towards the exit. Everyone had left now, so I walked towards the cafeteria alone, devising a plan to get the ring. There were a few Stormcrest City Potentials at the academy, but I only knew of two who would have the item I sought.

I had two options: take it by force from one of the Auger sisters or steal it without anyone seeing. The first would be detrimental to my end game, so not ideal. The latter required getting close to an Auger without them being suspicious.

Luckily, there were two Augers to choose from. Stealing one of their rings would be difficult, but at least I had multiple plays. Victoria was always surrounded by a gang of followers which meant increased barriers in my way, but on the other hand, having a lot of people around her would also be a convenient distraction of sorts.

Reaching the cafeteria, I shouldered the door open and made my way to the service counter to grab some food. After jumping the queue, I filled my plate then strode towards a nearby table.

"Move."

The Potentials sitting at the table I wanted quickly grabbed their plates and scurried away, leaving me alone. Perfect. Sitting down, I tucked into my pasta and contemplated my second option.

Fallon.

I eyed the table where the Stormcrest Princess now sat. I fucking hated myself for finding her so easily in a crowd, but she was like a magnet drawing my gaze. Zane and a petite woman with dark brown eyes and long dark hair were sitting with her. She'd found herself a little group of her own, but she must have thought they were beneath her. I could tell by the look in her copper eyes and the stiffness in her shoulders that she was still a lone wolf.

The younger Auger would be easier to get alone than her sister, but she was suspicious as fuck of everyone thanks to the constant threat of humiliation or abuse from either Victoria or

Kayden. If I were going to target Fallon, I'd need to win her trust or find myself some leverage. What would a rich bitch with access to anything that popped into her pretty head want enough to trade her family ring for?

I looked to where Victoria sat and knew instantly that Fallon was my target. She was the lesser of two evils, not that I'd let my guard down around her. Fallon was still the princess atop her sky tower, looking down at the rest of us fuckers fighting to stay alive. She had claws—expensive ones—but mine were sharper, and I wasn't afraid to draw blood.

# FALLON

My eyes fluttered open, and confusion clouded my senses as I felt strangely weightless. Flashes of blue and grey blurred into one, and with a sudden lurch of my stomach, I realised I was falling.

I screamed as I fully came to, my hair whipping around my face as I swivelled my body towards the ground. As I plummeted, my body passed through a forcefield of sorts, and I gasped, blinking at the world below. I knew Terrulia's geography well, but this ocean didn't look familiar, nor the land I was quickly dropping towards.

The sky was a sea of bodies as, one by one, students roused and the reality of their situation hit them.

They had parachutes strapped to their backs, but many still hadn't woken, and the window was running out to allow a safe distance to descend even with them deployed. My heart leapt into my throat as I spearheaded towards the ground, ready to stretch my wings when I got a good look at the terrain.

Freaking hell, they'd really started this trial off with a bang. My adaptation would serve me well, and I was grateful for the comforting weight of my wings helping to balance me out as I watched others struggling to get into a better position.

I hunted desperately for a sign of Zane and Kendra and was surprised to find terror filled me as I began moving in search of their forms among the sky, summoning my wings and weaving through the bodies.

I'd always found it hard to trust in others, thanks to the heavy fists and cutting words of my parents—not to mention their reputation, which people immediately judged me for. I'd learned to keep to myself, to build strong walls in order to keep others out. But there was something alluring about Zane. He was oddly calming, and I had never sensed any ill intentions from him. I didn't want him to be hurt.

Kendra was a breath of fresh air. The kind of girlfriend I'd always wanted, because dammit, yeah, I guessed I had quickly come to care about her. She'd had my back since day one without ever questioning me or asking for anything in return. That was loyalty, and I wasn't about to abuse it.

As I searched the sky, some students tried to clutch onto me, with their eyes wide and hands reaching to grab at my feathers. I lost my breath as someone latched on to my wing, causing us both to plummet as my balance wobbled and we tangled together, tumbling perilously towards death.

"Get off me!" I screamed. "Use your damn parachute!" But the black-haired guy didn't answer, frozen in shock and fear, his knuckles white where he gripped me. Guilt filled me as I looked into his pleading brown eyes, but I had no choice but to savagely kick him away. I couldn't open my wing, and if I didn't even out soon, we were both going to die. *To hell with splatting to death.*

I flapped away quickly, forcing myself to remain calm and feeling less anxious at the sight of parachutes deploying and a bunch of students descending, a mixture of relief and determination on their faces.

Ace, Kayden, and Noah were among them, the former two grinning smugly. At last I spotted Kendra and Zane, the two of them holding hands as she seemed to be yelling instructions at him. The poor merman was flailing, a look of utter panic in his eyes. I guessed the skies were as far from the seas as you could get, but it looked like they'd be okay.

I focused my attention below and frowned, my heart falling. They'd dumped us in a marshland of all places. Minimal shelter, resources, and a hell of a lot of bog to wade through. Just peachy.

I flapped my wings, slowing my descent so I could land smoothly ... and sucked back a scream.

Bodies crashed all over the earth, the limbs bent at impossible angles, blood and bones splashed across mud and soaked into the water. Oh gods. They must have either not awoken or hadn't deployed their parachutes quick enough, if at all.

My stomach twisted violently, and I had to hold back the urge to vomit, turning my attention to students still in the sky, most of whom had floated kilometres away as they controlled their descent. Kendra and Zane had disappeared.

Anger surged through my veins. Whatever we'd been dosed with must have been strong. The last thing I remembered was changing into the black jumpsuit and boots they'd instructed us to wear and stepping onto a jet, and who knew how long ago that was?

I inhaled deeply, assessing my surroundings. There was a tree line a few kilometres away, which would at least give me cover while I figured out my options. I'd need to find shelter and water first. The jumpsuits were lined, but it would be a long night if I didn't have access to fire. The problem with that was that a fire may as well be a beacon to other students, alerting them to my location.

A high-pitched screech echoed from somewhere close by and I crouched, the hairs on the back of my neck rising at the sound. I circled slowly, getting a good view of the marsh, but there was nothing but bog and muddy platforms as far as the eye could see.

Which meant...

Talons grabbed my shoulders as I looked up, the sharp claws sinking into my skin and making me cry out in pain. Heat blazed from the wounds, blood trickling down my arms as the creature lifted me into the air.

I screamed, punching at one of the sinewy legs and digging my nails into the creature's flesh. It screeched in protest before it let me go, and I tumbled, letting my own wings spring out and carry me higher.

It looked like something out of a horror movie. Huge batlike ears, fangs like a vampire and a piggish snout on its small skull. Its hideous fur was brown and patchy over its mottled grey skin— perfect for blending into this horrid environment.

More screeches echoed in the distance, followed by faint screams. I winced, circling my opponent as I frantically searched for what to do. I reached for my magic instinctively and frowned, feeling my power come up empty by the chip blocking it.

*Think Fallon.* I had no weapons, no magic, and being this creep's next meal was not an option. My only choice was to flee. I twisted sharply away, headed for the trees, and it bellowed in rage as it realised its prey was escaping.

The snap of leathery wings whipping through the air bled into my ears, and I grimaced. Shit, this thing was fast, and it looked hungry. I soared, forcing my wings to go harder, trying to keep my body straight as an arrow. Just a little further and I could at least seek some cover under the canopies where it was too narrow for the creature to fly.

I was so close when something latched onto my wing, the pain of pointed teeth embedding into the sensitive flesh of my wings and tearing down the tendons. I cried out, flapping hopelessly with my other wing as the ground rushed to meet me.

Barely managing to twist myself in time, I manoeuvred my body so that the creature cushioned my fall, and we rolled in a tangle of feathers, leathery skin, and limbs. My busted wing fluttered uselessly at my back, and I bit down hard on my lip, keeping my scream in check as my wounds barked from being jostled.

The giant bat came to a stop and I bolted, forced to sprint with my battered wing and wounds bleeding with each pounding step. I heard another shriek of rage, but I didn't look back as I careened around trees and logs, splashing through mucky water that smelled of rot.

I had to hide, because there was no way in hell I'd be outrunning this beast, and the trees weren't close enough together to keep me safe for long. My breath came in ragged gasps as I stumbled towards a tree with a root large enough for me to crawl under, and as I curled myself into a ball, I strained my ears to listen for the creature.

It was hunting me. The blood sucker was persistent, I'd give it that, but if I was lucky, it would be forced to give up and find its meal elsewhere. I frowned. There'd be plenty of other people on the menu.

The thought made me shudder. If there were more of these things, hopefully they'd be too preoccupied by the fresh meat of the splatters to kill anyone else, but I knew that was wishful thinking. I'd bet there were a whole lot of Potentials in a world of hell like me right now.

Not that that was a comforting thought. Damn, this whole trial was off to a bad start. Just twenty-nine days to go, no biggie, right?

The flapping of wings grew closer, the monster hissing angrily as it circled the trees above. Finally, its shadow moved on and the sounds grew distant as it lost my trail, seeming to head towards the sounds of another screech somewhere far away.

I let my head fall against the tree trunk, wincing at the damage done to my wing. It needed healing, but there was a slim chance of finding med supplies stashed anywhere. I just had to hope it was merely sprained and the wound wouldn't get infected, which meant I'd need to clean and bind it either way.

"Great start Fallon." I sighed, cautiously scrabbling out from beneath the tree. My jumpsuit was wet with blood from the injuries at my shoulders, and I gritted my teeth against the pain.

Everything hurt, and things would only get worse. Water, that's what I needed … which also meant I'd need a fire because in this swampy hell hole, there certainly didn't seem to be fresh water flowing anywhere.

*Fuck.*

Cautiously, I made my way through the trees, keeping my ears strained and my eyes open in case any other unwanted visitors thought they'd take a bite out of me. Not to mention other students. Mark and Victoria's faces flashed before my mind's eye. There were no rules, just a free-for-all and an all-you-can-eat buffet for any sharks that would come circling.

And I knew they would. This place would make people go mad. I'd seen it in movies and read it in books—it always started in places like this. The weak would fall prey to creatures or the beasts wearing human masks, and in the end only the strong would be left to assert their will over the masses.

It was a game of power and, right now, I was on the losing team. My determination hardened as I set my jaw. At least I had my wits about me. I was a survivor, and if my parents had taught me one thing, it was that common sense and a clear head prevailed.

They'd laugh if they saw me now. Wounded, miserable, and muddy as a wet dog trudging through the bog. They thrived off pain in all its forms. That was what they did—it was who they were.

And all of this, it was to put an end to their bullshit. To live in a world free from the vice-like grip of the Auger family and their thugs.

I looked to the sky. The sun was hidden behind the clouds, but I could tell it would be getting dark soon, which likely meant more monsters would come out to play tonight.

*Gotta find shelter.* I trudged on for what felt like an hour, my nerves shot and my instincts on high alert until I finally found a tree that seemed to have given up on life as it leaned heavily, its boughs providing a good hiding spot free from any predators.

I had no water or food, but it would have to do for now. Travelling in the dark in unknown territory would only sign my death warrant.

I just had to hope my wounds wouldn't fester overnight.

# KAYDEN

I slid into a landing, managing to brace myself as my boots sank into the marsh water. Unlike the rest of the Potentials, this trial wouldn't start with me being completely saturated. Unclipping my parachute, I let the pack drop into the mud and scanned my surroundings for threats, but I was struggling to see too far into the distance. The sky had been blue while I was falling, yet down here there was a fog that made it hard to get a look at anything more than a few feet away. Loud, unnatural screeching echoed around me and I whipped my head around to try and see the source. There were things flying around out here and I had a hunch there would be other monsters waiting in the shadows. It reminded me of a thriller movie I'd once seen where a city was trapped in a fog and monsters would jump out at people. The movie hadn't scared me, and the real deal was doing a worse job.

The screeching grew quiet and I rubbed my temple with the palm of my hand. It didn't help that I was also still foggy from whatever the fuck they'd given us on the jet to knock us out. My heart was thundering in my chest from the fall, adrenaline coursing through my veins, but I embraced the thrill running through me. It took a lot more than throwing me from a plane into a marsh filled with monsters to rattle me. I'd been brought up to take everything thrown at me and use it to make myself stronger. At the end of the thirty days, I'd still be standing and anything that had stood in my way would no longer be breathing.

A body crashed down beside me, knocking me to the side, and I quickly threw out a hand. I stopped myself from falling into the cold murky water, though I was saturated all the way up to the elbow of the hand I fell on. Righting myself, I looked over to where the guy was groaning in the fetid water, his parachute spread out ahead of him.

I marched over, grabbing him by the scruff of his neck and lifting him to his feet. "You'll need to work on your landings, bro."

"Yes, sir," Dick whimpered, attempting to stand on his own.

"Come on." I marched forward, leaving him to unclip himself and catch up.

We passed a body that was floating with their face to the heavens, and I couldn't help but wonder why most of these Potentials had signed up for the trials. They weren't made for this shit. Someone should have told them that they weren't cut out to compete. Didn't they have families or friends to dissuade them? Or were they so clouded by their own misplaced belief that they didn't listen?

"He's dead?" Dick asked from my side, looking at the body.

I nodded. Judging by the lack of parachute, I assumed it hadn't opened, though I was unable to tell whether the thing was faulty, or he'd simply never woken up to give it a go. Guess it didn't matter anymore; the fall had killed him. The body drifted away from us towards the tall reeds and I gave it no more of my attention. It was time to focus on my own survival. I needed to find the rest of my followers if I wanted to increase my odds over the next month.

It's not that I didn't have confidence in my own abilities to survive by myself, because let's face it, Dick wasn't going to help. I knew I had it in me, but it would be easier with other people following my orders. Playing smart was the way to go and besides, having people around me would be a convenient shield against whatever was hiding in the fog. And, sure, *maybe* a small part of me wanted to look out for my soldiers. I'd been training them after all. Especially those from the Crimson Steppes.

Walking through the cold water, I eventually found some dry patches of land. My feet were soaked and I hated the feel of wet socks in my boots. Living in an arid part of Terrulia meant that I wasn't used to this sort of shit. Give me dry sand and the hot sun any day. I dodged a couple more people falling from the sky, chuckling at their shrieks and wide eyes. I had no idea how they expected to last a month when a little skydiving scared the shit of them.

Amongst those dropping to the marsh, I spotted Flynn and made my way to where he landed. He was unclipping his parachute when I approached, a grin on his face.

"How sick was that, bro?" He laughed, slapping me on the back. I was amped to see he had survived, though I shouldn't have been surprised. He was tough as nails; it would take more than a fall from a plane to stop him. "Not as cool as base jumping in the canyons, but still pretty epic."

"It was alright." I smirked, putting my hands on my hips and glancing around. Back home, base jumping from the southern canyon was one of our favourite things to do. The adrenaline rush was epic. "Seen any of the others?"

"Nah, but I'm sure we'll find them," he replied with a shake of his head. "You made it, Dick!"

"Yep!" Dick grinned, puffing his scrawny chest out.

Yeah, I was just as shocked as my second to see the little guy. "Heard the screeching?" I asked.

Flynn nodded. "Saw some dark wings in the sky."

"We'll have to keep a lookout for them too. In the meantime," I said as a guy landed nearby, "eliminate anyone who attempts to get one over on us."

Flynn followed my line of sight and chuckled, eyeing off the blond guy who was struggling with his parachute clips. My friend angled his head in a clear question of whether said guy was a part of my murderous equation.

Blondie smiled, gesturing to the clips and shaking his head. "A little help?"

I shook my head, walking away. "Nah, don't think so."

Flynn laughed. "I'd hurry. Whatever is making those screeching noises sure does sound hungry."

"We need to find shelter too," I said. He strode by my side with Dick trailing just behind, our boots making disgusting squelching sounds with each step. "If we are going to camp out here for a month, we might as well be comfortable."

"Yeah, there's no way I'm sleeping in this shit."

I laughed, elbowing him in the side. "Not that different to your place back home."

"Like you can talk bro," he said, scoffing. "The only reason your room isn't a shithole is because you still live with your mumma. When will you get your own place like the rest of us adults?"

"When the need arises," I replied with a smirk. "I'm not moving until I have to. Why leave when I got it made at home?" I tapped my temple. "You're not going to shame me for living with my parents when it's the smart move, bro. Don't be snarky because yours got sick of your annoying ass."

"Harsh, man." Flynn laughed. "Don't hold back or anything."

We spent what felt like a few hours walking through the marsh, finding allies and disposing of only one other competitor. We managed to find five of my followers, though by now, those who survived the drop were already dispersing through the area, so the last hour went by without spotting another soul. The fog had started to clear as we got closer to the tree line and once we'd cleared the marsh and were in the forest, that's when I spotted the garrison.

The stone building was smack bang in the middle of the trees, towering a few stories high so that the top level was taller than the highest tree and would give a decent view of the surrounding area. A rampart was constructed around the outside, protecting the tower within. As far as I could tell, it looked dark inside, but that didn't mean it wasn't already occupied. I'd never been sloppy and I wasn't about to start now, especially when the stakes were higher.

"Stick together," I told my followers. "We move as a unit."

Flynn remained at my side. Despite the following I had, I didn't trust my minions to watch my back like Flynn could. We approached the garrison slowly and once I was satisfied no one was hiding around its perimeter, I gave the signal and we moved towards the building. Beyond the wall, we did a sweep, still finding no one, so we approached the only door at the base of the tower. Pushing it open slowly, I led us in, my eyes scanning the dark space. Flynn stayed close to my back and we scoped out each level. There were four in total; the bottom was arranged for hanging out and eating, and we found some cooking supplies piled on the floor. It was no fancy hotel, not that I expected or needed it to be.

In the Crimson Steppes we didn't have much beyond our basic needs. We learned to make do with what we had and be creative for the things we wanted. It meant making something, going without, or taking what you wanted. Like my parents, I had never been happy with any of those options. I used my strength and fought, gaining enough respect that people now gave me what I needed. Members of House Mars were gods among the people of the Crimson Steppes. Who was I to turn away from their devotion?

I ordered a couple of followers to open a stack of crates piled to the side while the rest of us cleared the remainder of the tower. Shitty blankets were piled on the second and third floor, so we'd use those floors for sleeping. The fourth floor was just one big empty room with a ladder in the centre of it that led to the rooftop overlooking the trees. I stood on the roof, the cool breeze blowing through my red hair, and scanned the skies. What looked like giant bats were circling something in the distance. They screeched as one dove to the ground to whatever—or whoever— it was they were preying on.

We needed weapons.

Once those monsters were done picking apart the easy targets, they'd come for the rest of us. The harsh conditions of my home city had taught me to always be prepared for anything, and this trial was no exception.

I headed downstairs to find the crates had been opened and more supplies were in piles on the floor. Rations, med kits, and a couple of swords and daggers. It wasn't much, but it would do for now.

"Not bad," Flynn said, picking up a scabbard and handing it to me. "Better than nothing."

I took the sword, strapping the sheath around my hips. "We'll need more."

"We can make some," he said, selecting his own sword. "Some spears would be good against those bat things."

"There were knives in the kitchen supplies," piped up the man who'd been going through the crate.

I looked around at the seven Potentials standing in a circle. I recognised all their faces but didn't have a fucking clue what any of their names were, apart from Flynn and Dick. My best friend was the only one worth remembering anyway. Dick, on the other hand, just had a way of weaselling himself into your mind with a name like that.

"Other than weapons and the possibility of making more, we have some food, medical supplies, and stuff for sleeping," I said, thinking about what I'd seen on each level. "We'll need to find water, hunt for more food and also recruit extra people."

"I can go look for food," Flynn offered, but I shook my head. I didn't want to risk sending him out there with those things flying around. Although I had a feeling they were going to be the least of our problems.

"Nah, we need to be here to hold the garrison and vet whoever wants to join us," I told him, then looked to the others. "This isn't a care home. Everyone needs to pull their weight."

A tall woman with delicate features pushed back her shoulders and set her chin. "I'll go find food and collect water."

"See." I waved a hand in her direction. "We want assets like her." I pointed to a muscular guy who was sporting a bruised face. "You go with her tomorrow."

He nodded, then winced from the movement.

"Someone give him the med kit," I ordered. "Patch yourselves up but don't be wasteful. Everything must last the month. If you're not a team player, you're out on your ass. I want everyone ready to act on a moment's notice. There are threats out there and I will drop any dead weight."

They all dispersed, moving into action to get the place in order. The rest of the weapons were allocated and then my followers set about sorting supplies or patching wounds. A woman standing by the door grimaced, trying and failing to hide the fact that she was holding her ribs as she made her way towards the med kit.

We needed to get more recruits and we needed them asap.

Leaving my followers to it, I climbed the stairs to the second floor and found myself sitting against the stone wall with Flynn by my side. I hated that I had to wait until morning to send people out. I wanted to increase our numbers and we needed more food. The rations, whilst good, were not enough. I'd been used to eating lightly when food was scarce at home, but there wasn't enough for the seven of us currently in the garrison to last much longer than a week. Out here, food could be used like currency. In a few days, people would be starving and once they found out that we had food, shelter, and weapons, they would want to be a part of that. They'd be desperate, and desperate people were easy to manipulate.

"We are gonna be like kings in this place," Flynn said, nudging my side. "Once we get some extra supplies and Potentials to fill our ranks, this month is going to be a breeze."

"I'm banking on it," I replied with a grin. "All those followers back at the House of Ascension are out there either searching for us or waiting to be found. I reckon we'll get a bunch of others too."

"What do you want me to do if Nellie is beat up pretty badly?" he asked, resting his head back.

"The chick with the injured ribs?"

"Yeah, her."

"Throw her out," I told him, tapping my fingers on my knee. "We aren't babysitting. This is a competition and only the strongest will survive. She can take her chances out there."

"My thoughts exactly."

As if on cue, a savage growl rumbled from outside. I smiled, anticipation spiking.

One hundred Potentials entered this trial. I couldn't wait to see how many would be left standing with me and Flynn at the finish line.

# A SKY OF STORMS

# FALLON

Istumbled through the marshland, my boots sticking in the muddy water, making it harder to find purchase as I sprinted. Something had been chasing me for the better half of the day. Something *big*.

The eerie screams of a creature followed in my steps, and I shivered as the discordant sound seemed to vibrate in my bones, sending invisible bugs skittering down my spine. My damaged wing fluttered uselessly behind me, dragging across the marsh, and I clenched my teeth. I wanted nothing more than to put my wings away, but if I did so now it would set wrong, and I'd never be able to fly again.

That thought alone was the only thing stopping me from giving in. Not being able to fly again felt like a fate worse than death. Nothing would take that gift from me. Flying was my freedom, my escape from all the bullshit, and my emergency measure in case I didn't have access to a portabracelet and ever needed to get Hadley away from our parents.

I just had to make it to safety. I swallowed as a shriek sounded, closer this time. The damn thing was persistent and, as horrible a thought as it was, I could only hope it would find someone else to prey upon. My strength was waning, and the injuries in my shoulders were taxing what little strength I had left.

If I didn't find water or meds soon, they'd fester, and I'd die of infection before anything else could lay a claw on me.

I looked around, squinting to spot somewhere to hide. In the distance, a dark shadow sprang up above the trees, and I almost wilted in relief. A building of sorts, which would at least give me somewhere to bed down out of the elements and away from the insatiable beast hot on my tail.

With renewed vigour, I forced my legs to keep pushing, and I sprinted into a set of trees to make sure I could do the last dash out in the open towards that beacon of hope. I frowned, glaring at the full moon above. Could it be any brighter out there? I may as well have a sign above my head that said all-you-can-eat buffet.

As I launched into the woods, I yelped as something crashed into my side, sending me tumbling into the disgusting water. I brandished my shoddy spear threateningly, only to find Zane's wide green eyes staring back at me.

"Starfish? Oh, thank my flippers, you're okay." He reached out and pulled me to my feet with surprising strength, twisting my chin gently with his other hand. "You're hurt," he said gravelly, his eyes hardening as he took me in.

My eyes widened in surprise at the sudden change in his temperament. For someone who was usually cool as a cucumber, he certainly had a dominant streak in him. I had to admit, it was kinda hot.

"Which fucker did this to you?" Zane snarled, his eyes searching mine as he shifted his arms to my body protectively.

I leaned into his touch, relishing his warm embrace as he adjusted his legs, placing one between my own. My skin warmed, my body becoming heated at the savage promise in his eyes to hurt whoever did this to me. A ripple of pleasure swirled between my legs, and I had to shift subtly to avoid grating against his junk.

Nobody had ever looked at me like that before, and I didn't know what to make of it. But that was a puzzle for another time.

I huffed, stepping back. "Some flying creature attacked me when I landed. It tore my wing. I can't fly."

He opened his mouth to speak, but the creature following me screeched at that same moment. Thankfully, it sounded further away. Silence rippled between us for a few seconds as we held our breath. And then the screams began.

My pulse raced as the sounds of Potentials dying greeted us, and I looked to him, setting my jaw as I pulled him along by the wrist. "Come on, I spotted a building maybe a few kilometres away. If we make a run for it, we might be able to get across while that thing is distracted."

He nodded, sliding his calloused palm into my hand and taking my spear in the other, holding it aloft like a damn water god. Vengeful merman looked good on him.

We ran together, him half pulling me along as I stumbled a few times, but I refused to die in this godsforsaken place. A watery grave just wasn't it. Besides, I had a shit list with some names begging to be ticked off and a throne waiting for my ass to warm it.

Queendom was calling.

My breaths came in gasps, my blood pumping loudly in my ears. Safety was so close—just another kilometre and we'd make it. Of course, the residents of this bog didn't take too kindly to that idea. A few screeches called from above and, alarmed, I glanced up to find more of those batlike things circling.

"Shit," Zane panted between breaths. "Faster, Starfish, we're almost there."

A strangled moan came from my lips as he practically dragged me through the marsh, and a strong beat of air from bat wings surged against my cheek as it approached. "Duck," I screamed, flattening myself to the ground as it soared over our heads.

We turned, facing off against two of the beasts with Zane brandishing his spear. "Go, get to the hut."

I glanced to freedom longingly, but as I looked back at Zane, I knew I'd already made my choice. I turned, shifting my stance. "I'm not leaving you."

His eyes gleamed with something deadly as he looked at me, and I realised beneath that calm exterior lay a predator just waiting to be freed if given the chance. The first bat dove, and Zane stood his ground until the last second, swivelling the spear with such precision he pierced its heart with a strangely sexual thrust ... or maybe that was just me. The bat screeched, flapping its wings for a few seconds until they slowed to a stop and it dropped lifelessly to the ground.

The other surged for Zane while he was distracted and I roared, somehow managing to land it on its back as I dug my nails in and snapped the bone on its wing, grappling with it until it fell beneath me and I pummelled my fists into its face again and again.

I put all my rage into those blows, seeing red as flashes of my parent's faces blurred before me, every hit I'd taken by their hands, every harsh word they'd ever said. Then I thought of Ethan in that position and every worker they'd forced into labouring for them, and my anger swelled tenfold.

Hands reached for me, pulling me away, and I finally realised the creature was long dead and I'd just been mashing at its still body. Zane looked at me, his brows pinching as he lifted my chin.

"Damn, Starfish, you're a fucking goddess."

My fists were bloody where I clutched him, but he didn't seem to care as a sob escaped me and a tear trickled down my face. All the emotions I'd been bottling up chose that moment to finally show themselves.

Two weeks in and I'd been thrown through the ringer and wrung the fuck out. I was useless. What chance did I have at becoming queen if I couldn't even hold my own against people like my sister? I'd thought I was strong, but even after everything I'd survived, I was still so weak. So pathetic.

Zane tugged me closer, and I breathed in his scent. His hair smelled like coconuts and mangoes, and his skin reminded me of a salty sea breeze. A tropical freaking paradise.

He pulled me into his arms, trailing a knuckle over my cheek, and I breathed in deeply as more tears fell. The walls I'd built to protect myself came crashing down as I struggled to maintain some semblance of control.

I'd dismissed Zane's strength too easily, when really, he was unphased by the shifting tides and had proven himself more than capable against new threats. Maybe there was more to his laidback attitude than I'd realised.

I leaned in and kissed him without thinking, the action coming so easily, seeming so right. His lips felt perfect against my own—warm and inviting, and I sighed against his mouth. Shit, he was so easily sucking me in again. I began to pull away, but he growled, sliding his hand around the nape of my neck and tipping my head up as his tongue curled around mine.

I moaned, needing this comfort, needing to forget my worries if only for a moment. His touch was bliss everywhere his skin met mine, but I hissed as his hand brushed against my wing and I sucked in a breath, stepping away on instinct.

He stared at me longingly, but made no move to approach again, and I took the opportunity to inhale deeply, letting my head clear. Harmless fun at the academy was one thing, but distractions in a place like this could get me killed. My emotions were getting the better of me ... and my body.

"Thank you," I breathed. "For helping me get here."

"You don't have to thank me, Starfish," he said quietly, tucking a strand of hair behind my ear. "I think we were meant to help each other through these trials."

I shook my head, frowning at him. "Why? I'm sure you've heard what people say about me and my family. Why are you so nice to me?"

He looked down at me, those green depths swirling with something I couldn't decipher. "Your parents may have made you, but you are *not* them. I mean, that's why you're here isn't it? To prove that to yourself?"

I cocked my head, studying the man before me. How could he see through me so easily? How could he possibly know? *I* didn't even know. If I thought about why I wanted to become queen, was it really to improve things in Terrulia? Or was it to punish Victrus and Eliana?

"I—"

The larger monster roared somewhere in the distance, and more screams followed, breaking the spell Zane seemed to hold over me. I grimaced, using the interruption to step away, my walls reforming instantly.

"We'd better get inside while we can. It's not safe out here."

He nodded, gesturing me forwards. "Lead the way then. I've got your back."

Something cold and sharp inside me thawed at those words, melting away into fuzzy warmth. Because I'd only ever had Ethan to care for me before. Because no one—not a single soul—had ever given a shit about what happened to me.

Until now.

# FALLON

We traipsed through the marsh on silent feet, ears pricked for any followers, creature or otherwise. Apart from Zane, I'd yet to see any other Potentials, which meant the marshlands must be vast. Thankfully, that meant we could focus on our furry, winged friends, rather than watching for any shifty backstabbers.

The cabin we'd slept in had been a rundown piece of shit that had looked like it'd given up on life, but it had provided enough shelter and relative comfort to get some sleep for the night—not that I'd gotten much.

I'd spent the night tossing and turning from my wounds and worrying about the month we'd yet to endure. Zane had at least provided some warmth, and I'd felt safer with his calming aura. Of course, the muscled arm that had curled around my stomach hadn't hurt either. I may or may not have rubbed my ass against his junk just to tease him.

Zane was unsurprisingly chipper this morning. In another life, he'd have made a great motivational speaker. The man was a walking endorphins-booster, not to mention some candy for me to eye-fuck when I thought he wasn't looking.

The damn top knot he wore when he meant business did

things to me that were entirely *unhelpful* in these circumstances.

I grinned, watching his ass as he stalked ahead of me, a shark circling the waters in search of his next meal.

"Gotcha," he roared, jabbing his spear and startling not only me but all the birds in the nearby trees.

I winced, almost afraid to look at the poor creature he'd snagged for our dinner. My stomach grumbled just at the thought of food. I hadn't eaten for a day, and my body was certainly reminding me of that. I was beginning to sweat despite the crisp breeze, and I felt weak, like every movement was too much effort.

At least we'd found some running water in a riverbed not too far away. I'd been desperate for a drink, but the marsh water wasn't worth getting sick for. Without something to boil it with, we'd be sicker than old king Theodore on his deathbed.

"How many does that make now?" I asked, cocking my head curiously as he held up his spear with a wide grin. He looked like a puppy with a new toy, and I couldn't help but smile too.

"Four," he replied happily, then his face crinkled with sadness. "I'm sorry my fishy friends, but even Zaney needs to make exceptions. Your deaths won't be in vain."

I raised a brow as he spoke to the fish like he was mourning his best friend's death.

"Starting a fire will be risky."

"We gotta eat, Starfish. You need the energy. In fact—" he looked me up and down with pursed lips. "You're looking a little peaky. Are you okay?"

I forced a smile, trying to ignore the nausea roiling in my stomach. "I'll be fine, but we need to get back to the hut. More of those creatures could come out any moment."

He gathered the fish in a sack we'd found in the hut and slung them over his shoulder, looking less than convinced. "When we get back, I'm gonna make you the best dinner, and maybe we can talk about that massage again."

I laughed. "We'll see." I turned to go when a high-pitched

voice floated across the water. I grabbed Zane, instantly clapping a hand over his mouth. "Listen."

"—It's not fair. I was here first, and that whore had to bat her lashes and steal him away. Kayden belongs with me."

My ears pricked up and I crouched, making my way towards some reeds where I could hide. A red-haired girl with wavy short hair and an arm on her hip examined her nails as another girl with long brown hair in a braid filled up some bottles of water.

"Yeah, but don't worry," Braid replied, a sneer on her face. "Crystal is a basic bitch. Kayden will get over her quickly once he realises she's a boring lay."

Red huffed. "Once he realises what it's like to be with a real woman, he won't bother with the trash anymore."

I rolled my eyes. *Well, that puts her out of the equation then.* I couldn't stand women like these two, placing themselves on pedestals and looking down their noses at everyone else. Getting out their claws—which were shabby, by the way—and degrading others simply because they could.

Braid laughed. "At least he's not fawning over that Auger bitch."

"Fallon?" Red scoffed. "She won't last the month. Besides, if my Kaydikins recruits more people for his army, the rest of the Potentials will be begging for their lives soon enough … if the monsters don't get them first."

My fingers curled into fists. So Kayden was building an army, but what for? To take on the monster or to make others submit to him? It would be so like that stupid beef cake to act like this was all one big game.

I bit my lip as I considered this information. If he had that many recruits, it must mean he'd found somewhere decent to shack up in, not to mention supplies. He'd have his cronies do all the work, sure, but if he really was planning on attacking anyone, they'd need weapons, food, and water. Maybe even meds.

I tried to overhear the rest of their conversation, but they'd turned their heads, and I swore under my breath.

An idea formed, and I grinned as I turned around to Zane, who apparently had been staring at my ass while I'd been on my knees.

"Change of plan," I said excitedly. "I say we have a little fun before we head back."

His eyes lit up. "We're going to Kaydikins's lair?" he asked hopefully.

"Yep. We've got new prey to track."

He fist-pumped, whooping silently as we crept as quietly as possible through the reeds. The girls were up ahead, splashing and talking loudly as they traipsed through the marsh. It was a wonder they hadn't called the whole horde of creatures down on us.

After tailing them for a while, they disappeared beyond a tree line and we slipped behind the trunks as we followed them cautiously. We didn't have to try hard—they didn't look back or check their surroundings once. They'd make useless guards, and the ditzes probably had no idea how to protect themselves if something attacked.

Turns out, they were good at leading enemies to their base. I gaped as a square tower popped into view where the trees formed around it. The stone was weather-worn but sturdy as the building loomed up several floors. There were a few Potentials keeping watch on the rampart on the top level, as well as a few huddled in pockets outside.

Kayden was nowhere to be seen, and my devious little heart pumped in excitement as I spotted supplies everywhere. Weapons, food stores, items to cook with and drink from and— my excitement surged—a med kit.

Holy shit. It was like a supermarket for survivors, except I had no plans of buying today. This was a robbery, and Zane and I would be adding to cart.

I looked at my beautiful blond sea monster with a raised

brow, and the dark smile he sent back had my toes curling. Oh yes, now this was what I called payback.

"How about you create the diversion and I'll nab the goods?" I purred, gesturing for the sack.

"I thought you'd never ask," he replied, his ass wiggling with excitement as he handed it to me.

I grinned. "Meet me back at the hut within the hour. And Zane?"

He turned his head, looking breathtaking as a beam of sunlight gilded his face. "Yeah?"

I kissed his cheek, sliding my hand against his junk and giggling as he stiffened beneath my touch. "Don't get caught."

His eyes lit with the thrill of the game, and a contented sound spilled from deep within his throat as he gripped my ass and tugged me towards him.

"And miss out on the real prize?" he said against my lips, his fingers curling down so that they slid over my pussy. I moaned breathily against him, excited by the promise of his hands and the hunt we were about to begin. "You can tease me as long as you like, Starfish, but when I have you, you'll be riding my wave so hard you'll never turn back."

I laughed breathily as I moved my hips, loving the friction of my jumpsuit shifting beneath his hand and kinda digging the weird way he spoke.

Then he was gone, and I forced myself to ignore the thrumming between my legs and focus on my mission. Most of the Potentials outside were rationing supplies, so it would be an easy hit provided Zane did his job well and everyone scattered like I hoped. That med kit was calling my name, and I licked my lips hungrily as I kept it in my sights.

A few minutes later, Zane ran out of the woods butt naked, one hand cupping his junk as he streaked towards the tower, roaring. "Kayden the boulder, Kayden the thick, had a remarkably tiny prick. He mounted his steeds and tried to ride, but it's hard to have sex when you're one inch wide."

I gaped, trying to stifle my laugh at the ridiculous song. Someone—presumably, Kayden—roared from inside the tower and the next minute everyone was swarming after Zane who disappeared promptly into the trees.

Bingo. I lunged, speeding towards the supplies like a dragon towards gold, and I grinned like a madwoman as I shoved anything and everything into the bag, starting with the prize med kit. Weapons, canteens, a pot, food rations, even food from civilised society ... I took everything I could carry.

At last I spotted some chocolate, and I just about bellowed my triumph. *You're coming home with me.*

When I heard some of the Potentials returning, I dashed back to the cover of the trees and waited, ever a glutton for a good prank. Everyone was grumbling and out of breath, and I smiled gleefully. *Zane you sly seadog, you did it.*

And then came the words I'd been aching to hear.

"Where's all the stuff?" a guy remarked, scratching his head.

"Oh my gods," another girl said, looking around in horror. "The med kit, the food rations, even some of the weapons, they're all gone!"

Something stomped towards them, and I soon realised Kayden, whose face kinda looked like a storm cloud waiting to erupt, was the cause of it. "What now?" he snapped, and I felt a little sorry for his minions as they shrank before him.

"I-I-I think someone has stolen our stuff," the guy said timidly.

"What!? I'm gone for two minutes and you dipshits can't even protect our shit?"

"Err ... But you told us to go after the blond guy," he replied, looking at his feet.

Kayden's face went bright red, and he stormed toward him, grabbing his jumpsuit and lifting so he dangled in the air. "You're telling me this is my fault?"

"N-no! I just—"

The guy never got to finish his sentence, because Kayden tossed him across the clearing like he was competing in a javelin tournament. Then Kayden roared, exploding into a huge boulder and rolling around the camp, taking out anyone in his way.

I burst out laughing, hefting my sack over my shoulder and feeling incredibly happy about my findings.

Yup. Payback's a bitch, Kayden, and we've only just begun.

I crept away, laughing to the sounds of Kayden's continued roars and the panicked screams of his people as they were forced to deal with his wrath. We wouldn't be robbing them blind again anytime soon, but it was well worth the effort.

I hurried back towards the cabin, hoping Zane had managed to escape whatever stragglers hadn't yet returned to their camp. An excited shiver ran through me at what had transpired between us before. Zane was sexy and so much fun, and it's not like we hadn't crossed some boundaries already.

So, maybe I was fighting a losing battle when it came to him. But it was like we were drawn together. He was my friend now, I knew that, but was it wise to cross that line together?

*And yet ... it's just sex, Fallon, it's not like you're committing to the man.*

I rolled my eyes, chastising my inner monster, who just wanted to get laid right fucking now because damn it, I'd nearly been eaten by a bat and it was going to be a long, rough, month. So what if I fooled around with him? Zane was the perfect candidate for some casual fun, because yes, now that he'd suggested it...

Yeah, I really freaking wanted to ride that wave. Ride it all the way next time.

I grinned deviously.

But maybe I could make him wait a little longer before I did.

# NOAH

"We need to pick up the pace," one of Mark's lackeys grumbled.

Wading through hip-deep water, I followed behind silently, stalking Mark's lackeys through the marsh. It was getting dark, the mist looking eerie as the sun set. Picturesque, if you were into horror movies, which I wasn't. I didn't let it bother me though. My mind was on the assholes in front of me as they rounded up those who had yet to find cover. From the outside it may have looked like they were well-meaning people with good intentions, but I'd been following them for a couple hours and listening in on their conversation to know better. They were rounding up those who either couldn't defend themselves or were too injured to try, letting their map and compass lead them.

The one who'd spoken put his hands on his hips as they stopped to hurry along one of their captives who was dragging their feet. He was tall with a bulbous nose that he stuck in the air as though he was better than everyone else. By the way he ordered the others around, he'd taken up leadership in Mark's absence. "Mark said the delivery is to be made at sunrise on day twenty-one."

I crouched low in the reeds, water lapping around my thighs

as something swam around me. I ignored the fish. At least ... I hoped it was a fish, my attention fixed on those shivering in the mud. I had no idea where Mark was, but I was banking on these people leading me to him. Screeching suddenly echoed around me and I ducked lower. Judging by the sound of it, the giant bat things weren't close, but I wasn't taking chances. I felt bad for whoever was in their line of sight though.

When I'd woken up in the sky, I'd had to scramble to work my parachute whilst my head attempted to clear. It had been the scariest experience of my life falling to the ground. I fucking hated heights, but the terror had turned to anger when Mark had appeared in the air beside me with a taunting smirk on his ugly face. He'd manoeuvred his parachute and I'd lost him by the time I'd landed in the marsh. The guy was always up to something, that I knew for sure, which is how I'd found myself in my current situation.

The group started up again and I crept along behind, being as quiet as I could in the water and trying not to make a splash. Seeing Mark's lackeys rounding people up was either a confirmation that his family were trafficking people to powerful clients, or they were going to use these Potentials as protection and slaves during this trial. I'd seen no sign of anything else, but that didn't mean Mark wasn't off organising that whilst his lackeys were doing some other job for him.

Despite spending nights following Mark around the House of Ascension while camouflaged, I hadn't found out any more of what he was up to or who he was meeting with beyond the mention of Stormcrest City's most powerful house. It was frustrating not being able to see the full picture. Were these Potentials the delivery House Jupiter was receiving or was it something else? House Jupiter may have been receiving a delivery during the trial, but it didn't mean they were the only buyers.

I couldn't discount anything that I was seeing, and as we trekked, I thought through my options.

I needed to catch Mark in the act to confirm his illegal activities and find out who the middleman was between him, Jupiter, and whichever other houses were buying illegal shit from him. He wasn't the mastermind behind the operation, so I needed the identity of the hooded guy. Mark was far from a genius, and he was also a cocky asshole who would have said something if there wasn't someone more powerful keeping him in line. I would make sure he would be punished once I'd gathered my evidence. Nobody treated the people of Verdant Plateau as a commodity or stole our precious resources and got away with it. And once I had Mark, then I would go after the head of this whole exploitation scheme and bring them down.

After reaching a dry patch of land, the leader barked orders and the group stopped to rest. One of the captives fell to the ground, exhausted by the hours of walking, only to be dragged into the huddle with the rest.

"Why do we need to babysit these people now?" one man whined, trying to steadily kick a rock along the ground. Instead, his boot pushed it further into the soft ground with each pass and he was getting angrier at it with each second. "Stupid rock."

The leader sighed. "Because there are monsters and other Potentials here that could kill them. You know Mark wants an exact number. Stop asking questions and just do your job."

"When's he going to show up?" a woman asked despite what the leader had said. She was standing guard of the captives with her arms folded over her chest. "Here we are doing all the work and he's off obsessing over that angel bitch. It's embarrassing."

*Interesting.* Either Mark was rendezvousing with Victoria, or he was off on another job and these people were only in on this part of his plans. Whatever said plans involving the captured Potentials were.

"Watch your mouth," the leader snapped. "He'll be here before the deal goes through."

"She's right though," a guy said, coming to stand beside the woman. He was wiry, with short curly hair. "He needs to just fuck her already and be done with it."

"Bit hard with the mermaid from Tritosa City always around," a tall, broad-shouldered guy said with a chuckle. "I bet you fifty credits those two are banging."

Apparently by angel bitch they meant Fallon, not Victoria. I rolled my tense shoulders at the comment and gritted my teeth. I didn't care if Fallon and Zane were sleeping together. Good for them. I just didn't like the way these people were betting on that. Yeah, that's exactly why I was getting annoyed. Betting on something like that was pathetic and immature.

The woman smirked. "I dunno, I reckon she has something going on with that Kayden guy, they're doing that whole hate each other thing but I reckon there's more going on there."

Once again, I found myself frowning at their comments. I needed to keep my mind on the mission, nothing else. Not that there was anything to dwell on in the first place.

"Ha, yeah I've seen that," the curly-haired guy replied, then turned to the tall guy. "A hundred credits says she's being dicked by them both."

"Together or at different times?" the leader asked, getting in on the conversation.

"Doesn't bother me." The tall guy chuckled, shaking the curly-haired guy's hand. "I'll take that bet."

They all laughed, finding themselves way funnier than they were. I clenched my fists. We were in a trial in which we could die at any moment and they were acting like hormonal teenagers discussing Fallon's sex life. Immature assholes.

"So, do you reckon they cross swords?" a low voice asked. I spun, my heart leaping out of my chest, to find Ace crouched behind me. I swung my fist, but he dodged the blow and my upper half joined the lower half of my body in the water.

I sputtered, trying to get back out before an arm tugged me up and I found Ace grinning at me, a finger over his lips.

Fuck that guy. If he'd just blown my cover, I'd skin him. I couldn't jeopardise all the work I'd done when I'd gotten so close to answers. I glanced behind me to where Mark's lackeys were, but none seemed to have noticed any sound I may have made. They'd been too loud, laughing at their stupid jokes.

"What do you want?" I grumbled, snatching my arm out of Ace's grip.

Ace shrugged. "Saw you here and thought there had to be something going on for you to be sitting in the cold listening in on these assholes. Turns out I wasn't disappointed. You didn't answer my question."

"Nothing is going on, not that I'd tell you anyway." I looked down at his bionic hand, the tips of his fingers in the water. "I thought you couldn't get that wet."

"Don't tell me you believed that too." He chuckled, flicking water at me with his metallic fingers. "It's waterproof. How useless would it be if I couldn't do basic shit like take a piss without it fucking up? Do you know how many times a day your hand comes in contact with liquid?"

"I'm gonna hazard a guess and say a lot."

"Ding ding ding." Ace grinned, his black hair falling into his eyes. He shoved it back, combing it with his fingers into the rest of the long strands at the top of his head. The sides were shaved and on his left side, black ink was visible behind his ear that snaked up from his neck. "So, why are you lurking out here? Didn't you hear all those crazy fuckers in the sky?" he asked.

"I like strolling around in the dark with monsters on the loose," I replied, swiping water from my face.

"Sarcastic fucker." Ace punched me in the arm.

I shrugged. "These assholes are holding people captive."

He raised a brow. "Any idea why?"

"Why do you care?"

"I have my reasons." He glanced away. "It's kinda interesting, don't you think?"

I sighed, turning my attention back to Mark's lackeys. They looked like they were settling in for a couple of hours, which meant I had to decide whether to act now or wait until they stopped again. If I continued following them, they would most likely lead me to Mark. But what kind of person would I be to let the Potentials they kidnapped suffer? I thought of Katie and Rena in a similar position and made up my mind. I wouldn't let Mark hurt any more people. The Potentials signed up to compete in this trial, not to be illegally traded like cattle.

"How much have you heard?" I asked, narrowing my eyes at him.

It shouldn't be much. They'd passed a few bits of information like the time of delivery and Mark's involvement, but other than the blatant round-up of defenceless Potentials, I didn't think there was any useful information for Ace.

"Enough," Ace said, his shoulder grazing mine as he came to crouch beside me. "You're going to play the hero and free them."

"Yeah, I am," I said without elaborating. I kept the part about stealing the compass and map to myself, and definitely didn't elaborate on my other reasons for following them. I barely knew the guy, so I wasn't about to trust him with my secrets.

"Reckon you can take them on your own?" Ace said, a hungry glint in his steely eyes.

"Is that an offer of help?"

"Maybe." Ace chuckled darkly. "What's in it for me?"

"A chance to beat the shit out of some lowlifes?"

He didn't reply at first, just watched alongside me as the leader of the group walked past the captives and kicked one in the gut for fun.

"Fuck it. I'm in," Ace declared, surprising me. "I'll follow your lead."

I hadn't thought he would actually help. There was nothing to gain and he didn't strike me as the type of guy to give a shit about anyone else. Ace usually sat on the side lines and observed from afar, sort of like me. Maybe we had other things in common too.

I conveyed my plan and we split up, Ace going left whilst I went right. There were about six of Mark's lackeys that we needed to deal with, so we'd be taking on three each. I stayed hidden, waiting for Ace to get into position.

"Banana split!" Ace shouted from somewhere opposite me and I hesitated only a moment before I barked a laugh and ran onto the dry land to punch a guy in the face.

I told him to give me a signal. I never expected that Ace, a member of the Drakes, would yell something like that before going into a fight. I was still laughing when someone hit me in the ribs. I turned to deflect another blow then let loose with one of my own. The guy stumbled but then someone else grabbed my arms, tugging them behind my back. I was pulled against a hard chest only to have the guy I'd just hit punch me in the gut. I struggled against their hold, but whoever held my arms had a firm grip and I was forced to absorb the blows to my stomach.

"This'll fucking teach you for trying to jump us!" the guy holding me growled in my ear. "Fuck him up real goo—"

He never got to finish his sentence as we were both shoved forward. I landed on the ground, my face colliding with the dirt with the weight of the guy on my back. Shouts came from overhead and I shoved the guy off me. He was a dead weight and when I stood, I noticed the knife sticking out of his neck.

"Holy shit!" I exclaimed, jumping back. "What did you do?"

"You're welcome," Ace called dryly, knocking the last lackey to the ground then strolling over and tugging the knife out of the other guy. He wiped it on his jumpsuit then pocketed it.

I gaped at his casual demeanour. "You killed him!"

"To save your life," he replied, folding his arms with a bored expression on his face. "Relax, take a couple of breaths."

"Yeah, sure, I'll just chill while you're over here murdering people."

"Breathe," Ace commanded, his tone allowing no room for negotiation.

I did as he said, calming myself from the shock of his blatant murder. "Where'd you get the knife?"

"Found it."

"And did you kill them all with it?" I asked, looking around at the six unconscious bodies around us. I knew Ace was dangerous, but it was one thing to see people die and another entirely to see someone take a life.

"Nah, just that one," he replied with a shrug. "The rest are still alive, just not up for a chat right now. You'll need to get used to it, you know. You're going to see a lot more death before this trial is over."

"All as casual as that I hope."

Ace barked a laugh as I stepped towards where the leader lay, keeping my eyes from the rest. "Let's free these people and get out of here."

Ace moved to help the captives who hadn't run off during the fight while I quickly checked the leader for the map and compass. Screeching howled overhead and I picked up my pace, finding the items stuffed in one of the guy's jumpsuit pockets. I transferred them to my own pockets before going over to help Ace.

"Got what you came for?" he asked, smiling at me slyly as he helped someone up. He didn't miss a beat, which made me think he knew more about what was happening here than I'd originally thought.

"I don't know what you're talking about," I replied, untying the last Potential so they could get away. Blood dripped from their nose and forehead, and they stumbled as they walked, but they weren't badly hurt. They darted away into the dark fog shrouding the forest. I doubted they'd last the night.

"Right," he said, looking at me with a faint glimmer of amusement. "So, what's your move now? Going to follow them all so that you can continue your superhero duties and protect them from the big bad monsters in this place?"

I shook my head. They signed up to be part of the trials so what they did now was on them. Whatever Mark's lackeys had been doing wasn't part of that. If those Potentials died now, as bad as it sounded, it wasn't my problem.

"What are you going to do?"

Ace hadn't been forthcoming at all, always asking questions and saying very little of actual importance.

"Still weighing my options," he replied smoothly with a casual shrug. "So, Mark then?"

"What makes you think I'm not going to find somewhere to lay low until the month is up?"

Ace stuffed his hands into his pockets. "I can see it in your eyes. I know what it looks like for a guy to have a vendetta."

"Or maybe you're just wanting to see something that isn't there," I replied dismissively.

"Doubt it," he said. "I'll come with you to find Mark."

"Why would you want to do that?"

"Knew you were planning to." He smirked, the tattoos on his neck drinking in the moonlight. "You need back up. Can't have the only normal person around here up and die on me."

His words were obviously meant as a compliment, but I saw straight through them for the tactic they were. "Why don't you just say what you want?"

"Who says I want anything beyond what I just told you? You're a suspicious fucker. Must be lonely thinking everyone is out to get you all the time."

I narrowed my gaze. "Not everyone, just a Drake."

"That's a bit prejudiced don't you think?"

I took a moment to weigh my options. Ace wasn't giving up. Either I agreed and I could keep my eyes on him, or I said no and he'd follow anyway.

"Fine," I told him, walking away. I needed to get moving; we were sitting ducks out here and I wasn't interested in becoming one of those giant bats' next meal. "Don't make me regret this."

# FALLON

"Are you sure about this Starfish? I don't like the idea of splitting up."

I smiled as Zane combed my hair with his fingers and then began massaging my neck, easing the tension that had built over the last few days. I moaned softly, relishing his touch as he worked.

He'd been insistent to the point of annoying yesterday with cleaning and patching my wounds, forcing me to take some antibiotics and even feeding me. Granted, the nausea and sweats had abated, and my wounds looked much better, but try telling that to *him*.

And as much as I'd love to stay in this crappy cabin and show Zane my appreciation, I couldn't erase the niggling feeling that we weren't safe here. Not after seeing Kayden's gang preparing for war, and not when people like Victoria, Mark, or that Ace guy could sneak up on us at any time.

"It'll just be for a little while. If Kayden is building an army, others might have the same idea, and I'd prefer to know what we're dealing with than be caught unaware."

He huffed. "It is strange we haven't come across anyone else, even with the size of this place. Do you think the m̲o̲n̲ster got them all?"

I shook my head. "Some, but not all. They're probably laying low like us. I just hope Kendra is ok."

"Kendra is smart, I'm sure our little possum is fine. She's a tiny little thing, probably hiding in the hollow of a tree somewhere," Zane said confidently.

"*Our* possum?" I laughed. "You've laid a claim on her, have you?"

"She's part of our threesome," he said, nodding seriously. "She's the bestie and I'm the comic relief. Together, we're the ultimate team."

"You seem to have given this a lot of thought," I teased, elbowing him in the ribs.

"Yup. I've got it all worked out. We just need to add Noah and we'll be swimming in our own little love pod in no time. We'll have everything you need, Starfish."

I twisted my neck, looking over my shoulder. "And what do you need?"

He paused, cocking his head as he thought about it. "I'm just here for the ride, don't you worry about me."

"Nope." I shook my head. "I refuse to accept that answer. Try again."

He sighed, his eyes glimmering in the glow of the morning sunlight creeping through the wooden slats of the cabin. "Truth is, I entered because I don't want to be the heir to House Neptune. I'll always be standing in my dad's shadow, never really knowing whether people respected me or the man behind me. Besides, I want an adventure. I love Tritosa City, but there's so much more to explore in the world, ya know? Sometimes I feel a bit trapped back home."

I leaned back into his chest and smiled, feeling pleasantly surprised about how easy it would be to open up to him despite knowing him for such a short time. "I get it. I feel the same in Stormcrest. My family is … well you've heard what people say about them. The sad part is most of it is true. My parents are monsters. All they care about is money and power, and they don't care who they abuse or use to get it. I can't go back to that house once the trials are done. I won't."

He ran his fingers through my long hair and nuzzled my cheek. "You won't have to, because if I don't win this thing, you will. You're strong, your parents should be proud to have you as their daughter."

Tears sprang to my eyes, but I refused to let them fall. Zane was right. I'd give my all to win this competition and if I didn't win then I'd just have to think of a different way to stop my parents from destroying the city. I'd try again and again to make things right. I would free the exploited workers and restore order, or I'd die trying.

I peeked at him over my shoulder. "You know, you're oddly wise for someone who comes across so flippant and carefree."

"It's all part of my charm, Starfish. Once people get tangled up in my net, it's a done deal. The trick is to get deep inside them, like all the way in, so they open up and I can thrust my trust upon them."

My nose scrunched up. "I take back what I said earlier."

"Too late. You want me, I want you, and I think Noah might want a piece of the Fallon pie friendship too."

"Oh? Friends, huh? Well that's a shame, I thought maybe we were heating up a little. Guess I'll have to set my eyes somewhere else. Maybe that Kayden guy…"

I smirked, trying to ease out of his grip, but he growled, clamping one hand on my thigh, the other snaking beneath my jumpsuit and over my bra, his fingers circling my nipple.

"*My Starfish*," he said.

I groaned, arching my back and feeling his length hardening against my ass. "I don't want to be caged, Zane. I'm not yours. I don't belong to anyone."

Not to mention I shouldn't want anyone at all, even if a small voice deep inside me wanted to play with fire with more than one Potential during these trials…

He pinched my tweaked nipple, then slid his other hand between my legs, rubbing me through the material. "Who said anything about that?" he whispered in my ear. "I'm not a possessive guy. You can have me and others too. Even at the same time, if that floats your boat."

I moaned, rocking my hips and pressing into his hand as he kissed my neck, biting softly at the sensitive flesh. His hand found the zipper of my jumpsuit, unravelling it slowly as he shifted his hand and placed it down my panties.

"You're so wet," he rumbled against my throat. "Does the idea of being shared turn you on?"

"Yes," I panted as his thumb circled my clit and he shifted me to face him. His other hand peeled back my bra to sit under my tits and push them up where he bit my nipple, causing me to cry out. Zane licked and sucked to lessen the hurt, scraping a finger up my centre as he did so. My pussy throbbed and I had to clench my legs together.

"You're so fucking beautiful," he rasped, his eyes glinting as he surveyed me. "I want to see those pretty eyes staring up at me when you're on your knees."

He began to unzip his jumpsuit, and I stared at him hungrily as his golden muscles peeked out. The zipper went down agonisingly slowly. I bit my lip, jumping into his lap and was just about to take charge when something crashed through the trees outside.

We both flinched, and I stared at Zane with wide eyes as a large shadow blocked out what little sunlight filled the room.

Zane groaned. "Come back to eat us later."

I raised a finger to his lips, shoving him towards the window on the far side. He grumbled, crouching low and crawling beneath the pane.

I zipped myself up, grabbing a sword and tying it to my hips with a sash, then slipped a knife into my boot. I tossed Zane another sword, because apparently the Overseer thought it would be fun to make us fight like freaking knights in one of her stupid tales, and then crammed as many of the meds supplies into my jumpsuit as I could.

Zane gestured at me frantically as something outside clicked menacingly. My eyes darted between him and the window frantically. At the last second, I threw my back against the wall, freezing in place as one giant eye peered in through the window.

Oh gods, it looked like—like—

It roared, the sound making me grit my teeth as fear blossomed in my stomach. It had stone stretched over its long legs, the tough texture transforming into a root-like system of pulsing veins over its chest. I'd never seen anything like it. My heart thudded in my chest, and just as I was about to bolt to Zane's side, the roof of the hut was torn off, exposing us to the giant beast outside.

"Run!"

I sprinted for the door, Zane hot on my heels as we scrambled through the threshold and out into the marsh beyond. I looked over my shoulder and yelped, shoving Zane again and diving the other way, narrowly escaping being torn in two by razor sharp teeth.

The creature turned, locking Zane in its sights. It lunged forward and I didn't hesitate to slash at its thigh. It hissed, swivelling towards me and gnashing its teeth. I darted back, staying just out of its reach as its yellow eyes gleamed dangerously. The damn thing kept coming. I backed up until my spine slammed into a tree and I realised it had me cornered.

Zane bellowed, running between its legs and slashing at its ankles. "The skin is too thick," he cried, sprinting out of the way before he could be stomped. "Go, Starfish, I'll lure it away."

No. *Hell no.* He was not going to be this thing's snack. There was only one item on the menu for today, and it was me … laid out as Zane's main course.

I unfurled my wings, testing the fragile membrane of the damaged one with a small flutter. It wasn't fully healed but it should hold. I launched into the sky, pirouetting in front of the creature's face, antagonising it as it tried to swat me like a cat would a mouse.

*Come on you stony little bitch, come and get me.*

It took the bait and I grinned before giving Zane an apologetic look and zooming away. The creature pounded the marshland behind me. It was damn fast, but if I stayed a few metres ahead it wouldn't catch me. I just needed to get it far away from Zane, then I could circle back once I was sure it was safe.

My wing barked with pain as I pushed and pushed, flying for another ten minutes before the creature began to slow and grow bored. Eventually it roared and lumbered off, and after a few more minutes to make sure I'd lost it, I sighed in relief and searched for a safe spot to land.

Something small flashed in the distance, and I frowned as I tried to make out what it was. A humanoid shape came into view when I gasped as I realised what I was looking at.

I landed in a running jog, sprinting over to Kendra, who had been tied up to a tree. Her cheek was bruised and she was unconscious, her head lolling to the side and her long brown hair dishevelled and loose.

*What the fuck? Who would do such a thing?*

"Kendra, hey, can you hear me? It's Fallon. I'm going to get you out of here, okay?"

"I was wondering when you'd show up," a deep voice rasped.

I stilled, my hackles rising. "Mark." I sniffed. "I should have known from the stench. It reeks of disappointment and failed dreams."

"Always so mouthy." He sneered. "But you won't be able to talk with my cock shoved down your throat. Your little sidekicks aren't around to protect you this time."

"Aw, it's cute that you think I need protecting. Do I need to remind you what it feels like to have your ass kicked?"

He rounded the tree and I backed up, one hand going to the sword at my hip. This guy was *everything* that was wrong with the world. The kind of man that felt entitled to a woman. Someone who had to put others down to feel good.

"Why don't we settle this without weapons? Just my fists against yours. And when I win, Fallon, you *will* submit to me. You'll be screaming, begging for me to stop before I'm done with you."

His eyes gleamed with malice, but there was lust in them too. A sick kind of perversion. As much as he hated me, he wanted me, and he wanted to fight me before he got what he wanted. It turned my fucking stomach.

I cocked my head, a smirk curling my lips. "Is that the only way you can get off Marky boy? By making women submit to your tiny dick? Okay, you want to touch me? I'll play, but don't say I didn't warn you."

"You stupid cunt," he swore, cracking his knuckles. "I'm going to enjoy this."

I smiled sweetly. "No one more than me."

Predictably, he lunged, and I sidestepped. I clipped him in the stomach with my elbow as I moved. He coughed, but recovered quickly, grabbing my arm and slamming me into a tree. I grunted as the breath whooshed from my lungs and my head whacked hard against the bark.

He smiled smugly as he approached. But I cracked my head into his, laughing as a satisfying amount of blood streamed down his nose. I followed up with a punch to his jaw, then a jab beneath his ribs. He groaned, stumbling back.

Quicker than lightning though, he slipped a knife from his belt and held it to Kendra's neck. "One more step and I'll slit her throat."

My heart hammered, my blood going cold as I put my hands

up. The bastard was too weak to hold his own, so he had to hide behind someone unable to defend themselves. It was pathetic. "Coward. Leave her out of it," I snarled. "Your beef is with me, right? So what do you want?"

The cruel, perverse smile he gave me made my stomach curl. "You know what I want."

I lifted my chin, letting him see the hate in my eyes as I stared him down. "You're disgusting. Not a week into the trial and you've already forgotten how to be human. You're sick."

"Keep talking, Auger scum, you'll only make things harder on yourself. The last one tried to be defiant too. It didn't end so well for her."

My nostrils flared, a primal anger surging from deep within. Drugs, torture, murder … I'd seen and done a lot of bad things, but if there was one thing I couldn't fucking stand, it was rapists and sex traffickers. This creep shouldn't be allowed to breathe. I needed to end this. *End him.* But I couldn't risk attacking him now, not with Kendra's life at risk.

He jerked his head, nodding to my blade. "Toss your sword."

I did as he asked. Slowly, he stalked towards me, slipping his knife into the back of his pants. My stomach recoiled as he slid his hands over my breasts and down my hips, pressing his wet mouth to my neck. His breath reeked, and I forced myself not to gag as he touched me. The sick bastard would probably like that.

"Get on your knees," he rasped. I complied, feeling bile creeping up my throat as he roughly grabbed the hair on my head and began unzipping his jumpsuit. "I've waited so long for this."

"Yeah," I agreed. "Me too."

In one swift movement, I unsheathed the knife from my boot, slamming it into his thigh. He let go of me instantly and I stood, pulling my knife out and sliding it home into his neck while he was preoccupied with his leg. His blue eyes widened and he clutched a hand to his neck, attempting to stop the blood pouring from it.

I pulled the blade out, his hot blood spraying over my face. Mark fell to the ground with red spilling into the water at my feet. I should have felt shocked, disgusted, even remorseful. But I felt nothing as his lifeblood spilled out and his body fell still.

This man was more a monster than anything in this marshland. He'd abused people, done unspeakable things to other Potentials. If I'd let him live, he'd never be punished for his actions, never atone in prison.

I was tired of letting people like him get away with their bullshit. I was tired of staying silent and submissive under the anarchy of a corrupt system.

No rules, they said? Fine. I'd promised Ethan that I'd do anything to become queen—anything to save my siblings and set things right once I got out of this mess.

I had been forced to kill before, but this time it was my choice. It didn't bother me like I'd thought it would. Mark deserved what he got.

He wouldn't have been punished in the real world.

But he'll rot out here.

# ZANE

Fallon was in big trouble once I got my hands on her. I was starting to think she was strong willed to the point of her own detriment. Why she had to play saviour was beyond me. Hadn't I proved with the whole Kayden thing that we could work together? I liked that she was independent, but the self-sacrificing thing had my insides squirming like a bag of slippery eels.

Fallon had me frustrated, and not in the sexually charged way. I didn't want to feel this way about her because I tried to think the best of everyone, and she was someone I wanted to only think the utmost amazing things about.

I clenched my hand around my sword, charging after the monster and the winged beauty in the sky. To survive these trials we needed friends we could count on; people to have our backs. No one was going to make it to the end on their own—okay, maybe Ace might—but the likelihood of anyone else being able to was slim. I was determined to be Fallon's back up, even if she refused to acknowledge that she needed it. I'd thought my father and siblings were oblivious to their needs, but it turned out a lot of people were. My poor Starfish was just as blind, but I would make it my mission to help her see that there were people she could rely on.

Like me.

At least until the final trial. We would be up against each other then, but building our little relationship now was a sure-fire way to make sure we got along once I'd beaten her to the crown. We'd look back on these trials and laugh about all our good times whilst relaxing beside the beach. She would be in a little bikini of course, and all would be swell. Maybe I'd keep her on as an advisor or something too. A sexy advisor who likes to swim between my sheets. Yes, life was going to be rad for sure.

Above me, Fallon and the monster were hurdling through the air too fast for me to keep up, but I didn't stop running after them. The monster had torn its way through the trees and underbrush and given me a direct path to wherever they were headed. The location the Overseer had chosen for this trial reminded me of the sewerage systems from the history websites, back when people used to dump shit in the rivers—like literal shit and dead bodies too. The only difference to this place and back then was the things dumping their waste here were monsters which didn't exist back then.

When people started to develop powers and adaptations, some of the animals rescued from Earth began changing too, turning into monsters. Humans were stronger than ever, but now so were the monsters. Luckily, the creatures were happy enough sticking to habitats generally far from civilisation. I'd only ever encountered one monster before now when I raced some of my siblings, Zeke, Zuri, Zariah, and Zion, into the depths below Tritosa City. Let's just say the swim up was a lot faster thanks to the giant monster that lived down there. So many tentacles…

My side started to ache and I rubbed my stitch as I kept going. I was fit and a pretty fast runner, though my exercise regime was usually water based. Why run when you could swim? It was the superior way to travel.

A growl ripped through the air and the next thing I knew

I was flying backwards like the monster had just tried to hit a home run and use me as the ball. My sword slipped from my grip and clanged to the ground nearby at the same moment I hit the dirt with a thud, snapping twigs from the low shrubs. I jumped to my feet, ignoring the smarting pain in my back and running for my sword whilst dodging another hit. The thing was an evolutionary disaster; no wonder it was so pissed off. Its mouth was full of sharp teeth that had no lips to hide behind. There was something seriously wrong about having no lips, food would just go everywhere when you ate. Completely undignified. Maybe that was why he was lashing out? He was embarrassed about his lack of lips. If he wasn't so invested in making me his dinner, I would have felt sorry for him.

Dropping to avoid a blow, I skidded along the ground and swept up my sword, spinning around and swiping at the thing. My sword clanged against its thick stone-like skin, the impact reverberating up my arm. I wondered if it was a cousin of Kayden's with its rocky skin and tendency to use violence before words. Distant relatives?

The monster made to swipe, its gnarly claws flying towards me.

"Fuck!" I shouted, rolling to avoid its blow as my shoulder throbbed from hitting the ground. Probably not the best move but I needed to get away quickly and it looked cool. At least I imagined that it did.

My eyes scanned over the monster, looking for a weakness. The bottom half of its limbs looked as though they were made of piled rocks that led to the upper part of its body which was less armoured. There, its torso and upper limbs were wrapped in what looked like tree roots, though there was something pulsing within them.

"Wearing your arteries on your sleeves?" I yelled at it, running between its legs. "I knew you were a softie at heart."

The monster roared, rearing back and opening its jaw to the

sky. It's five eyes—yes, five yellow eyes—widened in rage, and its spiky tail whipped around, knocking me off my feet. At first I couldn't move, winded by the blow, but then I saw its claws flying at me and resting was suddenly a bad idea. I rolled away, my shoulder unhappy about the movement, scrambling to my feet to run into the trees.

It chased me, keeping close. I was made for the sea not the land: I didn't have wings or super speed or camouflage, so it caught up quickly, knocking me to the ground. I gritted my teeth against the searing pain, my jumpsuit warming as blood dripped from my side from where its claws had ripped through the fabric and skin. Fuck, this is not how I wanted to go out. There was no way my final breath was gonna be on land.

The monster roared again and I braced myself for another blow that never came.

Shocked, I turned around and found none other than Noah throwing rocks at the thing's eyes. Look, it probably wasn't the best decision he had ever made in his life, but I was grateful, nonetheless. The monster turned his attention on Noah, stalking in his direction with a growl. Noah started stripping which made me question his mental health, but then he just went *poof* and disappeared before my eyes.

I laughed as the monster pulled up, clearly confused. But then it turned back to me and my grin instantly died. Shit in a sea sponge, I was the prime target again.

"Run!" Noah shouted. I rolled my eyes. Obviously, running was the right move. Did he think I was stupid?

I bolted into the trees again, my side screaming with the movement, the monster once again hot on my tail. Suddenly I was tugged to the right and almost fell on my ass. I swiped my sword through the air, my eyes going wide as Ace ducked to avoid losing his head.

"Easy, Merman!" Ace exclaimed, jumping back. "This way!"

He turned, not waiting to see if I would follow. Lucky for him,

I was a good boy, so I ran after him. Behind me, the monster was growing more agitated, its growls rumbling through the forest. It didn't come after me and Ace, so I assumed Noah was providing some sort of distraction again. Ace led me to where the monster's thorny tail was slashing around, smashing into trees and causing them to topple. I dodged a falling branch as Ace leapt onto its tail and started to climb, using its spikes for purchase.

The dude didn't baulk at anything, I'd give him that. I was no coward either, so I waited for the tail to come back down from its latest swipe and jumped up, grabbing the monster's stone flesh with one hand and keeping my sword in my other. It was going to be hard to climb it with only one hand and a bleeding side, but I had nowhere to sheath my sword, so I'd have to make do. Luckily, I was the future king of Terrulia and nothing was going to get in my way.

I followed Ace up, slipping a couple of times because no one was perfect—not even kings. The monster continued to roar and moved around like he had ants in his stony pants. Noah was doing an excellent job at distracting the thing, but I just wished he'd not make it move around so much. When I got past the rocky skin, it became much easier to climb as the root-like veins were easier to grasp. Ahead of me, Ace was leaning against one of the larger back spines, having a little break like climbing a monster was no big deal.

"Throw me the sword!" he called, holding his hand out.

I hesitated only a second. Friendships were built on trust and I had a feeling Ace was going to be a bestie one of these days. You didn't slay monsters with just anyone. I threw it to him and he caught it in his bionic hand, the metal clanking loudly. The monster must have heard it because it roared loudly and reared back. I quickly grabbed hold of the black vein before me, my fingers breaking the fibrous material, causing purple blood to rush out and coat me from head to toe. It must have hurt because the monster started shaking like a dog just after a bath.

I held on for dear life, my fingers barely able to keep my grip through all the blood. I couldn't stay where I was, so I tried to climb through the tossing and turning, scaling the monster like he was a mountain.

Ace must have had the same idea as he too was pushing on, using the sword to stay on the monster's back by digging it into its flesh with each move upwards. Below, I could hear Noah shouting and the monster stopped shaking as it began running through the trees. Branches and leaves flew around me as it sped away, the latter sticking to me thanks to all the blood that was coating my skin.

"Hold on tight!" Ace shouted as he made his way onto the base of the monster's head where it met the creature's neck.

The skin there was soft and a giant vein pulsed rapidly. I quickly gripped whatever I could before he lifted the sword and slammed it into that vein. Blood burst everywhere and the monster let out a strangled roar. It bucked and Ace slipped, but I reached out and caught his ankle before he could go flying to the ground. Every part of my body howled, the cuts on my side burning, but I held onto Ace in my bloody grip. Couldn't let my saviour die, could I?

To say the monster was unimpressed would have been the understatement of the millennia. It tossed and growled, its claws slicing in our direction as it fought to find what had punctured it. I started to worry that Ace's attack had done nothing until I noticed its yellow eyes starting to roll around. The monster's steps became clumsy and the next thing I knew we were falling to the forest floor.

I tumbled from the monster's back and landed on top of Ace, knocking him into the ground.

"Sorry," I groaned, rolling off him. I lay on my back, panting and trying to catch my breath as the monster took its last beside me. I ignored the fact that I was still coated in blood because if I thought too much about the purple stuff and how it was probably in my gills or mixing with my own blood in the cuts on my side, I think I'd be sick and now was not the time to throw up.

"Guys?" Noah shouted for us, his voice getting louder with each call. "Guys!"

He appeared at my side, completely in the nude. The guy was a unit that's for sure. No wonder I'd spotted Fallon fucking him with her eyes when she thought no one was looking.

"Are you both okay?"

"Not my best," I replied, gripping my side with sticky fingers. "Maybe give me a minute to fix my hair?"

Noah huffed a laugh then frowned at Ace. "How'd you know to stab it there?"

"A hunch," Ace said as he sat up and shrugged. "Things like that always have a weakness in video games and movies and shit. I just figured that looked like the least armoured area and went for it."

"You climbed that thing on a hunch from a video game?" Noah baulked. "Course you did."

"Fucking paid off though, didn't it?"

"Genius," I said, grinning, though it was pained. "You're one clever kelp cookie."

Ace rolled his eyes and glared in my direction, but I could tell that deep down it was all a façade. He liked me, I knew it.

"Are you alone?" Noah asked, glancing around as though expecting someone to be hiding in the trees.

Something clenched in my chest because Fallon had been trying to lure the monster away, but if it had come back then where was she?

"Get dressed," I told him, rising to my feet and rubbing blood from my face. I ignored how my body hurt. Starfish needed me and I wouldn't let her down. "We have to find Fallon."

Ace folded his arms over his chest and stood his ground. "Why should I help her?"

"Because she's my Starfish!" I stared at him with my mouth

as wide as a whale's at his bogus question.

Ace levelled a glare at me. "So?"

"Safety in numbers?" Noah suggested with a shrug. "Come on, we need to keep moving."

Noah ran off to find his clothes whilst Ace grumbled under his breath. He ripped the sleeves from his jumpsuit, revealing his tattooed arms as he handed them to me to dress my wounds.

"Thanks." I wiped the blood from my face then stuffed the sleeves down my jumpsuit, pressing them to my wounded side. It would do until I could get a proper clean up and some of the meds we'd stolen from Kayden's camp.

Ace didn't reply, instead striding towards the monster. He drew the sword from the monster's neck and came back to hand the bloody thing to me.

"I've got a knife," Ace said, as though he needed a reason for giving me my sword back.

"Okay, tough guy," I replied, grinning at him.

Ace's dark brows drew together, his eyes flashing menacingly. "I don't like that look."

"What look?" I said, staring at him adoringly. My saviour and inked knight. My grumpy little drake.

"That one," he said, scowling, though I knew he secretly loved it. "Stop it."

"There's no stopping it," Noah said, coming to stand beside me. "Accept it. You're never going to get rid of him now."

Ace punched me in the arm then strode into the woods. "Not fucking happening."

"I don't know what you're talking about," I replied, following with Noah by my side.

It was a lie, of course, because I knew exactly what was happening. The waves of destiny were calling the three of us, drawing us to her shores of friendship. Noah wasn't making a fuss and Ace would eventually stop fighting it. Nothing formed friendship better than defeating a hideous monster. Ace may have been a badass gangster from the Drakes, but even he couldn't fight fate.

# ACE

The princess was covered in blood when we found her and Kendra.

I shouldn't have been shocked to see Fallon like that. I knew she could take care of herself but seeing her splattered with a corpse laying by a tree had me fucking pause. I was no stranger to violence and gore but this was different somehow.

"What happened, Starfish?" Zane asked, rushing to her and cupping her face in his hands. "Are you both okay?"

"Well, we're alive. Kendra's just unconscious." She started untying her friend's bonds. "After I'd lost the monster an even sicker one found me. He was holding Kendra hostage."

"Is that Mark?" Noah asked, grimacing at the body. I guessed he wouldn't be getting any answers now. Kinda felt sorry for him.

"Yeah," she replied, an edge to her voice. She stood and gripped Zane's wrists. "He thought he could force me... he threatened Kendra's life just to get me on my knees."

I narrowed my eyes at what she was alluding to. Hearing about Mark forcing himself on her had my gut twisting with rage. Shit like that was the lowest of the low. No one deserved the invasion of their body. If she hadn't already killed him, I would have, and slowly too.

"Shit," Noah growled, looking how I felt. Even happy-go-lucky Zane had murder in his eyes.

"He can't hurt anyone now," Fallon said with a small shake of her head, releasing Zane and stepping back. Her gaze ran the length of him. "What happened to you guys?"

"Merman had a bath in the blood of a different kind of monster," I said, folding my arms over my chest.

She snapped her eyes to me as if only just noticing my existence, but quickly turned her attention to the bloody man in front of her. "The same one I tried to lead away?"

"Yeah," Zane replied with a grin. "But our little dream team—minus our fearless starfish, of course—took care of it." His smile dropped. "You shouldn't go running off on your own."

"Zane's right," Noah said. "As much as fighting for our lives is fun and all, we need to stick together. Not just for the monsters running around the place either. We can't be complacent with other Potentials around. If we want to get through the trial, the best way to do that is as a group."

Look at Noah, proving his worth. I wanted to get the Jupiter ring and here he was, leading me straight to the owner. Princess's copper eyes were back on me, dialled up to a full glare. Getting her to hand over that little piece of jewellery was going to be hard work. She was never gonna like me, so I'd have to get her to at least trust me somehow. A job that seemed fucking impossible, but luckily, I was like a dog with a bone when I set my mind to something.

"We need to find shelter," Noah added, his brown eyes narrowed on the darkening horizon.

Soon more creatures from everyone's nightmares would begin prowling the forest for dinner. I wasn't going to be anyone's meal.

"We could go back to our shelter?" Zane suggested, looking around at us all with puppy dog eyes. "It got a bit beat up, but it would do for the night."

"Is he really coming with us?" Princess asked, narrowing her eyes at me.

I glared back at her, my lips curving into a thin smile.

"We should stick together," Noah said, reiterating his words from earlier. He looked to the sky as if searching for the flying creatures.

"You want me to trust the asshole who watched me get beaten up and then threatened me after the fact," she snapped.

"People make mistakes," Zane said, slinging an arm over her shoulder. "Ace helped us. He's part of the dream team, Starfish."

I rolled my eyes. I wasn't part of any little team he had created in that warped brain of his. I was here for the ring, nothing more.

She didn't want to believe that I could have helped anyone, and I didn't fucking blame her. I didn't trust her either. Zane and Noah may believe her manipulative bullshit but I wasn't fucking buying it.

"Fine." She sighed heavily. "Help me with Kendra."

Noah picked her up, cradling her in his arms, and Fallon led the way to their shelter. The merman walked beside me, clutching his side and sneaking glances at me the entire time. If it weren't for my plan to get the ring from the princess, I would have decked him. Zane had gotten it in his head that now that we had killed together, we were friends. I'd killed with a lot of people, but that didn't mean that we swapped numbers and hung out. I didn't have time for this fucking shit. I needed to finish this trial and get the House Jupiter ring.

It wasn't a long walk, thank fuck, and when the building came into view I decided to take the opportunity to ask the princess about the ring. I jogged to her side and she gave me a death stare.

"Can I talk to you?" I asked, keeping my voice low.

"No."

"Why the fuck not?"

"Because I don't want to."

"Fuck it." I stopped, turning on my heel and striding back past Noah and Zane who both frowned at me.

It was a stupid idea to think the princess was going to be the easier target. She hated me as much as I hated her. I would have better luck with the sister.

"Wait!" a voice shouted after me and I slowed, letting the princess catch up. She'd have to work harder than that to get me to change my mind and turn around. She was dreaming if she thought I'd jump to attention like I was one of her servants.

"Can you just stop for a second?" she grumbled, grabbing my arm and pulling me to a halt. The others had continued ahead to the hut, leaving us alone.

"Give me your house ring and I'll stay," I blurted, pulling out of her grip.

Her eyebrows shot up at my demand and I cursed myself for my idiocy. It was fucking stupid to have come out and said it like that. My plan had all gone to shit but she made me act recklessly.

"Why do you want it?" she asked, her lips tugging up at one side.

Fuck, she had me on the back foot and she knew it. "Forget it."

She leaned forward, getting in my space. "You hate that you need something, don't you? Aw, is the big bad gangster feeling vulnerable?"

"Like hell. I just don't feel like babysitting a bunch of children." I turned away from her. "I'm leaving."

"I'll give it to you when we get back to the House of Ascension," she said, and I glanced back at her. "But I want something in return."

"What do you want?" I growled.

"Noah wants us to stick together," she said, her copper eyes narrowing on me. "And I'm inclined to agree."

"Why would you care what Noah thinks? Is that really what you want in exchange for your ring?"

"Not entirely." Fallon folded her arms over her chest. "But it will do for now until I can decide what I want. I'm not going to deny Noah's solid reasoning. Just because I don't like you doesn't mean that he isn't right."

"Are you worried about me Princess?" I smirked. "Using this as a way to keep me by your side?"

"In your dreams." She huffed. "We are safer all together."

"So you just want me to protect you?"

"We will protect each other," she said, then threw her hands in the air. "Don't be a dick and come back."

"If you need me so bad, then beg," I said slowly, looking her up and down. "Beg me to stay."

"You're fucking kidding me," she replied, raising a brow. "You're delusional if you think I'd ever do that."

My gaze dragged over her. Her cheeks were flushed beneath the splattering of blood, her breaths uneven as she licked her lower lip. "You like darkness, don't you, Princess?"

"You don't know a single thing about me," she said, stepping closer and invading my personal space.

She must have a death wish coming toe to toe with me. I held my ground because if she wanted to play with the big boys, I'd fucking let her. Equal opportunity and all that shit.

"I know that you taunt me, hoping to get a rise because you want to see what happens when you push too far," I said.

"Like … this?" She shoved me in the chest, her eyes glimmering.

"Be careful, Princess." I grabbed her wrists, restraining them at her sides. "Don't fucking test me."

"Don't be an asshole then," she snapped, tugging her arms. "Let me go. I'm not going to stand around and listen to your deranged psycho-babble."

"Then fucking go!" I released her, sneering as she stumbled backwards. "I didn't ask you to chase after me like some pathetic puppy."

"You are stubborn to the point of your own detriment, you know that?" She smirked and that look made a fire burn inside me.

"Then we must be two peas fucking in a pod," I shouted before realising how it had come out. I shook my head and pushed on before she could use it to her advantage. Fallon made me so angry I couldn't even speak properly, let alone think straight. "From what Zane was getting at earlier, you are obstinate. Who tries to take on a monster on their own?"

"I was protecting him!"

"Ha! Last I checked you did a piss poor job of that. Noah and I had to come help him because that monster you were so valiantly rescuing him from was trying to cut him in two with its claws."

"I just love how you're standing there all high and mighty, saying that I'm not a good friend when you have been the one waltzing around the House of Ascension all by yourself! Why do you have no friends, huh? Is it your giant ego or miserable personality?"

"Why would I want to make friends with the likes of you?" I stepped into her space and looked down at her. "You've spent your whole life sitting up in the clouds thinking that everyone else has to fall at your feet."

Fallon lifted her chin, holding my gaze and standing her ground. The sight had my heart racing in my chest. "And yet here you are, saying that you're better than me because you didn't grow up in Stormcrest city. Can you even hear your hypocrisy?"

"You don't know shit about what it's like to be me!"

"Right back at you, asshole!" she shouted. Her eyes held mine and we stood there, inches apart, panting with the heat of our fight.

She was so fucking infuriating. She ignited a dark rage inside me that was determined to make her burn with me. Instinctively, I reached for her hand, but she snatched it away and started punching me in the chest. I blocked most of her blows, growling as I tried to restrain her again. She managed to wriggle an arm free and came at me again, only this time everything changed. In one moment she looked ready to murder me and in the next her lips crashed into mine. There were no niceties, no build up, just a brutal force as her tongue battled with mine. She wrapped her arms around my neck, drawing me closer and I instinctively lifted her. Her legs instantly wrapped around my waist, pushing against my swelling dick.

I walked forward, shoving her hard against a tree. She moaned while her fingers twisted in my hair almost painfully as I ground my hard dick against her. I knew we hated each other, but I didn't fucking care right now. Princess didn't seem to give a shit either as she started unzipping my jumpsuit then shoved a hand down my front and stroked my dick between us. I ground into her again. She felt so fucking good, but her hand wasn't enough. I tugged her own zipper down then stepped back from the tree, letting her feet fall to the floor.

Fallon shoved her jumpsuit down so it fell around her ankles. She was fucking hot in her black bra and panties, her full tits almost spilling over the lace. We continued to kiss like we were still fighting, each of us trying to get the upper hand whilst we groped each other like teenagers. My hand slipped between the waistband of her panties and she spread her legs, letting me feel how wet she was for me. I slipped a finger inside, and she pressed herself closer, a groan escaping her lips.

Fuck, she was good to go and so was I.

Releasing her, I spun her around. Not needing any direction, she tugged down her panties then braced herself against the tree and bent over. What a fucking view she presented me with. She was an entitled princess but fuck she looked good bent over. I pulled my dick out then moved behind her, spanking her hard on the ass. Princess moaned loudly, pushing back against my dick. I rubbed her red ass cheek as I slowly pushed in and groaned with the feeling of her around me. She was so fucking tight and felt so fucking good. I drew out before slamming back in again and had her crying out in pleasure once more. I thrusted my hips in a steady rhythm, and grabbed her dark hair in my fist, my hold tightening as my pace quickened. Princess moved with me and when I spanked her ass again, I felt her clench around me in the most intense way.

Picking up my pace, I drove myself into her harder as my climax drew near. I reached around and rubbed her clit as I continued to pound into her. I could feel my orgasm building with each thrust and judging by her sounds I had a feeling she wasn't far off. I fucked her hard, pulling her hair, and she let out a cry as she clenched and contracted around my dick. Her fingers were pale as she gripped the bark of the tree, and I gave a few last thrusts before I pulled out and came all over her ass.

Silence fell between us and I swear my brain was going to short circuit trying to comprehend what the fuck we'd just done. Suddenly, Fallon shoved me away, knocking some sense into me.

"I still hate you," she panted, picking up her panties and wiping my cum from her back.

"The feeling is fucking mutual," I replied between breaths. I pulled up my jumpsuit and zipped it up, turning away as she dressed herself. "This doesn't change a fucking thing."

"Never said it did," she snapped back. "Do you still want the ring or are you going to let your pride get in the way of sense?"

"Did you fuck me so I would stay? Seal the deal?" I asked, facing her. Her lips were swollen, her dark hair even more of a tangled mess than it had been. "Is that how you keep Noah and Zane around? Have you made deals with them too?"

"You're such a dick!" She threw her hands in the air. "Fuck you!"

"You already did, Princess." I smirked because I could see she hated that she had. I bet she was fucking pissed that she enjoyed it too.

"You're such a miserable asshole!"

"And you are sugar and fucking spice." I scoffed.

"This was a huge mistake," she snapped. "One I won't be making again."

"Princess, you couldn't handle what I'm packing even if you did. What just happened? It was foreplay compared to what I can really give."

"You wanna talk about it, go see a therapist." Her eyes flared. "I don't care to hear about the dark shit you do in the bedroom."

I walked towards her, pressing her back against the tree. "In the bedroom, in public, after watching the light from my enemies' eyes go out…" I shrugged, wrapping my hand around her throat. Her breath sharpened as my hand tightened, but she didn't shove me off, instead she pressed closer. Fuck, despite what I'd said, I knew she could take it. All the fucked-up things she accused me of enjoying—the things I knew she'd enjoy too. If only she wasn't so fucking infuriating. I released my hand, stepping back and sneering. "Unfortunately for you, I'm not interested in Zane's sloppy seconds. He can keep you."

Her eyes burned and she stepped forward. "You fu—"

"Guys, hate to break up what looks like a pleasant discussion between two mature people, but can you stop for a second?"

I turned to see Noah striding towards us, twigs snapping beneath his boots. He didn't show any sign of knowing that we'd fucked, but then again, the guy was good at hiding. Not that I cared if he knew or not. It was a release. Nothing more.

"I'm leaving," I announced.

"Yeah, great decision. Really smart for survival, Ace," Noah replied. "That monster was proof that we need to all stick together. We made a deal to watch each other's backs before, this is no different."

Why were these people so adamant about protecting each other? I didn't need anyone. I had my gang, but even then I didn't expect them to stick around. Everybody leaves, it was just human fucking nature.

I still needed the ring though…

"Fine," I huffed, and without looking at the Princess I stormed through the trees to their shelter. When I reached the hut, Zane was sitting inside, a hand pressed to his side and Kendra asleep with her head on his shoulder.

"The roof is missing," I commented, looking up at the night sky. "You thought this place was safe?"

"They need to rest," Noah said, walking into the hut with Fallon a step behind. "We can find somewhere new in the morning."

"Whatever." I shrugged, my eyes unintentionally finding Fallon's like a magnet. I had a feeling I was going to regret my decision—among other things I'd done tonight. What had happened between me and the princess had changed nothing between us except for making me hate her more. I wasn't like Zane or Noah. I wasn't going to fall victim to her manipulative shit.

# FALLON

The marshland was eerily quiet for the first time since arriving after the guys had taken down that monster. We'd spent the better part of the morning searching for a safer place to bed down. Thankfully, Kendra knew of a garrison like the one Kayden had commandeered, and I was praying it would be empty when we arrived.

Guilt speared through me as I sneaked a peek at Zane. Naturally, he was in his usual cheery mood today, despite the injuries he'd received fighting yesterday. I'd done my best to lure the beast away, but it was smarter than I'd given it credit, turning back for easier prey ... or so it had thought before Ace killed it.

Zane had excitedly told me about it numerous times last night as I'd patched him up, much to Ace's delight. The guy had a permanent scowl on his face, and I was beginning to wonder if he knew how to crack a smile at all.

He was prowling on the other side of Noah now through the forest, his jaw set and his movements stiff as we approached the looming tower in the distance.

Zane's arm wrapped around my shoulder, and I snuggled into his warmth with a sigh, smirking at the lion's smile he gave me that promised we'd finish what we started yesterday morning.

I sighed. And yet, last night I'd stooped to cavorting with a psycho like Ace. I had to stop myself from groaning. What the hell was I thinking? I could admit there was something sexy about a bad boy—what is it about a dark-haired, broody asshole that makes me forget my morals and better judgements?—but Ace was a gangster, a murderer, and a thief … he was almost as bad as my parents, and I sure as shit wouldn't allow a guy like him to land his ass on the throne, fine as said ass may be.

Had it been the adrenaline? The realisation that any day out here could be my last? After what I'd done to Mark, what happened between Ace and me should have been the last thing on my mind. I'd killed a man, and not just in defence but in a violent, emotionally fired act.

I still wasn't sorry.

Maybe I was more broken than I realised. Maybe my parents had fucked me up so bad the lines between right and wrong had become too blurred. And *maybe* that's why I'd let my animal instincts take over and Ace and I had collided in yesterday's hate sex. As much as I despised the man, I had to admit, I could see some similarities between us. He was just as broken as I was and just as determined. We both had seen and done bad things and that sort of shit leaves a mark on your soul. We were branded by those who had raised us but were now forging our own paths. Ace was a survivor, just like me.

It made me hate him even more. No, it made me hate *myself*. I couldn't even deny how much I'd enjoyed having him inside me. Just thinking about it made me ache, and I had to clamp my thighs together. Sex with Ace had been savage, heated, and angry. And dammit, I … I wanted more. Wanted that hand clamped around my neck again, and every other fucked up thing he'd alluded to.

Ace might well be my biggest competition in this place. I could understand why he'd want to become king. I would never know how bad things were in Damascon Hollow until I saw it for myself, but from what I knew it was no slice of cake. That place bred dangerous beasts and when cornered, such creatures are vicious when fighting for their lives.

He likely had just as good a reason as me to take the throne, but since he'd asked about the ring of House Jupiter, I had to wonder if there were other reasons he was here. What the hell would he want that for? Or perhaps the better question was, *who* wanted it? He sure as shit had no use for it in the trials, which meant someone else could be pulling his strings. Someone like his gang leader, perhaps, hoping to rule through Ace.

He obviously had no idea I'd lied about it, and I'd just have to deal with his wrath when he realised. Victrus and Eliana had never deemed me worthy of a ring, and as for Victoria's ... I smiled to myself. I was worried that Ethan would get tangled up in this, but no one knew I'd given him her ring, and it was safe in our little hidey hole anyway.

Which meant Ace had no chance of getting one. That filled me with relief, but I was more curious than ever to keep both eyes peeled on his movements. I didn't trust his intentions with the others or myself, and I had no doubt he was involved in something beyond the trials. I just didn't know what.

"There's the tower," Kendra said excitedly, pointing to the stone building ahead. "The others will be waiting."

Ace abruptly halted. "Others?" he said in a low, dangerous voice. "There are other Potentials there?"

Kendra cocked her head. "Yes, but they're not a threat. In fact, I heard you saved a few from—from..." She trailed off, and I felt my heart swell as her face twisted.

Noah's eyes narrowed as he turned to me, the glint in his eyes telling me he felt the same. "Ace and I freed some Potentials Mark's men had captured. This has something to do with the hooded guy, I'm sure of it."

"Mark," I spat. My fingers curled into fists. I could only imagine what he had planned for those people, but I had a few ideas about the women. Disgust filled me, slick and oily in my stomach as I recalled what he'd said about another woman he'd assaulted. *The last one had tried to be defiant. It didn't end so well for her.* Noah and I shared a knowing look, but I didn't want to share anything else with Ace around. He could be in on whatever scheme Victoria and Mark were involved in for all we knew.

"What hooded man?" Zane asked, his brows furrowing as he looked between Noah and me. His eyes clouded with hurt. "You're keeping secrets, conspiring without me. My girl and my besties, forming their own team."

"I'm not your girl," I said with a huff. "And it's not like that."

"You're scheming and you left me out of it," he stated flatly, the tone unlike anything I'd heard come from his mouth. He shrugged his shoulders, though the movement was rigid and not as carefree as I presumed he was aiming for. "Cool, yeah, whatever. I thought we were friends but guess I was wrong."

"Zane…" I tried to put my hand on his shoulder, but he shrugged it off and stalked ahead.

I rolled my eyes, looking to Kendra. "A little help?"

Kendra laughed, shaking her head. "I'll go talk to him."

I stared as she jogged after him and hailed the Potentials on scout duty from the garrison's ramparts. It was the same setup as the one Kayden was in. Only this time, we hopefully had allies in the Potentials inside. I'd have to warn them about Kayden and Victoria, because something told me things were going to get ugly real soon.

Ace scoffed as we watched Kendra catch up to Zane. "Let the merman sulk. Guy's in a fucking marshland fighting for his life and he's crying over his little friends. What a joke."

"At least he's got friends," I snapped, glaring at him. "You wouldn't know the first thing about that."

Ace stepped towards me. "I don't have time to stroke his scales and grovel at his feet. If you had some dignity, you wouldn't either."

Oh hell no, he didn't go there. "You are such an asshole. You think you're some tough, violent thug who is so hard done by. Please. You just act like you're above everyone else."

He smirked, his steel grey eyes glinting. "I was above you last night when my dick was balls deep inside you. You didn't seem to complain about it then."

Noah cleared his throat awkwardly. "Guys, not that I don't love being the awkward third wheel here, but reckon you can give it a rest right now?"

I stalked over to Ace, looking him hard in the eye, and clocked him in the jaw. To my surprise and annoyance, he laughed.

"I like it rough, baby, but try that again and you'll be eating your words, and then something else."

"You'd like that wouldn't you?" I whispered in his ear. "You want me to submit, but here's the thing tough guy. The next time I feel like playing your little game, you'll be at my mercy." I leaned closer, letting him see my copper eyes, the touch of my lips grazing his. "Naughty boys get punished."

Ace's face twisted, his eyes flashing darkly with the promise of vengeance. Oh, this guy was fifty shades of fucked up.

"Let's go, Noah," I said sweetly, turning my back on Ace. "We've got more important things to do than waste our time with *him*."

He looked over his shoulder at Ace, seeming more curious than anything else. Noah was so hard to read; I couldn't get a feel for what he was thinking, which only made him more intriguing.

I now had three guys to navigate around and, if I was being honest, I didn't totally hate the idea about that.

I didn't mind it one bit.

———— ◆ ————

"I still can't believe Mark's really dead," Kendra said, shaking her head in wonder before her slender nose scrunched up and she frowned. "I'm glad he's dead. Now he can't hurt anyone ever again."

I laid my head against her shoulder as we sat in one of the storage rooms on the top floor of the garrison, swinging our legs from where we sat on a crate. "Kendra, I hate to ask but he didn't ... hurt you like that, did he?"

"Oh gods no." She gasped, clutching a hand to her chest. "I don't think he was planning to. He just delivered some payback from me beating him up. I think he was also using me as bait so he could capture you."

I wilted in relief, but a deep sadness filled me too. "I'm sorry. If it wasn't for me, none of this might ever have happened."

"Don't you dare," she said in a low tone, pulling back so I had to lift my head. Her dark brown eyes burned with fire as she looked at me. "Don't apologise. The only one responsible for his actions was him, and he paid in the end. He paid with everything he had."

I blew out a breath. "I know, but I still feel somewhat responsible. I'm just glad you're okay."

She relaxed, her features softening. "You know, we make an odd team, but I'm glad we're friends."

"Me too." I smiled, bumping my knee against hers. "Friends aren't really my speciality. The closest thing I have back home is my brother, Ethan." My heart sank, feeling empty just talking about him. "I miss him a lot."

Kendra cocked her head. "In the orphanage I grew up in, I'd had friends, but they came and went, and in the end, I stopped bothering. Even if my parents had still been alive though, many families where I come from only have one child. Times are tough and resources are hard to come by. The Crimson Steppes is a harsh place. In a way, it's like the marshland, just a hell of a lot hotter. Survival of the fittest, living day to day." She shrugged. "We pride ourselves on strength there, but a lot of hot heads can make it hard to find friends, ya know?"

I grinned, trying to lighten the mood. "With people like

Kayden as your neighbours, I can't imagine why."

She laughed, pulling out a chocolate bar from her pocket before snapping it and offering me half. I took it with a smile. *Girl knows a way to a woman's heart.* "Kayden is tough, but he's not as bad as he seems. I think deep down he's a bit of a marshmallow."

I blinked, bursting out laughing as I thought of the Kayden-boulder I'd seen roaring around at the other garrison. "Are you sure we're talking about the same guy?"

Kendra nudged me playfully, a suspicious smirk on her face. "We are, but I'd rather talk about some others."

"Oh gods," I groaned. "What do you know?"

"That there's enough sexual tension brewing between you and Ace that I'm expecting a ticking bomb to go off any second."

"Gross. When you put it like that it feels so dirty." I groaned again, covering my face with my hands. "It *is* dirty. He's disgusting, and awful, and—"

"A freaking beast in the sack?" I didn't answer, and she tutted at me knowingly. "And what about the merman?"

"Zane?" I bit my lip. What about him? I didn't even know how to answer that. "We're just friends."

"Ah-huh. *Good friends.*"

I looked at her, exasperated but also surprisingly happy to have someone to talk to about boys and other normal things. I'd never had someone to talk to like this, to gossip with, laugh, and just ... hang out. It was weird, but it also felt so nice to have a friend.

Kendra was the kind of girl I could just be myself around. She'd never judged me about my family or my House, and she'd never questioned my reasons to be here. Even though the world had already formed their opinions of me before I'd had a chance to show them who I really was, Kendra hadn't let that bother her in the slightest. Apparently, she'd found something in me to like, and that was all kinds of heart-warming.

I found I really liked her too. She was kind, genuine, and

funny, and she rocked her own unique style. I loved that about her. She was just unapologetically … her. Not bothered about society or its expectations, and not afraid to kick ass if she needed to.

"I don't really know what Zane is to me but I'd like to get to know him better. Maybe some others too." I stretched my neck so that I was looking at the stone ceiling. "I just don't want to be tied down. I've been living in a cage for so long, I can't be barred in another way."

"You don't strike me as the type of girl who follows societal norms," she said. "So don't."

I frowned. "What do you mean?"

She shrugged, looking at me with a cheeky grin. "If you want to explore things between more than one guy, what's stopping you? There are no rules, and girl, we might die any day. I need to live vicariously through you before I depart this shithole."

I chuckled. "You're not going to die, Kendra, I promise. We're going to get through this together and I'll rain hell on anyone who tries to get in our way."

She smirked, hopping off the crate and heading out the door. "I know you will. Just think about what I said. There are never guaranteed tomorrows, Fallon. Life's too short."

I sat there for a long time after she'd left, thinking on what she'd said. She was right. I hated to think that if today was my last day on Terrulia, I'd achieved nothing with my life. Never taken risks, never done anything of my own choice except for entering the very trial we were in right now. For the first time I didn't have my parents' prying eyes or rules over who I could spend my time with. Thanks to my sister's lies and gossiping, my romantic relationships—if they could even be called that—had been hidden in the shadows. Now, I had my very own friend and the possibility of other relationships in my life. The trials may kill me, but they also set me free.

I didn't know if there would be a tomorrow, or a day after

that, but I damn well wanted to make everything count while I could. And Kendra was right. I didn't need to promise myself to anyone or to be mutually exclusive to just one man. I was free to spread my wings and fly my own path.

My life had always been filled with pain. Agony had been carved into my heart and I'd been broken in too many ways to count. But bruises faded, and scars marked the victory of survivors.

It's time I took my own life into my hands and explored what I wanted from it. Found pleasure at the hands of another instead of torment.

And maybe that was within my reach after all.

I padded through the doorway and to the far room on the landing, finding Zane and Noah curled up near each other. I glanced down at them with a soft smile, seeing their faces relaxed in sleep.

Without overthinking it, I nestled into Zane's bedding and lay down next to him, his arms immediately wrapping around me and tugging me closer.

Green eyes blinked open sleepily, and I smiled as they glittered in the reflection of a lit torch on the wall. "Hello Starfish."

"Hello Zane."

I kissed him, long and deep, his tongue curling around mine in the most sensual way. Heat fired down my body, but I was content to just kiss him for the time being, and I think he was happy with that too.

Just exploring, lost in the comforting embrace of each other's arms.

# KAYDEN

"What did you get?" I asked, leaning back in my chair. It was the only chair in the garrison and might as well have been my throne.

"We found a group of random Potentials who weren't prepared at all," the woman before me snickered. Pam, I think her name was. "They just about shit themselves when we turned up. They handed over everything they had. Food, meds, and even a few knives. They weren't great at managing their supplies, so they'd gone through a bit."

I nodded, steepling my fingers. "If they were so happy to give you all they had, then why are there only three of you? I sent out five to scout that part of the marshland."

"We got attacked by those giant bats again," Pam said. "Lost a couple to the fight but saved all the supplies."

I smirked. Pam had her priorities in order. "Drop the supplies on the second floor to be sorted."

"Yes, sir," she replied, dipping her head then ushering those behind her out.

I loved how they'd all taken to calling me sir. It was like they had already submitted to my rule. All I needed now was for the next few weeks to go smoothly and I could wash my hands of the first trial. We were currently halfway through our month and so far, I'd managed to build and maintain an empire. We had a good stock of supplies and weapons, and we'd managed to keep the monsters at bay with minimal loss of life. Losing the two scouts was disappointing, but I was sure it wouldn't ruin what I'd built here.

"You've got someone else waiting to see you," Flynn said, leaning against the doorframe.

I raised a brow. "Who is it?"

"Victoria Auger."

Fuck. What was she doing here?

"Send her in," I replied and he nodded before striding away. I could hear his feet stomping on the stone steps as he made his way down. Naturally, my room was the biggest in the whole tower and on the third floor for extra safety. I had a big ass bed made from blankets and a stash of supplies including antibiotics and chocolate—necessities and luxury items I'd kept for bargaining. If someone wanted it, they'd have to go through me, and I gave nothing away for free.

I was curious to see what Victoria could possibly want from me other than trying to take what I'd built. Only over my dead body would she take what was mine, and I definitely wasn't going to worry that she was in my stronghold. I'd throw her out my window if I had to. Footsteps sounded and soon I found Victoria striding through my door, her hips swinging as she walked. She was wearing the same black jumpsuit as everyone else but hers was cleaner, not a speck of dirt to be seen, as though she'd just been valeted in.

"Kayden, Kayden, Kayden," she purred, stepping into the centre of the room and looking around the place. She flicked her long blond braid and whistled. "What a castle you have found yourself. A true lord of the marsh."

She laughed, though the sound was far from pleasant, and I gave her a smile that didn't reach my eyes. We were two predators eyeing each other. The problem for her being that I was the bigger, more dominant one. I'd send her scurrying back to her hole if she put a foot wrong.

"What do you want, Victoria?" I asked, leaning forward and resting my forearms on my thighs.

"I was in the neighbourhood and thought I'd visit," she replied, pouting at me. "Thought you'd like some real company in this tower of yours. You must be getting lonely with no one of your calibre here with you."

I angled my head to look past her and out the door. "Did you bring someone with you then?"

"Very funny." She laughed, that grating sound making me twitch with the need to punch something. "I always knew I liked you."

"What do you want, Victoria?" I repeated, tired of her dance already.

"Intel. Have you seen Fallon?"

"Why do you want to know where she is?" I asked. "Had a change of heart and feeling the need for a sisterly bonding session all of a sudden? Have the monsters in the marsh got you all frightened?"

"More like I don't want to waste the opportunity this place has presented," she replied. "And maybe I am feeling a little like helping my family."

"She's not going to join you. Even I can see how much she despises you."

"Who said that's what I want?" She chuckled. "I want to help my family, and if that means eliminating an embarrassment then I'll do just that."

I whistled. "Still as ruthless as ever."

"Don't say that like you wouldn't do the same thing. You're constantly touting shit about strength over weakness. We are the same, you and I."

"How so?"

"We both want the same things," she said as a woman I didn't recognise entered the room with a smirk on her face. "Power. The only problem for you is that there is no future in which you will have it."

I slowly rose from my seat, cracking my neck and focusing on keeping my temper in check. I shoved down the reaction she was trying to provoke out of me, forcing it to remain hidden so she wouldn't get the satisfaction she so desperately wanted.

"No one from the Crimson Steppes is ever going to amount to anything. House Mars? Your sad excuse for a ruling house? It's the most pathetic of them all. You have nothing to offer the people who follow you. Your people deserve to die out in the desert."

"Get the fuck out," I said through my gritted teeth. "Flynn! Get in here!"

Victoria grinned with a mouth full of white teeth. "It's comical, watching you trying to rise above your station. Just accept that you are the shit beneath my boot. You'll be happier once you realise your worth."

"Flynn!"

"So sad," she said through a pout, though the cruel glimmer in her eyes told a different story.

"Get out or I'll have you leave in a body bag," I growled, striding towards her.

"I think I'll stay, actually," she replied, slipping a knife from her pocket and pointing it towards me. "I want this garrison and everyone in it but you."

I laughed at the blade. "You think your butter knife is going to save you? Turn around and get the fuck out. I'll even pretend you didn't make this huge fucking mistake coming here."

"You just don't know when to quit, do you?" Victoria replied, pushing forward, and I let her have the ground as she backed me up towards the window. I'd let her think she was winning, give her that false sense of security before I brought her down a peg.

"I offered to be your ally and you turned it down. Now you are going to feel the consequences of your actions."

I looked to the doorway as the sound of something being dragged came to my attention. The smirking woman stepped aside and two guys hauled someone into the room, leaving a trail of blood. One of the guys nudged the body's head to the side, revealing a familiar face and slit throat.

My heart leapt into my throat. Fuck. Fuck, fuck, fuck. They'd killed Flynn.

We were meant to own these trials together. He'd been my right-hand man for so long.

Red filled my vision and I roared, charging as my skin shifted to stone. Victoria stepped out of my way but only by a hair's breadth. It didn't matter though, my fist collided with the smirking woman and I knocked her back into the wall with a loud crack. She dropped to the floor, blood running from her nose, and I turned to find my next target. The other three were already moving, drawing larger weapons. I wasn't afraid of swords. They couldn't cut through my stony skin.

I made for Victoria.

She laughed, swinging her sword. The metal hit my rocky skin with a clang as I blocked her blows, my back absorbing the hits from one of the guys. I spun around to swat him away when I noticed the other guy holding a fucking pulse gun directed at me. Where the fuck had they gotten weaponry like that?

"Make it count," Victoria shouted from behind me. Then the guy fired.

BANG.

The pulse slammed into my chest, propelling me backwards. I smashed through glass, flying through the window to the sheer drop below. Pain shot through my chest, and I thanked the fucking gods I had my rock skin on. If I hadn't, I'd have blown up rather than been thrown from the tower.

I landed outside, pain shooting through my limbs as I hit

269

the ground. I groaned, my skin turning soft again, and squinted to look up at the hole in the tower I'd just made. The Auger bitch stared down at me, a wicked grin on her face.

"Run along peasant," she said, waving her fingers dismissively. Patronising, usurping bitch. "You have ten minutes to get out of my sight or we'll come for you. And next time? You won't be breathing when I'm done with you."

"You think my people are going to let you take over?" I shouted up at her, each word sending excruciating pain through my chest.

"Who do you think let me in?" she called back, her horrible laugh echoing. "Tick-tock, Red, you're running out of time."

I was stuck between a rock and an entitled bitch. Groaning, I rolled to the side and got to my feet. Taking a few breaths, I walked away as best I could without limping or holding any injuries. I refused to give Victoria the satisfaction, but I swore I'd get revenge.

———— ◆ ————

Everything fucking hurt and I was starting to think that I would die out in the marshes if I didn't find shelter soon. It had begun raining about half an hour after leaving my tower and now I was soaked through. It turned out, it was over Flynn's body, not mine, that Victoria would take what I'd built. The sky was darkening, and soon I'd no longer be fuelled by my anger towards her. I could already feel it waning, the rain washing away my energy.

The monsters would be out soon and then I'd be royally fucked, and not in the way I'd been planning to be by the end of the year.

Victoria Auger was at the top of my shit list and she owed me payment in blood for taking my tower, my people, and worst of all, for murdering Flynn. The guy didn't deserve that shit. He was my right-hand man, and he was supposed to be by my side when this was all over, like he had been since we were kids. I'd rip Victoria apart limb from limb. I used to think she was a competitor, but now she was simply my enemy. I'd made it my mission to destroy her.

I stumbled over some wet rocks, falling to one knee with a growl as mud soaked through my jumpsuit. I couldn't keep going like this. I searched for any sign of which way to head. I had no idea where I was going, which was bad. I had no plan beyond payback and I wouldn't be able to do that if I got eaten by some giant flying bat or other fucked up monster out here.

I spotted the top of a stone tower through the rain in the distance, a grin spreading on my face. Flynn must have been watching over me. The guy would have wanted me to seek vengeance for his murder and take the crown. Being shot out of a window was a hiccup—a blip that wouldn't stop me from doing just that. I was going to make my parents proud, make the people of the Crimson Steppes proud ... make Flynn proud.

Victoria was a part of that plan now. Her death would be mighty.

Hobbling more than I'd like to admit, I made my way through the trees and mud towards the tower. There were a couple of Potentials standing guard, but they were no match for me. I was a big guy and, yes, I was injured, but I hadn't come this far in life without learning to be stealthy when I needed to. Before choosing this place to rebuild my strength, I needed to suss it out. Getting caught in another fight wasn't ideal and I hated to admit it, but I needed rest. I slipped past the guards as they made their rounds of the perimeter and as I drew closer, I could hear muffled voices from within. I waited, looking around and deciding whether I wanted to go through with seeking sanctuary or if I should just find my own space. Then the sound of one voice in particular had all thoughts of being on my own fall away.

I banged on the door and my brows rose to find Zane answering it with Twiggy peering over his shoulder. Since when did those two become allies?

"You look like shit," Zane said with a whistle. He held a sword out and pressed the tip to my chest. Not hard enough to pierce but the threat was there. "What happened to you?"

"Victoria," I grumbled. "Let me in, Tadpole."

"No fucking way," Ace said, holding the door with his bionic hand to stop it from opening further. "This could be a set up. I'm not showing you my back, only for you and your little followers to stick a knife in it."

"He makes a good point," Zane said, nodding like a bobble head stuck in a car. "Also, tadpoles are freshies, dude, I'm from the sea."

"Same shit," I huffed.

"Nah, dude," he replied with a pout. "They're—"

"Stop distracting the merman. You're not coming in," Ace said, cutting Zane off. "Shut the door."

Zane lowered the sword and started to shut the door in my face, but I quickly slammed a hand into the wood, holding it open. I hated being so desperate; my pride was taking a fucking beating today. When I spoke, my words came out strained. "Wait. Fuck, I'll get eaten out here."

"I see no problem with that," Ace said with a mocking grin.

A growl rumbled from my chest. "I can help you."

"What makes you think we want your help?" Fallon asked, stepping into my line of sight.

I puffed up my chest. "I'm strong."

"You don't look very strong right now," Zane pointed out. "More like a goldfish after a spin in a washing machine."

"Once I heal, I'll be strong," I said through gritted teeth. The rain continued pouring on me and I couldn't help the shiver it sent through me.

"I assume you want our meds and food too then?" Ace stated.

"It's a small price to pay," I replied.

"Let me think," Fallon said, tapping her chin. "No. We don't trust you."

"Do you trust Twiggy?" I asked, pointing at Ace.

"That's not the issue here," she said, though she smirked at the nickname.

"Why is he allowed in and not me? What's the difference?"

She glanced at him with pursed lips. "We have an arrangement."

"Then I'll make a deal with you," I replied. "You let me in, feed me and give me meds, and I'll be on your side for the rest of the trial. I'll even kill your sister for you. How does that sound?"

Fallon narrowed her eyes. "Why would I want you to kill Victoria?"

"She's coming for you. Told me herself before she usurped me, murdered Flynn, and threw me from my tower," I said. "I'll kill her before she gets a chance to draw the knife on you. You're getting the better end of the deal on this, by the way."

Fallon exchanged a look with Zane, then sighed heavily. I'd convinced her. Who would have thought offering to murder her sibling would be the thing that brought us to the same side.

"Get your miserable ass inside then," she said, rolling her eyes. "I want you to tell me everything about Victoria and the garrison you just left."

# FALLON

My sister wanted to kill me. It was all I'd been able to think about since Kayden rocked up at our door last night, looking more than a little sorry for himself. Under other circumstances, I'd have found some satisfaction in that—okay, maybe I did feel a smidge—but the bombshell he'd dropped outweighed that by far.

Victoria was a monster, but a small part of me had always hoped that deep down, there was some good hiding away in her black heart. That one day, after I'd destroyed Victrus and Eliana's empire, we'd be able to make amends and start fresh.

How foolish I'd been. Our parents had carved every good thing out of her, filling her head with lies and corrupting every inch of her soul. There was nothing my sister did that didn't benefit the House or herself.

I knew why she wanted to be queen.

If she ruled Terrulia, our parents' dynasty would be forever set in stone. They wouldn't just have Stormcrest City under their thrall, but all the others too. I wouldn't allow it. If things were bad now, they'd spiral into chaos with Victoria on the throne.

My parents didn't know how determined I was to prevent that from happening, so I had the advantage there. Victrus thought my rebellious nature was something I'd grow out of something he could temper and bend to his will, but he was dead wrong. Not that he was taking any chances. Victrus and Eliana had told me not to come home if I didn't win the trials ... I just hadn't realised Victoria would never give me the chance.

*A back-up plan*, Victoria had said of me. Someone for our parents to manipulate if anything happened to their precious first-born daughter. She obviously wasn't happy with even that scenario and was taking matters into her own hands. My sister didn't plan for me to succeed, and I'd signed my own death warrant in these trials.

Any affection I held for Victoria had died a long time ago—she made it impossible to love her after all the things she'd done—but something inside me cracked a little more to know that I was just another target. Not a sister, not family, just a mark to be disposed of and cleaned up.

I sighed, strolling onto the ramparts of the top floor, surveying the grounds below. My gaze snagged on the men digging trenches and setting up blockades, their jumpsuits rolled down to reveal muscled arms and slick abs.

Ace and Kayden were bickering about something, and I couldn't help but smirk as they got in each other's faces. Noah was muttering to himself beside them, and Zane had stepped in to mediate. I couldn't help but laugh. It was freaking testosterone city down there, and to be honest, I wouldn't have minded a show.

It was a hot and humid day after the rain yesterday, and sweat was gleaming on all their naked torsos. I just about salivated as I looked between them all. Kayden towered over the others, his bronzed muscles threatening to jump ship from his arms, but smaller as he was, I knew Ace could hold his own. He was the palest of them all, and I wondered if Damascon Hollow ever saw the sun.

Noah looked like a god with his umber skin gleaming and the green shimmer of his adaptation snaking down his neck. And then Zane, with his blond hair billowing in the slight breeze, his golden skin slick.

Well, if death was planning on knocking on my door any day now, I couldn't think of a better way to go. Actually, scratch that, there were some things I had in mind ... I shook my head, chastising the girl downstairs. I'd already made one mistake with Ace this week, and I certainly didn't need to cause more complications with Kayden and Noah.

I eyed Kayden as whatever Zane had said seemed to break up their fight and he returned to his work. He was cocky and pig-headed, but I got the feeling there was more to the Crimson Steppes Potential than muscles. There had to be more than rocks rattling in that skull if he had been running his own army ... then again, he had lost them all in a swift and calculating move from Victoria.

He'd never stood a chance. He looked like a lost but not so little lamb and seemed to have no clue how to work as one unit. I got the feeling he'd only ever looked out for number one, and frankly, I don't think he knew how to treat people as anything but underlings who served his every whim. Now it would be a matter of seeing whether he could play nice and take orders as well as give them.

I didn't trust the guy, but between Zane, Noah, Ace and me, he stood no chance of taking over our garrison here, which meant he'd have to play ball or get kicked out on his ass. I had to give him credit though after he provided valuable information.

Victoria now had around twenty Potentials under her command, according to Kayden, and they were fully stocked with provisions, not to mention weapons. It was hard to estimate the number of Potentials left alive, given many would be hiding around the marsh and fighting amongst themselves. My sister had everything she needed to attack, hence why Noah had suggested building extra precautions to defend our building and to increase the number of watchmen.

A smart idea and, to my surprise, no one had argued. It

seemed the Potentials who had already been here automatically looked to our group for leadership, maybe because Noah and Ace had saved a bunch of them, or maybe just because we came from the strongest Houses—or in Ace's case—the most notorious gang. We were born leaders in our own rights, and I just hoped having too many alphas in one room didn't backfire on our asses.

"Fallon."

I blinked, turning to find Kayden approaching, and I cursed myself for zoning out. Vigilance was key now more than ever. I analysed our newest recruit, raising a brow. "If you're here to insist we attack Victoria again, the answer is still no."

His nostrils flared as he halted. "It's the best time to attack. She won't expect me to have teamed up with you."

"That's exactly what she'll expect."

His brow furrowed. "You don't know that."

I twirled a strand of raven hair around my finger, contemplating. "She told you she wanted to kill me, right? Why would she bother dropping that little nugget of information unless it served her? She wanted you to find me, and she wanted me to retaliate. I know my sister, and she's a clever snake. No, we won't be walking into her trap today."

He ran a hand through his red hair, turning his curious brown eyes on me. "What is it between you two? She's your sister for Mars' sake."

I smiled sadly, weighing up whether I should tell him, but it didn't really hurt either way. Anyone who cared enough to investigate the Auger family would be doing it for the wrong reasons, and everyone at the academy already knew how much my sister hated me.

"Victoria wants to destroy me because she's intimidated by what I could do. I'm a threat to her—to her ascension in these trials. My parents won't care if she succeeds. They only care if an Auger sits on the throne."

"Damn," he breathed. "That's harsh little angel."

I swept my eyes over his face, taking in the chiselled jawline and golden-brown eyes that seemed gentle despite his usual macho bullshit. "Are you close with your family?"

He smiled genuinely; a hint of pride etched in his eyes. "Very. They've always pushed me to do my best and to make them proud. Everyone looks down their noses at the Crimson Steppes, but things are going to be different when I become king. It'll be better."

"So there's a heart beneath all that brawn after all," I teased.

He folded his giant arms and scowled. "I didn't say it would be better for everyone else. Maybe I just want to see the other Houses squirm beneath Mars' boot."

"Sure." I smiled sweetly, striding over and placing a hand on his bare chest. His huge muscles stiffened beneath my palm. "Big bad Kayden is going to punish everyone."

He growled, stepping forwards and forcing me to back up. "Don't mock me little angel. No one's watching, I could push you over the edge right now."

I enjoyed this game, getting under each other's skin. Kayden was a puzzle I wanted to figure out, if only so I could understand his motivations. His ego was overinflated and he was definitely an asshole, but if he genuinely cared about improving things for his city, there had to be a softer side beneath all that muscle.

The dominant energy that he exuded was no joke and frankly was impossible to ignore, but I was beginning to wonder if it was partly a mask. To cover what, I wasn't sure, but I'd be lying if I didn't admit a part of me wanted to explore not only his head but other things too. Maybe I could have some fun finding out if this sexual tension I was feeling went both ways.

"Would it make you happy to see me dead?" I asked curiously, cocking my head and stepping into his space.

"What?" he asked with a frown, caught off-guard by my sincere question. "No, I—"

I laughed, sliding my hand down his chest to trail my fingers along the vee above his pants. He quivered beneath my touch, his cock hardening as he leaned in and grabbed my ass, a low growl rumbling in his throat.

"You don't really know what you want, do you?" I breathed, moving my hand lower so I was stroking him through his jumpsuit.

"I'm beginning to get a few ideas," he said roughly.

I laughed again, thrilled by the idea of anyone being able to see us like this if they only looked up. "Do you want me, baby?" I asked in a husky voice, batting my lashes as I looked up at him.

"Yes," he groaned. "Fuck, yes, I want to see those pretty eyes staring up at me with my cock jammed down your throat."

He pushed his leg between my thighs and I had to stop myself from grinding against him. "Do you want to hurt me?" I breathed against his lips, trying not to pant as heat ran down my skin.

"Only when you beg me to."

I stood back abruptly, leaving him gaping at me. "Good. You've been very helpful." I winked. "We should do this again sometime."

Without hesitation I stepped backwards, letting myself fall off the ramparts as he rushed to the edge with a cry. My copper wings burst from my back in a flurry of feathers, glinting in the midday sun as I flapped higher, laughing at Kayden's shocked expression.

"Cya, Rocky, you've been a real treat."

I left him standing there in his full, hardened glory, and joined Kendra below. I pulled in my wings as I landed and she smirked, handing me a spear.

"So, what's the deal with Kayden then? Think we can trust him?"

Straight to the point. It was one of the things I liked about her. "I don't think he's a threat. Victoria bruised his ego and he's out for her blood, but he seems harmless enough. In fact, I think you're right about him being a marshmallow deep down. He could be an asset to our group here."

She rolled her eyes. "Speaking of the other three fools, can you deal with the mean, scary machine over there? He's threatening to rip out eyes and break necks. It's not doing much for morale."

I looked over at the Potentials who were glancing at Ace nervously, giving him a wide berth as they worked to set spears and sharpened branches into the earth. I snorted. "You want *me* to deal with him? I'm more likely to end up with a spear in my gut than anyone."

She looked me up and down with a raised brow. "Well you're the one that ground up and down on *his* spear, you sort it out."

With a huff, I gave her a look that promised death and stalked towards him. "Hey."

"Come back for round two, Princess?" He sneered.

"In your dreams," I scoffed, glaring at him. "Stop fucking around with the other Potentials and let them work in peace. Or maybe it'll be your head on one of these spikes."

"You think because you've got the other guys wrapped around your little finger that you can tell me what to do?"

I pouted, bending over and talking to him as though he was a child. "Do I need to put you in the naughty corner? Does Ace need a timeout so he can get all his raging hormones in check?"

He hissed, storming towards me, his grey eyes flashing like lightning. "Trying to get me alone so you can bounce on my lap, Princess? You could just ask if you're so desperate to go again."

"Been there, done that, won't be trying it again." I smirked. "Just play nice, okay? These people are your allies, not your enemies. When Victoria comes knocking, one of these Potentials could save your life, but if you treat people like shit, you'll be on your own."

"I've always been on my own," he snarled, his words tainted by bitterness. Was that regret I'd heard? Or sadness? "Always was, always will be."

I looked at him sadly, and his lips curled as he gazed back, his fists shaking by his sides. He was hurting, I realised. Something had happened to him to make him lose his faith in humanity, and life had twisted him into this bitter creature. Ace had seen and done things people don't forget, and I couldn't imagine what life had been like growing up in a gang.

I'd considered it before but … we really weren't that different after all. Just swap out the monsters and the shoe fit. Ace was hateful and brutal, but I had to believe there was a light in there too. I had to … for me as well.

My heart fluttered with sadness, because maybe he didn't have an Ethan or a Hadley to uplift him or remind him that it was all worth it. Maybe he didn't even understand what true love or loyalty was.

I sighed, shaking my head slowly. "If that's what you really think, then I feel sorry for you. I know what it's like to be treated like shit, to be abused, beat down and forgotten, but the world is so much more than that, and people have so much more to offer. So you better try harder, Ace, to make friends or find your family, or you'll die alone, just like you lived."

"I like being alone, Princess. I'm the only one I can rely on." He looked at me in disgust, his lips curling into a sneer. "Take your pity and give it to someone who gives a shit."

I opened my mouth to retort, but he'd already stormed off. A violent hurricane that could not be tempered. The question was, why did I even want to try?

# NOAH

Tomorrow I'd be one step closer to discovering what was happening to the people of Verdant Plateau. Mark Leroy may be dead, but whoever was coming from House Jupiter to collect the delivery on the twenty-first day of this trial was not.

I had been careful to keep the map and compass hidden, working out the best route to get to the meeting spot marked on the map I'd stolen in quiet, private moments. I felt a little guilty not showing the others, but I wasn't ready to let them all in on my investigation. I couldn't let them jeopardise my work. The twins needed me—all my people did.

"Are you going to meet them tomorrow?" Ace asked from where he leant against the tree. His face was a mask of calm, but the way his steely eyes scanned the perimeter suggested he was itching for some action.

Dammit, how did he know about tomorrow?

"Who?" I asked, rolling my neck slowly, playing pretend.

Ace flicked his eyes at me knowingly, the scowl on his lips lifting to a thin smile. "Don't play dumb, Noah, it's beneath you. I mean whoever the fuck Mark was planning to trade those people to. I was there, remember? I heard bits and pieces of what they were saying."

We were on guard duty outside the garrison. Ace and Kayden had gotten into another brawl, so I'd suggested I take Kayden's spot. The two of them together spelled trouble … and not just for each other.

Besides, I needed time to think and Ace needed to cool off. Seemed like a win-win. Except now he was asking questions I didn't want him to. He helped me rescue those people from Mark's lackeys and I was all for him working with us to get through the trial, but that's where our alliance ended. Katie and Rena's lives weren't worth the risk.

"I don't know what you're talking about," I said, trying not to let my irritation show.

He raised a brow as he toyed with his knife. "Are you sure about that?"

"Yeah, I have memory loss. It's a heavy burden to bear," I said, folding my arms as I gave him the side-eye. "But let's say I was meeting them, what then?"

"I'd say you could use some backup," he said. "This place is overcrowded and Zane is doing my head in. Unless you'd rather I stay and take my frustrations out on him?"

I grunted noncommittally.

I didn't know how I felt about his offer and whether I could actually trust him not to be working an angle. Ace was not the kind of person to do something out of the goodness of his heart—if he even had one. Everything was a deal, a give and take.

"What's in it for you? Aside from potentially shedding some blood, what else do you get?"

Ace huffed, running a hand through his dark hair. "If I have to listen to another order from the Auger Princess, someone is going to get hurt. She's a bossy, stubborn, entitled—"

"Why did you have sex with her if you hated her so much?" I asked, genuinely curious. I'd overheard them the night we'd found Fallon, Zane, and Kendra. They had sex like they spoke to each other; angry and full of hate.

His face darkened, his scowl immediately back. "Call it a lapse in judgement. A brain aneurism, I don't fucking know, but it won't be happening again."

"You're not into her then?"

"I'd rather my dick fall off then stick it in her again."

I leaned against the tree, amusement lifting my lips. "A bit aggressive but okay."

Ace looked at me, cocking his head. "You like her."

"What?" I lifted my hands. "We're just allies. I was more sussing you out because of Zane."

"You're worried about what the merman will do?"

"Not worried, but he's been, you know, nice to me. And we are sort of allies too. I know he likes Fallon and he's not a bad guy so…"

"You're worried I'm going to cut his lunch?" he asked, his lips pressing together. I could tell by the glint in his eyes he was holding back a laugh. "How thoughtful of you."

"I'm a real stand-up guy," I drawled, running a hand over my face. "I want to get through this trial in one piece. That involves everyone getting along. Think you can manage that?"

"Fine, but I'm coming with you."

"I'm not going anywhere."

"Whatever you say, champ," he said. "So, what's your plan for tomorrow?"

I looked at Ace. I couldn't trust him yet, but as long as he was getting something out of it, Ace would fall in line. And he *was* getting something out of all this, I just didn't know what yet.

"Meeting's at sunrise so we leave a couple of hours before then," I told him. "Tell no one that we're going, and follow my instructions. I don't want you stuffing this up for me."

Ace raised his hands before him. "I know how to play with others."

"Oh, I'm sure you know how to share and everything," I said, kicking the dirt with my shoe. "Judging from experience, that's a damn lie."

"Too fucking right it was." He smirked. "You have no alternative back-up, so it looks like you're stuck with me."

"I could get Zane or Fallon to come."

"The guy would annoy the shit out of you and the Princess is as bad as me when it comes to playing with others."

I bit my lip, looking away. "Fine, but stuff this up for me and I'll kill you."

"Note taken," Ace replied, though his chuckle as he strode away spoke volumes of whether he thought I was capable of such a thing.

————— ✦ —————

It was a couple of hours before sunrise when Ace and I slipped past the sleeping Potentials and downstairs. True to his word, Ace hadn't told anyone what we were doing today. I didn't want them to know that I was investigating something or have any reason to believe I wasn't here for the crown at the end. I'd already spilled too much to Fallon—the woman had a way of making me want to tell her everything I knew, every thought I had. As for Ace, not only did he know more than I wanted, but I had a feeling he gathered intel like it was second nature. I'd managed to keep my plans from Fallon, but I had given up on trying to dissuade Ace. If I'd left without him, he'd have just followed me. Unless I used my camouflage, but then I couldn't bring weapons ... or clothes.

"Where are you going?" one of the Potentials on guard asked as we stepped outside.

"Scouting," Ace said smoothly.

The Potential didn't bat an eyelid, just nodded and went back to what he'd been doing, which was blinking sleepily. Once we made it a safe distance from the keep, I took out the map and compass I'd stolen from Mark's leading lackey.

"Which way?" Ace asked, looking over my shoulder.

I looked from the map to the compass. "North."

We trekked through the dark, sticking close, and I held the sword I'd taken firmly in my hand. The monsters hunted primarily at night—especially the giant bats. Turned out the thing we'd found attacking Zane wasn't as common as the flying monstrosities. Right now, they were screeching, their shadows visible in the sky above.

"Hopefully they don't spot us," Ace said, his eyes trained to the sky.

"Stay quiet and just keep moving," I replied, turning and heading downhill.

The screeching grew louder above us, and I had the sickening feeling that we'd been spotted. I picked up my pace, seeing thicker growth ahead. If we could make it there, we'd be harder to see ... at least, that's what I hoped.

I ducked as the bat swooped towards me, causing me to stumble as it missed me by a mere inch.

"Run!" Ace shouted, gripping the arm of my jumpsuit and dragging me forward.

We bolted, sticks snapping and scratching into legs as we forced our way through the undergrowth. The bat dropped from the sky, then began jumping between the trees, its long claws tearing at the foliage and sending bark flying overhead. It bared its sharp fangs, the hair on its face speckled with blood from its last meal. Its beady red eyes glowed in the darkness as it screeched, launching to the tree in front of me.

I skidded to a stop and raised my sword, seeing Ace do the same. There was one thing that could be said about the guy, he didn't back down from a fight. Ace was lean, but he was somehow more intimidating than the biggest guys I'd ever seen. He had a presence about him and a look in his eyes that screamed bloody murder.

The bat may not have considered him a threat, but I was glad to have him on my side at that moment. The monster threw itself at us, almost felling the tree it was hanging from. I jumped out of its way but didn't stick around for another attack, swinging my sword and cutting into the thick membrane of its wing. A howl of pain blasted my ear as it turned on me, but that was its mistake because Ace took that moment to throw his sword and pierce the thing straight through the eyes. At least I thought he did.

It dropped to the ground with a thud and I found Ace opposite me, sword in hand and a frown on his face. I scrunched my brow in confusion. "How?"

"You can thank me later, bro," came a booming voice, and I turned to see Kayden striding closer to the bat. He pulled his sword—no wait, it was a spear—from the monster's skull, wiping the point on its furry head.

"What the fuck are you doing here?" Ace growled, pointing his sword at Kayden. The movement wasn't threatening, more like a maths teacher pointing to an equation on the board.

"Saving your ass," Kayden replied casually, though he stood still, his gaze focused on the tip of the blade that was precariously close to his chest. "Don't be ungrateful, Twiggy."

"That's rich coming from you," Ace said, raising his sword so that the tip rested below Kayden's chin. "You've been nothing but an ungrateful ass since stepping foot in the garrison. You'd be dead if it wasn't for us."

Kayden narrowed his eyes at Ace. "I'd think my debt was paid now. Don't you think?"

I didn't bother waiting around to witness the argument go further south, instead I took out the map and compass and continued to the meeting point. There was just over an hour until sunrise if my calculations were correct and I didn't want to waste my time with their constant posturing.

Adrenaline was coursing through me, not just from the fight, but from being so close to getting answers. The next piece of the puzzle was within my reach. I was so close to finding out what was happening to the missing people in Verdant Plateau.

"I'm coming, girls," I promised under my breath.

The sound of footsteps alerted me to Ace and Kayden's nearness, but I didn't slow. They were wasting my time.

"Noah!" Ace called. "Don't leave me with this blockhead!"

They caught up easily enough and walked on either side of me, like I was some kind of barrier between them. The meeting point was close now, we just had to cross part of the marsh and we'd be at a large section of flat, dry land.

"Are you two finished with your shit?" I asked, my boot sinking into the mud as I took my first step from the tree line.

"For now," Kayden replied, giving Ace a death glare. "Where are we headed?"

"You're not here to ask questions," Ace snapped. "You shouldn't be here at all."

Kayden shot him a crooked grin. "You have some serious anger issues, Twiggy."

"Fucking rich coming from you."

"Shut. Up!" I shouted, turning on them furiously. "I've had it up to here with your tantrums. If you two don't stop making jabs at each other, you can both go back to the garrison and neither of you will get to find out who's at the meeting point. Am I clear?"

Kayden and Ace exchanged a sheepish look before nodding, though neither looked pleased about having to make a truce.

"Good." I huffed, running a hand over my shaved head and straightening my jumpsuit. "Let's go."

We waded through the marsh waters until Ace found a cluster of reeds for us to hide in while we waited for the sun to come up.

"Noah, I don't think they'll show with no one there," Ace said quietly. "If I was them, I wouldn't fly down if the guy I was supposed to meet wasn't standing there waiting for me."

"You think I should go out there?"

"Who are you meeting?" Kayden asked, but we ignored him.

"Nope," Ace said. "I should go. You look nothing like Mark

and they'll know straight away something is up."

"You just want intel," I said, narrowing my gaze at Ace. "What are you playing at?"

Ace smiled darkly. "Maybe I do, but I'm your only option if you want them to land. You, on the other hand, have zero fucking chance. What's it gonna be cupcake?"

"He's got a point," Kayden said, surprising both Ace and me. We both looked at him, but he only shrugged. "I'm not Twiggy's biggest fan but I'm not an idiot either. His logic makes sense."

I clenched my jaw, deliberating. Apart from the hair colour, Ace and Mark did have similar builds. It was a big risk, given the hooded guy had met with Mark before, albeit in a dark room. We were banking a lot on the mystery guest not recognising him—and therefore Mark—but if Ace was successful, he'd get the answers I wanted. But what if he refused to give them to me once he had them?

I contemplated using my invisibility but I was exhausted and I wasn't sure I could hold it for very long. I'd get zero answers if I appeared out of thin air and scared whoever rocked up.

My choices were limited.

"Once whoever it is lands, you bring them to me to question," I said finally. "If they question where Mark is, you tell them he's dead and House Jupiter asked you to step in. It's a long shot, but it's worth a try."

"House Jupiter?" Kayden asked.

Ace didn't question it, nodding. "Done."

He strode towards the centre of the low island in the marsh, and we waited for the sun to rise. It didn't take long for the sky to begin turning orange. I stared at Ace's back, praying that he wouldn't screw me over. Soon the sound of helicopter blades whirling filled the air and I instinctively crouched lower. Kayden did the same at my side.

"Here we go," he whispered as the source of the sound came into view.

I started to worry our cover would be blown as the reeds were almost flattened by the wind, but whoever was piloting the helicopter must not have noticed. Ace had to turn away and cover his eyes with an arm as it landed nearby.

When I turned back, I noticed a drake was painted on the side of the helicopter. *Interesting.* Is that why Ace had insisted on coming? I cursed under my breath. I knew he was out for himself. Was he going to sabotage this whole thing for me?

I waited, holding my breath with my fists clenched at my sides as the helicopter blades slowed to a stop and the door opened. A hooded figure stepped out, took five steps, then waved Ace over. Ace didn't hesitate, walking over confidently. It all seemed to be going well until the hooded figure backed up slowly and pulled a gun on Ace.

Fuck.

Ace froze, raising his hands. Was he in danger or was this all for show? I could see his mouth moving but had no idea what was being said. I just hoped it was exactly what I'd told him to say and not him giving us up. I was tempted to run out there and get the answers for myself instead of waiting to see if Ace had betrayed us or not. I made to move, but Kayden gripped my arm.

"If you show yourself, your mystery person will shoot," Kayden said in a low voice. "They'll be on the helicopter in a blink and you'll never get the answers you seek."

"For all we know, this is all some show Ace and his Drakes planned," I gritted out, watching my only lead helplessly.

"Maybe," Kayden replied. "Or maybe not. Best bet is to get Ace alone either way."

"Fuck," I grumbled, hating that he was right.

A gunshot sounded, my heart racing as Ace fell to the ground and a flock of birds took to the skies. Kayden kept his grip firmly on my arm as the hooded figure ran back into the helicopter.

"We need to help him!" I shouted at Kayden, tearing my arm from his grip. Ace couldn't die, not before I got answers.

He launched himself on me, pinning me beneath his weight and almost shoving my head beneath the water. I struggled against his hold, but he was stronger than me, and there was nothing I could do to get him to ease his grip. What the fuck was Kayden playing at? I'd been so delusional to think that he was on our side, and yet here he was, trying to drown me. Were they working together?

Kayden shouted at me, but the sound of the helicopter propellers lifting it into the air blocked out his words. The aircraft flew away, taking all my hope with it. Finally, his grip eased and I launched myself at him, throwing a fist at his jaw for good measure.

"I just saved your life," he ground out, defending against my next attack. "They would have been searching for witnesses. Did you want to get shot too?"

I jumped to my feet, adrenaline pumping through my veins. Kayden and Ace had both sabotaged me, no matter what they said. I shook my head. Lesson damn well learned. I strode through the marsh, already saturated by the disgusting water, with Kayden close on my heels.

"He better not be dead," I snapped, seething. Ace had some serious explaining to do. Shot or not, I wanted answers.

By some miracle, Ace was already on his feet, storming back and forth when we reached him, blood trickling down the side of his head.

"What was that all about?" I asked, not bothering to check in on his well-being. If he was up and moving after a gunshot wound, then he was fine to answer my questions.

"He knew I wasn't Mark and tried to kill me, what do you think?!" Ace shouted, throwing his hands in the air.

"Did he say anything before he decided to murder you?" I asked, hands on my hips.

Ace shook his head then winced from the movement. "Nah, nothing of use. Our little chat was me trying to convince him not to put a bullet between my eyes."

"Did you see what he looked like? Was he a Drake? I saw your logo on the side of the helicopter."

"Logo," Ace scoffed. "We aren't a fucking corporation or sports team."

"Answer me."

Ace narrowed his eyes. "Didn't recognise his voice so, no, not a Drake. As for the helicopter, I don't know why this mystery guy had access to it."

"Not as high up in your gang as you thought," Kayden said, attracting an elbow to the side from Ace. Kayden laughed. "Tough break."

Ace strode towards me, his gait wobbly. He probably was fighting a concussion. "I don't know what's going on," he said, looking me dead in the eyes. "But I plan to find out."

# ZANE

"They said they were going scouting," the Potential said, looking between me and Fallon. "Were they not allowed to leave?"

"We don't run a dictatorship here. Everyone is free to come and go when they want," she said. "Thanks, Nick."

The Potential smiled then left us to it, and I spun Fallon around to face me. "How are you so calm when our friends have abandoned us?"

"They're not my friends."

"Hush, little one," I said, stroking her black hair like she was a cat. I was already feeling calmer, so it had to be working wonders on her. "We will endure their betrayal. Don't worry, I'm still here with you and I'll never leave."

Her lips quirked as she tilted her head, looking all kinds of cute. "I'm not worried."

"You don't need to put on a brave face with me," I told her. There could have been any reason for Ace, Noah, and Kayden to be gone, but my mind was diving into the deepest of oceans. With Victoria outright declaring her intentions to kill Fallon, I was already on edge and now that my three besties were gone,

"They've left us to form their own group," I said, whimpering.

Fallon smoothed the crease between my brow with her thumb. "Let's just wait and see, water boy. No jumping to conclusions. We should prepare ourselves for Victoria to attack though," she added, stepping back. "With our numbers down, waiting around could get us all killed. We are an easy target right now."

"You're presuming they're coming back," I said. "For all we know, they've allied with each other and left permanently."

"Kayden and Ace?" She laughed, her eyes twinkling. "Not a chance. Those two can barely stand being in the same room."

I sighed. It was sweet of Fallon to try and be positive for me. She was the clownfish to my sea anemone. "Maybe they discovered that they are truly meant to be the best of friends. It happens, you know. One minute you are enemies, then a defining moment happens and you're buddies for life." I groaned. "I missed their defining moment."

"No one had a defining moment," she said, planting a quick kiss on my lips. "Take a breath. I'm going to go check our defences and see what we can improve."

She strode away, off to organise the others. Fallon was born for leadership—strong, intelligent, and strategic, but also caring and considerate of those around her. She had a good heart and shined when she felt needed by those around her. I hoped she'd start to see that she needed others too, even though she liked to hide behind her independence.

It was a bit of a bummer she'd never become queen. She would have made a good one.

Everyone in the garrison was moving with purpose, erecting extra defences or sorting through weapons. My heart just wasn't in it. I still couldn't believe my new besties had up and left without telling me. I'd thought they were warming up to us all being friends, but maybe Fallon had a point about them being up to something sinister. It's like my aunt always said, you can never trust an orca at a seal's birthday party.

I scratched my chin. Is that how it went or was it a football game? My aunt always handed out her advice at family events when the alcohol was flowing. Anyway, the point was Ace and Kayden were orcas and poor Noah was a majestic seal. That realisation had dread pooling into my gut and I gasped aloud. Had they done something to him? Had they taken him hostage?

"Starfish!" I shouted, running down the stairs. "Starfish!"

"What?" she called, appearing at the bottom with wide eyes. "What's wrong? Is it Victoria?"

"We need to organise a rescue mission," I said as I came to stand before her. "They've taken the seal."

"Who?"

"Noah! Ace and Kayden have taken Noah!" I gripped her upper arms. "They must have kidnapped him and taken him to Victoria. That's the only rational explanation."

"Um, I'm not so sure," she replied, biting her lip, her body shaking with ... fear? Yep. Definitely fear. "How could they have kidnapped Noah without us knowing? He would have put up a fight and someone would have heard."

"Not if they knocked him out before he could," I countered. "Starfish, take this seriously, he is in trouble."

"I am taking it seriously," she said, nodding. "I just don't think it's possible. And why would Vic—"

I put my finger over her lush lips. "Save your tears. I'm going to organise a search party."

"For who?" another voice said.

I turned, dropping my finger from Fallon's face to see Kendra standing behind me.

"Noah," Fallon supplied, one brow raised.

"No need," Kendra said. "He and the other two were just spotted walking towards the garrison. Should be here any minute."

"They're back?" Fallon asked, already making her way outside with me following close behind. Was that a hint of relief in her voice? I knew she'd been as worried as me.

The sun beat down with a vengeance and, sure enough, Noah, Ace, and Kayden were striding towards us, looking like they'd been making mud pies all morning. I stood at Fallon's side, folding my arms over my chest as I waited. Looked like Noah wasn't kidnapped after all and they had gone on an adventure without me.

With. Out. Me.

"Where have you three been?" Fallon called out as they got closer.

"Went for a morning stroll," Kayden replied, stuffing his hands into the pockets of his jumpsuit and knocking the sword that was sheathed there. "Miss us?"

"Yes," I replied sulkily under my breath. At the same time, Fallon asked if they'd gone to see Victoria.

Kayden's lips tugged to one side as he looked me up and down. He made to step closer, but Fallon held out her hand, stopping him. He rolled his eyes. "Why would I go back there?"

"You tell me," she said, planting her hands on her hips.

"Noah had business to deal with." He shrugged. "If you're pissed, talk to him. I'm just the muscle."

I looked to Noah, but he kept his mouth shut. My slinky seal was keeping secrets.

"Before you ask, I have nothing to say and if I did, I wouldn't be telling you," Ace said, pushing past us, the dried blood on the side of his forehead making him look more menacing than usual. "Last I checked, you aren't queen yet, so quit being a bossy princess."

"*Yet.*" She smirked, then flipped her long hair in his face. "There are other people in this garrison. If your actions are putting them in jeopardy then we're going to be a problem," she replied. "I'm trying to keep us all safe."

Ace's chest rumbled. "No, you're trying to control everything, but reality check, we aren't your servants back in Stormcrest City so back the fuck off."

Kayden snickered as Ace stormed into the garrison, frightening a Potential who'd been standing near the door. "He is not your biggest fan."

"Feeling's mutual," Fallon grumbled. "Doesn't change the fact that he can't fly solo on a team. It's a recipe for failure."

"Fair point," he replied with a huff then turned to me. "What's the matter, Tadpole? You look like someone cracked your surfboard." Kayden laughed, slapping me on the shoulder as he strode after Ace, leaving us alone with Noah.

"Tadpoles are freshies!" I called to his back. I'd have to sit him down for a lesson on aquatic creatures. I was getting second-hand embarrassment every time he mixed up his references.

"Why didn't you tell us you were going?" I said to Noah. "I can't believe you asked those two to go on an adventure with you and not me. Low blow, dude."

"Technically I didn't tell anyone," he replied. "Ace did what he does best and Kayden followed us. If it were up to me I'd have gone alone."

"Oh, that's a relief." I sighed, putting a hand to my chest. "Wait, no it's not, because you still left without saying anything. Doesn't our friendship mean anything to you?"

"Friendship?" Noah asked, quirking a brow.

Fallon made a noise that sounded suspiciously like a laugh as she leaned against a wall, watching us with a small smile quirking her perfect lips. She mimed eating out of a box of popcorn. Everyone was out to get me today. That cut me deep.

I pouted at her, then Noah, until realisation hit and I barked a laugh. "Oh, I see what this is."

Noah looked between Fallon and me, the former shrugging. "Please, enlighten me."

I smiled brightly. "You're just playing it cool in front of Starfish." My voice dropped to a whisper. "But I know you were trying to protect me. That's what bros do, right?"

"Uh-huh, sure."

I launched myself at Noah, wrapping my arms tight around him. "I knew we were still besties."

Noah patted my back, trying to extricate himself from my love. "So, what happened here?"

"Starfish went into defensive mode after you all left," I replied, hugging him tighter and patting his back soothingly. "You'll soon learn all about her quirks."

"What's that supposed to mean?" she said, raising her brow.

"I think that's smart, considering we're in a trial," Noah said, carefully avoiding her question and saving me from trying to explain myself and most likely receiving some slaps. Such a good bestie.

"So why did you leave?" I asked, getting things back on track. "Now that you're back safe and sound."

"Not sure if Ace getting shot falls under the category of safe and sound," he replied.

I felt like an icy wave had crashed over my head. "Ace got shot?!"

Without waiting to hear Noah's confirmation I bolted inside to find my favourite grizzly bear. He needed me and I wouldn't let him down. Ace had saved me from that monster, like a knight in shining armour, and now I was going to be his protector. A little late, perhaps, but better late than never was the old saying. I found my little bundle of grumpiness on the second floor, leaning against the stone wall with a small red case in front of him. His brow was scrunched as he shoved around the contents like a racoon in a trash can.

I dropped to a crouch before him and searched his body, my hands grabbing at the fabric of the jumpsuit. "Where did you get shot?"

"Piss off," he growled, shoving me back and holding a bionic finger up. "Touch me like that again and I'll give you a demonstration of what I have hidden in this finger."

"Sounds like an incentive," I replied with one of my cheekiest grins.

Ace narrowed his eyes, pushing back his hair and revealing the dried blood on the side of his head. "It's just a graze, now go."

"Dude, chill," I said, moving to his side and sliding down beside him, taking the med kit from his lap before he could argue. "Let Zaney look after you."

"No fucking way," he grumbled, trying to take the kit back, but I held it out of his reach. "Give it back and find someone else to annoy."

"Ace," I said soothingly, smiling. "You're a crabby dude but how about you mellow for a couple of minutes and let me do my thing?"

"Leave me alone or I'll punch you in the fucking face."

"There are no mirrors in here. The quicker you let me do it the quicker you can go back to being the resident storm cloud."

I shuffled closer, only to dodge out of the way as Ace swung a fist at me. "Mellow," I said slowly, dragging the word out. "It will only sting for a second."

Ace muttered under his breath but didn't outwardly argue again or follow through with the threat of what was hidden in his metallic finger, so I got to work, finding some antiseptic wipes and a sticky bandage. The wound was close to his face and in the shaved part above his ear, but the longer strands from the top of his head were in the way. I gently brushed away his hair, being as careful as I could to not hurt him. It was a sweet moment if I do say so myself.

"Can you not do that?"

"Do what?" I asked, cleaning the blood from just above his ear. Ace hissed, glaring at me murderously.

"Did I hurt you?"

"No," he grumbled. "Don't be all soft and shit. Just clean and patch it already."

I smirked but didn't change my touch. Poor Ace was so hellbent on being the toughest dude to ever walk the planet that he was depriving himself of his basic human needs. I wished I had my power so I could help him more, but I guessed I'd have to rely on my top tier people skills to help heal his damaged soul behind the walls he'd built around himself.

Covertly, of course. There was no way he'd let me help him if he knew about it. Luckily, I was a sneaky sea snake. I'd slowly penetrate him and exude my healing vibes all over him before he knew what was happening.

"Can't believe you got shot in the head," I said, wiping the last of the blood. The graze wasn't too bad now that it was cleaned up. "Gnarly as."

"Are you finished yet?"

"Almost." I unwrapped the bandage then carefully applied it over the graze. "Okay, done."

"Finally," Ace grumbled, rising to his feet just as an alert sounded outside. We both exchanged a look. "What the fuck was that?"

# A SKY OF STORMS

# FALLON

Shouts rang out and the clamour of steel met my ears as I raced to the ramparts. Victoria's army was upon us, ready to rain hell on our people. I gritted my teeth, drawing my blade and conjuring my wings. We'd prepared for this, and we sure as shit weren't going down without a fight.

With a ruffle of my feathers, I took to the sky before speeding like a bullet towards the ground and knocking a cluster of Potentials into the trench we'd dug in front of the garrison. They screamed as they fell into the ditch and I saluted them with a wicked smile as our people surrounded them with swords and spears.

Scarlet was already splattered over the grassy hill and marsh. I clenched my fist tighter around my sword when I spotted some of our people being felled by swords and axes.

This wasn't a game. It wasn't a coup, a disagreement between parties, or a means of taking over new territory. Victoria and her people were out for blood. I smiled with closed lips. If she'd expected us to lie down and take it, she was dead wrong.

Adrenaline surged through me as I landed, jogging to a stop right before swinging my blade at a Potential cornering Kendra and another girl. The woman screamed as I nicked an artery in her thigh. She'd be dead within minutes.

Kendra nodded her thanks with wide eyes, turning her gaze on the other Potentials streaming up the hill and altering her stance. I noted she didn't have a weapon, probably because she had the strength of freaking sledgehammers for fists.

"Fall back," I yelled. "Get behind our defences. Use the ramparts for long range."

Bodies swarmed around me as our people came flooding in with Victoria's minions on their tails. I did my best to hold back the tide. We'd built a wall of spears closer to the garrison entry, with a narrow path heading through the middle. So long as we maintained our ground, they'd be vulnerable while having to squeeze through the pass and we could ambush them on the other side.

Victoria thought she was powerful because she controlled others through fear, but what she didn't realise was that there was strength in numbers—in working as a team. She'd never learned that fact, and one day it would get her killed.

I grunted as I blocked a blow from a huge unit, his eyes glimmering as he sneered behind his sword. The guy was freakishly strong and my guard was slipping at my chest, my blade dipping dangerously close. Sweat beaded on my forehead as my muscles barked in protest, and I was just about to lose it when Kendra shouted, coming out of nowhere to swing a fist into the guy's head.

My opponent toppled to the ground, felled instantly by her incredible strength. I blinked, looking between the mountain of a man and my friend. Kendra winked, smiling brightly before darting away to take down more Potentials.

I blew out a breath, running back to take care of anyone who'd snuck through. I hadn't felt so alive in a long time and my veins sang with the call of battle. I felt strong and ready to take down anyone standing in my way.

That was the thing about being caged—about being forced

to do things you didn't want to and not being able to act when you needed to. Treat an animal badly enough, it will become the very thing you fear. Well I was free of my bonds and it was time to bite back.

I snarled, narrowly escaping a thrust to my stomach and kicking the Potential hard enough so he was impaled on one of the spearheads. Someone else managed to slash my arm while I wasn't looking, and I grunted as I turned around. Thankfully it was just a flesh wound on my left arm. But I retaliated with a cry, kicking their feet out from beneath them and readying to pounce.

Ace stabbed them several times in the chest before I had the chance, and when he looked up it was with cold fury, a sort of predatorial gleam in his eyes.

Did he just save my ass?

He slipped back into the chaos without a word, his black hair pushed back and his tattooed skin slick with sweat.

Zane appeared at my side and fought like a born warrior, his blond hair gleaming in its top knot, the muscles in his arms flexing with each swing of his sword. Most of the Potentials were trained, but few moved with the grace and fluidity he did. Like he was parting the seas with his sword. A true tidal king.

"We need to circle around and corner them against the palisade," Zane commanded after chopping the arm off one of the Potentials. He didn't even blink, his green eyes hard and determined.

I nodded, smiling approvingly. It was a solid plan and might just give us the edge to win this thing before many more people were killed. I scanned the sea of bodies, searching for Kendra, Kayden, Ace, and Noah, while whistling to get their attention. Noah and Kendra were nowhere to be found, probably fighting by the steps leading into the garrison.

Ace scowled at me, no doubt wanting to punch my head in for being summoned, but he jogged over with Kayden regardless.

I relayed Zane's plan and we split up, slashing our way through to come to the back of Victoria's people. They turned in surprise as we advanced, the four of us smiling menacingly as we forced them to back up.

Their numbers were dwindling, and though we'd lost a few people, we had the advantage. "Press the attack," I shouted to the others. "Force them back!"

Kayden boomed a laugh, cracking his knuckles and rolling his neck as he strolled forward, smiling like this was the best day ever. The guy really needed a better hobby.

Ace jogged forward and lunged mid-air, embedding two knives into a dude's chest and slamming his back into the ground. He really was a brutal bastard. I swallowed, eyeing off the tattoos on his arms as his muscles flexed as well as the ass that jumpsuit fit like a glove.

"Eyes on the prize, Starfish," Zane said with a shit-eating-grin. I snarled, ducking a swipe at my neck and thrusting my sword into a Potential's chest.

The other enemy Potentials yelped and I smiled at them, letting my inner bitch come to the surface as we approached. "Yield, or become part of the furniture," I said, nodding to the deadly wall of spears behind them. "It's your choice."

They dropped their weapons quickly, holding their hands in the air. Zane and Kayden walked forward, kicking the backs of their knees so they fell to the ground with a thud.

I looked ahead to find the fighting was nearly over, and the knots in my stomach eased as I saw Kendra barking orders at the others and rounding up prisoners. She saw me and jogged over.

"We won," I breathed, running a hand through my braid.

"Of course we did, Starfish," Zane said triumphantly. "We snared them in our net and filleted those foolish fish."

I couldn't help but laugh as he pressed a quick kiss to my lips then whooped loudly, running along the hill to the cheers of other Potentials. It wouldn't surprise me if he stripped and decide to run naked again, not that I'd complain. The last time had given me much to ponder over.

I bit my lip, shoving that enticing image away as I scanned the grounds. Zane might be ready to celebrate, but a sick feeling in my gut told me something wasn't right. I looked over the heads of both our people and prisoners alike as I stormed across the grass, beginning to fear the worst.

"What's up your ass, Princess?" Ace said from where he leaned against the stone arch.

"Not that you give a shit, but Victoria isn't here." I sheathed my sword, putting my hands on my hips and trying not to let him see how worried I was. "Why would she send her army and not join the fight?"

He shrugged, his grey eyes raking over me, making me feel naked. "Isn't that what you Augers do? Make everyone else do the hard work while you watch from on high?"

"You're right, I had a great time watching everyone else defend our camp just now," I scoffed. "Clearly you don't know the first thing about Victoria. She wouldn't miss this. She revels in a fight and enjoys watching people suffer. Something's not right."

Zane caught my eye, his brow bunching as he trotted over, dragging Kayden along with him. "What is it, Starfish?"

"Victoria isn't here." I frowned. "Did we lose many people?"

"A few," Kendra replied. "But they lost more."

"Where's Noah?" Ace asked suddenly, pushing off the wall. "Have you seen him?"

Dread pooled in my stomach as I realised what was wrong. "She took him. Godsdammit, she fucking took him while we were fighting. We played right into her trap."

Kayden folded his arms, his brown eyes sharpening. "What would she want with Noah?"

"She knows," Kendra said, her lips twisting. "She must know he's been spying on her. Maybe the guy she was meeting got in contact with her, or maybe Noah wasn't as stealthy as he'd thought."

"Oh gods." I looked between the three guys and Kendra as guilt speared through my chest. "We need to get him back. Victoria is ruthless, there's no telling what she'll do to get information out of him."

Kayden huffed. "If that psycho woman has him, he's as good as dead."

My heart sank as I thought of my sister sinking her claws into Noah. She would torture him for pleasure, and then she would have her cronies dump his body and she'd wipe her hands of him. This was so much worse than I'd realised. Rigging the trials and smuggling in goods was one thing, but whatever Victoria was up to was clearly much bigger than the Terrulian Trials if she felt the need to silence anyone on her trail.

I couldn't let my sister get away with it. I felt responsible for the actions of my family and I wouldn't let them hurt Noah.

"Well, good luck with that," Ace muttered, his face carefully blank as he turned to walk away.

"Are you kidding me?" I gaped after him. "You're not helping? I thought you two were friends."

He shrugged. "Noah's a good guy, but I'm not about to go making friendship bracelets with him. This is a competition, Princess. There are no friends, only enemies. The sooner you realise that the better off you'll be."

"You fucking—"

"Let him go," Zane said, holding me back. "He's made his bed. Let him sleep in it. You and I will get Noah. What about you, Kaydikins?"

Kayden glowered, looking all kinds of murderous. "Don't call me Kaydikins. And the answer is no," he stated, gesturing at the frantic Potentials running around. "I'm staying here."

"I'm surprised you care about these people enough to stay," I retorted.

He laughed. "I don't, but I'm not stupid. There's safety in

numbers and a roof over my head. Why would I want to lose that?"

I pursed my lips as I studied his face. For someone so big and brutal, there was certainly a glimmer of softness in his eyes he couldn't hide. Something told me he was lying and that maybe, deep down under that tough exterior, a caramel centre was waiting for someone to take a bite.

Now wasn't the time to ponder that. Besides, there was no reason for him to jump ship. He hated Victoria after what she'd done.

"I'll watch him and Ace while you guys are away," Kendra said as the big guy strode off, barking at the prisoners as he went. Gods help them.

"Thanks," I said, hugging Kendra.

"Be safe," she replied, grinning as she pulled away. "Give that bitch hell."

"Okay," I breathed, looking at Zane. "We'll wait until nightfall, then we'll make our move when it's dark."

"I'm pumped," he said, rolling his shoulders. He clapped his hands, rubbing them together. "Rescue mission then orgy."

"Who said anything about an orgy?"

Zane rolled his eyes. "Noah is gonna want to repay our kindness. Obviously."

I snorted, swatting his arm. "Zane, not everyone wants a piece of your fish pie, okay?"

He looked genuinely affronted, but then he smiled slyly. "You do though. Don't try to deny it."

I smirked. "Maybe. I might reward you later if you're a good boy."

"Oh, Starfish." He chuckled, running his gaze over my curves and licking his lips. "You don't want a good boy. And when this shit dies down, I'm going to prove exactly why."

Heat rolled through me at his dark promise and I had to stop myself from shivering at the thought of him dominating me in every way. Gods, we'd been fucked with at every turn during this trial and I was so ready to make the fucking be on my own terms.

With so many people around and having to share quarters with the boulder, the Drake, and Noah, it had been impossible to find some quiet time to get to know Zane more … intimately.

I gave him a slow once-over to let him know I had no problem with that and shook my head, forcing myself to remain on task. I turned to assess the damage instead. Most Potentials had minor scratches and bruises, but a few were sporting some serious wounds that needed attention.

Kendra was already tending to some, but I flew up to the ramparts to quickly grab some extra bandages and solution to clean and wrap wounds. Then, flapping back down, I distributed them among the more medically-minded individuals.

"What are we going to do about the prisoners?" Kayden mumbled to Ace.

"Gut 'em," Ace growled. "Leave them for the monsters."

"Hmm, or we can tie them up so the monsters can feast on them while they're still breathing."

I couldn't help but chuckle under my breath. I didn't think they'd really do it—though knowing Ace, it was very possible—even so, it was a little satisfying to see these people quiver with fear. They'd attacked us after all. Even if it was under Victoria's orders, they weren't much better than mindless sheep.

Ace drew his knife, twisting it faster and faster as he considered. "We'll keep them under watch until the trial ends."

"And let them eat our food and use our med supplies?" Kayden scoffed. "No way."

"Don't think I haven't noticed you hoarding extra supplies," Ace said, smirking. "Or having your little cheerleaders doing it for you. Your hiding spot under your blanket isn't so inconspicuous when it's a mountain high."

"I am not hoarding anything," Kayden said indignantly.

"And it's not my fault I have minions who worship me just for existing."

Ace barked a laugh and my jaw dropped at the alien sound coming from his lips. Even Kayden blinked, looking lost for words at the noise. Ace immediately scowled, storming off before Kayden could say anything.

"Did he just…" Kayden said under his breath, then walked away, scratching his head as though unsure what to do with that information.

I was inclined to agree.

"Fallon," Zane called. "You'd better come look at this."

I ran over to find a hawk perched on Zane's arm, which Zane was beaming about. "It came out of nowhere and landed right on me," he said excitedly. "It's got a note."

"Hello," I said gently to the creature. I stroked the bird's brown head tentatively, cautious it might bite me, but it just ruffled its feathers impatiently and pinned me with one eye. "Err … you want me to grab the note?"

It bobbed its head and I reached out, untying the message carefully. I swallowed my trepidation, reading the contents quickly.

"What does it say?" Zane asked impatiently.

"Nothing good." I took a breath, reading the words several times over before opening my mouth and relaying it to him.

*On the final day of the trial, follow the beacon to true glory. But be warned, those without a key cannot pass the gate. Redemption lies in gold, and death awaits all who fail to purchase their freedom.*

The hawk squawked and then took to the skies. I gritted my teeth. When I got out of here, I was going to strangle that Overseer. We'd overcome all obstacles, only to face a final hurdle at the end.

I was beginning to think surprises like these would be a

running theme at the academy.

Whatever we had to face at this beacon, it couldn't be good. There was no way in hell we would all survive this—they'd made the threat clear enough in the message.

Gold.

Gold was the answer to our freedom and I would damn well make sure I'd get it. Zane and Kendra, too, if I could manage it.

But at the end of the day, this was life or death. As much as he was a bastard, Ace had a point when he mentioned there were no friends in competitions like these. Anyone who stood in my way of becoming queen was my enemy. Anyone who prevented me from getting that gold and getting out of here was no friend.

I had a job to do. So where did the line blur in a trial like this? At what point could I forget my humanity and look out only for number one?

I didn't know if I could. And maybe that was stupid, but I couldn't turn my back on Kendra and Zane. For the first time, I'd found others who I could imagine myself coming to care for deeply. People who were kind and brave and loyal and wanted to see change in this world just like I did.

If they needed me I'd be there, just like Zane and I would be for Noah. I wasn't going to let my family hurt anyone else.

We had two days to rescue Noah, get the gold, and get the fuck out of here.

Or die trying.

# NOAH

I gritted my teeth. My ribs screamed as I hunched on the floor and tried to calm the twisting pain and anger coiling within. Victoria Auger and her lackeys didn't play by the rules and they certainly didn't play fair. Her minions had grabbed me back at the garrison and teamed up to overpower me before shoving a gag in my mouth, a bag over my head, and tying my wrists behind my back. I'd been stupid enough to be lured away from the others and I'd put up a damn good fight, but four against one, not to mention the pulse gun they shoved in my face, had me quickly on my knees with a couple of broken ribs and a smashed nose.

They'd dragged me from my garrison before dropping me here—wherever that was—earning me a couple of extra bruises and a whole lot of pain. Broken ribs combined with being dragged through marshes was not ideal in the least. Not that they cared.

I hated that my power was blocked. Not being able to use my restorative power to heal myself was infuriating. I'd never felt so weak in my life and if I didn't have the stupid chip in my arm, they'd never have been able to capture me.

Victoria may have me tied up, but she wouldn't have gone to the effort unless she wanted something from me. That's what kept me going. She hadn't won because I still had something she wanted and I was *never* going to give it to her.

"Noah Hawthorn," Victoria purred, pulling off my hood and crouching beside me.

I blinked, looking at my surroundings. It looked exactly like the garrison we'd come from. Same stone walls, same supply crates. It must have been the one she'd stolen from Kayden.

I cursed at her through the gag, cracking my forehead against hers. She swore viciously, and her cronies kicked me in the ribs. Repeatedly. My vision blurred and I hung my head, pressing my forehead to the floor as I waited for it to pass. If it weren't for the adrenaline coursing through me, I'd have gone into shock and probably thrown up all over the place.

"As I was saying," she continued, a little further back now. Blood trickled from her forehead and the sight made me smile. She still saw me as a threat, even with my hands bound. "This is how our little meeting is going to go. You're going to tell me everything you know about Mark Leroy and his business dealings, then you are going to tell me everything you have learnt about Fallon. Your death can either be quick and painless or slow and agonising. If you don't tell me anything, I'll tie you up and dump you in the marshes for the monsters to tear you apart. Got it?"

One of the Potentials pulled the gag from my mouth, and I swallowed, wetting my dry mouth and tasting blood.

"Sounds like a terrible offer, so you can understand why I must politely decline," I told her, earning a punch to the jaw.

"Don't make this harder than it has to be," she hissed.

"Wouldn't dream of it," I spat. She flicked her hand lazily and suddenly I was dragged back by the shoulders and slammed hard into the wall. I groaned, my arms barking and my ribs smarting at the impact with the stone. Yeah, I could definitely use my power right about now.

One of Victoria's lackeys brought a chair over and she sat down in front of me, her position forcing me to look up at her cold-hearted face. Her copper eyes glinted dangerously and the smirk on her face showed how much she delighted in having power over people.

She was such a contrast to her sister. In my short time of observing both I'd concluded that Fallon used her power to help people. Victoria used it to instil fear and punishment. The Auger family was well known in Terrulia thanks to being one of—if not *the*—wealthiest families in existence. They mined and sold energy crystals and were influential beyond belief. From what my mums have said, Victrus and Eliana were ruthless business people. If Victoria's actions were anything to go by, I'd have to say that ruthless was too kind a word. But Fallon … there was definitely more to her than meets the eye. She seemed genuine, caring, and kind—beautiful, inside and out. An image popped into my head of her lips when she smiled, and the sparkle in her eyes when she was teasing. I cocked my head. *Interesting.* Elevated heart rate, rising temperature, a surge of jealousy if my instincts were correct. Not ideal during a torture session, but then again I was only a rookie at these sorts of things.

"Why were you and your little friends in the meeting spot instead of Mark?" Victoria asked, leaning forward in her chair with her hands on her knees. Even after nearly a month in the marshlands, her nails were near perfect and her blond hair was coiled neatly in a bun on her head. She was flanked by two Potentials and a third stood by the door, pulse gun in hand directed at me.

I held her hateful gaze, refusing to say a word.

"Why are you making this so hard for yourself? You're going to be dead soon. I could make it quick and painless. Why drag the process out?"

"Maybe because I give a shit about other people, not just myself."

"That's not the answer I was looking for," she replied with a pout.

Victoria flicked her wrist and the Potential on her left

pounced towards me. I turned my shoulder, aiming to block the blow, only to have excruciating pain burn through my foot. I bit my lip, drawing blood as I clamped my mouth shut. It had been a fake attack that had left me open for the other Potential to shatter the bones in my foot with their bat. My heart rate kicked up and I kept my eyes from my foot, refusing to look at the damage.

"Let's try again. Tell me why you were there instead of Mark," Victoria said calmly.

"Mark was busy. He asked me to go for him," I lied through gritted teeth. Might as well try and get some information out of her while I was here. Despite her saying I'd die here, there was still a chance I would survive. I'd fight with everything I had.

"I know you weren't working together. Mark hates the Hawthorn family and I share the sentiment." She sneered. "So much wasted potential, it's disgusting."

"That was a ruse. Another layer to keep our business under wraps," I said. "How else do you think he had access to all the stuff he was selling?"

Victoria tapped her chin. "Where is he then?"

I raised my chin, letting a smile grace my lips. "I believe he had a run-in with your sister. I assume you're smart enough to know how that turned out."

She narrowed her eyes. "That bitch has always been a thorn in my side. She isn't worthy of the Auger name."

"I agree with you on that," I replied with a huff that had pain shooting through my chest. To be worthy of the Auger name was to be evil and Fallon was far from it. I didn't voice that part aloud though. "I had to get close to her, especially after she murdered my business partner."

Victoria started laughing, the sound hollow as it reverberated around the room. "You're a poor liar, Hawthorn. I've seen you looking at my sister like a lost puppy since we arrived at the House of Ascension. It's pathetic, really. She's manipulating you; don't you see? And you're blinded by, what, her pretty smile? Or has she just fucked you into submission?"

Heat rose within me at her words. How could someone speak of their family that way? My family meant everything to me and my community as a whole was the reason I was in this trial in the first place. I didn't want to rule Terrulia. I had no interest in power. Victoria's greed and animosity towards her family, even her people, was so foreign to me.

"I can see you're not going to tell me the truth about Mark," she said, steepling her fingers. "Perhaps you'll be more accommodating about why you were at the meeting spot with Kayden Hale and Atticus Warner?"

I raised a brow. Ace's name was Atticus? I locked that one away and clamped my lips tighter together. At first Ace had said he wanted to be back-up, but he didn't do anything without something in return and, judging by the Drake's emblem on that helicopter, there was definitely more going on than he'd said. Even if he'd told me he didn't know about the Drakes being involved, I'd be stupid to fully trust him. As for Kayden's help, I didn't have a clue. He may have given an excuse, but I didn't believe him either.

"Has Atticus betrayed his Drakes?" she pushed. "I'm sure Cormac would be very displeased to hear one of his members is working with the enemy."

Was she telling me that Ace actually knew about the Drakes' involvement in all of this? Were Victoria and Ace working together?

"Pity," Victoria sighed, when I didn't answer. She leaned back in her seat and both of the Potentials by her side moved towards me.

They swung their fists in unison, which left me only one option. I curled in on myself as best I could to protect my head and as much of my body as possible. It was a feeble attempt— each blow brought another bruise or broken bone. Agony fired through my body with every hit, but I refused to cry out. I wouldn't give Victoria the satisfaction. When they were finished, I hadn't the strength or desire to move from where I lay on my side.

"Lift him up," Victoria ordered, and I was hauled back into a sitting position. She looked me in the eye, the hard set of her jaw betraying her anger. "Talk now or I will have them cutting off body parts. And believe me, these things will be missed," she said, eyeing my crotch with a wicked smile. "Now, what do you know about Mark?"

I kept my mouth shut. I'd known Mark had been involved in some really bad shit, and I'd felt disappointed about what had happened with the meet-up that morning. Victoria's reaction to finding out I was on Mark's trail was a balm to that. Yes, I was being tortured for information, but she was unwittingly giving me what I'd been searching for.

If what I'd gleaned so far was correct, Mark was in the slave trade business and it appeared Victoria was in deep as well. The Drakes seemed to have a stake in it too. Were the people of Verdant Plateau being sold to the corporations in Stormcrest City and Damascon Hollow?

Did Fallon know and was simply acting like she didn't?

"Noah, Noah, Noah," Victoria sang, stepping closer and crouching before me. She held a knife in her hand, the blade swinging with each mention of my name. "Looks like you need some time to think."

She lifted the knife, slamming it down into my thigh. I screamed, the pain blinding as she twisted the blade with a wicked grin on her face.

"Hopefully that will help to loosen your tongue."

"Fuck you," I growled.

Victoria slapped me on the face then stood. "I'll be back soon to continue our little chat. You'd better have something to say."

"I won't talk."

She leaned on my injured leg, clamping her hand around the

knife embedded there and twisting it more. Pain fired through me and I cried out, slumping further on the ground. "Oh, you'll talk, Hawthorn. You'll fucking squeal when I'm done with you. I know you have information on Mark's business dealings. I know you have access to Fallon, Kayden, Atticus, and Zane, all of whom pose a threat to something greater than you could ever imagine."

Maybe it was the delirium from the pain, or maybe I had a death wish, but I laughed, spitting a wad of blood in her face. "You're insane if you think I'm going to give you information."

"And that's the kicker," she said, smiling coldly, the blood on her cheeks making her appear psychotic. "While information is high on my list, it's not the only reason you're here. My sweet sister has a saviour streak and a desperate need to protect people. Fallon will come for you, Hawthorn, so rest assured, you win nothing by keeping your mouth shut. When my wretched sister comes, I'll have another kill to add to my count. So rest while you can, knowing I'm victorious either way."

A cold chill ran over my body and I curled up, nearly passing out from pain. Victoria left with the two Potentials, leaving me alone with the guy holding a pulse gun and the very real threat that I would not survive till morning—or Fallon either.

# FALLON

Zane and I crept through the marsh on silent feet, using the cover of trees as much as possible to hide us from monsters and stray Potentials. The moon was hidden behind clouds tonight, giving us the advantage to slink like shadows through the night.

I had hoped Noah would return to the garrison before nightfall—that he'd escape Victoria's clutches and show up unscathed—but that had been a fool's wish. Of course, that would be too easy and, when it came to my sister, nothing ever was.

Zane grabbed my hand, putting a finger to his lips, and we froze as a few giant bats passed overhead, their screeches echoing across the expanse of the water. His fingers were warm as they slipped between mine, and I leaned into his touch as we waited.

I hated this place. Hated the creatures, hated traipsing through the water, and the stink … oh, don't get me started. The bog-like smell clung to my skin and hair, making me feel constantly dirty. What I wouldn't do for a hot shower and some freaking soap. Maybe a burger and some fries too.

We'd been living off rations and whatever wildlife we'd managed to hunt and I, for one, was over it. Even the junk food wasn't hitting right anymore. Most of my chocolate stash had melted, and any sweets had turned to jelly with the hot summer days. It was a crime. There had been tears on one occasion.

Zane leaned in, tucking a stray piece of hair behind my ear. "Coast is clear. We'll need to make a run for it to the next tree line. Ready?"

I grinned, leaning in to whisper, "Last one there goes down on the other." Then sprinted away.

An excited noise that sounded a little like a dolphin followed me and I laughed under my breath as he barrelled along beside me, a smug grin on his face that said he knew he'd win.

I was fast, but damn, Zane had some speed on him. I conjured my wings, speeding to the finish line, and hovered gracefully while shooting him my most innocent smile.

"You cheated, Starfish," he growled, coming to a stop and tugging me into his arms. "You'll have to be punished for that."

His hands slid down my waist to cup my ass, and he turned us, slamming me into a tree and kissing me hard, his lips bruising and his tongue circling against mine. He tasted like gummy bears, utterly addictive and driving me mad.

Zane leaned against me and I moaned as his incredible length pressed against my clit, making me wild with need. He pressed kisses down my neck, his teeth grazing the sensitive skin above my collar bone before he grabbed the zipper with his teeth and unravelled it ever so slowly. I bucked as he took my breast in his mouth, licking through my bra and rubbing against me so much that I was panting as I rolled my head back.

"I'm a generous guy," he said, leaning back and capturing me, his eyes glimmering with hunger. "You'll get your prize. I want you to sit on my face and fuck my mouth when we're out of here," he breathed, claiming my other nipple with his tongue. "And when we win this trial, I am going to make you cum so hard you see stars."

"Yes," I breathed. "Not later. Now."

I wrapped my legs around him and shivered as he put his hand down my pants, circling my clit lazily. "Oh baby," he said with a smile. "You're soaked for me."

I ground against his hand, groaning and hurting with anticipation. I needed release, needed to feel him inside me, but he pulled back, his lips twisting into a smile.

"Zane," I growled, feeling frustrated with his endless teasing.

"Uh-uh, Starfish," he said with a broad smile. "That's your punishment. Only good girls get their rewards. You'll have to wait."

I scowled as he set me down on the ground. "Are you freaking kidding me?"

He winked, his gorgeous face alight with amusement. "We've got a job to do. Get your head in the game, sweetheart. We can finish this later."

Oh gods. He was such a tease, and I freaking loved it. I supposed I kinda deserved it, but the endless back and forth without ever getting the goods was giving me whiplash.

He was right though, now wasn't the time. My sister had captured Noah and was most likely hurting him too. I didn't fully trust him yet, but so far, he'd proven a good asset and a reliable ally. He didn't deserve Victoria's brutality. No one did.

I huffed, staring at Zane's ass as we stalked towards the garrison looming into view. Fine, if I had to wait, I would, and next time it would be on my terms ... though if he meant what he said I certainly wouldn't be turning down his offer.

He was so hot. I would savour him like the last square in a block of chocolate, and there would be no holding back.

"Starfish," Zane whispered, jerking me from my fantasies and ushering me forward. "Look."

The garrison lay just ahead. There weren't as many Potentials guarding it, given we'd captured several of Victoria's people, but the place was lit up like a Christmas tree with the amount of torches staked around the grounds.

"It will be difficult to get in unseen," I said with a frown. "But I might be able to manage it if we fly up?"

Zane looked at me uncertainly. "Are you sure you can carry me?"

"Nope. But there's no way in hell Victoria would be keeping Noah on the ground floor. We'd either need to sneak past the guards and everyone inside or take them out directly."

"It's risky either way," Zane agreed, scratching the stubble on his chin. "Let's go with option one, but be warned, Starfish, heights aren't my thing."

I smirked. "I promise I won't drop you, but let's get a closer look first, see if the guards patrol or stay stationary."

He nodded, slapping my ass as we crouched low and scampered through the trees. I bit back my surprise and smiled, shaking my head. Only Zane could make me grin when we were about to walk into the devil's dungeon. We could die trying to save Noah, but I wasn't afraid. My body hummed with energy and anticipation. It felt good to do the right thing, to help save someone from my family's clutches for a change.

"We're coming, Noah," I whispered in a quiet promise.

The guards had a predictable patrol. They walked the same path once every five minutes, which gave me ample time to fly up and duck into the entry on the top floor where Noah would most likely be. Victoria might be expecting me to fly up, but I just had to hope she was preoccupied with other matters and wasn't in the middle of interrogating him.

The question was how to get down? Going through the garrison meant we'd for sure come across other Potentials. Noah could be injured, which meant we'd be vulnerable if we had to support him. I told Zane as much, and he sucked on his lip while he thought.

"What if we found some rope?" he asked. "You could fly him down and I'll rappel."

I nodded. "That will work if you can find some. And if not…"

"Then we'll take them out quietly," Zane finished, his face grim. "I'm all for second chances here, but these people knew what they signed up for. We're doing what we must to get him back Starfish."

I sucked in a breath. It's not like we both hadn't taken lives today. We were survivors, and Zane was right. We'd do what was needed to get through these trials. But even so, I didn't feel right about killing someone like that. In a fair fight, I'm game, but this felt cowardly.

*Eyes on the prize. Get in, get out, get the job done.*

"You've got this," Zane said, tugging on the front of my jumpsuit with a smile. "Ready?"

I nodded. "Ready."

My wings burst from my back, and I wrapped my arms tightly around him, cradling his ass as he circled my calves with his legs. It wasn't ideal, but I wasn't strong enough to carry him like a baby, and my wings were powerful enough to compensate for the imbalance of weight in front.

"It's a good thing … you're not … super muscled and all," I huffed, hefting him up more comfortably and waiting for the prime moment to fly.

Zane nuzzled into my neck. "Could be worse," he said. "I could be Kayden."

I could only grunt in reply, taking off just as the Potentials were both standing at the edge of the ramparts, overlooking the grounds. I had around twenty seconds to get us in that door, or it was all over.

Sweat beaded on my temple as my arms quivered beneath Zane's weight. My wings flapped furiously as I soared towards our goal. The Potentials below were facing the other way, so I had timed it perfectly.

One of the guards on the ramparts started turning early, and my heart jumped into my throat as I forced more power into my wings. Shit, shit, shit! I swooped into the room in the nick of time, skidding along the floor and somehow managing not to crash into a stack of crates in the corner.

I knelt double, panting for a moment to catch my breath. No one was in this room, thank fuck, but I had to hope Noah was nearby and that the guards hadn't heard us. Zane slipped into a crouch, drawing a knife from his pocket. I slid mine from my boot as well.

Warily, we approached the doorway to the next room, and Zane ducked his head through. "Clear," he mouthed, gesturing for me to get behind him.

We stalked through, my heart pumping so loud I wondered if it would alert anyone to our presence. Panic fluttered in my chest. If Noah wasn't in the next room, so help me…

I almost cried out when I caught a glimpse of a body on the floor, blood splashed over the ground. It took everything in me not to dart forward, forcing myself to be cautious in case we gave ourselves away.

When it was clear he was unguarded, I bolted in and dropped to my knees. "Noah," I whispered, feeling suspiciously emotional as I looked at his crumpled body. He'd been beaten brutally, his gorgeous face near unrecognisable. One eye was swollen so badly it was closed and his nose appeared to be broken. His cheeks and lips were an ugly purple-yellow, and his jumpsuit was wet with blood on his thigh.

If we didn't get him patched up, he'd be in serious trouble. I swore under my breath, running to a threadbare blanket in the corner and tearing a strip up to wrap around his leg. He winced, whimpering slightly in his sleep as I bound the wound, tightening it to stop the blood flow.

His breathing was shallow, which meant he probably had a few broken ribs. I just had to hope he had no internal bleeding and that his organs were okay. Fuck. My vision went red, rage overcoming all else as I thought of the person responsible for this mess.

I was finding more and more reasons to destroy Victoria. Family bonds only went so far and dammit I had tried so fucking hard for too long to make up excuses for her. To pretend it was because our parents had made her this way. Maybe that was partially true, but the real honest truth was that she was in full control of her actions.

She had done this of her own agenda, and I knew she'd enjoyed it.

"Noah, man, you gotta get up," Zane said softly. "It's Zane and Fallon, we're here to rescue you."

Noah didn't answer and my stomach tied in knots as Zane continued to try and rouse him. Zane looked at me hopelessly, and I swallowed. "Noah," I tried. "Wake up. We're getting you out of here."

He cracked an eyelid, his one good brown eye widening in surprise. "You came," he breathed, reaching out to stroke my cheek. Then he seemed to realise his situation, his voice becoming gravelly. "Wait, you shouldn't have. You need to leave. Go!"

"I—"

Shouts sounded from the stairs and outside. I stiffened, looking at Zane fearfully.

"Get him out, Starfish," he ordered. "I'll buy you some time."

"No." I shook my head, refusing for this to play out. He was not going to be some freaking hero while we ran with our tails between our legs. Not today. "No fucking way am I letting you stay behind. We're all going, and I don't care what it takes."

He opened his mouth to argue, but at the sharp look I gave him, he must have thought better of it because he nodded and got to his feet. "You take the ramparts. I've got the stairs."

I turned, tightening my hold on my knife as one guy came running in, roaring as he charged. I slipped beneath his guard and ran at him with all my strength, wrapping my arms around him and taking to the sky. He screamed as I flapped mid-air, shoving him off me so he fell to his death.

Fuck this. I was so done with being attacked and having to fight off these assholes. I missed my magic. If I had access to my telekinesis, things would be so much easier. I could control the situation, use my surroundings, but the block on my power was like a wall I couldn't crumble.

So here I was, flinging people from freaking rooftops and swinging swords. I just wanted it to be over.

I zoomed back to the rampart, landing in front of the guard who was standing like a stunned mullet—*ugh, Zane, he was rubbing off on me too hard.* The guard looked at me with hatred swirling in his dark gaze. "You fucking bitch," he spat. "You're going to pay for that."

"You're probably right," I said, lowering into a crouch. "Guess I'll see you in hell."

He roared, slashing at me like a madman, but his form sucked balls and he clearly had no skill with a sword, so I punched his armpit and finished by angling my blade into his heart. His eyes widened, mouth opening and closing, but no sound came out before I removed the knife and kicked him over the edge.

There went my plan to get Noah out quietly with no casualties. Death and misery followed me everywhere. Why would it stop now?

The sound of scuffling greeted my ears, and a cry made me rush back into the building.

"Zane!"

He was fending off two Potentials, his sword locked with one while the other came up to stab him in the back. Nope. Not on my watch.

I lunged, stabbing him in his side at the last second. Blood spilled over my hand, warm and sticky, and I shoved the guy away from me. Zane finished his opponent off with a savage thrust of his sword, and I looked at his blood-flecked face.

He was breathing heavily, his eyes wild, but he seemed to be unhurt. I sighed in relief. "We need to get out of here. Now."

He nodded. I grabbed Noah as gently as possible and bundled him into my arms. I don't know how I found the strength, but I managed to carry him easier, putting all my weight on my back foot. Noah was muscly, but he was slimmer than Zane, so I'd manage.

I turned towards the ramparts, but a feminine voice curled into my ear, making my blood run cold. "Going so soon? But I was just getting started. Don't you want to stay and join the party?"

The thing with villains is they always like to talk. And the heroine *always* indulges them. Well, I had no interest in standing around and listening to that viper spit her venom. Victoria wouldn't have much to gloat about when we escaped. I'd deal with her later, one on one, like it was always meant to be.

I ran to the ramparts, seizing my chance to fly while I still could.

Victoria shrieked in anger, and I heard the pounding of her boots as she ran after me. Fuck, if she caught me in the sky, I'd be a goner. With Noah in my arms, I had no way to defend myself, and I was slow with the extra weight, my wings beating double time.

A bellow reached my ears, and I turned to find Victoria's arm outstretched, her wings sprouting to follow me, but I was more focused on the blond warrior behind her.

Zane jumped—freaking jumped into the air—latching onto her back with one hand on her shoulder, the other slashing a knife through one wing. She screamed in pain and they spiralled down. My heart just about exploded as they tumbled, but at the last second, she managed a few feeble beats of her wings, stopping them from crashing to their deaths.

He whooped loudly, jumping off her and sprinting into the trees. I bellowed my own victory cry, flapping to meet him before my wings gave out. We'd done it. Somehow, some-fucking-how, we'd escaped. I caught up to Zane, who took Noah carefully.

We turned to face the rising sun. Dawn was coming, which meant it was the last day of the first trial.

A final hurdle awaited, and I glanced at Zane and Noah with worry clouding my heart. We were so close, but with Noah in tow, we'd be lucky to make it at all.

Time was running out, and if the sand stopped falling before we found the gold, well…

Only the gods knew what awaited us.

# A SKY OF STORMS

# ACE

I strode through the mud and cracked my knuckles, with my head a mess of unanswered questions. I knew the Drakes were up to some shady shit, but I'd been kept completely in the dark. People disappeared all the time in DH, so it was nothing to write home to your mother about. After what I'd seen during this trial, I was starting to think there was more to it.

The helicopter had been one of ours. I'd ridden in it more times than I could count and would have recognised it even without our emblem on the side.

There were bigger players in this game than Mark Leroy. The guy had been doing grunt work, which was fucking evident when a bullet grazed my head. The asshole who shot me? I had no fucking idea who that was, and it left a bad taste in my mouth. Who the fuck was Cormac in bed with and why hadn't he let me in on the plan?

I'd trusted Cormac to keep me in the loop on the gang's movements, but I'd been a fucking idiot. And now he wanted the House Jupiter ring?

Fuck that. If he wanted me to finish this job and steal the ring, then he'd have to give me answers first.

And then there was Noah. He was suspicious of me even

after I'd told him I had no idea what the Drakes' involvement was. I'd taken a fucking bullet for him out there. I could have stood by and let him try to meet the hooded guy, but no, I went and got a nice bullet graze as a thank you. I don't know why I fucking cared whether he believed me or not. We weren't friends. None of us were.

I reached the drop, mud slicking up my thighs as I looked down at the giant crater in the ground. Water spilled over the edge, falling to the foggy marsh below. Not that I could see much with the fog obscuring most of the centre, leaving an outer rim of foul water and mud with shit floating in it. I lifted my elbow to cover my nose from the disgusting smell coming from the place. It was where things came to die. On either side of me, other Potentials were standing around the perimeter, staring into the crater, and not one of them looked stoked about going down there.

A roar rumbled overhead and I looked up to see a huge shadow rippling through the clouds and flying off into the distance. Great, just what I needed, another monster to add to the collection. A chill ran down my spine at the thought of that thing flying down from the sky, but I used it to solidify my resolve. I should have died more times than I could count. This would just be another on that list.

"That thing better not come back," Kayden commented beside me, glaring at the sky.

Both Kayden and Kendra stuck with me when I'd started to follow the beacon, the former occasionally making obnoxious comments that I ignored. The three of us may have walked here together, but we were each other's competition. Nothing that had happened in the last few weeks would change that and frankly, that's how I wanted it. Kendra was alright, but Kayden... I'd been tempted more than once to slit his throat and be done with his shit, but the threat of monsters had made me hesitate. I needed to come out of the trial alive and if enduring the brick head's

340

bullshit kept me from dying then so fucking be it.

I focused on the crater before me instead of the asshole at my side. There was very little light thanks to the clouds and fog surrounding the place, making it look like something out of a gothic horror movie. Movies like that just so happened to be my favourite.

"Come on, you two," Kayden said, slapping me on the shoulder. He strode forward and smashed right into the invisible force field, causing a wave of sparkling dots to dart across the air in front of us. "What the fuck?"

A laugh burst from my lips as he skulked back over, rubbing his nose. Nothing beat watching that shit-for-brains do something stupid.

"Not funny, bro," Kayden grumbled.

"It totally was," Kendra replied, not bothering to hide her laughter either.

The guy was so impatient, always demanding something as soon as he wanted it. Thinking like that would get him into a shitload of trouble.

The Overseer obviously wanted us to start at a certain time. Part of me—a microscopic speck—wondered whether Zane, Noah, and the Princess would make it here for kick-off. It's not like I cared if Noah was okay, or if the other two succeeded. It was only so I had an idea of what I was going up against. Keep your enemies close and all that.

"More survived than I expected," Kendra commented.

I turned to see where she was looking and sure enough, more Potentials began arriving. Some were from our garrison, but there were others too. Everyone looked like shit warmed up, and that was putting it nicely. The month had not been easy and judging by the number of Potentials sporting fresh injuries, the trek here hadn't been a walk in the park either.

It was a mystery to me why most of these people were here. What had crawled into their heads and told them signing up to a set of deadly trials to become the ruler of Terrulia was a good idea? I could understand the motives behind those from Damascon Hollow and the Crimson Steppes. Fighting for what we wanted had been beaten into us from day-dot, but those from the other cities that looked like they belonged in a country club?

Ego, all of them. They'd never been told 'no' a single day in their lives, so why was getting a crown any different? I bet they thought it'd be handed to them on a silver fucking platter. Double that bet they were deluded enough to think it might still happen.

A piercing electronic noise had me slamming my hands over my ears, which was followed by the sound of the Overseer's voice. Not much fucking better.

"My heart is warmed to see so many of you valiant Potentials having come so far in your quest for greatness," Celeste began in her usual drawn-out way. I assumed she aimed to come across theatrical to those she was speaking to, but it had the opposite effect for me. It ground my nerves and infuriated me that she wouldn't just get to the fucking point. "It is a testament to the people of Terrulia that we have a wealth of talent in the coming generation."

I rolled my eyes. More like literal wealth that supplied extra weapons and advantages to those with access to it.

"To be a royal in Terrulia is to be the guardian of all people. A ruler who will lead us to great things and a future so wondrous and bright," she continued. "We are a prosperous people, made to endure the struggles that befall us, as those in history have attempted time and again. We continue to triumph, and our future monarch will do the same as the trials are rained down upon our valiant Potentials."

I blew out a slow breath, my irritation rising.

"She talks a lot of shit, doesn't she?" Kayden said in a low voice. "I think she likes the sound of her own voice."

"Mmm," I grumbled noncommittally. Just because I agreed didn't mean I was going to get chummy with him about it.

"Reminds me of some other people I know," Kendra said, giving Kayden a pointed look. I chuckled. The little woman had spark and zero fear of the big asshole despite him being more than double her size.

"And now you are to face the final step of this first trial that will take you to the next level on your journey," Celeste said. "As Overseer, I have had the pleasure of planning this and believe it is a test that will make our future monarch shine. At the centre of the crater is a chest filled with golden coins, but be warned, its numbers are limited. You must obtain a single coin and make your way to the other side of the crater. You have until the sun sets to succeed. All who fail will be abandoned."

I scratched my stubbled chin. Get the coin, get to the end point. Piece of fucking cake. The air shimmered as the forcefield disappeared and Celeste shouted for the test to begin. Then chaos ensued.

Potentials leapt, launching themselves into the misty crater in a panic to seize the prize, whilst others decided on eliminating their competition beforehand. Weapons were drawn, blood splattered, and I decided to join those who'd escaped into the crater, with a quick glance to where Kendra and Kayden had run off to. She had disappeared into the fog but Kayden was still visible, his fists pounding into whoever he could catch. I jumped down, landing in putrid filth. As much as it felt like water, the smell alone suggested it was far from it. I didn't want to think about why Kayden hadn't started a fight with me, being the bigger competition, instead going after the other Potentials. Who knew how that asshole's brain worked? If it functioned at all.

Shouts rang out behind me as I crept towards the centre where the fog was thickest. As soon as I stepped through it, my sight cleared and I was able to see deep within the corrupted marsh. I passed a dead tree, following some Potentials as they worked their way to the chest. My plan was to stay out of sight. Someone would retrieve a coin and when they did, I would steal it with them none the wiser. No fights, just stealth. Not that I didn't mind throwing a few fists, but we were given a time limit and I needed to play this smart.

The chest was exactly where the Overseer had said it would be, the gold practically glowing. She'd said they were coins, but they looked more like the size of my palm. There was no way you'd be able to carry one without someone noticing. I watched as two Potentials gathered multiple coins, stuffing the pockets of their jumpsuits. The thought behind the strategy was clever, culling the numbers of Potentials returning to the House of Ascension, but what those two idiots weren't banking on was the huge targets they were painting on their backs. Those coins were not only obvious in their pockets, but they would weigh the two Potentials down.

A spear shot between them and they ducked to the ground. At times like this, it's hard not to feel like a cocky asshole. The Potentials scrambled to their feet, but their greedy asses weren't fast enough and whoever had thrown the spear ran through the dead trees and launched themselves at the thieves with a knife in hand. Let's just say there was a lot of stabbing, even in my book. The attacking Potential clearly had other issues, that fact becoming clearer when they raised their knife and smiled at the eyeball pierced on it.

I could hear more Potentials drawing closer behind me, either running for their lives or running to end them. I dodged behind a blackened tree to avoid the onslaught and watched as the area around the chest became a fighting pit. I'd seen some dirty fights back in Damascon Hollow, but nothing like what I was watching. These people were fucking savage and that was putting it nicely.

Kayden was amongst them, his skin like solid rock as he picked someone up by the throat and threw them into a tree before targeting his next prey. The guy was living his best life, his brown eyes alight with each hit. People from the Crimson

Steppes were raised to fight and favoured the strong, so it was no wonder he revelled in inflicting as much damage as possible.

Out of the corner of my eye, I spotted a Potential sneaking away and took it as my cue to leave. Screeching sounded overhead and I ducked down as giant bats descended on those still fighting around the chest. The Potential I was trailing picked up their pace and I wasn't too far behind, glad to be out of sight of the flying monsters. I followed them as they attempted to disappear, keeping to the cover of tree trunks and gnarled low lying branches.

Once the sound of fighting faded, I flicked a bionic finger to reveal a small scalpel blade, then ran towards the Potential. Before they could register my arrival, I sliced their pocket and let the coin drop into my hand, then slipped away out of sight. From behind one of the creepy ass trees, I fought back a laugh at the dumbfounded look on the Potential's face while they searched their pockets and surrounding area of the marsh for the coin.

It was tempting as fuck to whistle like a cocky bastard as I strode away. All those Potentials fighting each other, and they were so blinded by the fox in their hen house. I was on a high no drug could give.

Tossing the coin in the air and catching it, I strode towards the other side of the crater. I grinned because fuck, I not only had the coin, but I was most likely going to be the first person over the finish line. I threw it in the air again only to be shoved forward into the cold mud.

"Fuck!" I growled, spinning around to see who had dared come after me, only to find Danger Dog—the rat from Hallow's Griff—crouched beside me.

He pressed a finger to his lips, gesturing at the sky. "Chill man, I just saved your life. There was one of those bat things up there," he said in a hushed tone. "I got your back Atti the Ant."

I shoved him onto his ass with a growl. I fucking hated that name. It had been my nickname as a kid when Cormac first took me under his wing. I'd been stealing scraps off the street after my parents died and the good old foster system of DH didn't bother to sort me out a new home. I was a small, skinny thing, barely getting by as I lived day to day. I wasn't beaten and I hadn't been picked up by child traffickers, so I'd counted that as a win, but one day my luck well and truly ran out. I'd gotten caught stealing a slice of pizza from a street vendor. Rather than turn me into the cops, the merchant had cut my hand off and left me for dead.

Cormac found me, gifting me the bionic hand and that shitty nickname. Once I'd shown I could hold my own, the nickname fell away naturally. Okay, fine, I beat the shit out of anyone who used it other than Cormac. I wasn't an ant; I was a Drake. Using it was a slap in the face for all I'd become.

"Meant no harm," Danger Dog said, his eyes wide as he raised his hands before him and sat up. "I've been thinking about how you said we shouldn't work together."

"Still not interested."

"No shit, but—" He looked above me, pointing to the horizon. "Fuck! I think it's coming back."

I had to fucking look, didn't I? A big mistake because Danger Dog took the opportunity to grab my bionic hand and twist, pulling the limb off.

"What—" I mumbled, attempting to shove him away, but my whole body went into reboot mode at the loss of my hand.

"How does it feel to know I have the upper hand?" he snickered. "Get it? 'Cos I have your fucking hand?"

My vision darkened and I felt myself fall sideways. How that fucking cunt had known that disconnecting my hand would make me lose control of my senses and body was beyond me, but I made it my mission to find out. He'd pay for pulling a stunt like this. Slowly and painfully, he would come to regret every choice he'd ever made in life.

# KAYDEN

If I never saw a fucking bat again it would be too soon. I spun, grabbing a wing in one hand and slamming the creature into the ground before launching on top of it. The monster gnashed its teeth, struggling against my hold. I tightened my grip on its wing and snapped with both hands, tearing the thin membrane in the process. It howled but I continued, moving onto the next wing and splintering more flesh and cartilage. The thing didn't give up though, despite me rendering its limbs useless. It was desperate for my blood.

I punched its ugly, patchy head as it tried to bite me with its frothing fangs. They couldn't penetrate my rock-hard skin, so I laughed like a mad man as I sentenced it to death with my fists. I loved how the adrenaline of a fight rushed through my veins and took me on a high that intensified with each hit I made. At times like this I was a fucking god amongst men. Mars reborn.

Something jumped on my back and I shook like a dog after a bath, throwing it off me. Turned out it was a Potential—one of Victoria's, no less. I recognised his face from the attack on our garrison and couldn't help the grin spreading on my face.

"I'm going to enjoy this," I called, prowling towards him.

The cocky bastard held no weapon, obviously blind to the

threat right in front of him. I removed my rock skin, giving me more range of motion and preserving my energy. It wouldn't take much to finish him off.

The guy didn't back down as I drew closer, spreading his feet and eyeing me with hatred. Most people submitted to true leaders, but he obviously had some pent-up rage churning in his chest. Must suck to believe you were more important than you actually were. To want something and not be able to take it. I chuckled, having no experience with that. If he didn't have the power to challenge Victoria, then he definitely didn't have it to beat me. His dumb ass was about to get a serious wake-up call.

I didn't wait for pleasantries, striking first. My fist connected with his jaw, but the guy pushed through and aimed a few punches my way, if you could even call them that. I let one of his efforts land, using his momentum to grab one of his arms and twist. He struggled against me, flapping around like a flag in the wind, but I held firm, twisting further until I heard a satisfying crack. I was going to break his limbs just like I'd done with the giant bat.

The Potential screamed and I threw him away from me. He fell, sliding through mud and glaring daggers at me. He clambered to his feet, sneering, his mouth frothing like a wild beast as blood dripped down his face.

"Fuck you!" the guy yelled, charging at me even though one of his arms swung limply at his side.

"Nah, bro, think I'll pass," I replied, easily blocking his punch and kicking his feet out from beneath him.

He fell, howling in pain from landing on his broken arm. I presumed he'd stay down but the little weasel scrambled to his feet and came at me again. His fighting was getting sloppier by the second and it was like batting away a child as I shoved him to the muddy ground once more. The little bastard made to rise again so I knocked him onto his front, pushing his face down into the mud. He squirmed and after I slowly counted to five, I grabbed the collar of his jumpsuit and dragged him up so that his ear was near my lips.

"Bet you regret coming after me now." I chuckled, letting him go and tossing him onto his broken arm.

He turned his filthy head, spitting curses at me. I had little patience for anything, let alone this runt, so I stamped my boot down on his spine with a *crack*. And not in the good way that osteopaths do. I stared down at him with a wide grin. Now to finish the guy off.

I was about to bend down and end his misery when a deep roar rumbled through the air. The next thing I knew, a huge shadow flew overhead, making the misty marsh even spookier. I decided the guy wasn't a high priority anymore and jogged out of the death pit. The dragon was making its descent and I wasn't about to get caught up in a battle with it. I wanted to prove to everyone that I was the strongest person in Terrulia, but even I knew when the stakes were too high. The monster's face appeared through the fog, its long yellowed fangs and bright red eyes immediately drawing my attention. It was travelling swiftly, its jaws opening wide as it swooped down. Moving faster than something that size should have been able to, it captured Potentials in its mouth before they could escape and crunched down, blood coating its teeth and silencing their screams before carrying them away.

It flew up but I knew it would circle back for more. Why miss out on the smorgasbord down here? I didn't plan on becoming lunch and I definitely wasn't going to waste my time battling the thing to save anyone. Around me, Potentials were still fighting over the coins, the gold scattered around the marsh and sunk into mud. I needed to grab one soon before they were either taken or buried in the filth.

The dragon whirled, ready to make its descent, and I moved to stand in what little tree cover I could find. From my vantage point, I watched as it swooped to scoop up more Potentials in its huge jaws, their screams quickly silenced as it snapped its maw shut. Blood rained down over the pit. Once it was satisfied and rising again I made a dash for the chest. Potentials scrambled beside me, some to get to the chest while others tried to get the upper hand on an opponent. I flattened anyone who got in my way, my huge arms no match for them as Potentials flew from my path like I was flicking bugs.

As I reached the chest, I grabbed my coin and stuffed it into my pocket, elbowing the face of the guy beside me for good measure. I shoved the cry-baby aside with a laugh, earning a howl as a torrent of blood spilled between the fingers that had been holding his nose. Served him right. He should have gotten out of my way quicker.

I ran through the mud, only to flatten myself in the disgusting shit as a roar boomed and the monster swooped. The tip of a talon scraped the top of my hair, but I'd avoided being scooped up and becoming monster dinner. I jumped to my feet once it ascended, noticing Fallon and Zane in the distance with Noah drooped between them as they dragged him through the misty marsh. The guy looked to be in pretty bad shape.

"Grab coins!" I shouted at them, my voice carrying over the fighting still going on between the other Potentials. "And watch out for the thing above!"

Fallon's gaze snapped to mine and her copper eyes widened. Truth be told, I didn't blame her for being shocked. Keeping her alive was another way I could stick it to her sister for usurping me. It was petty, but I still wanted that bitch to pay and until I could fight Victoria one-on-one, I would use her own tactics and fight dirty. I watched Fallon and Zane drag Noah towards the chest, only to see the bitch I wanted to punish arrive with her favourite followers right behind them. Victoria stormed towards Fallon and co like a hurricane ready to destroy everything in her path.

There was no way they'd be able to defend themselves against the Auger bitch and her cronies with Noah hanging between them. It was the perfect time to get my revenge, but first I was going to take Victoria's people like she'd taken Flynn from me. I raced towards the Potentials, my skin turning as hard as stone as I rolled into them like they were bowling pins. It was one of my favourite moves. Not only was it fun as all hell, but it was hard to defend against. Whatever the outcome, whoever the target, they always ended up on the back foot.

I knocked one of the Potentials over but the other two escaped me, falling over themselves in the mud to get away. I flipped into standing and squared my shoulders, blocking the others from getting to Fallon, Noah, and Zane. I could hear Fallon shouting at the merman about Victoria behind me, already knowing she'd be gearing up for a fight with her sister. The Augers had bad blood, there was no denying that. I turned my attention back to the Potentials and smirked at their weapons. They held swords and knives, but not a pulse gun was in sight.

Ever tried to cut a rock with a knife? Sure, you could chip away, but it took a lot of force to make any real damage. I doubted the three fuckheads in front of me could make a dent combined.

"And to think I was hoping for a challenge," I said casually, looking at my hand and rubbing mud and dried blood between my thumb and fingers. "Pity."

"I'm going to enjoy killing you," one replied with a sneer. "Crimson cunt."

I laughed at his pathetic insult. He made me sound like some kind of superhero. "All I need now is a red cape."

The dragon roared from above, its call echoed by the screeching of more giant bats on their way. We would be overrun soon. Time was running the fuck out and I needed to deal with these three now. They had played a role in Flynn's death and it was damn time they paid for it.

"Are we doing this or are you three going to stand around shaking in your boots all day?"

It was all the incentive they needed. They came at me as one, their blades raised high. I didn't carry any. Why bother when my fists were all the weapon I needed? The first to reach me swung their sword and I raised my arm to block, following up with a punch to their gut. The breath escaped their lungs as I sent them flying across the muddy ground. I didn't wait to see where they went, turning on the other two as they swung at me.

Metal clashed with rock as we fought blow for blow. They were skilled, but not enough to better me. I was the strongest of all in the Crimson Steppes and I wasn't about to let some upstarts from wherever the fuck these two came from try and best me. I sent my rage into each punch and quickly gained ground, pushing them back from the chest and deeper into the dead marsh. The blackened trees grew thicker and more plentiful around us, the smell of rot making me gag. It was just the three of us now, having left the fighting and scrambling for coins far behind.

The monsters' growls and shrieks grew louder and I knew they would make their dive any minute. Once they'd devoured those near the chest, they'd come for anyone else in this place. I needed to finish these two off and get the hell out of this crater. I swung at one of their faces with my giant rock fist only to stumble, pain shooting up my leg. I turned to see the third Potential had scurried back to the fight and stuck a sword into the back of my calf.

Fucking coward couldn't even face me. He wasn't fit to rule Terrulia.

I roared a sound that could rival the monsters flying overhead and lunged for him, ignoring the blade that was wedged in the crevice of my rocky skin like that famous sword from the kid's story. Motherfucker had found a way. If I wasn't so pissed, I'd have given him props for creativity. As it was, my fury was in charge and I shoved him to the ground, pummelling his face into the mud. Blood splattered and bone cracked as he became unrecognisable beneath my fists. One down, two to go, then

Victoria would get what's coming for her.

I panted as the anger died down and stood slowly, pulling the sword from my leg. I slammed the blade into the mud then searched for the other two Potentials. They were nowhere in sight, having scurried away like frightened little mice. Typical.

Thunder clapped and I looked to the sky as rain began pouring. I was running out of time and fighting internally with my options. Would I let them go or finish what I'd started? They needed to pay for what they'd done to Flynn. I owed my friend that much, but I had to finish this test, end the trial, and move on through to the end.

I shifted out of my rock skin and ran a hand over my face, wiping the rain from my eyes. What if they ran back to Victoria and made it out? Worse, what if they helped Victoria kill Fallon and the others?

Fuck. I shouldn't care if the Augers had some feud. I shouldn't care if the merman and nudist made it out. I shouldn't care about any of those things. This was a competition and the only person fit to make it past the final trial was me. Everyone would either fail or die eventually.

Was helping them and Flynn's vengeance worth losing this trial and everything I'd worked my whole life for?

Since I'd first started walking, my parents had been moulding me into the person I was today. The person who would bring glory and prosperity to the Crimson Steppes. I was not only made to be the ruler of Terrulia, I was shaped to be the saviour of my people. Would I throw it all away to avenge my friend and help my competition?

"Shit!" I shouted at the sky, the sound rumbling in my chest. Lightning flashed and thunder followed as if in answer. I clenched my fists at my side and took off through the trees. I'd made my decision and I fucking hoped it wouldn't bite me in my rocky ass.

# FALLON

It was chaos. A blood bath of epic proportions. Potentials fought each other viciously as blood sprayed in every direction of the crater we'd found ourselves in. The red beacon surging into the sky was still glimmering, as if it was proud of the destruction surrounding it.

The smug fucking thing.

We'd left one hellhole and walked into another and this time I didn't know what we were up against. All I knew was that our lives depended on getting the gold and getting out of the kill zone.

Zane and I stumbled forward, half dragging Noah through the mud and blood as we tried to avoid the attention of other Potentials to make our way towards the chest at the centre of the arena. It had taken us all night to get from Victoria's garrison to the beacon and I was already tired from hauling Noah's near dead weight through the marsh.

Saving him had cost us dearly, but there was no way in hell I could have left him behind. My eyes landed on the chest and a burst of panic coiled in my stomach. It was nearly empty now and every second it took for us to slowly manoeuvre through the throng of bodies was one step closer to costing us our lives.

There was no choice but to head into the thick of the battle. Once we'd got our gold, we could get the fuck out of there. At the far end of the crater, Celeste and the other Masters watched behind some kind of forcefield, their faces revealing nothing. Those assholes got to sit back and watch Potentials killing each other like it was a freaking sports match. All they needed were hotdogs and beers for the big game.

I didn't have to guess that the forcefield they stood behind was the gate mentioned in the note and our only way out was with the gold. Wisely, they'd spelled it to keep everything else out, including the bats flapping around and feasting.

One of the bats swooped towards us and I ducked as Zane thrust his sword into its chest, killing it on impact. The creature slumped to the ground and we continued our painfully slow progress.

I almost sighed in relief as I spotted Kayden barrelling towards us. I never thought I'd be so happy to see the cocky bastard, and yet, a little piece of me was thankful to see he was safe. His jumpsuit was soaked with blood and mud, and blood was crusted in his hair and on his cheeks. Not his blood though, I noted.

"Grab coins!" he shouted, sprinting towards us. "And watch out for the thing above!"

A giant dragon in the sky roared ferociously right on cue, swooping down to clutch a woman in its talons and rip her body apart. I grimaced as a shower of slimy pieces rained down on us. Nope. Mm-mm. I would not fucking think about what just landed in my hair. I swallowed down bile and yelped as a Potential with crazy eyes came at me, forcing me to drop Noah's arm to defend myself.

His eyes gleamed with bloodlust as he threw an axe at me and I narrowly dodged it, watching as it sailed past my nose and took out some other poor fucker. Nah, I wasn't going to stand for that. Dropping to a crouch and slipping my knife from my boot,

I rose and tossed my blade back, mirroring the guy's movement. Mine hit my mark right in his chest.

Blood dribbled from his lips as he fell to his knees, and I sprinted over to retrieve my weapon before hurrying back to Noah's side to lift him up again, noticing Kayden squaring off with a bunch of Potentials behind us. And beyond them … Victoria.

Her eyes were cold fury, blazing with anger and hatred as she looked at me, stalking towards us like a big cat. This was it. The moment of reckoning. I turned my head towards the gate, getting a glimpse of the chest through several people's legs.

"Zane!" I cried, pointing towards it. "The chest is dead ahead. Take Noah, get your coins and go."

His green eyes swam with uncertainty as he looked between Victoria and me. I got the feeling he realised this shit was between me and my sister, but I knew he didn't want to leave me.

"Fallon…"

My heart skipped a beat. He never called me by my name and somehow the depth of his fear for me shone brighter than ever from that one word. I shook my head. "I'll be fine. Noah needs you."

He nodded, hefting Noah's weight as I stepped back. "If you die, Starfish, I'm going to kill you."

I grinned. "Get going you sap."

Noah croaked, reaching his hand towards me, but I never got to hear what he said as the dragon above us roared and they disappeared through the crowd of people. I looked at the sky, my stomach dropping.

It was coming straight for me.

I ran like my life depended on it—because yeah, I was in no mood to be ripped in half—and skidded to a halt just as Victoria swiped at me with her blade. I dodged, trying to angle my body, but her blade slashed my back and I screamed, my nerves on fire as pain ripped me apart. My body jolted as I fell into the water, red staining it an even darker shade of brown.

She laughed, but her glee was cut short as the monster reared up before her, its long talons extended. Victoria grabbed one of her cronies and shoved them in the way instead, appeasing the beast as it clung to them and took to the sky.

This bitch. This. Bloody. Bitch.

I *hated* her. Despised everything she'd become.

With a grunt of effort I pulled myself up, sliding my sword from its sheath as I faced her. Victoria's blond hair spiralled out from its braid, her copper eyes flaring in the darkening sky. For a long moment, we simply stared at each other, ignoring the chaos around us.

Thunder crackled and before long the heavens opened, spitting on our feud with torrential rain. Lightning flashed ominously and sweat and rain slid down my jumpsuit, the water easing the burning in my back.

"What did they do to you, to make you so fucking cruel?" I yelled, shaking my head.

She knew who I meant. The two people on this planet who were supposed to love, nurture, and protect us like only parents could.

"They made me stronger," she said with a manic grin. "House Jupiter weeds out the weak. Just like I'm going to do to you."

I spat on the ground, gesturing at the death all around us. "Do you really think they give a shit about you? Victrus and Eliana only care about the power you can bring if you become queen. They don't care if you live or die, they are using you for their own gain. You're just a puppet whose strings are being pulled."

"You're lying," she hissed, beginning to prowl around me again. "They love me. I am their future, their heir! One day I will be queen, but you won't be around to see it. This ends now, sister."

She really was a fucking psychopath, deluded in all the worst ways. Our parents had warped her brain, manipulated her so deeply that she truly believed everything she was saying. And that kind of thinking only made her more dangerous. She would be anything for them. Do anything for them, including killing me. Their rebellious, strong-willed, weak spare.

Why had I ever wasted any tears on these people? They didn't deserve my love or even my pity. I was done.

"You can try to kill me, but I swear to you, Victoria, before you die, my face will be the last thing you see. Your punishment is coming sooner than you think."

Her face crinkled with rage, her eyes flashing like the lightning forking around us. The monsters had disappeared into the sky of storms and few Potentials were left alive in the crater.

It was just her and me, dancing to a discordant tune. The same way it had always been. The same way it always would be.

She advanced, running at me with a scream as I shifted, pirouetting and bringing my sword down, but she blocked the move and proceeded to attack quickly, getting me on my back foot.

Her sword smashed against mine again and again, her fury igniting even further as I gave it my all. I was losing too much blood and my wound made me weak and sloppy.

As her cockiness increased, I saw my opening when she thrust too far and, with a cry that took all my strength, I lunged, slipping my blade into the soft flesh of her stomach.

She gaped at me, her mouth opening and closing as she gasped for air, staggering forward with my sword still in her gut. Blood trailed down her stomach and she clutched at it in confusion, her brows pulling together as she stumbled and fell to her knees.

I stood there watching her, just as shocked and hurting badly. When she looked at me with eyes as wide as a child's, her blond hair plastered to her scalp, I could almost forget what a monster she'd become. I remembered the few good memories I had of us playing together when we were little. Of the times she'd been a kind older sister, protecting me, looking out for me, caring for me.

It was so long ago, but I still remembered what she was like before being initiated into Auger Enterprises. She might have become a monster and forced me to do horrible things, but I couldn't force those memories aside as I saw her now with my blade sticking out of her.

"You won," she said, her voice barely audible over the rain. "You really beat me."

I took a step forward, my heart raging against the unfairness of it all. "I never wanted this Victoria," I cried above the storm. "I never wanted to be your enemy."

"It could never have been any different," she said calmly, her face almost serene as she looked at me. "You never understood what they were trying to build. There is so much you don't know."

"What?" I cried frantically. "Tell me!"

Fuck. She couldn't die now, not before she gave me some answers. What did she know about House Jupiter? About the trials? About our parents?

She ignored my question, her eyes seeming to lose focus as she sat in the rain. "Will you take my body back to our parents?"

Tears blurred my vision as I looked at her. I'd done this. I was just as much a monster as she. "I—of course I will."

"Come here," she said softly. "I need to tell you something."

I padded forward slowly, kneeling before her in the mud and leaning in so I could hear her over the rain. She took the back of my head, pulling me closer in the nearest thing to an embrace that we'd had in years.

Her lips brushed against my ear as she whispered, her voice turning hard. "You will never win."

Then she thrust a blade into my gut.

I flinched, barely feeling the cold sting of the metal, gasping as she pulled me closer still, hugging me until her strength gave out and she toppled onto her side. I wheezed as scarlet spilled down my front, the water turning red as the blood of Augers ran freely.

My body began to shut down, my strength failing me as I felt the overwhelming need to lie down and close my eyes. I curled onto my side, mirroring Victoria as we lay head to toe, two sisters defeated by each other's blades.

The beacon glimmered above and the odd shimmer of a gold coin shone within the murky water. Bodies floated around us, the area filled with death and destruction. Never had I seen such a display of human savagery and wasted life.

We weren't just in a crater anymore. We were in a mass grave.

As I turned my eyes to the finish line in the distance, my last hope was that the others had made it. That Kendra, Zane, and Noah were safe and would live to see another day. Maybe one of them would even go on to win the crown and rule this kingdom.

I smiled at that thought, even as my life drained away little by little. Death had come for me, but I could take comfort in the idea of a better world. I trusted Kendra to keep Ethan and Hadley safe.

Free.

Just like I would soon be.

# ZANE

I ran for the edge of the crater with Noah slung over my shoulder. The rain soaked me through, making the whole thing worse than trying to swim with jeans and a woollen jumper on. As I reached the top, I stumbled through the forcefield, landing on the muddy ground on the other side. Noah groaned, rolling off me, and I took a moment to catch my breath. We'd been travelling all night and nearly the whole day, and my legs were as jiggly as jellyfish.

"Another two worthy Potentials!" the Overseer called and for a split second I was ecstatic instead of tired because I had finished the first trial. Then reality hit and my happiness dissolved like a bath bomb in a tub.

Crossing the finish line of a race should have been an epic moment when streamers got thrown and you were showered in sparkling wine, some hot girls handing you a massive gold trophy. Turns out that's not what happened at all. Instead, my bestie was barely alive, Starfish was off fighting her bitch of a sister, and Kendra and my other two best friends were nowhere to be seen. I expected an adrenaline rush at the end of each trial, but not like this.

A nurse came to my side, handing me a med pill which I

swallowed like it was a lifesaver. Once I felt like my energy was coming back, I stood, glancing around at the other Potentials who'd made it here. There weren't as many as I'd thought there'd be which was good, but also a total bummer. These conflicting emotions were totally bogus. I wanted to beat the competition, but it seemed like a lot of unnecessary death.

I began pacing back and forth in front of the forcefield. The rain was pouring all over me, which I couldn't complain about because it was both refreshing and comforting being wet, but my anxiety was at an all-time high. Not a single drop of water was going to wash that away.

"Where the heck are they?" I groaned, throwing my hands in the air. "I need to go find them."

"You can't go back once you've crossed," Nolan said from where he was kneeling beside the nurse, helping to patch my bestie up.

"These rules are bogus," I grumbled, focusing my eyes back to the crater, then whispering to myself. "Where are you Starfish?"

She'd better arrive any minute. Fallon had promised she would get here and I'd be so pissed if she broke it. We'd come so far after saving Noah and then following the beacon all the way to the test. As usual, Victoria had to ruin it. That woman was like sand in your underpants.

"The sands have almost fallen. This trial approaches its end," the Overseer announced in her calming voice. Fallon always made a face when the woman spoke, but I liked hearing Celeste speak. She really knew how to tell a story. Though right now, I wasn't entirely impressed by her words. "Our victorious Potentials will soon be known."

"There's more coming!" one of the Potentials shouted. I looked to where she was pointing eagerly, my stomach plummeting into my boots.

"No one good," I mumbled, my shoulders dropping.

Five Potentials were running to the finish line, covered

in blood and mud but with grins on their faces as wide as a blue whale. They obviously hadn't noticed the shadows looming on the horizon. Shouts came from my side of the forcefield, but they couldn't hear the warning and soon loud screeching told them all they needed to know.

The Potentials' wide smiles morphed into panicked screams as the giant bats came into sight. They really were horrifyingly ugly things. Flapping their wings with a vengeance, they sailed through the rain towards the terrified Potentials who were desperately trying to run through the slick mud towards us.

They never stood a chance.

The bats dove, some carrying their prey off into the skies whilst others landed on the Potentials, clawing at their backs and tearing into them with their fangs. It was a massacre, but the bats weren't done once the bodies were lifeless and shredded beneath them. They launched back into the sky and flew towards us. Screeching loudly, they propelled towards the forcefield, hitting it with a loud boom that rivalled the thunder.

"Shit!" I shouted as they backed up and flew towards us again. Each hit against the barrier seared their flesh and left blood dripping down the side, but they kept going, like sharks in the heat of a feeding frenzy.

"The barrier will hold!" the Overseer called out over the commotion with a creepy smile on her face.

"We should take the injured back to the House of Ascension just in case," the nurse said. I took my eyes off the massacre to focus on her conversation with Nolan. "If those things break through, they'll be defenceless."

"Agreed," Nolan said, rising to his feet. "We'll get them into a helicopter now."

Another boom echoed as the bats attacked, and the barrier rippled violently.

"On second thought, perhaps we should return all victors to the academy, just to be safe. Do we need to risk having no one to crown?" asked the nurse, following him to where the Overseer stood with a bright pink umbrella over her head.

The three exchanged words, then the next thing I knew Celeste was announcing for us all to follow the Mind Master, Jeremiah, towards a ring of waiting helicopters. I frowned. There was no way I was boarding now. Fallon, Kendra, Kayden and Ace weren't here yet.

Despite the giant bats trying to beat themselves bloody against the forcefield, a Potential walked past me, swinging a familiar metal hand around and whistling. The guy looked like a ferret, and not the cute and cuddly kind. He was giving me some seriously bad vibes.

"Hey," I called out, snatching the hand from him. With one swift move I slapped him across the face with it like a good old-fashioned glove slap. "This doesn't belong to you."

He stared at me like a stunned mullet, then a sneer dragged across his face. "Fuck you, give it back."

"Nope," I replied, stuffing the hand in my pocket. "What kind of friend would I be if I did that, hmmm?"

"I don—"

"That was a rhetorical question, you slimy sea snail," I said as his face burned red. He stormed forward, pressing his chest up against mine. I rolled my eyes, prodding him back with one finger. "Bit close, dude."

"Give it back you little fucker."

"Little? You're looking up at me."

"You have no idea who you're dealing with," he barked. The guy could really do with some mellowing out. He was gonna pop a vein in his eye if he didn't chill soon. "Now fucking give it back before I break every bone in your body then do the same to your friend over there."

I narrowed my eyes, grabbing a fistful of his jumpsuit and lifting him up. He squeaked as his boots flailed in the air. "No one threatens my bestie."

Before the ferret could say another word, I threw a punch, clocking him in the mouth. The dude fell to the ground, holding his jaw and crying as he spat teeth into the mud.

"Walk it off," Nolan said with an impatient shake of his hand. He strode over with a stretcher under his arm. "Loch, help me with this."

The hand thief scrambled to his feet, darting away, and I crouched beside Noah.

"I want to stay," I told Nolan.

"No can do," he replied. We lifted Noah out of the mud and onto the stretcher, my bestie groaning with the movement. "Overseer's orders."

"But I'm waiting for someone," I insisted, watching as he strapped Noah down.

"If they are worthy and finish, you'll see them back at the House of Ascension," he said. "If not, I doubt there's much left of them to see anyway. Now hurry up. Pick up the other side and get your ass moving."

With a dramatic sigh, I took one last look at the bloody bats and the crater beyond then picked up the other side of the stretcher. Noah was out cold as we marched through the mud to where another forcefield awaited, but Nolan walked through without hesitation, dragging me with him. Suddenly, the helicopters came into view.

"Why isn't it raining here?" I asked, looking up at the clear dusky sky.

"Not in the trial anymore, are we?" Nolan shot back as we strode across the tarmac.

"Who has the power to control the weather like that?" I knew some had the power to manipulate water and air, but not to that extreme.

He scoffed. "No one. It's called science and engineering."

Crew members ran towards us, taking Noah from me and loading him into a helicopter while other Potentials followed suit.

There were just under half of us left from the original hundred, give or take. I turned from them to stare one last time in the direction we'd just come. Still no sign of the others.

A dude came to stand in front of me, his face half obscured from the helmet he was wearing, blocking my view. "You need to get on board so we can take off."

I nodded, though I felt like the shittest person for leaving. This was what it must have felt like for the mother emperor penguins when they had to leave their eggs to go hunting for food. It must have broken their hearts because mine was not having a good time.

Following the dude, I strode towards the helicopter Noah had been put on only to pull up short. Tattooed around the guy's neck were a bunch of swirls that all led to a simple central circle with a cross in the middle.

"Nice tattoo, dude."

"Thanks man."

"Mean anything?"

"Just this," he said, pointing to the circle. "It means Earth, but the rest I thought looked cool."

"Gnarly," I replied with a slow nod. The dude chuckled, patting me on the back in a not-so-subtle nudge forward. I climbed up and sat in the seat closest to Noah.

"Buckle up," he said, sitting in the chair next to the pilot. He looked back at me and the other Potentials, making sure we were following his orders. "Good, we're all set."

The pilot nodded. "Roger that."

As we took off, I looked down at my bestie, then at the forcefield once more. Only a few giant bats remained behind the now bloodied shield, not a Potential in sight. The sun had almost set. There wasn't much time left.

We rose higher, the helicopter blades whipping through the air. The dragon roared, its massive wings clearing some of the fog to reveal two figures in the mud.

I let out a whoop as I recognised Fallon's long black hair as she leant over her sister's fallen body. My starfish was victorious, and she'd be diving over the finish line and back into my arms in no time.

That's when I saw it. A flash of silver in the sunlight.

The dragon roared and began its descent, angling to scoop up the meal laid out before it. My stomach dropped, my heart pounding in my chest as I realised what had happened. The last thing I saw before grey clouds obscured my view was the wicked curve of the sword rammed right into Fallon's stomach.

# WANT TO KNOW WHAT HAPPENS NEXT?

Yeah, we know, we kinda left you in the dark there, but we do so love a brutal cliffie, and we promise you won't mind so much when you're starting the second book!

Is Fallon still alive? Did Ace and Kayden escape the marsh? Will Zane ever see his Starfish again? Is that grapefruit *really* still a virgin? Find out these answers and more in Book Two, A Forest of Fire.

In the meantime, join the ASOS Discussion Group:

www.facebook.com/groups/asosdiscussiongroup

Need some more content? Follow our reading groups for teasers, freebies, and to keep up to date with all our bookish content!

Chloe Hodge's Reading Coven -- www.facebook.com/groups/chloesreadingcoven

Rebecca Camm's Reader Group --www.facebook.com/groups/rebeccacammsreadergroup

# ACKNOWLEDGEMENTS

You know when you're thinking something wild or entertaining, and you give one of your besties *the look*™? The one that conveys all the mischief you're thinking, or whatever grand scheme you've concocted? This series was that. *The look*™, sent through an Instagram DM asking, from one author to another, if that friend wanted to dive deep into treacherous waters and explore the story that is this weird and wonderful book.

We know this story has some kooky characters, weird dialogue, cocky assholes and grumpy men with bionic hands, and you know what? We're here for it. And we're so thankful that you are too! To keep this short and sweet, thanks for being weird, friends. For loving our men and our fierce leading lady, the smut that you know is absolutely going to turn full throttle real soon, and the brutal chaos yet to come.

Thanks to Fran for making our beautiful covers, to Emily and her magical editing wand (no, not that kind you damned freaks in the sheets), to Sima (Simarts_) for the gorgeous character art, and to the amazing beta readers, the booktokers/tubers/grammers, and every reader who made it this far.

We promise, it's only going to get crazier from here.

Much love,
the Overseers. xx

# ABOUT THE AUTHORS

Chloe Hodge has always had a fondness for the fantastical. Before her love of books led her to publish the Guardians of the Grove trilogy, she completed a Bachelor of Journalism and Professional Writing and worked as a journalist. She currently lives in Adelaide, Australia, crafting new worlds, running editing business, Chloe's Chapters, drinking copious amounts of tea, and playing video games.

Stay in touch!

Instagram
@chloeschapters

TikTok
@chloehodgeauthor

Website
www.chloehodge.com

Reading Group
www.facebook.com/groups/chloesreadingcoven

# MORE BOOKS FROM CHLOE

## The Cursed Blood Duology

 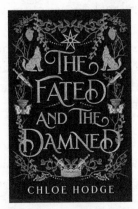

## The Guardians of the Grove

# ABOUT THE AUTHORS

Rebecca Camm was raised in Melbourne by a single mother who encouraged her passion for reading and all things magical. She has been writing stories since she was a child to help manage her anxiety and make sense of the world.

Rebecca strongly believes in the power stories have in changing lives. Just like her, Rebecca's characters are flawed, yet they are continually learning. Unlike her, they are confident, witty, and just generally more exciting.

Rebecca lives with her husband and two children. When her children allow her free time, she is either writing or attempting to conquer her ever-growing tbr pile.

Stay in touch!

Instagram
@readingwritingdaydreaming

TikTok
@readingwritingdaydream

Newsletter
www.rebeccacamm.com/contact

Reader Group
www.facebook.com/groups/rebeccacammsreadergroup

# MORE BOOKS FROM REBECCA

## The Valmenessian Chronicles

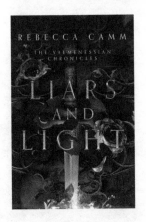 

## Novella

9 780645 625011